The Butterfly Prison

Tamara Pearson

For Jeaneth Lopez and all those who so humbly change the world.

Who made the story rules? Once, stories had been an oral tradition, a way to teach. Then they were stolen, canned, and sold. But now and then people tried to reclaim stories. They told them in order to redefine corrupted ideas and to name injustice. They broke the rules, making a new awareness, dreamfires of non-acceptance and possibilities.

Every human was a living metaphor for the social and economic world they lived in, and people together were a patchwork quilt of stories. Stories touched; revealing as they did the complex connection between individuals and the bigger issues. Readers questioned, and became, with each reflection, a little more alive.

Mella's garden

Nineteen-year-old Mella lived in a small fibro house in north west Sydney. The windows of the house squealed when opened, and the paint on their wooden frames peeled off and formed powder piles in the corners. Possums lived in the roof, and cockroaches lived behind the fridge. The bathroom/toilet/laundry floor and walls were covered with four different types of tile, and there were squares and triangles of bare concrete where tiles had come loose.

The little house was in a street with similar little fibro houses, in a suburb with one library, two bread shops, three pubs, four banks, and a main road eight lanes wide going through the middle of it. The street behind Mella's street was the same as her street, and the street behind that was also the same, and all the parallel streets came off a secondary road called Adelaide Road, which was lined with red brick flats of one and two bedroom apartments. Immigrant families, single mothers and their children, supermarket and bank workers, and the sporadically unemployed lived in those apartments, with often large families in a single bedroom. In front of each building were brick fences with forty letterbox holes in each, the metal covers flapping shut after the postie left yet another unpayable electricity bill.

It was the height of summer and already there had been more days of 43 degree oven-air this year than any other year, and the blue sky cracked, electricity wires drooped, and gasping house sparrows sat in the middle of the droop before being chased off by a magpie. The wind whispered of a summer thunderstorm that night.

Mella was working in the front yard in the shade made by the two metre high timber fence. Her dad had erected it after her mother had died a few years ago. Since then, she had done all the housework; the washing, ironing and cooking. This morning he'd told her to "work in the garden, water it, and sweep up the leaves." The leaves had blown in from late night wind journeys and settled there. "Clean it up, get rid of that mess," he'd said. (Sweep up leaves, tidy up the forest; put the trees in perfect rows and columns, comb the branches so they point in the same direction, spray the air with deodorant, vacuum up the beetles, replace the flowers with perfect plastic petals, tell the breeze which way to blow, teach the toads to sing in tune...).

Mella gathered the leaves and threw them into the empty otto. They made pigeon feet patter sounds as they landed at the bottom. She filled a large old pasta pan with water, and with shoulders hunched, as they always were, got down on her knees to water the strawberries. She wondered why she bothered. What seedlings had managed to shoot up were already shrivelled into brown strings. Most of the yard was barren dustdirt or clumps of grass and weeds. The flowers she had planted had grown a little then turned down and buried themselves in the ground. The rhubarb was pink mush, and the garlic cloves she'd planted had rotted, the dirt above them then collapsing into the space they'd occupied, forming pockmarked groundskin.

Mella stroked some of the seedlings and held them up as if showing them which way to grow. And In the yard behind her, ants walked backwards, retreating into a pile of brick rubble in the far corner. Worms came to the surface and were cooked by the hot air. The pebbles she'd gathered and arranged as borders to mark the different sections of the garden sat like an audience waiting for a play that would never start.

A pair of lorikeets walked along the top of the timber fence then flew off, taking their colour with them.

Damaged
In the very end, the land was cratered, scorched, shattered, exhausted, abused and bruised. And so were the people. The only things that grew were bombs. Millions stuck out of the desertland, watered by money, colouring the dreamstarved horizon metalgrey. The last few butterflies died of boredom.

Paz's walls
Every day in Macquarie Fields, to the south west of Sydney, police cars parked in groups of three outside the supermarket, the station, and the park. Officers patrolled the quiet public housing streets, and their shadows stuck to the public housing walls, haunting people even when they weren't around. The suburb was surrounded by bushland, and half public, half private housing. Most of the residents

were unemployed or living off low paying, sporadic casual work. The area had originally been inhabited by the Darug people. Its rich soil had meant abundant vegetables, fruits, kangaroos, and emus. The British came and pushed the Darug off their land and introduced smallpox, and now just seventy-five people living in the municipality identified themselves as Aboriginal. Their shadows didn't stick to walls.

Forty minutes' walk from the centre of Macquarie Fields was the train line, and on the other side of the tracks three storey houses with six car garages, private pools, cinemas and table tennis flanked an extensive golf course. The train line was part of an invisible wall that surrounded Macquarie Fields. It told the people within that they weren't ever going anywhere.

And on the brick fence of one government owned house in Macquarie Fields, nineteen-year-old Paz sat waiting. Behind him, another small fibro house with windows that also squealed and a shower head that leaked and drew brown rust trails between the tiles and into the drain. There were two sponge mattresses in one bedroom, and in the kitchen there was a small pan for coffee in its permanent place on the stove and a cookie tin first aid container on the shelf (inside it, two bandaids and lots of painkillers). One unwashed fork slumbered in the sink.

While Paz waited for his mum to come home, he took photos. Only with his eyes. When he'd first started taking them (imagining them) as a child, he'd used his fingers. He had crossed two long fingers on each hand to make a rectangle, a photo frame, and with that discovery he saw photos everywhere. His mum had made a rare joke and laughed, her eyes rolling, and he had wanted to remember it, to frame it, so he had held his fingers up to her and taken a photo. He had taken finger photos of many things; the edges of trees, flushing water, and the things he thought ought to happen in life even if they didn't. As he grew up he stopped using his fingers because he could see the life paintings without them. In his mind he adjusted light and contrast, deepened colour, focused on faces and blurred backgrounds. Now, sitting on the fence, he imagined/remembered a photo of his mum's eyes as she slept. A close up of one eye that was still, but not peaceful. The thin eyelid skin was pulled tightly, as though it were toiling. Paz gave the photo detail; skin lines crossing, the eyelashes dark and gentle.

Meanwhile, his mum, eyes open, was fast walking, and almost home. She'd become pregnant with Paz when she was seventeen, and hadn't been able to afford an abortion. After that, she'd lived through years of unemployment and the occasional boyfriend. She spent a lot of her days trying to feel busy; walking around the house and picking things up noisily then banging them down again, making three separate trips to the shops for three different grocery items; racing there and racing back with her head pointed forward, telling anyone who would listen how much she had to do and that there weren't enough hours in the day. A perpetual frown lined her cheeks and thinned her hair.

Paz lay on his back on the fence, his legs folded, his feet in a line, trying out lizardlife. He felt warm brick lines under his back and the hot sun sitting on his stomach. There was nowhere for his arms so he let them flop down. He photographed a skink; the patterns on its foot next to the textures of red brick. He wondered about the smell of lizards. He thought perhaps they smelt just like clay, and toast, and other brown things.

And just then his mum turned the corner into their street, racing towards their house, her head even more forward than usual. She was angry and hot, and it seemed that a bit of the day's orange sun had attached itself to her back, giving her a mane of flames. She raced past Paz, into the house, and slammed the door behind her. Paz gave his mum a look of sympathy as she passed, guessing that something had happened while she was handing in dole forms at Centrelink. But the slamming of the door made him forget his photo; it vanished like masterful sleight of hand. What was it? It had been nice. Coming from inside, he heard a lone fork fly across the kitchen, hit the wall, and fall onto the tiles, where it would probably stay for weeks.

He tried to go back to photos—he'd lost one, but he made new ones; a fingerprint in water, bird skidmarks in the sky, the doors of ant castles, the scars left in the earthskin by new asphalt, the soft pillows around the seeds of passionfruit, a groan in a dustcloud, the useful disorder of soil, and the walls of his house slumped inwards, despondent.

Thunderclouds drifted across his view. Followed by an empty wine bottle and the passing shout of midday partiers going past in a dark blue Jaguar XFR. The bottle landed right in the middle of Paz's front yard. It wasn't the first time people from the other side of the railway line had flung their rubbish there, or into houses nearby. He supposed because the lawn was uncut, they mistook the area for vacant land.

One last photo for the evening, a photo he saved and stored at the front of his mind, the place for priorities of the live-or-die kind. A photo of dignity: it flew delicately, somewhere particular. It was intensely artistic. It meant one day not being rubbish, disposable, disrespected, unprotected.

He photographed two butterfly wings, open and announcing themselves to high blue sky.

Where rubbish goes

The UK shipped its electronic waste, used tires and hazardous rubbish to Tamil Nadu, India, Vietnam, and western Africa. Barcelona sent its rubbish to Torticoran port, southern India. Japan also sent its hazardous waste to poor countries. The US sent its electronic waste to China, and old paint cans to Nigeria. The first world sent its refuse to the third world, and in West Africa children extracted metal from used circuit boards so that it could be melted down into bullets.

Child's point of view

When Mella was five, she carried a small cotton bag around with her. She talked to it, hugged it, stroked it, and people would comment, 'Boy, she sure loves that bag', not realising that in Mella's mind it wasn't a bag, but a pouch with a baby kangaroo inside.

When Mella was six, she took one leaf with her everywhere. Sometimes she held it in her hand, sometimes she stored it in her pocket, and when crossing the eight lane road near her house, she held it up to her nose. Because someone had told her that people need trees to survive, and there weren't any trees on the eight lane road. Also because she thought nature was magical. She touched concrete with her leaf, hoping to change its colour. She touched the road tar, hoping to turn it back to dirt. She touched the recorder a friend was playing, hoping to soften its sound. When her friend was sad, she touched his eyes with her leaf. Once she came across a dead bird on the side of the road and she covered it with wattle flowers from a nearby tree.

When Mella was seven, she taught her mum about plants. Opening a big book from the library, she pointed at the colour photographs and explained to her mum how:

The drakaea glyptodont flower formed a shape just like a wasp, to attract male wasps.

The silver torch cactus liked cold weather.

The dragon's blood tree had red sap that could be used for toothpaste.

Hydnora africana grew underground, except for its flower which sat above the ground, trapping beetles with its poo smell.

Victoria Amazonica was a lily up to three metres wide. Round and flat like a plate, Mella said she would like to sleep on it.

The pine tree called Methuselah was 4,800 years old.

Mimosa pudica's leaves folded in when touched, and the telegraph plant rotated its own leaves to catch sunlight.

The resurrection fern curled itself into a ball and turned brown during droughts, appearing to be dead. When it came into contact with water, it uncurled and came back to life. It could survive for one hundred years without water.

When Mella was eight, she stuck flowers on a card and gave it to her mum's friend, who was a holocaust survivor. Mella wanted to give her life, but the old woman gave the card back to her, "What would I do with this?" she said.

Child's point of view

When Paz was six, he learnt that Aboriginals had drawn on cave walls and rocks, left storyprints. So he decided to draw on footpaths. He would draw stories with his box of broken crayons over all the footpaths of the world, which at that age meant the footpath from his house to the supermarket, the bus stop, the bank, and back again. He would make the boring concrete exciting and interesting, and he would cheer up his neighbourhood.

So he set out with a carrot in his pocket, his huge t-shirt covering his too-small shorts, and his bare feet dodging the bindi-eyes in the month-long grass next to the footpath. He put his box down beside him and kneeled down to draw giant pink ants all in a line, kind dinosaurs, singing snakes hanging from lampposts, coral reefs bedding sleeping sharks, air balloons to new places where the people walked sideways and spoke only with their eyes and hands and the air was sweet-tasting and pens were gigantic and tanks were tiny. He drew winking windows and hairy squeaky capsicums, bubbles which, like dogs, got excited about everything, salty clouds, ticking ponds, and stretchy grass. He took another bite of his carrot and held it in his left hand while his right picked up another crayon gone slightly soft from the sun. His knees and palms were all red-dimpled from the rough concrete. Coloured crayon crumbs lodged in his fingernails, making little coloured fingernail moons. A pink ant got an extra leg on top of its head when Paz's crayon slipped. He drew and drew until his crayons were short stubs and the fingers holding them rubbed on the pavement and became a bit torn and red.

Then two shadows drifted across the pink ants, the dinosaurs and snakes. Paz looked up and saw four blue uniformed legs, and two batons and two guns.

"What are you doing?" one pair of legs with a gun and baton asked.

"I'm drawing stories."

"Looks like a mess of scribbles to me. Hasn't anyone taught you that drawing on public property is vandalism? Are you a vandal?"

Paz didn't know what a vandal was, but it didn't sound very good. His bottom lip trembled, and he bit it to keep it still. His sweaty palm dropped the red crayon it was holding. He noticed that the police smelled like metal and oil and a horse in blinders.

"Wash it off now," the legs said. Four oil-smelling legs blocking the sun, two guns hanging down near his head, four shoes treading all over his story drawing, six smudged pink ants.

Paz filled his little hands at a garden tap and washed away the drawings. His head was lowered a little. A little dream was gone, or deflated, or trod upon. He went inside with his hands wet, his head still lowered, and a line of crayon stubs and a carrot end left behind in the bindis.

The butterflies of Zimbabwe

It was October 2008 and the butterflies of Zimbabwe were falling out of the four metre tall grass onto piles of dead dry wings. A new butterfly slipped out of its cacoon and its wet wings stuck to the hot dirt and tore. For a few days it walked around and around and fell over and got up and stumbled more. It flapped uselessly, then after a long torment, it died too. So went the lives of many people in Zimbabwe as their wings were torn by hyperinflation, closed hospitals, unemployment, scarce food, and no transport. They buried their butterflies every day at 5:00 pm.

That same month and year, the private media and business people (monarchs without crowns), declared a financial crisis because the banks of North America and Europe started to collapse and some stockbrokers lost some of their unproductive investments. Butterflies had been falling for years in Zimbabwe, and six million children in the world had been dying each year from hunger for a long time, but a crisis was only declared when the rich were worried.

The holes in the walls

By the time Mella had finished year ten, she knew the names of thousands of plants, flowers, fruits, vegetables, and herbs. And she knew all their dirt, sun, and water needs, and where they grew. But then her mum had gone and the fence had gone up and she had left school, and that was that. On the fence and walls of Mella's house were the shadows of vines that weren't growing, and the shadows of missed conversations haunted her too. It was still hot and that made Mella's period cramp and her head ache even worse. She massaged her stomach as she kneeled on the kitchen floor to scrub the corners the mop couldn't reach.

She was getting towards the end of the list of tasks he had given her for the day, and when she was finished she would have to go to her room. That was his rule. She had already cleaned the bathroom and the toilet, scrubbed the mould off the bath curtain, waxed the dining room floor, watered the front yard, ironed the sheets and pillow covers, tidied his ties, and defrosted the freezer. She bent over to reach under the cupboards and her hair grazed the wet floor, causing its tips to stick together in short rat tails. She had a cotton bag tied around her waist, but it wasn't a kangaroo pouch. It was full of cleaning liquids, rags, and scrubbing brushes. The taste of the cleaning liquids stuck in the back of her nose. The dustdirt accumulated inside her gradually. Along with the collection of accepted bruises, it trickled like a sand timer into her feet, and up her legs.

Sometimes it had occurred to her to explain to him that there were natural cleaning materials they could use, that ironing the sheets was pointless, that the yard needed compost, the dirt needed aerating, that cardboard would keep water in and the topsoil down, but she knew he wouldn't listen. He would have told her she was stupid and to shut up. She had grown used to justsayingnothing. And she'd become accustomed to hiding her stupid self under a huge white t-shirt or her huge cream wool jumper, her eyes bowed, her shoulders closed, and her feet of insects making the sound of socksonfloor, a controlled scuttling sound as she tip toed around the house. The fridge cockroaches, scattering as humans entered their warm space, were louder than she was. Massaging her head, she wished she could read that night. Read away the headache with an adventure story about a place with purple trees that muttered when people pulled their leaves and aqua eagles that gave advice. A story with a hero that followed a path, finding puzzles for her to solve, and the longer he walked, the more knowledgeable he and she became.

She made his dinner—pasta with white mushroom sauce, then went to her bedroom. The place where he stored her till morning. She curled up on her single bed with nails in the wooden bed head that squeaked when she nightmare-twisted. She was a curling up type of person, always crossing her arms and rolling them up against her as much as she could, or perching on a chair with her feet tucked underneath her. Now she held the pillow to her stomach.

Her room was at the front of the house, and from her knot position she could still look out the window at the yard. The fence was so high that it made a fake horizon, a single line with the sky. She imagined poking her finger through the space between the gate's hinges. A duck that happened to be walking past licked it. Palestine's walls had gates too, with guards to decide who could pass from one world to another. Her gate didn't have guards, yet she couldn't go through it.

How long could justsaynothing last? When did it expire and spill over into its opposite, into outrage? She needed to be on the other side of that fence. She needed dignity wings to take her to a place where she was heard. For her too, it was a priority saved at the front of her mind. But she didn't know how to reach it—she wasn't at outrage yet, she wasn't starving, she just had a huge 'and yet' dangling off the end of each thought.

The nightstars were out of order

Paz walked to his mate Matt's house, carrying his mum's floor fan and spinning its electric chord in small circles. Because that's what you do with long things that have a weight at the end.

The day had been another 40 degree one, and his mum had moved the floor fan from room to room with her, unplugging it and plugging it back in, positioning it in the most strategic places with its head pointed right at her. Then in the afternoon it had stopped, ending the gentle drone they had both gotten used to, leaving weirdsilence hanging in the air, which within minutes became warmer. Matt would be able to fix it, just as he had fixed their back door handle that had refused to stay locked, their stove that had leaked gas, and their bathroom tap handle that spun and spun and never closed.

Night time, and as Paz spun the chord in front of him, he walked with his head pointed at the sky. He noticed that although it was cloudless, he could not see the endless starfields. Sky glow caused by Sydney's light pollution; all those cars, stadium lights, glowing shopping centres, street lights, neon signs and commercial lighting displays made the night sky fuzzy. The whole city saw the night through fogged-up glasses; the Milky Way and Andromeda galaxy all disappeared, millions of stars reduced to fifty.

Paz knocked on Matt's door with the electric plug. Matt opened it and noisyblast gushed out. A stereo radio turned up as far as it would go, and a drunken father yelling mashedupwords, believing he was singing, but actually he was vocally tumbling and crashing. Matt saw the fan and gestured with his chin towards his room. Drunken father slammed his beer bottle onto the kitchen bench and there was breaking glass sound, followed by, "Oh no no nonono the beer is broken broken." Matt rolled his towel up length ways and put it at the bottom of his bedroom door to try to keep some of the sound out.

"Every night this week man," he said to Paz, who was now lying on his bed. "We're the same, me and him, we don't know what to do with our time."

"Ask him to turn it down a bit."

"Nah, better to justsaynothing."

The towel helped, but enough radiosound, enough drunkdad leaked in for it still to be hard to talk.

So Paz just watched as Matt undid the screws of the hub with a pair of nail scissors and removed the cover to reveal the motor. Wedged into it, he found a small orange pompom. He didn't wonder why, just took it out and cleaned around inside with a cut off t-shirt sleeve. Then he plugged the fan in, sat it on the floor, and pointed it up at his single bed. He turned it on and pushed the button down so the head would rotate. The fan spun air at the room, causing Matt's map of the moon poster to flutter and beat against the wall, the dust on his bedside table to jump up and settle back down again, and some of the three hundred and thirty-seven glow in the dark stars on his ceiling and the tops of his walls to tremble and wiggle. Matt lay next to Paz, his head at his friend's feet. He watched the stars on his ceiling dance with routine-eyes. Eyes unlike his childhood ones which had wanted to look inside everything, which had read about the solar system and the galaxy really fast. Now his eyes were routine and his mouth always straight; he slept too much and he would start his day at eleven in the morning with heavycheeks and fuzzyhead. He didn't know it, but in his sleep he would laugh hysterically. During the day, he rarely laughed. If he felt that it was expected, he would raise his left eyebrow and force a gentle smile.

Yesterday he had wandered around the house slowly, poking his head into the different rooms, then had decided to go to the shopping centre because it was the only place with any activity during the day. There he'd sat in the food court on a plastic chair, at a plastic table, and watched the people. After an hour, he went back home and watched television. The blinds had projected stripes onto the screen as he watched *Quizmania* with a pillow on his lap and a beer on top of the pillow. After four hours in that position his neck throbbed and his underarms were sweaty, and he had gotten up from his death and made some toast. He'd called his girlfriend Tracey, but she didn't answer, so he had walked to Paz's place. All floppybody, his feet had followed behind him like rocks tied to his waist. He walked like an off light, knowing he was just half alive. Sometimes though, someone—Tracey, or Paz, or a complete stranger, pressed a button at the bottom of his back where a little life lingered, and his light turned on. For just a minute he would imagine things, and be a little beautiful. Matt wanted Dignity too, though he hadn't found that word yet.

Now, for the umpteenth time, he counted the stars on his ceiling. Stereo sound bashed against his bedroom door.

"I gotta get out of this place," Matt said.

All Paz heard was "out", and saw Matt's face. He understood.

"Me too," he replied, but Matt didn't hear that.

One star slowly trembled and wiggled its way off the ceiling, hung by one of its corners for a second, then fell and landed on Paz's forehead. On the front of his mind.

Her eyebrows

Tracey's eyebrows were lines for his finger to follow. Matt started at her nose bridge and his finger drifted up and down the eyebrow curve then went back to the start again, like a child on a slide. Each time, the smoothness surprised him. A contrast to the pair of tripping caterpillars on his own forehead. He would do it for twenty minutes, if he thought she was sleeping. Each time it happened that she wasn't, the touching rocked her to sleep anyway. Matt's own kind of lullaby.

One day she asked him, "Why do you do that?"

"Umm, dunno." Embarrassed, caught.

But he dared to keep doing it, and she stayed awake that time, and her wide eyes watched him. Then she touched him back, on his so faint smile lines.

Too much. He stopped. Twisted around on the bed and picked his comb off the floor and cleaned dust out of its teeth with his long thumb nail.

Pink river dolphin

Tracey would have liked a little more; for Matt to hold her hand in the street sometimes, for him to answer her questions. Instead, when they talked and got a little closer, his eyes would do circles around her. He had his list of excuses to look away, walk away, or change the subject. And she pretended that it was fine.

Her armour: apathetic and tough, thick skinned shrugposture, you can't break me, drink whisky fast and look unimpressed, fall over in football and keep running with deadface. Just three weeks ago she'd had her wrist tattooed. She'd chosen her wrist because it was better to seek pain than have it pursue her. The tattoo was a pink Amazon River dolphin, a complex creature that got its colour as an adult and had an unusually flexible neck and spinal column in order to manoeuvre among the underwater tree trunks of flooded forests. It liked to play with turtles, rub against boats, and was curious about strange objects. It wasn't often kept in captivity because it tended to die, and it was harder to train than other dolphins. It was also facing extinction in some areas due to the ongoing destruction of the Amazon rainforest.

"What does the tattoo mean?" people would ask her. And she would do her shrug, her not-that-it-matters gesture, and respond, "Most people don't know about the pink dolphins. But they do exist, in Bolivia, Venezuela, north Brazil, Ecuador, and Peru. There are things outside our worlds that we don't know about, and those things are possible. I'll go to Bolivia one day to see the pink dolphin."

Matt had stroked her new tattoo. He'd moved his finger up and down, petting the dolphin.

Birds drew their language in the sky

A few days later, Paz was sitting on his fence when seventy-two corellas landed on the grass strip on the other side of the road. They walked about, eying, pecking, and pulling at things in the ground. Then, with no signal, they lifted into the air and flew off. Their wind touched him and cooled him.

Mella was in the front yard, looking at the sky, when seventy-two corellas flew over and filled the yard with mottled shadow. As they flew, they invented corella-constellations, broke them and made new ones. They left her feeling a little cooled too.

Mella in the bath

Tongues are like sea monsters, Mella thought as she wagged her own about. She was alone in the house, and she was going to take advantage of it to have a long bath. Breathsteps to the bathroom. Rubber doorstop wedged underneath the door as tight as it would go, because the door didn't lock. Her towel with the big turtles printed on it, in a heap on the floor in the corner, as far from the bathtub as possible. Because that was the only bit of the floor that wouldn't get wet.

She lowered herself into the hot water, rested her head on one end of the tub, and her feet on either side of the tap. She wanted giggles, and she tried to make some by clicking her fingers on the water's surface. But her mind wanted to do the bath thing, and it wandered quickly to the 'and yet' part of life. She saw a world full of houseworkers or houseslaves, busy in so many houses, and no one knew they were there. Or no one cared. Bitter words and migraine words and 'and yet' over and over, she quickly went from tongue-playing to an internal tantrum.

Bath steam bumped the ceiling. With nowhere to go, it continued with the slow process of making green-grey mould and peeling off the cream-coloured ceiling paint.

There she was, a soft little human submerged in water, getting wrinkled quickly, not just from soaking but because she was upset. The things her father said, the things the magazines said, expensively dressed superstars, and her, hidden away with her shoes breaking at the toes and her one pair of old black jeans that didn't fit properly, scrunched-up by a belt around her waist. Her legs were wrong, her stomach was wrong. She used finger-scissors to cut lines up her legs, over the sides of her hips, her waist, arms. She wrote with her fingernail on her thigh: I am worthless.

Lowlife in a bath. She lay back and looked at the ceiling, just as Paz had looked at the stars coming unstuck. She looked at the peeling paint but none fell on her.

She rocked herself sideways in the bath: first she rocked the water, and then it rocked her. Her hair under the water became soft snakes swimming. And then she pulled the plug but remained in the tub and felt the water draining out, pulling her down. When the last of the water fell down the pipe with a thunderous gurgle, she was left naked in an empty bathtub, still without the urge to get out.

What seas do

There's a place in the Alaskan Gulf where two seas meet. One is light blue, the other is dark, and between them, a line of foam. Because of runoff from Alaska's glacial rivers, they have different salt proportions and therefore different densities, and a surface tension forms between them, acting like a thin wall, though the water does eventually mix. And what do the fish do? Perhaps they look at each other from their respective seas and wave.

Portrait of a town of unemployed and unwanted

Midday, and Paz climbed onto a car hood, then from there onto a dumpster, then onto the roof of Macquarie Field's little U-shaped shopping centre. From there he had a great view of most of the suburb; of the people and their absence of looking-forward-to, of their smoko wrinkles and their salty voices, of unfinished graffiti—quick flags of people trying to exist, of the housing commission homes with one window smashed and their rooms without furniture, of the long grass everywhere hiding the broken glass that snowed the streets, of the corner shop and its chico rolls soaking brown paper bags in oil, the pub, the McDonald's, the KFC, a few clothes shops, an ATM, and of the fluoro green golf course off in the distance. From up there on the shopping centre roof, he decided to make a complex photo, a portrait of the town. It consisted of:

—A conversation at the bus stop: "You're like a hobo with no socks on," she told her husband. His teeth were broken, yellow, or missing, and the tattoos on his legs green and washed out. One of their kids, two years old, wearing just a nappy and with a mouth lined in orange lollypop, drank coke through a straw and climbed on to her dad's lap. "Get orf me! Eh!" he joked. The two year old passed the coke to her brother; the father passed a bottle in a brown paper bag to his brother. Uncle refused to pass it to the wife—"you've had enough"—but she took it anyway and slapped him playfully on the head.

"Whattaya gunna do?"

—And one by the shopping centre doors: An eleven year old boy said hello to an old man in pants that looked like pyjamas. "I just had a seizure," he replied. The boy yelled out to someone on a bike, "Hey you, what time is it?" Then he looked back at the old man, "Hey, you got a spare two bucks?" The old man showed him a handful of silver coins. "Hey, you're right," the boy said. And then his sister, twelve, in make-up and a push-up bra, offered him a smoke.

—And a fair bit of impotent anger: After a short relationship with Sophie because Andy hadn't felt like sharing all the nothing he did with another person, he'd thought, 'I'm useless, pathetic, good for nothing'. Then a new girlfriend, Emma, and she'd asked him the wrong question: "What dya wanna do with ya life?" "How the fuck should I know?" he screamed again and again. He was being the person he hated, but couldn't stop. That time, she listened to him, touched his shoulder to show him she knew. Another time, though, he hit her hard. He wanted to break and bash that thing that meant he couldn't do anything at all with his life, but it wasn't there, and she was.

—And an imagined conversation: Jono imagined he was talking to a journalist who was unusually very interested in what he had to say. "There's nothing to do. From about ten you start smoking, and at twelve you start experimenting and try cones, and by thirteen you're already aggressive. At fifteen, you can try and leave the place cos you realise it's all fucked, but if you've got no way out, you stay. You bully, or get bullied, cos if you're bashed by one person and ten other people hear about it, it happens again. From fifteen to eighteen you steal. Everyone here has done something to put them behind bars. You're bored, you're jealous. You see people with their iPods and feel they're looking down on you, and it provokes you. And the cops are corrupt. They protect people selling drugs, and if you pull out enough money, then they leave you alone. And if you don't, the cops say that you did stuff, and you think, well then I may as well do it. Going to a party or something costs money, so you do crime to have a bit of fun." The imaginary journalist nodded seriously, as though she cared.

—And not the moon at night: It was a 7/11 shop, a bright cube of light on the corner, telling one and all that profit never sleeps. A teenager, like a moth, tipsy and attracted to the white cube moon, sought the mini-orgasm of a small purchase. Deodorant. For fun, she tried to jump over the soundthing at the door, but it dinged anyway. The guy behind the counter looked her up and down, saw her thongs, and became a bit nervous. She was going to pay for the deodorant, but to hell with it. She held it to her side and walked out as if she had changed her mind.

And to finish his photo portrait of his town: the butterflies of Macquarie Fields walked along the footpaths, walked in the shopping centre with their achromatic wings dragging along the ground behind them, collecting dirtdust.

What is a hero?
Are the real heroes seen or unseen? Why?

While Mella contemplated her fence, someone who would later become important to her contemplated his own. In Woomera refugee detention centre, South Australia, Rafi, a young man with grass-like hair and a cheeky smile leaned against the edge of the world and tried to see out. The fence's thick bars separated the surrounding nonstop desert into vertical strips, and it was hard for Rafi to put them together. He wanted that orange sandy sea so badly.

He looked around, a meerkat, tentative, and for once there were no guard looking his way. He twisted his arm between the thick fence bars. Mella had thought of a duck's lick, but Rafi only imagined that it would be windy out there on the other side of the fence. Beyond the bars, the air could go where it wanted.

A guard came into view, and Rafi pulled his arm inside too quickly. He knocked his elbow and a day later a purple bruise would appear. Of course, he'd forget by then how he'd got it. Behind him, the concrete land of linked cabins where the refugees slept could have been the grey moon.

Rafi the story teller, they called him. He turned his journey, his memories and his hard days into little stories about big things. Like how he had fled Iran, left tender streets and his big, broken brother behind, travelled in a boat that almost sank. He'd imagined arriving in Australia and things not being broken there, and being comforted and cared for. But he'd been in Woomera for two years now. Two years of doing nothing but waiting on the concrete moon. An old man inside.

Each day in the detention centre was the same, becoming one nonstop day, one desert day. Rafi worked in the kitchen from 8:00 am until 6.30 pm, then showered, ate dinner, and spent an hour teaching English to some friends. Then he'd read the newspaper. There were cameras on every corner; guards calling them by their numbers, never their names. Sometimes the monotony was broken by a letter from family or friends, or ruptured by a swift, quiet suicide. Now came a small rip. While Rafi still sat cross-legged on the ground, resting against the fence and squinting at the sky, there was a sudden crawling scream. No formal name for that sound that combined built-up desperation and physical pain. Rafi knew at once that it was Haman the Brave. He had had a toothache for a month now but wasn't allowed to see a dentist. In a month Haman had gone from sporty and uncle-like to a fidgeting fetusman. He groaned, he pinched and cut his arm, he swallowed shampoo, and he hard-hummed all night to distract himself from the pain that colonised his nerves and his imagination.

Rafi ran to Haman's room in Cabin #12, knocked, and looked inside. It was a bare room with four bunk beds, four bedside tables, and a small window near the ceiling. There were pages of notepaper and blue and black pens on Haman's little table, and on the paper he'd drawn angular frowning faces that overlapped and were etched so deeply that the paper had torn in places. Haman didn't look up, but he dulled his hard-humming and groaning to intermittent whimpers. Rafi entered and sat next to him on his bunk.

"How are you?" He watched Haman's dry eyes.

"My tooth is hurting still. It's such a small part of my body, I don't want it." He massaged his jaw, and his dry eyes didn't move. "I hate myself for talking about nothing else. I can't seem to remember what else there is."

"Sky," said Rafi. He pointed at the window. "Look how it changes," he said, as a pink scarf cloud drifted in, marking sunset time.

"Nothing changes."

"Checkers?" Rafi asked.

Hopping pieces around, click-clack sound, and Haman relaxed for a moment. Then the six o'clock knocking started, six o'clock check. The guard went from cabin to cabin, and the knocking got louder as he moved closer, and Haman started humming again. Then, "Five seventy-two, stop that ridiculous racket; four sixty-three, why aren't you in your cabin?"

Haman hummed even louder. He hummed his eyes big and his stomach tight and his skin red-blue. He gargled a long foreverscream sound; Brave turned inside-out as though it had been dissolved by salt. Haman made that sound, and the guard saw the multitude of drawn angry faces and the pens, and he took the pens and put them in his pants pocket.

"You'll get these back when you shut-up," he said, then left.

The salted-Brave sound stopped.

"Haman?"

So quiet now.

"Haman, I've got a few pens. You can have one of mine."

A blink.

He seemed to want to be alone. Rafi touched his shoulder and left.

Night, and there were no corellas. Stillness, then a rupture; something in the sky, finally. A pointy fire funnelling upwards, its grey smoke spilling out and staining the night. The smell of the demise of Cabin #12 was interesting. Hot wine. The refugees came out to watch; the guards came out with batons ready. Burning white sheets shrivelled into black balls, and a bloody white tooth rolled away. A Brave man was temporarily calm.

Damjan's legs

It was one of those rare moments when all of Damjan's large family was out. So he rang Paz and asked him over, and Paz passed by Matt's place, where he found him and Tracey and brought them both along. The four of them were now squeezed onto a three-person, sponge-pillow brown couch watching midday infomercials on television. Damjan on the left, then Tracey, Matt, and Paz. They each turned their shoulders in and put their hands on their knees so they could fit. They stretched their legs out straight and Tracey, Matt, and Paz's feet all lined up, but Damjan's stuck out twenty centimetres more.

When Damjan was a kid, people had said he had springs in his legs; when he was talking to people he would jump up and down on the spot. Once he made himself a tail out of a stuffed stocking, put on his dad's giant shoes, and kangaroo-ed all the way to the station and back, yelling "boing". Another time, he'd become convinced that by climbing the tallest trees he would be able to touch the sky. He climbed a lot of trees, but he supposed the ones in his area just weren't tall enough. And there was the day he announced to little Paz that he had invented a new dance; trampoline dancing. "They'll ask me to be on TV and I'll be famous," he said. Damjan the roadrunner/roadjumper/streetskipper, always walking along the tops of fences instead of the footpaths.

Now, Damjan's knees were falling asleep. He clacked them together and woke them up, but soon his toes would fall asleep. On the TV: ten minute long infomercials for all sorts of blenders, stretchy things for exercising, comfort wipes, wearable towels, potty putters, Ginsu knives (that came with a peeler, a fork, a steak knife, and a grater), Bark Off, music vests, Mighty Putty, and Blublocker sunglasses.

Damjan's legs twitched. Their springs were squeaky and rusty. They wanted to do something but Damjan paid them no attention. He focused on the television. Because it was better than focusing on the giant family that wasn't home right now. Some of them were unemployed, some of them worked night shifts, a sister was failing at school, being told she was a failure every ten weeks as each term ended, but never asked why, never helped, and two uncles in prison. Damjan was three years out of school and had worked a bit, but mostly he didn't see the point. His angular angry faces were undrawn, unmentioned. Instead, nausea curdled him back into bed in the mornings; his body screaming anxiety and Damjan not understanding it, blaming instead his smoking and drinking. He got used to always feeling a little bit off, and to not liking anything, even himself. Back to the television, the beer, to anything distracting, even the occasional lottery ticket. Damjan was lazy now, but mostly he was uninspired. And Paz had noticed. He thought Damjan needed some kind of project to work on, something to care about.

And then, finally, Damjan's legs couldn't take it any longer. They wanted to run around the world. They wanted to run up steep mountains then run back down again. Damjan wanted to want to join them. But his heart wasn't running. He got up though, climbed on to the couch back and lay straight across it. Paz followed and lay in the same direction, but on the floor, and Matt and Tracey also lay along the couch seat. Four twisted, craning heads in a row, and an infomercial for invincible glue.

And like that, with his head bent at a 90-degree angle, held upright by one hand, Paz had a big idea. A little too easy, a little too convenient. But he said it anyway.

"There's a place—three bedrooms, bit of a wreck, cheap—that's come up for rent. We should all move in together. Start something new."

Something. Something sounded good.

(Paz photo-dreamed. Fruit trees growing and bananas, pineapples, oranges and apples multiplying. A fruit salad yard. Damjan, Tracey and Matt among them, growing too, glowing too. Music blowing wind playing).

Necks hurting from 90-degree angles, the four of them squeezed back onto the couch again, hands on knees, feet dozing off.

The missing thing

Mella opened the gate and walked out. It was late night. After hours of wondering what it felt like to be okay, she had made two lists. One had lots of risk, the unknown, and the possibility of a meaningful life, and the other just had easy. Nothing else. So then she had gathered all the air that she could inside her cheeks and under her wings, as though to sustain herself, to hold herself up, and she had opened the door of her storage room, walked through the garden that wasn't, and opened the gate. She walked out of it hoping to find places where gardens grew.

She walked past the little fibro houses, and past the redbrick flats full of fractions of families, until she got to the eight-lane road. Then she walked past the first pub, then the second, past the first bank, then the second and the third, until she got to the Coles with its automatic double doors opening and closing and eating up late night grocery shoppers who tucked their car keys into their shirt pockets then irritably tried to ply apart a shopping trolley from the stack in the trolley queue.

Mella sat on the tiled ramp outside the Coles and looked for the muttering purple trees and aqua eagles and other adventures she'd hoped to find on the other side of the gate. Instead, she saw that dustdirt was here too, caught in the shopping trolley wheels and hiding under supermarket shelves and hovering in the air and coating the world's windows. She saw a supermarketworld of people muttering to themselves, one man with a trolley wheel that would only go left, mumbling, "No one listens around here", another man hissing after stubbing his toe on an unseen stair; she saw sighs and one brown eye twitching and someone with a lot of fallen out hair stuck to the back of his shirt, and short patience and tempers and two people telling exaggerated stories and rows of canned food wrapped in advertising. In the street, it was just-after-rain, and snails came out to draw their goo-lines across the footpaths, and in the dustdirt; the empty beer bottles, the broken feathers and broken leaves rode the rainwater, raced down the gutters, and disappeared into the nameless tunnels of the world below the pavements. And a small dead bird, the colour of rainedonpavement, got stuck in a drain corner. Its wings were full of water. Its stomach was vacant. And the boots, high heels, office shoes, and sandals walked past it—a bored war march. The small bird had thought it might find seeds on the road. Cars would have turned it quickly into part of the black tar had it not bounced sideways off the first wheel that hit it.

Mella's head filled with heavy rain and trafficsound and the supermarketbreathing of automatic opening and closing double doors. Shoppingpeople; little fires encased in jam jars. The asphalt city where the birds made roof gutters into their trees and the children fell out of the doors of storage with unkind sleep lingering in day like a dim death and one line monologues of here I am, I guess. All the hesitant whispering, and then hurricanes of the same argument repeated, pyjamas of a thousand sighs, and history hidden under the tar road.

And Mella there on the tiled ramp, aware of her state of barely existing, because she didn't touch or alter this world, barely dented it with her presence. Her and her justsayingnothing. She tried to say something to the crowd hurrying past her, brushing their bags against her knees and not stopping. She tried to say, "Excuse me," in a breathwhisper. But no one heard her, or no one stopped.

"Sorry," she said to the people who bumped into her, who accidently elbowed her. Help? She asked the jam jar fires but forgot to say it out loud.

She had thought she would feel something nice if she got up the guts to walk out the gate. But so far all she felt was that giant hole in the air that had clung to her back when she was at home. She felt it even bigger. It pushed her shoulders down further and her eyes more into ground. It was the Missing Thing. Life's big gap, big hole in the air, that gave her migraines sometimes, made her throw up, made her never really sleep well. What was it that seemed to be missing from absolutely everything, no matter which side of the gate she was on?

Whatever it was, she wouldn't find it in the garden that didn't grow, nor in the corners of the kitchen floor that the mop couldn't reach. Mella hopped down off the ramp. The backs of her legs were crisscrossed in tileprints. She walked around the side of Coles and through the arcade, to the train station. She caught the first train that pulled in, and spent the night curled up on a train seat, knowing that in the morning she would wake up somewhere new.

Someone stole the world

Paz in bed with his pillow folded in half, the room black and white because when the sun went down it took the colours with it. Noise, too, seeped down a drain somewhere and he slowly fell asleep.

Mella rested her head on one arm and was lulled by the

clickety-clackety sound of the train carriages on the rails.

Then they dreamed the same dream. The whole world had been stolen, and people tumbled about on it like hungry and lost refugees in a foreign land. All spaces seemed to be owned by private companies. And the world had fences in strange places. And many long walls.

Paz couldn't move, and his real leg jerked as though he had fallen down stairs. Mella murmured. In the stolen world they walked carefully, trying not to upset anything, like visitors. Barbed wire between their toes. They bumped into another wall and got a new bruise, and it seemed that there were bluebruised people everywhere discovering new walls.

A queue then to buy back a bit of the world: a little bit of space for $2.5 million, so they could have somewhere to sit down. But they had no money, so they walked and walked and bumped into walls.

Inside and outside
The morning was chilly and it stretched itself with yearning, and the air floated and rippled and picked up Paz's arm hair, and he got up and stretched too. With no barbed wire between his toes, no bruises on his legs, he had just a little bit of warningfeeling that he should ask someone for permission to move house today.

The place was a privately owned, three-bedroom house just a few blocks away. Matt and Tracey would share one room, Damjan and Paz another, and Damjan had a cousin, Ashley, with a three-year-old kid, who would have the third room. The lounge room was big, with a floor of thin grey carpet. The kitchen was in order apart from a detached oven door leaning against the wall, and the bathroom/laundry had just a cold water shower, a low toilet, and pipes jutting out for a washing machine. Three sponges, worn down to their bases, had dried in the gaps around the metal sink, making sponge-landscapes. The grass was knee-high in the medium sized back yard, and on one side the vinyl fence leant over towards the middle then fell down completely at the back. The Hills Hoist washing line was also leaning a bit, and with some oil or grease, the handle would work.

First thing that morning, the six of them walked around the town collecting every single milk crate they spotted, as well as a few broken bricks and some corrugated iron. Eva, Ashley's daughter, carried one crate in each hand, and wore one on her head "like a hat I can see through". From her position at the end of the line of six milk crate carriers, she muttered to people they passed, "These boxes are empty but they are HEAVY", and panted dramatically with her tongue all the way out. Another day she would ask her mum why a dog tied up outside the chemist was panting with its tongue out when it "wasn't even doing anything".

At their new house, Damjan ran backwards and forwards, carrying in the crates, bricks, corrugated iron, as well as some chairs they'd found the day before, and their mattresses they'd tied to the top of a friend's car. He ran around for an hour then lay on his bare mattress on the floor in his and Paz's new room and had a snooze with half an unlit cigarette hanging from his mouth.

The lounge room and kitchen were full of almost-dead cockroaches with their hairy legs peddling the air. Ashley calmly swept them into one corner. A few cockroaches got stuck among the broom bristles, and she picked them off. Then there was a plastic bag full of almost-dead cockroaches in the otto, and Ashley washed the kitchen all over with vinegar. The twenty-two milk crates became shelves and seats. The broken bricks and corrugated iron became a barbecue. Paz's grandmother had sewn them some curtains out of old sheets, and those went up about the house, with a thin rope used as a curtain rod. Matt reattached the oven door, Tracey scrubbed the bathroom/laundry, and Paz picked up rubbish from the front yard. Matt made some strong glue out of polystyrene and oil from orange skins, and used it to fix the letterbox, the lock on his and Tracey's bedroom door, and a few window panes. Eva asked him what he was doing then went and informed Ashley that "glue comes from oranges".

With most things set up, they all became cats in their new house; exploring it and doing little things to make it theirs. Paz knocked on the curled-over fence to listen to its echo, he smelt the bathroom/laundry, touched the lounge floor with his palms, poked his finger in all the house's holes and cracks, tried all the taps, and looked out all the windows with his nose and forehead pressed against them. Lastly, he checked the walls for shadows that might have stuck there. He found some from previous renters; some had left stuffysound stains, and a few others some shadows of deaths from drugs sadness aimlessness pointlessness.

Ashley measured the walls of her room and her bed with her feet then drew a diagram to work out the best way to arrange her bed, clothes rack, and four milk crates. Damjan woke up and smoked his half cigarette. Tracey stuck a map of Bolivia on their door, and other drawings, magazine cut-outs, and photos on their walls, moving them up or down, standing back, frowning, and adjusting. Matt watched her, and that was enough for him. Little Eva hid in every corner, called out for her mother to find her, then poked her head out to see if she'd heard.

(Outside: The slow sound of a hopeless town, the smell of twisted heat and swallowed tongue. Breath sliding out between clenched teeth. A woman with dragging feet and no expectations zigzagging nowhere. And the town's clock stopped, and bodies greyed and dropped on treadmills, and watched the train go past the length of borders, all because of the poverty bomb. Plants stopped growing and everything was might-as-well. The bodies of the town had stopped waiting years ago because they knew the buses would never come and the happy clown with jobs for everyone had caught an expensive flight back to Shinytown.)

And soon it was afternoon and they were exhausted. They went out the front and sat on the brick fence with its bricks that weren't quite attached and wobbled underneath them. Legs dangled. Damjan ran to the bottle-o and got a six pack and they sipped beer out there on the fence, that line around their world. Paz said he wanted their new house to be a place where they could support and respect each other, because no one else did. He said when mates got out of jail they could stay there too. Then it was like the sunset got inside them, and they felt free to do strange things. Damjan did handstands in the middle of the road, holding them for thirty seconds, each time doing different things with his legs; scissorlegs, peddlelegs, dancelegs, chairlegs, flamencolegs. Tracey watched and made little dolphin noises, and snuggled her nose into Matt's shoulder-space. Ashley hummed her own songs. Matt chatted about outer space, about what happens when two galaxies collide, about Saturn's weight (so light, it could float in water), about the smell of fresh moon dust and how astronaut footprints there lasted for millions of years. Eva planted a few of her marbles near the fence, then filled a cup and watered them. She liked to plant things and was sure she would have marble trees soon. And Paz took quickphotos because he wanted to remember. He mentally clicked Damjan in a handstand, Matt and Tracey together, Ashley relaxed, and the afternoon dropping down over the house and blanketing it in pink, then darkness. Then he made a few more photos, because he felt like it; itchy rain, bubble wrap thunder, and all their window ledges and all the window ledges he could remember, for a photo series about the different ways of looking outside.

(Outside: More police arrived in Macquarie Fields, a war march of officers in vans and cars. Thirty-eight new police officers in dark blue riot uniforms occupied, patrolled, inspected, watched, stalked the town, the streets, the skies and sunsets, poked people with batons—nudge-nudge—are you behaving well? Stern talk with the night, stern talk with the town. Giving lessons in dignity is for others, don't even try. Don't crave it, Paz. Police outside the bakery, outside the bank, outside the supermarket entrance, guarding the giant slippery floored, lit-up glow dome. Standard Glock .22 pistol, spare magazines, Saflock handcuffs, capsicum spray, expandable baton, and UHF portable radio clipped to belts. Maglite rechargeable torches in the boots of their cars, which at night were lightbatons pointed into car windows, house windows, late night walkers' musty eyes. During the day the German Shepherds came out, did what they were ordered at whistle or a word—it was the people who didn't quite do as ordered, who one day might bite, apparently. A week later they intensified the night patrol, parked in front of different houses and put on sweet sirens screeching and screaming to the song "Bad Boys", and they'd yell out to the people in their houses who were trying to sleep or study or argue out a stress rage: "Housies coming out to play tonight?")

Inside and Outside
Mella was waking up. With her head resting on her arm, she reached out with her other arm and her hand did a dance trying to find a bedside table and an alarm clock that wasn't there. She opened one eye all the way, and remembered the train, opened the other eye, and jerked fully awake. Two and a half million to buy some world. Trace of a dream walked slowly backwards into the distance, and blue train seats and passengers came into focus. Mella's hungry stomach sent off rumbles. "Shush," she told it, "I know already".

Then the feeling of a hard stare upon her. Heat on the top of her head. She looked up and there was a young man, his eyes doing elevators up and down her. She pretended not to notice the eyebrush. Instead, the train, tin can with ads on the ceiling and unreadable words scratched into the windows with keys or knives, and through the windows the morning colour of suburbs. The guard two carriages down blew his whistle and announced the next station over the speaker system, "Next stop Kingsgrove, Kingsgrove next stop". Then a recorded voice interrupted the guard, "Stand clear, doors closing", and that was also joined with another recorded voice from the platform, "Next stop, Kingsgrove". Mella noticed a don't care smell here too.

And the staring elevator-eyes man was talking to her: "I'm Ben. Are you okay?"

All she had with her were the clothes she was wearing (too big jeans, belt, white t-shirt from one of those packets of three) and in her shoulder bag, a small notebook, a black pen, an over 18 ID and a pink comb with two sizes of teeth spacing. No ticket, no money. But yeah, she was okay, she supposed.

Ben was going home from a night shift. She was pretty, she needed help, come back to his place; he had a couch, some food. And more soft words and pink words and he leaned forward to hear her whispered replies. "This is my stop," he said. Mella thought that the man seemed a bit strange but she had nowhere to go. So she followed his pink words off the train and to his third floor apartment.

There he took her by her hand and led her straight to his bedroom. It smelt of carpet cleaner and hair gel. And of no plants. Of no lifeleaf greenbit scratching itching to grow. He took a towel out of the built-in wardrobe and placed it on top of the bed, perfectly in the middle, perfectly parallel with the sides of the bed, and he flattened it out with his hand. He went to the kitchen, and brought back a carton of chocolate milk, opened it, put a straw in and put it on the bedside table. He squirted some anti-septic foam on his hands, rubbed them thoroughly, then took Mella by her shoulders and placed her down on the towel. A few more pinkwords carefully selected from a hand book of advertising jargon, then...

(Inside: Her stubs of butterfly wings with their urge to unfurl already, her blank canvases waiting to be shaken out and painted with all kinds of...confused by glue drops touching fragile wings, sticking them together in places, wreaking havoc among the chitin. Her half unfurled wings tried to curl back into themselves.)

Now there was a towel barely moved, a Mella barely moved, a half-drunk chocolate milk with a drop hanging from the end of the straw. There were lazywords coming from a stranger who was falling asleep beside her. There were various kinds of wet patches. Ben wiped his hands on the towel then rolled over and started to snore. Mella felt a strange solidarity with the towel.

Missing Thing was there loud and clear, big hole in the air nagging louder than her stomach. She still hadn't eaten. And despite it all, she wondered if now, this time, things would get better.

Nigeria 1: Money or life

Women were drying washing over oil pipelines in Odi, a town of 60,000 people in Bayelsa, Nigeria, when it happened. There, the pipelines leaked crude into the Niger Delta, into the surface water, ground water, and crops. Odi oil air, oilskin, oil fish, oil stained landscape. It was 1999, and President Obasanjo used the murders of seven police officers to crack down on resistance to Shell. Heavy artillery, grenade launchers, and mortars were pointed at Odi and wiped out crops, burnt yam barns, wrecked garri processing plants and the entire town except for three buildings, except for a few people. And for many women, when the soldiers found them, there was no towel, just wing colours falling.

Two weeks later, the washing was still draped across the pipelines. The defence minister said the "operation" was aimed at protecting property, particularly oil platforms. Odi barely made the news, and the soldier in command was promoted.

Busking days

On Monday, Paz met Ashley at Circular Quay. She had been busking long hours to cover her part of the rent, and he wanted to see how she was going. It had just rained heavily, and all the slugs, lizards, and centipedes had come out to crowd the footpaths. At the quay, seagulls, pigeons, and jellyfish bobbed about in or on the harbour water, unintimidated by the relatively giant ferries and RiverCats docked there. The ground was still wet in patches and puddles, and a few people still had their umbrellas up. Either they hadn't noticed that the rain had stopped now, or they were protecting themselves from the feeling of overcast, heavy air.

Ashley was leaning against the quay's cast iron fence, with one leg bent, and one hand holding out a white Macdonald's cup. She sang half-heartedly, face straight, low energy, weak words, because she knew that people were always more distracted and uncharitable during and after rain. Paz leaned against the fence next to her, and still holding her cup out, they talked quickly. Though she had a whole room, she should pay less rent, he argued. She agreed. And Paz wanted the conversation to go a little longer, so he asked, "What's it like, busking?"

"Oh, you know, no matter what you do, or how well you do it, people don't see it as real work. They'll stop and listen for a bit, but they won't talk to you or give you anything. I usually get about twenty-five dollars a day, in ten and twenty-cent coins."

"Your cup's too small, and you need to project a little

more confidence and commitment. Let's try this," Paz said, taking off his cap and placing it on the ground about a metre from her feet. He thought people might be more willing to give if they didn't have to go right up to her. "Let me busk too," he said. He purposefully didn't use the word 'help'. "You sing, and I'll mime."

Ashley shrugged, so Paz sat down next to her. She straightened up then and sang feelings and flywords and freefall. Paz, like a translator, put her song into his face and hands, added story to it.

A five dollar note landed in the cap. "He was just trying to impress his girlfriend," Ashley said.

Six coins dropped into the cap. "She was just trying to get rid of her small change."

A two dollar coin landed in the cap. "He's got a guilty conscience about something," she said.

On Tuesday, Paz arrived at Circular Quay with purple eyeliner in a thick ring around his eyes, and wearing a black and white striped long sleeve top, black jeans, and black gloves. Ashley sang solemn, nostalgia, disappointment, and Paz moved slow, soft, heavy-feet. She sang red anger and blue anger; he clenched his muscles, glared his whole chest. He was already listening to her; that other kind of listening where you don't just hear the sounds but try to work out what they mean. She felt less tired. "What are you seeing?" she asked.

"Oh..." He smiled. He didn't know where to start.

"There's a thousand pictures trapped inside you, isn't there? Eager to surface. That's why you always look a bit frustrated," she said.

So he was hearing her and she was seeing him, he thought.

Later, they took a break and sat in wharf four with their legs dangling over the harbour water. They counted jellyfish, and Paz tried to ask questions.

"What's your thing when you're down? Beer? Music?

Old Star Trek episodes?"

"I don't like beer. It's bitter and foul, and basically just cereals broken down by micro-organisms mixed with yellow flowers. Honestly, I'm always down. I'm used to it."

That night he lay awake thinking that it was like he had been tipsy all day. That clouds had tickled his ears and his self-control had gone. He'd crossed his arms tightly to keep his body still, and the excitement and laughter inside him. She'd asked him if he was cold. At one point, for no clear reason, he'd skipped around in circles. He was looking forward to tomorrow.

Ashley, on the other side of the wall in her room, felt this friendship fall from nowhere, and knew it seemed prettier now than what it would eventually be. Like everything else in the world. She thought it would be nice to have an adult friend and serious conversations, but no more than that. She calculated her caution and kept strong walls up around herself.

On Wednesday, Paz thought she was angry. They both went to the public toilet under Circular Quay station, and he finished first. He could see her washing her hands at the sink, turning on the tap violently and letting the door slam closed as she came out. Ashley always did that though. She had no urge to be quiet. She squinted, bit her upper lip, and her legs had some red dots where she'd plucked hairs out against their direction, on purpose. But just with the tone of his voice when he greeted her outside, Paz stroked her bitterness. So she explained it to him.

"When Eva was born, it was hard—the lack of sleep, the expenses. But Dylan didn't get it; he wouldn't let me complain. He thought my job was to make him happy. He said I'd ruined it all, and he hooked up with someone more cheerful. It's not rational to trust people," she said. And as soon as she said that, Paz wanted her to trust him.

On Thursday, sixteen minutes into busking, two patrolling police officers told them to move on, as they didn't have a permit. Paz asked where they could get one, but the police both shrugged. "That's not our job," they said.

Living with James Bond

With Ben gone to an afternoon work shift, Mella was alone in this stranger man's apartment. She had said to him as he left, said with a deep breath and a mouth half full of shame or something like that, "Can I stay here a while? I don't have anywhere to go". And he had said, "Well, I'll think about it", which wasn't the worst answer, but it made everything vague and uncertain, to go with the weather that day. Wandering weather, air undecided, storm or break into sunshine, or conjure an earthquake.

Mella walked slowly about the small apartment, looking at its details, looking at Ben without him being there. In the lounge room there were three pendant lamps hanging from the ceiling, and grey egg footstools on either side of a glass coffee table with a base of joined teak wood strips. The television was mounted in a black display case that spanned one wall to the other. The cream leather couches were too-perfectly clean, and the white walls were plain: no pictures, posters, or photos.

She walked quickly past the large rectangular mirror hanging in the hall, avoiding her reflection, and knocked over a vase of plastic long-stemmed peonies. A label where a leaf should have been noted that they had been grown with injection moulding in one of the hundreds of artificial flower factories in the Pearl River delta area of Guangdong province, China. Fuzzy pink petals were scattered about the carpet. Mella got down on her knees and gathered them into her palms. Then, even though Ben's apartment was spotless, she vacuumed the area around the vase, tidied the remaining plastic peonies, and dusted the vase. As though to make up for her mistake. Then on tiptoes, sound of socksonfloor, controlled scuttle, she went to look at the display case.

The first thing she saw was the gun. According to the packaging, it was a James Bond replica, a Walther PPK semi-automatic, "a small, flat, easily concealed and stylish weapon and James Bond's signature firearm in most of his movies". On either side of it were model cars; a Lotus Turbo 1/36 from *For Your Eyes Only* and a Corgi James Bond BMW Z8 from *The World Is Not Enough*. The model cars included interior decoration, spoke wheels, working side missiles, and chrome mirrors. On the shelf below, there were chronologically ordered box sets of all twenty-one James Bond movies, and two special James Bond ties in see-through display boxes.

Ben believed in James Bond. The character had taste, knew how to dress, wear watches, drink cocktails, seduce fashionable women, talk to the rich, and drive a range of cars, boats, and planes. Unlike Superman, he was also a regular human being; it was his gadgets that were 'super'. Ben liked the idea of being able to buy super things. Every 26 December he sold his old gadgets on Ebay—his phone, mp3 player, tablet computer, laptop, game consoles, television, wireless modem, printer-scanner, digital camera, and his multi-functional watch, and bought newer versions of each. He usually bought some new gadgets too; a handheld projector, a pen-thermometer, an electric foot massager, a musical blender, a battery operated car vacuum cleaner, a battery recharger with a touch screen, and a fingerprint operated coffee machine. He would have bought more things; a special bed, a better car, but his salary as assistant manager in the Westwood Hotel was average. The hotel was four-star, had a large entrance hall and lobby, art in its main stairwell, two honeymoon suits, bathrobes and slippers in all rooms, a pillow menu, a small gym, and a conference facility. Ben oversaw the front desk, monitored the staff, contracted extra cleaners and receptionists for the busy season, and was responsible for general presentation. His favourite task was the bar menu, which he constantly updated according to seasonal availability and demand. He felt he had a similar work ethic to James Bond. He worked hard, alone, and was loyal to the hotel. He would do whatever it took, including firing workers and overtime, to get his job done, but unlike James Bond, he did get stressed, exhausted, asthma, and intensely blocked nasal passages.

Mella fingered through the books Ben had on the lower shelf on either side of the television. There were car, train, and financial magazines and electronics catalogues sorted into coloured cardboard holders, James Bond novels, books about the history of the series, a Roger Moore memoir, Indiana Jones DVDs, and a Jurassic Park novel. She pulled that out and like a tiger, spread herself across the full length of the couch. She opened the book in the middle and read a few paragraphs. She closed her eyes and she was there, and she kept reading with her eyes closed. She gave the dinosaurs details the author hadn't mentioned—hairs and wrinkles and eyebrows and neck horns and blue claw nails and spotted tongues. And they smelt like cake and felt confused, and she was talking to them. A few more paragraphs from the book, and then she closed her eyes again. Toes curling and uncurling, quiet breathing, pleasant smell of printed words. Half a waterburp escaped and floated away on the air like dandelion seeds. Sunbathing tiger reader.

A few hours later, there was the sound of key rattle, and Ben walked in and woke her up. He tapped her on the shoulder and held out a fitted grey t-shirt in a royal blue box. "For you!" he said, big grin and eyes wide.

"Oh, what's that?"

Ben pointed at the word across the top. "Givenchy! It's a big clothing brand."

"Why does that matter?" She felt intimidated. Her eyelids went hot red.

"Go on, try it, and throw out that awful thing you're wearing."

Ben turned on the television and sat on the couch next to Mella. There they were, Mella in a brand t-shirt, compromise of a reading tiger, legs adjusting to this man who was a compromise of a James Bond. She read dinosaur stories and her eyelids cooled down. Ben's tired eyes half followed a program while one hand held a cocktail shaker. He drank his martini straight from it.

Paz's forbidden fruit

It was Sunday and overcast and there were too-early autumn winds painting the trees orange, yellow, red, brown, brittle. The people in the Macquarie Fields house weren't going to wait for blue skies though. They were holding their housewarming that day, and they sent messages, made a few phone calls, yelled out at the people across the road and on the other side of the curly fence, and word spread. By eleven o'clock the backyard was full, and there were neighbours in the lounge room, in the doorways, three people squeezed onto the Cracked Step, another kid rocking on the loose brick in the front fence, and people sitting on the kitchen bench, legs swinging. Matt and Tracey went around asking people to chip in a gold coin for food, then Ashley and Damjan went with a neighbour in his van to the supermarket, and returned with a box of cheap green grapes, four kilos of the pinkest sausages, a kilo of onions, a few bottles of tomato sauce, six loaves of white sandwich bread, and six slabs of beer.

Soon barbeque smoke was splitting like hairs around gum tree branches. Flies and mozzies drawn by the smell of well-burnt sausages hovered and dashed through smoke holes, through conversations, and into beer cans. The mozzies bit ankles, toes, thumb knuckles, and necks, and then disappeared into the grass, leaving behind a crowd of absent-minded scratchers.

Improvised ash trays became people-circle makers. An old pickle jar left outside and half filled with water was eventually three quarters filled with ashes. A few days later Damjan put sticks and twigs in the pickle jar too, snails slid around it, mosquitoes bred in it, and a weed flower grew out of it. Time and nature made it part of the yard-house landscape, and Eva thought it was a special thing, and dared not touch it.

Ashley had given Eva some electronics catalogues. Junk mail from the last week, and as her mum had told her that junk meant 'rubbish', Eva wondered why people would mail junk and why people would eat it. Now she turned this mailed junk into paper planes—one for each guest. She handed them out, and people looked at their gift and thanked her with unsure expressions. They held the plane in one hand with their beer in the other, planning to get rid of it once Eva had forgotten and moved on to something else. But when everyone had a plane, one teenage neighbour threw his into the air, then suddenly everyone was throwing planes around: seventy-two flying papers. Summersaults, eagleflight, owl dives, then smooth landings; planes parking themselves between people's feet, on the hot barbeque grill, on a few heads and shoulders, pulling in on window ledges, getting stuck on the roof. Eva tapped on a nearby leg and asked its owner why there hadn't been lots of little clouds?

"Why would there be?"

"Because that's where clouds come from; they are made by planes," she said.

Meanwhile, Paz was sitting on the grass with some people around a margarine lid ashtray. He listened to the chatterstories and pulled a worm out of the ground. It was really just a wiggling digestive tube with a mouth at the front for eating dead organic matter, an anus at the end to release the humus, and five hearts. Paz dropped it back on to the ground, and by the time he'd taken a sip of his beer, it had disappeared underneath the dirt. He wanted to photograph worms close-up. And learn one language from every continent. And understand rocks, read the ground's stories. And try many different fruits and vegies. The supermarkets sold perhaps twenty kinds, always the same. He wanted to try giant chachafruto beans, yucca bread, fried plantain with guacamole, salty mangoes, guanabana juice. And photograph the huge, awkward red papaya, the hairy red rambutan and its pearly centre, the hard purple-shelled mangosteen, the bumpy patterns of the jackfruit, the little cloudberries, cocky apple and dead man's fingers just because of their names, the coarsely wrinkled chayote, the white, yellow-dotted noni fruit (sometimes called vomit fruit because of its smell when ripening), the lantern husk of the physalis, the translucent langsats, the Amazon aguaje fruit with its red scales, and the romanesco and its Fibonacci patterned exterior. And all the photos he took, he would print them out on A1 paper and stick them in hospitals, to make the walls less bare.

Someone put the Whitlams on very loud, and Paz went into the lounge room and air-guitar danced. He sang along too, as loudly and as out of tune as he could. Then, as though imitating crabs that think danger has gone, people came from the kitchen, back yard, front fence, and bedrooms, and crowded into the lounge room. They danced, little Eva among them clenching her fists and jumping up and down on the spot, her head angled up towards the adults, certain she was copying them perfectly. Damjan's legs jogged hard in quick dance; Tracey was smoother, like she knew what she was doing; Matt was happily awkward. Ashely stood in the doorway, not joining in. Paz noticed and his urge to air-guitar deflated. He asked her questions with his eyes from across the room, weaving his look in and out of the people until it reached her and she looked back, shrugexpression, shake of a head, No I don't want to, but it's okay. Paz considered insisting, wanting to grab her by the hand and pull her into crowddance, but deciding to leave her. Remembering that more than anything he wanted her trust. Four more songs, then most people left the lounge room again, back to the yard, the fence, the bedroom, kitchen, but puffing and cheek flushed, eyes grown just a little bit bigger.

(Outside: Two police officers in a van parked out front and counted seventy-two people from the community in the house where Paz and Matt lived. They wrote it down in their notebook).

When birds yawn

Carrying one hundred and eighty-eight printouts of her resume and a reference in a manila folder under her arm, and wearing her too big jeans and her new fancybrand t-shirt, Mella took the train into the city to begin her week of job searching. Starting in the business district then moving out to the inner city, Mella walked into restaurants, shops, pubs, laundromats, offices, food courts, shopping centres, cinemas, ice-cream street stalls, game arcades, juice bars, flower shops, and even hairdressers.

Ben had designed her resume and written her a reference as assistant manager of his hotel. He'd spent hours playing with fonts, line and paragraph spacing, and styles, trying to make her "hospitality" skills look impressive. Marketing her. She had felt uncomfortable, seeing her name so huge, double underlined, Gill Sans font. Ben's reference had come with a condition. He wanted her first two weeks' pay cheque "to cover your expenses so far in the flat".

Mella walked and walked and smiled and smiled and said please please please accept my résumé my leafletadvertisement with my life in Gill Sans. In doors, out doors, until her shoes squeaked and her ankles squeaked and her smile squeaked. Even out there she walked on the edges of her toes, whisperwalking to go with her mumbledvoice. But she walked extra fast past the windows and glass doors with reflections, and in the same kind of movement she dodged-ducked under people's gazes as they took her résumé. She trekked up the moving mountain escalators in shopping centres, fell over traffic lights, tripped on the edges of gutters, glanced into drains, forgetting about the sky above in the city where people lose their shadows because only sunpatches made it through the sky scrapers, skyblockers, sky-eaters. She forgot, for a while, about trees and lifeleaves because the roads had deleted the forests like ruthless erasers. After a few days her t-shirt didn't look so new anymore, and she wore holes into the pavements and her squeaky heals blistered. The people who received her résumé would look at it, at the glowing personal reference from a hotel assistant manager, then look her up and down and not bother hiding their surprise. She would excuse herself using their words, "It's just that I'm walking all over the city. Once I start work I'll have good personal presentation." She felt she had to use a different voice, one with five fruit flavours added. And that was the hardest part, harder than the walking—changing her voice. Then accepting rejection after rejection. And there were blisters formed somewhere inside her too, near that place where wings were meant to grow.

Still, Mella kept walking through the insomniac city. Streets set to brown and grey. A man tried to walk through the automatic doors of a bank. They didn't open so he backed up a step, and walked towards them again, his head pointed forwards in concentration. Again they didn't open, and again he repeated his dance. Then a flood of people, released by the beeping green man of the nearby traffic lights, all walked towards the bank doors, and this time they opened. The man walked in with them and went straight to a counter to fill out a yellow withdrawal slip.

Elsewhere in the city, on its corners and in key building entrances, were people wearing all their clothes all at once, dirt under their averted eyes. Like city street furniture, the beggars, the homeless, became permanent, expected, unseens. Ghost-like, they unintentionally haunted the city, watching its people move through its veins, predictably, but watching as though from another dimension, as though behind a one-way mirror. The police, wealthy young drunks, and others with something strange to prove, or too much boredom, would beat up the homeless, knowing nothing would come of it. Other people flung their cigarette ashes at them, or left them a half-eaten sandwich that they didn't like, filled with the notion that they were being generous. Recently, a man sleeping in the entrance of a suburban arcade had been set on fire. But when the homeless died, it didn't make the news. Another man had lived twenty years next to one of the George Street ATMs. He had fine cotton hair—grey, white, blue. It climbed the tiled walls behind him, following the groves, like a bean plant. He hummed to himself and read the newspaper with one hand, with the other always out straight, cupped, ready for some spare change. One day, he wasn't there, and no one asked why.

And the fifth day, Mella walked slowly home from the station. She stopped, just once, when she saw a red bird singing its I-am-here songs. She breathed in, and dared to say out loud, "Hello, little bird". Then she kept walking and came home to a Ben set to brown and grey. She sat down on the couch feeling full of no we don't need...no we're not interested...no you're not what we're after...no you're not presentable enough...no thanks, not today. She left her dinosaur story book where it was, and instead picked up the remote and flicked through television channels without noticing what each one was yelling. She wondered if anyone would call her.

No camera

Two weeks behind on rent, and two reminder notices for the electricity bill, with a third due in three days, incurring a fifty-dollar fine. Paz called a house meeting for that night, and they made cereal with bananas for dinner and sat in the lounge room. They decided they would all increase their efforts to find work, or would work more, turning down nothing. From the start they had ruled out illegal ways of getting funds, wanting the house to be a clean start for all. But Matt was tilting his head at Damjan, and Damjan was small-shaking his head back, and Paz saw them. He decided to get work that week, no matter what it was.

Each morning he got up at 6:00 and bought three newspapers, and came back and sat on the lounge room floor with them. He colour-coded his search; highlighted in pink and yellow with a cereal flap ruler for straight lines, jobs that he liked and jobs he thought he could get. Then he listed and columned and numbered them all, and spent the next few hours on the phone.

On the third day, he saw an ad for an assistant photographer in a school photo company. He called the number straight away, and was told to come into the head office for an interview. Paz then had a measured morning of quick porridge for breakfast, an eight minute shave, a timetabled train trip, a calculated walk from the station, a too-quick glance at a waxed blue sky and a gentle sun, straight collar, extradust flicked away.

From the third floor of the ANZ tower, he stood in the reception area looking down at the street, as he waited to be called. A woman in a grey t-shirt and too-big pants, carrying a manila folder under her arm, went into a shop, came out, and then went into the one next to it. Each time, she tripped a little as she came out. Then he was called, and his interview was over in four minutes. Afterwards, Paz only remembered snippets of it; the courtroom layout of the room, empty except for a polished wooden desk, a multifunction phone on one corner of the desk, an executive tall-backed chair on one side of it and a standard office chair on the other. A look up and down at him and a decision made. Then questions, as though to taunt: three cameras placed in front of him; "Which one has the greatest aperture range? Which is best for indoor photography and why? Which brand is more reliable?" Then, "You don't have a portfolio?" "You've never owned a camera?" "You haven't even finished high school?" And Paz waiting for them to ask him about what he was interested in. "Well, good luck", and he walked downstairs then out the door, and tripped.

Over the next few weeks, Paz got three days' work at a local 7/11 filling in for a sick neighbour, but no interviews. The fast-food places said they were after teenagers, and most other jobs, no matter how menial, demanded experience and references. He felt like he was wasting money and time on all the phone calls, newspapers, and resumé photocopies, and looked for work every second morning, then just on Saturdays and Wednesdays. He wondered why he had dreamed of languages and rocks when it was becoming clear he wasn't good for anything. Other times he would tell himself it was "normal to spend months looking" and that "something would come in eventually". But between those two views, he was frustrated, and frustration tends to make its victims mad. He became vulnerable to exaggerated responses to small annoyances, to yelling at strange times, to inappropriate impatience. He was often tired by late morning, got dry skin and dry brain, and swore the phone had begun to smell a bit. Like it was going off from too many rejections. And the lounge room floor newspapers were bare of pink, hopeful highlighter.

So many smithereens

The people of the world all had trees growing from their heads, in a way. The tree branches curled across roads and fields, meeting with other people's branches and twisting around them. Their leaves fell to the ground and formed an endless carpet-sea of crackling orange-green, and no one ever knew to which tree the leaves belonged. If the moon could see, it would have seen one giant forest.

Zooming in, it would have seen a knitted jumper of branches, an endless dance. There were hundreds of millions of different flowers and fruit too. Better than fireworks.

But when people were unemployed, used, abused, or sad in a long-term way, their headtrees did other things; buried down into their stomachs and the leaves fluttered into their feet and stayed there. For some, their headtrees stayed little and the leaves brushed someone's cheek, but not much more. The moon looked down and saw a broken forest; too many smithereens.

The spaces between people

One day Tracey and Matt were sitting in the yard. They kissed, but not for long, never for too long. He talked to her, but with a table or a joke or a vast rumbling river between them.

"So, what did you do today?"

"Same old... And I went and talked to mum; she's so angry about everything."

He sat back; she leaned in closer. She didn't like the river.

Another day Matt didn't touch her at all. He sat among the weeds, the barbeque, and the mozzies. She watched him from the back door, then went over and put her hand on his shoulder. Finally, he touched her, but not the way she wanted. He stood up, put his hand firmly on the back of her head and pulled it to him, and then he kissed her hard, and his tongue teeth, her teeth, all clashed, and his lips tongue moved quickly like a child in the throes of a tantrum. She went with it. Better than nothing.

And one afternoon she tried his moves back on him. She grabbed his head and kissed. He felt shy, kissed back, called her something awkward like darling, and looked past her at anything, at the wall, at the waxed sky, at the curly fence.

The next day he had his river around him, and she

respected it; they sat a little apart. They shared beer from a can, he talked about stars, and she talked about Latin American river creatures. But there were shadows. Felt but not seen, they ghosted the walls, gurgled in the river. Shadows of bills, and landlords, of police patrols, of employment sections of newspapers with just one or two yellow highlights.

Anxiety's pace

Damjan lounged in floppygorilla position in front of the television, and Matt paced triangles in the backyard. They now had an unpaid bill with a fine, and daily phone calls from the landlord, and Damjan's anxiety took the form of lounging, of legs with less energy, of long sleep-ins followed by morning television. Matt, on the other hand, spoke less. So far their only income was Ashley's busking, Tracey's reduced dole payments, and Paz filled-in one more night at the 7/11. Matt had been asked various times by neighbours to fix things, but the neighbours were often even worse off than they were, and he found it hard to charge them. Usually, he just asked for a coffee.

Damjan took out a half-smoked cigarette and lit it, then remembered that in the same pocket he had three scratchies he'd bought a few days before. Buying them was habit, like his sleeping in. It was another quick rush, and he never expected to win. But just for the sake of doing something, he scratched them with his nails, flicking the latex coating dust onto the old newspaper with his cigarette ashes. And the first ticket revealed three rainbow symbols. He had won one thousand five hundred dollars. "Ha!" was all he said. He put the scratchies back into his jeans pocket, and kept watching television. A little later, though, he made lists in his head, and some calculations. One carton of ciggies, some cask wine; dry white, a bit of pot, and a four-litre box of no-frills Neapolitan ice-cream. He would fill out the claim form, have a bit of fun, and it would still leave one thousand, four hundred for house expenses. He flicked channels.

Outside, Matt was calculating too. Just one rorted camera from a disorientated tourist with insurance, two hundred and fifty dollars or so as a quick sale on E-bay. Tell the others the money was a loan from an auntie, just this once. Matt's pacing stopped abruptly, changed into walkingsomewhere. A feeling of sweaty relief to have somewhere to go and to be able to help out.

What is beauty? The price of dolphins

Tracey entered the western Sydney strip club aware of leaving behind the gentle black night as she walked down the stairs to the below-ground venue. She had got work for Friday nights, and she told herself, in red pen, over and over, that it was basically getting paid to dance. Though she'd never sewn before, she made her own costume. She laid out some light grey, skinny jeans and a pink georgette blouse on her bed. Then she drew the two sides of the dorsal fin freehand on an old grey t-shirt, rubbing bits out and re-drawing them. She used a ruler to measure the stitch holes along the fin's edge, three millimetres apart. Dipping a size 00 paintbrush into white paper glue, she drew small water drops all over the blouse, jeans and fin, and sprinkled silver glitter onto the glue.

At the entrance to the club, neon outlines of women on poles flashed redgreenredgreen, and inside big bouncers in black took men to their seats. Five-dollar cocktails, and no windows. Around a wooden stage lit by dimmed, recessed lighting, men drank beer from Styrofoam cups and red wine from clear plastic cups and ate peanuts from little plates off tables with plastic tops so they could easily be wiped down. At side tables, buyable bits of body moved up and down poles in the same rhythm as the neon lights.

Tracey on the wooden, somewhat creaky stage holding a bucket of water, wearing lipstick, eyeliner, body glitter—takeaway beauty bought for twenty-two dollars from Kmart, sold for...well, she'd see how much she could sell it for... She danced, and eyes began to eye-eat, to calculate with wallets in one hand, fingers rubbing notes. Men protected by the watching-audience state, a state that gave them permission to yell out whatever they wanted at the thingperson on the stage. Roars, wetgrunts, growls, bubbledribble, cupbeer flung in comatose overstated excitement, and yells of "Show us!" "Take it off!" "Bring it!". They threw money, and at the end of it all she scrambled around onto naked knees and picked it up and walked-almost-ran off the stage, leaving a trail of wet floor, glitter, beer foot prints, and a tanglepile of dolphin skin behind her.

Dragged

Ben came home at 6:00 pm on the dot.

"Hey babe! God, I've been thinking about coming home to you all day."

(She had been looking for work, and hadn't thought about him at all.)

"I like having you around."

(Really?) She smiled. (He wants to...I'm not in the mood.) "Well, that's good. You sound like you've had a nice day."

"Let's not talk about work. Come on, come here..."

"Wait, wait... I visited twenty-five places today, and people kept asking me for a copy of my..."

"Later, babe."

He put one hand on her waist, and moved her towards him. He kissed her. She let him. He stopped to breathe, she tried to talk. He plugged her up again with another kiss, then prince-like (Bond-like), he dragged her into his room.

In his mind, she floated.

He threw her onto the bed.

More smithereens

"How many times can you do it in one night?" John asked

as they lay in bed.

Jane stared. "What is it with you and numbers? Always measuring and scoring..."

She turned away and rolled to the edge of the bed. Then she built a tight, opaque cacoon of sheet and blanket around herself.

John masturbated calmly, came coldly, and wiped his hands on her cacoon.

"Goodnight, Jane," he said to a disturbed bed lump.

And he huddled as far to the other side of the bed as he could.

Bees go home

It was another Sunday in Macquarie Fields, but this one was windless, hotdogless, and full of bees. There were bees by the bus stops, bees in the grass around the street bins, and bees in little lines, efficiently pollinating the weed-flowers that grew along the front yard fences. There was a gentle peace, but it was marred by an awareness that calmness is a fragile thing, and tends to be short-lived.

In the house they were having a late Sunday breakfast of spaghetti, cheese, and peas. They stood hunched together in the small kitchen, their bowls in their hands, eating with big bites because they were hungry, and chatting. Six peas rolled and dived off Matt's plate onto the floor, then scattered quickly and disappeared into another dimension.

"Find them, otherwise we'll step on them, or Eva will eat them, or the cockroaches will," Ashley said.

Matt bent down and looked between legs into the dark recesses of under-the-stove and kitchen corners. "They aren't here. They've gone."

As they finished their spaghetti, every now and then one of them looked at the floor out of the corner of an eye, or tilted his or her head to the side, trying to spot a pea. Damjan collected the plates, Ashley ran water into the sink, and Eva, with the aid of a pick-up from Tracey, shook green "ghost" detergent into the water, then bashed the surface with her hands to make bubbles. Matt washed, Paz dried, and Tracey put away, while Damjan told them all about the best and worst Australian television series.

It was a day for cleaning and grass-cutting. Half of them swept their rooms, and half swept out the kitchen and lounge room, then they cut the grass. Having no lawnmower, they spaced themselves around the backyard and cut handfuls of grass with scissors or knives. Damjan was impatient and distracted, and pulled clumps of grass out with his hands. Bees drifted in to inspect their work, and finding nothing sweet, circled twice, then flew off. When they'd finished, Eva offered to collect all the grass "and put it in a box so we can feed it to a horse one day", but Ashley said they should just leave it on the ground; it was good for the soil.

As time passed, rules and customs evolved in the house. Those who came home late from work were never the ones to cook dinner. When Damjan's occasional girlfriend, Melissa, broke up with him again, he pulled a crate up to the couch, put a beer and a margarine lid ashtray on it, and put on a movie. Then, like worms sensing rain, the others would come out of their rooms and sit around him. Sometimes someone would leave his or her money on the television or the couch, and someone who needed it would take it. No one worried, though; they knew the person would pay it back soon.

Now, with cleaning and cutting all done, Damjan brought his mattress into the lounge room and the six of them listened to TripleJ radio. Damjan, like all of them, had been affected by the unemployment in one way, but he was also affected by the house in another, and he wanted Matt and Paz to get up early and jog with him, counting houses as they went. Tracey was spending Saturdays being tough and distant with aggressive eyes, but from Sunday onwards she would warm to her housemates and become playful again, hide their spoons while they were eating, or write them letters and put them in the mailbox. Ashley was grating her teeth less and making up stories for Eva at night. The more ridiculous and fantastic they were, the more Eva liked them, and the other housemates would often listen and modify the stories.

"A dinosaur..." Ashley would say.

"A one-legged dinosaur!" Tracey would interject.

"A whistling, one-legged, twenty-toed dinosaur!" Paz would say, and it would go on.

Paz, though stuck in his slightly mad frustration, and believing his dreams to be futile and dignity a privilege for others, was nevertheless composing photos more and more. Ashley had brought him a guide to photography on one of her library trips, and after reading it, his photos included things he hadn't been aware of before; light tone and quality, deliberate overexposure, and angles to add depth. Matt was becoming known as a fixer of things, and people were calling him from all over the block, and then three blocks away, and five. Gifts now included not just a coffee but also a few tins of tuna, bags of oranges, and mini-packets of cereal.

The radio shifted from news to music; the afternoon grew old and night came, and a bee dropped dead on the lounge room window sill.

Then the phone rang, and they all imitated getting up by straightening their backs and leaning a little toward the phone, but hoping that someone else would get it because they were in a state of lovely relaxation on the mattress. But the ringing of a phone is hard to resist, and eventually Ashley grunted, stood up and answered it. From the gentle way she talked, and the glance she directed at the couch, they all knew it was another kid running away from the boys' home. And they knew what would come. The kid (tonight it happened to be two), put in a home because his parent or parents had financial, psychological, or addiction problems, had run away from the home because he was frustrated with being treated like he was the one with the problem, like he had committed a crime, and he would come to their place on his first stop in his search for something like freedom. Paz, who had spent a short time in one such home, would stay up with him for hours, listening as he described it and joked about his future— joked, because it was impossible to talk about it seriously. Eventually, talked out, the kid would fall asleep on the couch with one foot scraping the floor, and Paz would take the sheet off his bed and cover him. The next morning, or the one after, the kid would go back into the world, lost still, but with a few names and numbers.

Another time, it was a woman who had had a fight with her twenty-year-old husband and stayed for a few days until things cooled down. Or it was Ned, who refused to stay with his violent father, but who at fourteen couldn't get any Centrelink support. He had stayed on their couch for a few days then gave up and went back too. Once, two brothers that had stolen a car from a driveway which always had four cars parked in it, had been spotted, and needed somewhere to hide for a week.

"It's not morally wrong, you know," one of them said, "stealing from people who have more than they need, and with property insurance too."

Those staying left traces; beard shavings in the sink, a body dimple in the couch where they had slept, or a warm spot on the floor if there were two of them, or a tap that squeaked after they tried to turn it the wrong way, or a blocked pipe or a fixed one. And traces of notes in the notebooks of police shadows outside.

When the two kids from the boys home arrived, Ashley cut up some apples for them, then everyone called it an early night. The boys, one on the couch and one hugging a pillow on the floor, were asleep within minutes. Ashley opened Paz's door a little, and with a plate of apple slices, signalled to him to come out. She climbed onto the roof first, Paz passed her the plate, then he climbed up and sat next to her. Night was strong now and the dark sky heavy in a comforting way. The smell of hand-cut grass tickled their backs as they looked at their street and beyond.

"They say we're lazy because we don't make it to the top of the ladder. We're drinkers, abusers, unintelligent, we're a mob of anonymous ugly people who are undeserving of the few bits of help we're given, like the cheap housing or subsidised medicine. Of course, you put beer or drugs or a night out in the hands of the upper classes, and it takes on a different tone, it becomes glamorous," Ashley said.

Paz put his cold hands inside his pants pockets; he was surprised to find a pea in one, and in the other, a dead bee.

"Sometimes I imagine that it's a trick. That we're all born as wrinkled, short- sighted naked little babies, all the same really, but all the babies have labels on their heads that say either 'Doer' or 'Controller'. There's six thousand Doers for each Controller. The Controllers live in luxury; own four cars each, you know. And the Doers work, and for them working is the same as living, and they live in dark tunnels and don't really see much. Their mouths slowly close up from disuse. Sometimes a Doer escapes, but outside the tunnels there isn't much to eat, and of course they are called 'lazy' or 'useless' for wanting to escape. But it's all a trick, Ash, because the Doers all think they were born with those labels on their heads, and the whole set-up has to be like that, but actually, it's a Controller who puts the labels there."

The strong night smiled, briefly flashing its millions of white teeth, then closed its mouth over them with a burst of thick cloud cover.

Orange blood

The woman that rang Mella didn't offer her a job. Instead, she asked Mella if she could attend training on Friday, Saturday, and Sunday, and told her to bring her tax file number, bank details, and ID, and to wear a white shirt, black skirt, stockings, and polished shoes. Mella borrowed money from Ben for the clothes, and sex that night was quick and efficient.

Mella arrived at the BBB department store half an hour early. It was located in the centre of the city, opposite the Queen Victoria Building, and directly above Town Hall Station. It had four sales floors; the top one was a restaurant, the one below was clothes and haberdashery, the ground level one, where Mella was to work, sold souvenirs, junk food, toiletries, cigarettes, film processing and music, and the below ground floor, which led straight into the station, sold groceries and hot food like chips, nuggets, chicken wings, and the infamous chicken chips. BBB was known for its large discounts, regular sales, and cheap t-shirts.

To get to the administration floor where the offices, training area, and staff room were located, Mella caught a large goods lift from the delivery bay, after a security guard in a cubicle checked her name off a list. In the training room there was a small television, three cash registers, five other trainees, and a woman in orange high heels who spoke with an orange voice, whose condescension squeaked out high pitches in overly pronounced words. The woman handed out stapled booklets, which included all the BBB rules and regulations such as dress codes, sign-in rules, what to do when sick and so on. In the top corner, on the front of the booklets, each person's name was written, and below it a number which they had to type into a little machine in the security area at least five minutes before their shift started. Standing up, they watched a fifteen minute video about all the security cameras installed above the cash registers and in the money counting rooms. Then the orange woman showed them how to scan a piece of cardboard with a barcode on it and got each of them to do it twenty times. Then she showed them how to scan something and type in a quantity, and they did that twenty times too. They spent seven hours that day and the next practicing scanning barcoded cardboard, and the third day rehearsing again and again, the dialogue on page four of their stapled booklet: "Hello, how are you? <smile> That's x dollars, here's your change, would you like a bag? Have a nice day" <smile>. And there was orange woman poking Mella, telling her to "Stand-up straighter, do it again" until there was blood swelling in her feet from all the standing and her scanhands froze into scanclaws in the ready to grab barcode and move it past the little scanner's window position. The other hand in ready-to-type position on the keypad, like getting ready to run. And mouth hurting too from too many forced smiles. Sore smiles. They were meant to have a break for lunch, but on the second and third day the orange woman forgot, and they wanted this job so they decided they had forgotten too and kept scanning and standing in front of their registers while the orange woman left because she remembered to eat her own lunch. Last hour of the last day and she brought in a stop watch, and she played the customer, and she timed them as they scanned and pressed 'total' and asked 'cash or card', and she was pleased—forty-eight seconds. To Mella, it seemed like orange woman felt that she'd cleverly trained stupid mice to perform complex tricks.

As she finally walked out again, past the security guard and into the street, her eyes blinked and squinted and she tried to adjust to all the human movement and their regulated street crossing and trains pumping them out of the station in aggravated puffs, and the lights, all the different kinds of street lights, traffic lights, sign lights. Her left hand tried to keep scanning, side to side.

She thought to herself that the city was in fact a desert, since deserts have few trees, but no one had noticed because of all the buildings everywhere. She thought that her blood felt orange and that things seemed upside-down. That it was too easy to be trained into, turned into a robot, that it was strange that smiling had to be rehearsed, and that hours were drained tea bags, and that there was algae on the train roof and plastic rocks in fish tanks, and oil and gas in the roads and the air while the rain refused to fall and stayed sulking in the heavy black rainclouds. That such a basic right as dignity was too hard. On the train there was a squinting woman with a white Macdonald's cup, singing. It was a sound that let Mella's breath out, and let her relax and curl her back and put away her scanhandclaw. She thought it was upside-down that this woman sounded more beautiful than anything she heard on popsong radio.

A new union

Ashley was scrunched-up in a shell that was lodged into wet beach sand, and the ocean's arms reached out and caressed the shell then fell back into the ocean, then pattered over it again, and retreated again. She was in a state of bodycurl around a pillow on the couch, after a long day of busking. She was imagining and she was thoughtful and she was analysing, and it showed in her body; her clenched knuckles with tight skin webbing between them, her mouth murmuring quickthoughts, her eyes jerking under their closed lids.

Paz stood a metre away and watched. He wanted to trace the line that her body made. He wanted to paint the shell around her, paint an outline then colour it in pink and very light grey.

She opened her eyes and caught him looking at her. In a groggy voice she asked, "Do you like me?"

"I like talking with you, I like the rare occasions that you smile, I like your hair and I like the way you think." He held his hands behind his back to stop them gesturing and flying about.

"But you think I'm ugly?"

"Ah, compliments are easy Ashley. And would you even believe me if I said I thought you were soft and sexy, and that I often want to kiss you..."

"When you say it like that, with that expression on your face, yes I would."

And that was the moment when something changed between Ashley and Paz; because he had admitted he felt things, and because she had believed him.

"I have a lot of faults, you know," Ashley said.

"I know, but I like them. You're angry, bitter, intelligent, and strong. The combination fascinates me. I want to know more, to explore your mind. You go deeper than me Ash, you question more, and you take me out of the clouds, and I think I need that. On the other hand, you need a few clouds."

Ashley, as usual, said exactly what she was thinking: "I'm confused. Guys tend to be very good at saying the things they think we want to hear. Yet I believe you. You listen to me."

"What you say is important."

He wasn't trying to persuade her or calm her or change her. He seemed to value her and that had Ashley so surprised and overwhelmed that she had to get up and walk into her room on the pretext of checking on Eva.

Five minutes later she came back. She sat where her shell had been on the couch and she pointed at Paz, who was still standing in the same spot, and then with the same finger she pointed at the space of couch next to her. He sat down, she took his hand, his stressed hand which also had knuckles with tight skin over them and webs between, and she massaged the knuckles.

"What's this?" she asked, pointing to a large freckle near the base of his right thumb.

"It's penguins."

"Penguins?"

"Sure, it's looking down on them, that's the tops of all their little heads as they huddle together to stay warm."

There are many kinds of unions, of people merging to make something new. While Paz and Ashley remained separate people, as workers in a union remain separate people, they also created a new thing, an Ashley-Paz thing, like the Matt-Tracey thing, or the trade union thing. But none of these unions were simple, because they existed among the noise of the world and its many-coloured troubles, its havoc, terror, and wallshadows. The shadows, like drafts, crept into their house through the gaps under the door, the holes in the broken windows, and then into their unions through their own little gaps and holes.

Ways of reading

Eva had been "reading" a lot lately. Paz and Tracey both read a lot, consuming whatever newspaper, magazine, or book somehow found its way into the house. Ashley read too, but was pickier. Eva couldn't be left out, and would push her way onto the laps of readers and make them do it out loud. They would pick up her little pointer finger and move it along the words. Eventually, she started to "read" books to herself. Feeling quite grown up, she moved her finger over the book pages and, muttering out loud, made up stories about dogs, mothers, cereal, and dinosaurs.

Then she did it to walls, couches, or legs that happened to be nearby. She "read" the fence, Ashley's hair, and Damjan's shirt, stroking her pointer finger over those too, and muttering words. Now she was standing in front of the television reading the moving actors, her finger making all sorts of loops and zigzags as it followed them around. Damjan, Matt, and Tracey moved their heads to one side and the other in synchronisation as they tried to see the bigger part of the screen. Ashley and Paz sat in the kitchen going over the employment section of the paper, their legs touching.

Then Eva fell over dramatically. "Argh, the cold is attacking me!" she cried. Tracey picked her up and Ashley went to get her a jumper. Then: "You never listen! You don't get it! You should bloody see a doctor..." rattled in the windows from the neighbourly space outside.

"Why don't they just break up?" Matt said, and turned up the volume of the TV.

"Because it's not easy to find housing, and they have a kid," Ashley replied.

Damjan closed a window. "We've got to get a washing machine," he said. Matt started to reply but was drowned out. "They should ... lock you up again!" came the voice from the other side of the house, then a thump of the kind that only soft bodies make as they hit a wall or floor or cupboard corner.

Eva took a cigarette from Damjan's pocket, and maintaining her assumption that anything long could be used to draw, gave him the cigarette and her hand, and commanded that he draw a house here, and the noisy neighbours there. "And on my thumb I want Mummy; this finger is Paz, this finger is Tracey, this one is Matt, and this finger is you!"

"Why do I have to be the little finger," he groaned.

Where all the flowers went
In a giant department store in Melbourne there were one thousand red and white roses arranged into giant heart-shaped centrepieces. People in sleek black suits steered easy paths between the hearts, the stacked and shelved product displays, in-store seating, and interactive kiosks. Money went in at the checkouts on each floor like a one-way store respiratory system.

But one child had wandered onto it without sunlight, and he didn't want to linger among product displays, he didn't want to try anything on, he didn't want the floor mirrors and column mirrors, nor did he want the designer plastic bags so that he could display his shop choice to the people in the street, and he didn't want to buy anything because he didn't have any money. He was tired. He went up to one of the heart-shaped centrepieces, and he scrambled onto it and fell asleep amongst the roses.

The contour of days

Start-up: Mella started all her days by peeing. Then she splashed cold water onto her neck to turn on her skin. She rubbed and pulled the dry bits of sleep off her eyelashes, and opened her eyes wide, to turn them on too. Then she got into the shower to try to turn on thought, but it never seemed to work very well. She sat cross-legged when she showered, right under the spray. Then she combed her hair slowly and felt thin fingers massaging her. Ben was sleeping-in after a late shift, so she got dressed silently. She opened the fridge and stood there eating some cold leftover pasta, then put it back into the fridge and quickly washed the spoon. She tripped on her own foot as she ran out the door, and as usual, she accidently slammed it.

Work: Mella stood at the register, repeating the short play with each customer. The whole thirteen hour shift (with compulsory two-hour break) was spent surrounded by artificial light trapped by walls with doors—more doors that she could go through but didn't—so the passing of time was marked instead by the increasing stiffness in her fingers, the pain that started in her feet and extended slowly up her legs, the increasingly desperate urge of her toes to wiggle, and the development of leg-rods.

Shut-down: When she got home, an almost wooden Mella with almost wooden eyes, without an urge to wonder or contemplate or read, crumpled onto the couch like a pile of wood shavings dust dirt, and stayed in that spot and watched somethingorother on the television. Her wing stubs, grey, stayed still. Soon, Ben came home from his shift and they sat at the table in the kitchen, him eating take-away, her eating the rest of the leftover pasta. Ben asked her to pass the soy sauce, and she did, adding, "Would you like a bag?" accidently, automatically. Later, as they climbed into bed, he bumped his knee on the side of the bed and she said quickly, "Can I help you?" in that same work tone. Back at BBB, the last shift workers were logging out and the security guard was turning off the lights at the main control. The cleaners had polished the floors, the shelves were fronted, the round fruits arranged in pyramids, and the four-dollar souvenir t-shirts were folded perfectly in the square bins on the ground floor.

And Mella couldn't sleep. A Bob Dylan song in her head: "That he not busy being born, is busy dying... is busy dying..."

Nowhere

And if they couldn't even finish a soccer game? The best place for it was in the cul-de-sac at the end of their road. While Ashley and Damjan debated where the goals should be, Eva showed Matt her animal picture book. Matt pointed at a rooster and asked her what it was.

"Clown pigeon," she replied. Then she quizzed him back. "What's the opposite of nowhere?"

"Everywhere?"

"Yeswhere!"

Then Damjan impatiently kicked a goal, and everyone ran into the centre of the cul-de-sac, and the game started. Eva understood that she had to chase the ball, and therefore followed it wherever it went, like a magnet. Damjan and his legs always managed to do surprise interceptions, only to then be intercepted himself by Tracey, who distracted him by poking her tongue out or yelling. Paz, as goalie, watched the ball as seriously as he watched the top of the broom when he walked around the house balancing it on one finger. He was good at that and would often walk between people chatting in the lounge room, absorbed and focused on the broom. The other team didn't get a single goal.

Then the sound of a siren winding through streets and heading towards them, followed by the appearance of a white police car with the blue stripes along the side. It parked in the first goal and two police officers got out. The soccer game stopped abruptly, and Eva, thinking it was a new game, froze in position with one foot raised slightly and her arms stretched out behind her.

"What are you doing?" one police officer asked. All of them thought it was obvious what they were doing, but swallowed sarcasm and looked at Paz, silently appointing him spokesperson.

"We're playing soccer."

"Shouldn't you be out looking for jobs?"

"Shouldn't you be stopping rapes?" Ashley said.

And Paz was seeing four blue uniformed legs. Indignity once again interrupted his thoughts. While watching the ball, he had been thinking about Matt and the way he vented to him sometimes in long strings of disjointed thoughts and pieces of words, and how Paz told Matt his fears. Because they had been friends since they were children, it was pointless to try to hide or pretend, and so they both spoke all-things with each other. Now these police officers were here, making him remember the blue uniformed legs that had called him a vandal so long ago.

"We have been looking, but there aren't a lot of jobs, and it's not something you can do all day," he said.

"Yeah, well, we know how you're really getting by. We've got our eyes on you," the first officer said, and the two of them got into their car and drove off.

Over the next few weeks, at different times during the day and night, a police car would arrive, siren whining, blue light dizzyspinning, and park outside the house for an hour or two. Now and then a police officer would yell at the house, "Yous coming out to play tonight?", or get out and shine a torch through their windows and look inside.

Unarmed 1
In Haiti, the banana trees squawked under slow sunrises, then roosters and chickens dropped out of them and

quickmarched to their favourite spot of grass. Serious pecking. The hot air made the banana leaves quiver. Centuries ago, generals and rich people from Europe had sailed the Caribbean and bagsed bits of it, smothered it in an infestation of pompous greed and fights over the bits. Then in the Dominican Republic, decades of dictatorship in the early to mid-twentieth century, and Rafael Trujillo, gold coins in his eyes, infested his side of Hispaniola with 1800 statutes of himself.

In October 1937, soldiers herded 30,000 Haitians on the wrong side of Hispaniola towards the river. Rain imposed semi-darkness, and Sonson, hiding, covered his face with his sugarcane hands, and watched, swallowing rainclouds. But he needed a giant blind across the world to not see the quick cuts through the heads of parents and siblings by soldiers' machetes. Like cutting cane. Wings broken. Gunshots ricocheting up and down the river. That day, the river became a blood line, just like the border lines that crisscrossed the Caribbean, red war scars of European business ventures, of bagsing bits.

Unarmed 2

As Mella walked past the security guard, he called out, "There's new rules now! You have to spin around." Mella laughed and spun once.

"Not good enough. Do it again." She did, and he looked at his watch.

"It's five to..." He turned on the PA. "Three o'clock starters to their registers."

Mella logged in to hers and stood straight, shoulders back. She looked at the first customer and smiled, saying in a clear voice, "Hello, can I help you?" Soon, though, there was a long queue, and every few seconds someone would peer out from the line at her and yell out, "Hurry up, would you? We've got places to be." Others in the queue would turn and look gratefully at the person who'd spoken. Mella's shoulders fell forward a little and her back curved, indicating the start of her daily loss of straight-back. She started to say "umm" a lot, and to the next customer she only whispered, "Have a good day."

"What?" he replied. Mella's eyebrow twitched and she scratched her forehead to hide it.

Another customer came up to her, waving an electric razor around. "This is broken, I want my money back." Mella picked up the phone to call a supervisor. "Who are you calling? I don't have all day you know!" the customer said, shaking the razor under her face.

"I'm sorry sir, but I don't have authorisation to do refunds."

"Well bloody hell!" the man yelled, and stormed off, leaving the razor and its packet on the counter. Mella's shoulders fell further forward, her back curved more, her eyes lowered, and her head moved forward. After four more hours working, her legs were tired and she bent her knees as though to sit like she sat in the shower, as though to make herself shorter and hidden by the counter so no one would yell at her. Eventually, her whole top half was curved and dropping and she had scared eyes, possum eyes. She was slowly shrinking her body, and she put one hand on the counter even though that was against the rules. Just then the boss, in his black suit jacket and the cup of coffee he always walked around with, passed by. "Don't lean on the counter!" he yelled at her. "The customers have to feel that you are ready to serve them. All the time! Do it again, and you're out of the job," he said. "And, by the way, your name badge is upside-down, and your shoes are shabby; get some new ones."

Still possum-eyed, Mella bit her cheeks to stop herself from crying. The shop would be closing in twenty minutes, and the boss told her to log out of her register and clean the party shelves. Hunched and looking at the floor, she bumped into a corner of a display shelf on the way. "Sorry," she said to it faintly.

Shop assistants closed the doors behind the last

customers and took the cash draws out of their registers. Mella dusted the lower party shelves then got down on her knees and used a wet rag to clean under them. The boss, gold coins in his eyes, sipping from his coffee cup, stood behind her and watched. Mella felt familiarity as the taste of cleaning liquids stained her throat and the dustdirt gathered into her fingernails.

In the delivery bay, a shop assistant with hair like grass and cheeky eyes tapped her on the shoulder, then grinned when she turned around. "Hey, quiet girl, how are you? Hard day at work, hey?" he said and patted her on the back, then offered her his hand. "I'm Rafi." They called him Rafi the storyteller at BBB, because he was forever following people around on their lunch breaks and telling stories. He also told a lot of jokes involving really bad puns, or when calling supervisors over the PA, he would sneak in a rhyme or a pun.

"I'll let you in on a secret, quiet girl. They tell you what to do because they would never have the patience to do it themselves. That means you're actually stronger than them, even if it may not feel like it sometimes." He winked. "Hey, see you tomorrow?"

Mella wanted to touch his hair. She managed a small smile in reply.

The 40 hour

wasted work week
recycled
piles of bodies
like a lonely teenager at the top of concrete stairs, looking out at ten train tracks and the hundreds of electrical wires and all he saw were sticky cobwebs, a hazy maze to dive into, engulf his jelly bean body, prickle his face into
wrinkles

like the silver spider that was carried away in neat little parts by mechanical, ingenious ants.

The 55 hour week

A neighbour's friend told Paz about a man who hired people for cleaning and wasn't bothered with résumés. Paz called the man, and was asked to start on Saturday. Saturday came, and Paz met the man at the office building he was to clean.

"I'll pay you eight dollars an hour."

Paz tried to keep his face flat, but his forehead narrowed without his permission.

"That's cash, you know. It's like fourteen if you include tax."

"No extra rates for working late at night?"

"Mate, you're not a doctor. That's good money. I'm doing you a favour and offering you a job despite your lack of experience. Consider yourself lucky." The man added a bit of disgusted-injured to his expression, that face used by most people trying to sell something with a negotiable price. But Paz wasn't in a position to negotiate; he didn't have any other offers. He accepted.

"Good. I'll pay you every Saturday."

The building was simply called 170A. In the escalator lobby there was a sign with the companies and their corresponding floors in metal lettering. Most of them were PR or Internet companies; Huset Communications, Simon Fontell Associates, Halifont Mcknight, PLFN Accounting, Frech Verdoben, and Speedsta. They had city offices where they met the clients, and they saved money by doing their administrative work in the suburbs. Paz had never heard of them, all he knew was that he had to clean all seven floors in his eleven-hour shift. The man gave him a sheet of instructions that said that Saturdays, Tuesdays, and Thursdays he had to clean the toilets, refill toilet paper, mop toilet and kitchen floors, clean microwaves and coffee machines and refill cup supplies. On Mondays and Wednesdays he had to vacuum carpeted areas, dust everything, and empty bins. The work hours were long, but Paz was looking forward to being exhausted. He imagined after a night of work he would feel like someone at the end of a long distance race, breathing hard, a sweaty neck, but satisfied.

On the first day, alone in a giant building with people's work lives sprawled across desks and photos of their families on cubicle walls, he imagined who they might be, peered inside cupboard doors, inspected stationary supplies, made himself cups of coffee with four spoons of sugar, and played with the squeezing mechanism on the mop bucket. But as he discovered that his paid hours were less than the amount of time he needed to complete all tasks, he ran the vacuuming, skipped the cleaner toilets, raced the mopping, timed his toilet cleaning, and swore at food that was burnt onto microwave sides. His head and lower back hurt and the huge floors seemed to fill with traps; tricky corners, door stoppers, low shelves where he bumped his head again and again.

He started at 7:00 pm and worked until 6:00 or 7:00 am He spent one and a half hours each way in travel, as the building was far from any public transport. The walking, too, started as something pleasurable; the streets were interesting, the exercise invigorated him, and his thoughts matched his walking, stopping at traffic lights, taking new paths as he turned a corner, relaxing as the temperature dropped. But it, too, quickly became tedious. He chose landmarks like a closed down hairdresser and a letterbox hidden in long grass to mark how far he'd come. Going there or walking home, he walked in daylight, so it seemed that night never came. He fell asleep in the morning with the sun burning orange on his eyelids, and with his breathing too fast because he was aware that soon he would have to wake up and do it all again.

What Paz didn't know was that the man who had hired him was being paid forty dollars an hour for the cleaning that Paz did, and that the man had gold coins for eyes. At the end of the fifth day of work, Paz's own eyes wanted to make a photo, any photo, a sad one, a tired one, a photo of a silver spider, but all he could see was a plastic bag full of dirt-drenched dish cloths, and three buckets of grimy water.

Nigeria 2: Cleaning up someone else's mess

As the sun set over the Niger Delta, the sky caught on fire. Slow, silky fireworks, with a subtle end. Little worms wiggled along windowsills, fidgeted down the insides of walls, and slipped comfortably into little ponds among the pans.

And the landscape; gas flares that cracked the walls, mangroves burning, a wasteland panorama of petroleum oozing black, blotted earth, sodden, rank and the wrong colour. Oil pumps like giant mechanised land leaches on the skyline. Animal carcasses in regular piles along the river stones and charcoaled creeks. Nets that once swelled with fish and lobster harvest now abandoned, string knots amongst the oil saturation. And no one much over forty to be seen. There, some people in a boat, travelling several kilometres to get drinkable water from the Opuekaba platform: water used for the cooling of engines. Chevron, Shell, Exxon-Mobil oil spilled every month into the Delta. They had been there since 1958, stealing the region's oil and shipping it to the US and Europe as though it were the most legitimate thing to do. The wetland and livestock died, and farmers wondered how they would survive.

Sometimes oil companies set fire to the spilt oil to burn it away, sometimes they buried it in pits and covered it with sand, sometimes they left it there; often they paid contractors to pay locals and non-locals to clean up the mess. At five dollars a day, children, youth, and older people would mop up the oil with cotton rags and collect it in bottles and buckets and hand pans. Youths patrolled the rivers to cart away the dead animals. They soaked up the mess with their skin too, ordered the oil, untangled the rain out of it and tried to put it back where it was meant to be. But with all the rags in the world, the oil kept coming, year after year drenching people and land in thick black slime that was gold for the companies.

Chemical burn
When 4.9 million barrels of light crude spilt into the Gulf of Mexico in 2010, BP buried it into the ocean's floor, out of sight, using 10 million litres of highly toxic Corexit dispersants.

On US land, companies unburied shale gas using over 500,000 wells (more mechanised land leaches, all connected to each other by specially slashed roads, like a country-sized circuit board), billions of tonnes of water, and over 750 chemicals, many of them toxic.

When no one can see you
Sometimes Mella would get up in the middle of the night because she felt like walking around the house and being alone. She left the lights off and tip-toed around, touching the furniture and walls to guide her. She liked the feel of the cold kitchen tiles under her bare feet. She would light a candle using one of the matches near the stove, then drip wax into the bottom of a plastic cup, stand the candle up in it, and place it on the kitchen floor. Then she would sit down on the floor and read. The candle projected her long shadow onto the fridge. Sometimes she stopped reading and examined the ends of her hair in the candle light. Sometimes she chewed on an elastic band. Often, she felt too exhausted to read, and instead she would go through the latest newspaper, drawing triangular eyebrows on the faces. Then she would tidy the kitchen, arrange the spices, put the two half packets of rice into one container, dry the dishes, and go back to bed.

When Paz was alone, he liked to smell the vinegar, the basil, cilantro seeds, and coffee. He also liked to nibble on paper, to doodle-invent mazes, and to look around him and imagine the house was a different place. The floor was moon dust, the curtains were string bridges, the couch a steep rocky mountain, the television was a chatty cube alien, and the bedroom doors were the chorused yawns of a family of blue whales. The photos he composed were more surreal when he was alone.

When Rafi was alone he would imagine he was in a musical and sing about all the things on his mind and the things that were happening to him or he felt like imagining were happening to him. Or he would put some music on loudly, lie on his back on the floor, and stick his feet straight up in the air. He found that position relaxing. He also liked to weave blue ribbon in and out of his toes.

When no one was home, Matt liked to dip a finger in the sugar and walk around the house sucking on it. Or he would spread some vegemite on a cracker and lick it like a cat until the cracker was clean, then he would put more on. He would systematically pick at the ingrown hairs on his knees with his uncut thumb nail. He enjoyed leaving the door wide open while he used the toilet.

When Damjan was alone, he felt itchy and uncomfortable. He scratched his knees, his underarms, his knuckles, hard. Confusion rose, salty on his tongue, and he would leave the room in search of a beer and the cover of loud noise, turning on the television to full volume.

Spacing

On his first Sunday off, Paz took slow photos with tiny apertures. He took a photo of someone on an exercise bike peddling fast, but their upper half barely moving, so that in his photo they looked like they had no legs. Likewise, he took a photo of a traffic police officer standing on the pedestrian strip waving cars past, and he seemed to have no arms. Another photo was of a person who was talking very fast, and seemed to have no mouth. Then there were people selling coffee from large thermoses. They sat on benches and seemed sad, but because they barely moved, they were clear and detailed in his photo, whereas the people walking around were faint ghosts.

Then he composed a photo of a young woman he'd seen working at the city BBB. A man with hair like grass was working at the register next to her, turning towards her now and then to share a joke. Later, Paz had walked past the delivery bay on his way to the station and had seen them taking a break, sitting together on a pipe that jutted out of the wall. Both of them could only half fit onto the pipe, so they stuck their outside legs out straight to balance. Paz liked the symmetry. He noticed how the registers had spaced the sales assistants evenly apart, and how the pipe sat them close together, thighs and shoulders touching. The woman was commenting that the grasshair man was always cheerful. He replied that he liked to make people smile and to counter the "tyranny of boredom" with jokes, and that he preferred to keep his sadness out of sight.

"Why are you sad?"

"I worry about my mates, and sometimes about the whole world." He had fled Iran when he was eighteen, he told the woman. He was put in detention in Australia for two years and four months, until he was given permanent residency. He said he had had a good human rights lawyer that helped him for free, and now he was allowed to work, but many of his friends weren't allowed to, and many more were still in detention.

Paz made a third photo in the series; next to the registers and pipe photos, he had them restocking on either side of a shelf, looking at each other through the gaps between the products. The man was taking her stock and hiding it in the gaps, and she was laughing small, trying not to be heard by the boss with his coffee cup, walking around nearby. Then he was whispering to her to "resist them, everything they do to you, tire you, empty you out...think about joining the union, I know its magazine is crap, and full of ads and give-aways, but it's a start". Paz's photo had two people on their knees, looking at each other through gaps. Next to the woman was a large white space, a non-photo, a something missing.

Patience

Saturday came, and Paz asked for his wage. He had caterpillarskin, jumpingskin, buzzskin, and he smiled at his boss.

"Oh, no; you get paid on Sundays," was the reply.

Sunday was his day off, so he asked again on Monday. He had turtleskin, and a slow, cautious smile.

"I don't have it here; ask again next week."

Next Saturday Paz asked his boss to have his wage ready for Monday, as he didn't come in on Sundays. It was strange to have to explain that.

Monday came, and he asked again, his skin this time tense and thick. Opaque moonskin.

"Oh, I forgot. Next week."

Paz got sick of asking, but on the fourth week, he asked again. With armourskin and no smile, he said, "It's been a month now; I'd like you to pay me."

"I'm a bit short right now. Next week, I promise."

At the end of the fifth week, Paz asked again, and walked home unpaid. He started to wonder if he'd ever get paid, and how long he would keep working unpaid, until he decided to stop.

(And thousands of people got sick of waiting after Katrina hit New Orleans on 29 August 2005. The levee system failed, the city was flooded, houses choked and burst. With no assistance to get out, a total of 1,833 people died, and 20,000 people with just the clothes they were wearing shuffled into the Superdome and were told to wait.

Inside, it was boiling. There was little food or water, little information, no electricity, and faeces piled up in the stairwells and corridors, urine air wafted around the leftbehind people who waited, waited, waited for help. They stared at a wrecked ceiling, swallowing the rancid aftertaste, avoiding the torture of the stoppedclock and no rush to help them, to stop death, indignity. They wandered in a confined, sweating stadiumcastle. One woman used her bags to build a shelter around herself, sat cross-legged, and the space was so small her earlobes grazed her knees. A man told everyone he saw that he needed a towel, but no one knew why he needed it—maybe because the city was under water. Another man spun a toilet role in circles, flopsulking away the time, ignoring his watch, ignoring the drip falling all the way from the dome onto his sparse, white haired head.

After a few days, the tourists and the sickest people were taken on buses to another stadium in Houston. Most people had to wait four to seven days. When they were all gone, there was a stadium with two holes in its roof, and among the puddles, butterfly wings trampled into the floor.)

On the last day of the sixth week, Paz finished off in a bathroom and started to kick a toilet roll around the floor, vaguely watching the quirky circles it made. A sink tap that wouldn't close properly dripped water straight into the drain. More quirky circles. Then he packed away the cleaning detergents, mops and buckets, and met the boss outside. One last time he asked. And then, "Fuck you, I'm not coming back." Towelskin flashing red.

The sound that silver makes
There was a mountain in Bolivia that was filled to overflowing with eight million dead bodies. It was Cerro

Rico in Potosi, where from 1545 Spanish capitalists forced indigenous peoples and African slaves down the mountain's throat and into its veins to mine silver. And the mountain went into the women, men, and children's veins too. They worked up to sixteen hours a day, learning that fresh air and sun were for other people. Over three centuries a gradual massacre saw eight million of them die young from mercury poisoning, hard work, and mine collapses.

Meanwhile, the capitalists and royalty of Spain wore silver rings, and necklaces, and their churches were adorned with it. For centuries, Europe's development was funded by 45,000 tonnes of silver. And the silver jewellery jingled and jangled. People thought it was the sound that silver made, but actually it was the sound of rich Europeans walking over a mountain full of bones.

Methylated spirits

Rafi watched a drunk woman on the bus scan the air in circles. "I've been living on the streets for thirty years, ya know. Yep. And I've got five beautiful children. Dux three times she was and made it into every single university in Australia," she announced to the bus window, the air, an inside-the-bus advertisement, the person on the other side of the aisle. The other passengers felt uncomfortable and they all looked out their windows as if absorbed. A few passengers nodded to show that they had heard, then looked down, hoping she'd leave them alone.

"Ya see that intersection there?" she pointed. "They buried my uncle alive there. Ah-ha. Buried him alive! I'm an Aborigine, ya know. From Wagga Wagga tribe. They buried him alive, ah-ha. But they'll pay to that man up there, they'll pay." Saliva gathered in the corner of her mouth where teeth were missing, and she crumpled her eyebrows into a quizzical expression. "I got into parliament, you know, but I couldn't stay, cos of this," she waved a water bottle in circles. "This ain't water, you know, it's metho."

A student sitting behind her leaned over and said with concern, "Don't drink metho; it'll make you blind."

"I know that, but I don't care anymore," she shrieked. The bus stopped, and she got up and stumbled off it, mumbling to herself.

Rafi knew that the highest cause of death for Aboriginals after heart failure was unnatural deaths like accidents, suicides, and police violence. He thought to himself that the gradual massacre of the Australian Aborigines was still going on.

Forgetting spirits

A touch of quiet cloud and snug sun. Matt was burning pen lids over a lighter, watching them turn black, then bubble, then flop over. Damjan had some pot, and this time Tracey wanted to join him, but she didn't like to smoke. So they drank it in a banana milkshake. They watched some TV, flipping between the infomercials and ads, avoiding the programming. Tracey got up to go to the toilet, and thought the pot wasn't affecting her at all. Then she looked in the bathroom mirror and saw that she had a very awkward, scary, and huge smile on her face, rather like a fair clown. It was so funny that she laughed out loud, and walked back to the lounge room laughing and holding her stomach, and laughed a good ten minutes more before she managed to say anything to Damjan. She started to say, "You know, in some countries people don't drink water, they only drink Gatorade," but then she remembered that that was in a movie...or was it?

They were hungry. They ate some plain crackers, and started laughing again when they noticed that they both used their fingers to get the chewed cracker out from behind their teeth. It was hilarious. But they were still hungry and Tracey started to feel that the pot wasn't enough, she wanted to drink wine or beer. Then she forgot about that. She thought a sentence, started to say it, but forgot it half way through, and left it there in the middle. Damjan laughed at her halfsentences, and he started to say halfwords. Tracey thought they were just random noises, and as she laughed, she herself made funny noises accidently. She laughed more, and more noises came out— squeaks and creaks and tweets.

"I've lost half my brain," she said, ashamed. She hid her head under a couch pillow to stop Damjan from seeing her sillyface and sillylaughter. Her thoughts had definitely slowed down... they came...in dotted lines...she noticed. Dotted...thoughts, she saw them scrolling in front of her. Half her head now hovered thirty centimetres above her body. She sniffed, and her nose was blocked too. Lots of her was blocked.

Damjan was amused. He giggled and giggled and rubbed his head. He noticed that that didn't happen when he smoked alone. "Forget what you are and be what you're not!" he sang.

Spaces: Park benches and restaurant chairs
Mella was tilting her head back and forth, physically enacting her indecision. Rafi wanted to meet her in the city then take her to a workers' rights meeting afterward. But at the same time as the meeting, Ben and his family were going to a restaurant she couldn't afford to celebrate his birthday. Indecision head. The right thing verses the right thing in a different kind of way. Awkward restaurant conversations and undignified digs at complicated food and a disgruntled boyfriend or something meaningful with a man who was gently becoming her first friend. She tilted her head some more then headed out to meet Rafi: she would work out her dilemma later.

She arrived first and sat on a bench in the triangular park just before the NSW Art Gallery. Mella watched the ferries pull in and out of the port and the day's fallen cloud glitter bobbing off the ends of things nearby. Then Rafi arrived, wearing a zipper jacket similar to one she had on, and spinning his small umbrella by its chord. Seagulls and pigeons lazing in the grass by the bench she was sitting on looked up as he approached, moving their heads in circles to follow the movement of the umbrella.

Rafi greeted her with a big smile and a shoulder pat, and sat at the other end of the bench, leaving a large space between them that allowed them to sit diagonally and face each other—unlike the registers or the pipe that jutted out. Park bench was a different kind of conversation, it was more than just workmates, it was get-to-know-each-other, and that excited Mella, gave her buzz skin, prickly skin. A story in the shape of a person was sitting opposite her, an adventure story.

"What was it like in Iran?" she asked.

"Things weren't so different...sometimes workers didn't get paid for months or years, and when they protested, the military got out their clubs and tear gas... It's hard being a union leader, it's considered an act against national security." Rafi talked about chemical warfare, the Iran-Iraq war, how the first George Bush had supported Saddam Hussein with money, information, and weapons, and then about union struggles in other countries. His words were raw, cut, crying, angry and roaring, yet soberly hopeful. He spoke so directly, *without hairs on his tongue*, that Mella felt him naked for the lack of drama or politeness. Then he asked her questions that were direct, that gave her seethroughskin and a soft face, and she fidgeted with the Velcro on her own umbrella, then left it and took to her jacket zipper. Rafi, however, had put his umbrella on the bench, and his hands sat calmly upon his knees.

He looked at her with limpid eyes, waited for her opinion. She looked away because she didn't feel like she had much to say. Instead, she wanted to take notes about what he'd said and then think for a very long time. But he was waiting, so she said, "Insecurity is everywhere. I need to think about it." Rafi saw that she was affected and cared, and that was enough. Their conversation travelled across continents. Mella's world began to expand. People lived in bubbles, with their problems inside them, she thought, but Rafi wiped the mist off her bubbleskin. As she peered out, he pointed things out to her, "Look at that, look over there."

Ferries honked. Seagulls dropped down from overcast sky and stood in front of Rafi and Mella, knowing that park bench people often threw food. Fifteen minutes till she had to meet Ben, and she still hadn't decided.

Now Mella and Rafi sat closer, just a few centimetres of warm air between them, and Mella's umbrella was on her knees, and her hands were still. And faraway places were a little less far away. World spacing changing for her.

Finally, she said, "I can't come."

"That's a shame."

"Sorry, it's Ben's birthday."

"Hey, it's cool. See you at work tomorrow."

The harbour restaurant was Arranged, like the roses in the department store. Calculated pleasantness. Round tables with white-laced tablecloths, art-vases, and long wine glasses with folded light blue napkins inside them, were positioned next to the all-glass walls so that passers-by could look inside and see a theatre of happy, backlit families and couples. A centre staircase, the ceiling, the waiters' uniforms, and the tables and chairs were all part of an alternating white/blue colour scheme, and there was just the right amount of space—cold space—between each chair.

Ben, his parents, two sisters, their husbands, and a friend of Ben's from school walked in single file to their reserved table. Mella hurried along behind them, feeling like a tiny bird with little legs trying to keep up with another larger flock, bobbing its head to their noises, getting distracted by a cow or a tree, then sprinting to catch up again. At the table, Mella continued to be an estranged bird. Two forks, one slightly smaller than the other: she knew about desert spoons and soup spoons, but not about different sized forks; she would have to watch what others did, and in the meantime, try to fit into the conversation.

"I heard that Scarlet Johansson bought a baby."

"Oh, who's that?" Mella asked.

"You don't know?" There was closed-mouth laughter followed by a list of movies.

"Speaking of which, Thomas Newtown wants to have a baby."

"Oh, and what movies has he been in?" Mella asked.

"He's Ben's boss!" More closed-mouth laughter.

Then the meals arrived. Mella's salad had wings—a colourful dragonfly. She tilted her head again at her meal and wondered where to start, while the conversation moved onto spaghetti straps verses cap sleeves on cocktail dresses, then island vacations, weather on island vacations, the best way to make béchamel sauce, then a list of things that were easier to Just Buy, which led to the prices of furniture, then the prices of oil. Suddenly, Mella had her segue, and she mentioned Nigeria.

"Oh, don't talk about such gloomy things!"

"They're all fanatics, Mella," Ben said, confusing countries and continents. "They don't know how to govern themselves; look at all the dictators they keep choosing." He patted her head.

Estranged bird morphed itself into sea clam, which shut and locked its shell with a snap and finished its plate of dragonfly salad then claimed full stomach when it came time to order desert.

Couches

So far none of the adults in the house had cried. They had often smiled without teeth or told jokes that had bitter, unsteady edges. They laughed sometimes with small aches pinching at their cheeks, but they hadn't cried or lost their temper. Then, one night, while everyone else was asleep, Ashley got up and cried quickly into the bathroom sink, without even knowing why.

Also that night, one of a pair of stay-overs, while his friend slept on the couch, had fallen asleep on the lounge room floor. During the night he had rolled, snuggled, and flipped his way towards what the household called the 'hallway', the space between the lounge area and the doors to their bedrooms. The next morning, thinking of cereal and bananas for breakfast, Ashley and Eva came out of their room. Ashley stepped over the sleeping teenager without a second thought, and Eva tried to imitate her mother's nonchalance, but she had to lift her little legs up to her neck and leapstep just to pass over the chest, then she ended up catching her bare foot on an underarm, and stopping her fall by tumble-running into the kitchen.

The latest stay-overs had been there for a week now. They slept until midday, chatted away the early afternoon, then as evening came, they eyed each other with a sense of sudden purpose, and walked briskly out of the house. Sometimes Matt went with them. Paz went once, because of the unpaid bills, the often empty fridge, his shoes that opened like grinning mouths at the front.

Then, a week to the day that Ashley had cried at night and no one heard, the stay-overs were gone. Damjan came out of his room, walked straight out the front door to a large tree, jumped up and grabbed a branch and lifted his knees up to his chin twenty times. He dropped down, jumped on the spot a few times, and then did a back flip. He went back inside, and it was then that he saw the empty couch and empty floor. Two empty spaces where backpacks had been. "Oh, they're gone," he said to the room, and walked into the kitchen, yawning loudly.

He hadn't yawned loudly when another stay-over, Lissa, had left. Lissa who had feet freckles, skinny hard eyes, a hard smile and hard hair and who knew that it was better that she didn't live with her broken and burnt-out parents any more. She worked at BBB for a while, and though she only stayed a few nights, she asked them if she could use their address to receive pay cheques. She couldn't be paid without a permanent address, and she knew she'd be moving around for a long time to come.

She'd only talked of practicalities. How many nights? What meals? Who? How? Get out of this suburb with its streets of quicksand. Ashley had seen some of her old self in her, and Damjan had also seen something. He wasn't sure what, but he enjoyed watching this practical, freckled person get up, go out, come back. He had felt disappointed when he saw the empty couch and empty backpack space.

Matt was up. He put some coffee on and leaned against the fridge to wait. Matt's lights this morning were back down to dim. He was back to floppy, to slumping in chairs, flopping across his bed, to never totally standing up. Damjan said to him, "The stay-overs are gone," but he seemed to know already. Stretching and yawning, Tracey wandered into the kitchen and peered at the boiling coffee. "The stay-overs are gone," Damjan said to her too.

Hearing poverty

When Mella wrapped the towel around her, it was normal that it didn't make a noise. Then she closed the bathroom door, opened the bedroom door, and they didn't make a noise either. She sat down on the bed and it didn't squeak. She opened the bedroom window, an action which would normally suck in the sounds of traffic as though there were a vacuum in the previously quiet room, but this time the cars glided by quietly. So Mella sat down on the bed and tilted her head until the water was suddenly released from her ear and trickled down her shoulder. She tilted her head the other way, and more water ran down her other shoulder, and the world was turned on again, busy and screeching and aching.

At the staff meeting at work there were bouquets of

plastic tulips and glitter balloons stuck into heavy green foam in the four corners of the room, and two trays of gourmet sandwiches cut into triangle quarters on a table at the front of the room. Mella sat with the ground floor staff at a back table, but instead of listening to the manager's speech, she looked around the room. The night before she had read an article that Rafi had photocopied for her called, "What Is Poverty?" by Jo Goodwin Park. It had made her all tissuebody and sad and had drawn lines from herself to others, filled in the outlines of life with solid colours and causes. Television world of puppets had become a world of historic and economic processes, a complex place, and unfair. So now when she looked around the staffroom, she saw the things behind the things. When she tuned into the manager saying, "...certain staff members have put just that little bit extra in to making BBB the best, most popular supermarket in the city...they understand that a job is more than just a wage, but also a commitment..." she heard bright yellow cheese in a spray can. She heard plastic flowers and a throat cleared because its user was uncomfortable and had to force out the fluffwords. She saw that his thumbs hung from his front pants pockets on either side as though he were trying to show casualness, but his pointer fingers scratched and picked at his pants. She wondered if other people, like politicians, did the same thing with their fingers when they spoke to the press.

A ground floor shop assistant called Valerie was standing next to the manager. Her plastic name badge had been exchanged for a metal one, meaning she was being promoted to supervisor. She was a woman with a smile that curled and eyes that flirted. "Hi, Mella!" she would say with so much intonation, each sound a party, a multicoloured firecracker. "Hi?" Mella would respond, her voice mousing, her eyes bouncing off Valerie's disco light eyes onto the floor. "Ya like to keep it short, don't ya?" Valerie would joke, and Mella would walk away, taking her boringness with her, wishing her voice had balloons and streamers in it too.

But today she heard something different in Valerie. She heard a warehouse of faulty fireworks packed up in light brown boxes. After the speeches, Mella asked Valerie quietly, "Hey, are you okay?"

"'Course I am, lovely! I just got promoted!"

"You seem different today."

Valerie's bottom lip trembled, and Mella cocked her head, ready to listen. "The first thing they told me to do after they promoted me this morning was to fire Luisa and Wei. They are two of the oldest staff here, and they know everything, Mella. The rest of us love them; they're like our mothers. They should have been promoted ages ago, but instead they promoted me and I have to fire them, because younger people are cheaper."

Mella realised the two of them had more in common than she had thought.

What is poverty?

What is a beggar? Why are the most common definitions of these things limited to material well-being? Isn't poverty also workers with insufficient time to live? And places that are all roads and shopping centres; don't they have a poverty of parks and public spaces, a poverty of socialising? Couldn't poverty also be low quality or insufficient education, culture, healthcare, information, stability, rights, and dignity?

What is Poverty by Jo Goodwin Park (1971): In her personal account of poverty in the US, Goodwin Park wrote; "Poverty is getting up every morning from a dirt-and illness-stained mattress. The sheets have long since been used for diapers. Poverty is living in a smell that never leaves... Poverty is being tired... In summer poverty is watching gnats and flies devour your baby's tears when he cries. The screens are torn and you pay so little rent you know they will never be fixed... Poverty is an acid that drips on pride until all pride is worn away."

The median salary for CEOs in the top 100 US corporations was US$33.4 million in 2002, and at large companies, the median CEO pay was US$1017 per hour. In 2008, according to Forbes, Warren Buffett was the richest person in the world. His fortune was US$62 billion, more than the GDPs of Croatia and Jordan combined. That year, Lev Leviev, diamond magnate, bought a house for US$65 million. It had a bullet proof front door, a gold-plated pool, an indoor cinema, a night club and a hair salon.

What if poverty were inequality? Because meanwhile, 1.6 billion people lived without electricity, a billion people were unable to read, and eighty percent of the world lived on less than ten dollars a day, according to UNICEF.

Life cycle of the poor: they were born, becoming statistically alive, then they spent their lifestorm struggling to put off death. If they were to ever see a Hollywood movie, they wouldn't have understood it, because it was made in a different life language. These people without bank accounts watched the rich play in their backlit dollhouses and then they died—unheard, untelevised, so quietly.

The advantages of hunger
While Haitians mixed mud, salt, and oil to make mudcakes to beguile their hunger, companies in the US, Canada, and Europe burnt food and converted it into fuel. According to the New Statesman, US vehicles burned enough corn to cover the entire import needs of the poorest eighty-two countries.

When US companies stole Haiti's rice market, Haitians could no longer afford to buy what they had previously been able to easily grow in their own backyards. The IMF had made Haiti cut its tariffs on imported rice from thirty-five percent to three percent, while US rice companies benefited from massive subsidies, so that Haitian rice farmers lost their lands and livelihoods and three-quarters of the rice eaten in Haiti then came from the US.

"Control oil and you control nations; control food and you control people," said Henry Kissinger.

Damaged 2

Before the land was one giant grey garden of bombs, an undeclared war on the poor was waged, with concealed sharpshooters aiming at them, subtly stealing their colour and selling it again for high prices. Making markets out of their hopes, pillaging their land, their ideas, their time, and leaving them as husks of people. Intentionally starving them, sickening them, ridiculing. Steamrolling oblivion, peppering indignity ash, words like lazy, stupid, ugly, foul, rank, useless, all over their unprotected hearts as they slept and worked. Abusing them, canning them, clipping them, bagging and branding them, hoarding them into the factories and whorehouses. They numbed them, blistered their bent banks, glazed over their eyes, margarined their minds, subtracting softness, selling them poisoned food, translating them into ghosts. The poor hung around life, carrying their bruises and cuts in plastic bag bundles over their shoulders while the sharpshooters shot big holes of missing thing at them.

Undeclared war 1

Rubbled Iraq, invaded by the US, struggled every day to repair the damage, the broken birdcage, ribcage, bus stop, water supply. Broken sleep and the sound of broken air, of smashed up sunlight penetrating every day.

Bombing made housing cheap, and one man thought he would buy a house and make money by selling it after the war. But the house was bombed, his friends were killed, and shrapnel ripped his arm off.

With Fallujah's population halved, the Iraqi people were shadows in psychological shock, internally torn up for years and decades to come, blue sky fallen over.

Undeclared war 2

It was early night when it happened. Paz and Ashley were sitting cross-legged in the kitchen doorway facing each other, their backs against the doorframe. Ashley, with Eva in bed, felt a little released and was chatting away at double speed, with red cheeks, flying hands, and a glowing gaze. She had been talking for an hour now, wondering from one idea to another, always expecting Paz to get up and leave with some excuse, but he didn't. He never interrupted her, his eyes never retreated and glazed over so he could think about other things. He was all there. In fact, he really wanted to fetch a pen and take notes.

Damjan mirrored Paz's face of concentration as he watched television, with Matt and Tracey on either side of him, a little less focused. Their eyes wanted exercise and did bike circuits; quick circles around the room, which bumped at a common point, jumped across each other to continue the circuit, then returned with acquiescence to the television.

In Ashley's room, Eva was a sleeping turtle. Her legs and arms were curled under her back and her head stretched forward on the pillow. Now and then she farted, and Tracey would look up as though searching out the source of the sound, because the farts were so small and unpretentious and they puzzled her. Damjan, without moving his eyes, wondered out loud, "How does she sleep so deeply, trusting that we won't sit on her or something?"

There was a small hole in the ceiling in Ashley's room, a crack shaped like a canoe, and it was dripping dirty water drops on to the bubble part of Eva's big toe. It was a soundful reminder that above the ceiling there was roofspace, a sealed pyramidal darkness with cobwebs and splintery beams and bug families. To the rhythm of the water drops, black buckled boots were walking over the backyard grass, all squishy and torn from a day of rain. The boots belonged to two figures with black leather belts and holstered guns. In the lounge room though, they mustn't have heard the drops or the boots because Paz stayed focused and Damjan stayed focused and Ashley kept chatting and Matt and Tracey's eye circuits were perfectly symmetrical.

(Did the anxious bewildered children of Iraq wonder why police-like people from another country who couldn't speak their language were suddenly telling them where to go? Were, overnight, walking about the children's streets and driving about in big army vans and tanks...bringing an earthquake of sad neighbours and parents, but at the same time taking on the role of the moral Authority?)

There was a loud bashing not much like a knock on the lounge room window, the one closest to the back door. Then, "Hey, yous!" and the lounge room-kitchen door scene was interrupted. The windows became tent holes, rips in the peace bigger than the leak in Ashley's ceiling, letting in the cold and the angry putrid air. Two police officers shined their torches into the lounge room and around its walls in circles faster than Matt and Tracey's eye circuits.

"What are yous up to?" one officer said with an accusing tone.

And five heartbeats lost track of their rhythm, as five heads looked in disbelief at the window.

"How did dole bludges like yous get this place, hey?" the same officer asked.

"Bludgers alright, look't them, pretty comfy aren't they? Bit sus if you ask me. Must be doing something dirty," the second officer replied.

Then the two of them pointed at them with their chins, first officer drew his finger across his neck, second shook his head in disgust. They tucked away five bits of cake sized dignity into their uniform pockets, and said, "We're watching you..." and left. A minute later a siren sounded.

Dole bludges. For the second time in his life, but not the last, Paz imagined some kind of monster, a dirty couch potato, and that was meant to be him. Ashley wondered if she should keep talking where she'd left off, and decided not to. "What did I tell you? They won't leave us alone now," she said.

Paz looked at her, heart rhythm still tripping all over itself, stumbling and fumbling. "We haven't actually done anything wrong; the most they can do is annoy us," he replied.

Matt pulled his feet up onto the couch and held his knees. "I thought we might get a bit of peace here," he said. Eva the turtle slept on.

Undeclared war 3

It was dinosaur day at BBB; a day of dinosaur promotions, and the staff had to wear half dinosaur head hats and say, "Happy dinosaur day" to each customer. The boss, his coffee mug in one hand, a clipboard resting on his forearm, and a pen in the other hand, patrolled the shop floors and noted pay reductions. Fifteen minutes off Rafi's pay, because a customer said he was rude; thirty minutes off Valerie's pay for getting stuck in the lift when it broke down; One and a half hours off Rafi's pay the second time the lift broke; twenty minutes off Saba's pay because his friend came into the shop to say hello to him; fifteen minutes off Maria's pay for scanning something twice and needing a supervisor to key in the code and cancel it; fifteen minutes off Ali's pay for doing leg stretches during a six-hour shift standing at the registers; one hour off Mella's pay for going to the toilet twice, then to the bag lockers to take migraine medication; fifteen minutes more off her pay for having her hair out; fifteen minutes more off Valerie's pay for putting her name badge on upside down, and for sucking on tic tacs.

At the end of the day the staff accountant added up the income. Customers had seized the discount items; the 200g chocolate, the gummy lollies, the 2-pack of soap at 50% off, and feeling they had earned it, bought more extra items than usual at the normal price. Dinosaur day was a success.

Toucheye

An old man in a mall playing a violin was joined by an old lady playing bass, then a teenager playing clarinet. A crowd gathered, and as more people joined the street orchestra, the crowd grew and grew. Paz was in that crowd, and he looked at people's faces. His eyes stopped on one woman, and just as they did, Mella's roaming eyes were caught by a man. They found themselves looking at each other through all the faces, hats, children on shoulders, phones held up taking photos. They did that thing people sometimes do when the person they look at looks back; they half-smiled, a vague movement of acknowledgement, then looked back at the musicians.

Vanilla or margarine

Rafi was prattling with Mella at the loading dock before she left to catch the train home. Nights of purple quietness, eagles falling gracefully out of the sky past waxed stars that bleated goodbye. Rafi listed all the dreams he could remember having recently. Mella listened and watched ant lines move like a series of cable cars up the tree. The ant trail arrived at a fork and chose one branch, and she imagined them calling down to each other in a chain of whispers: this way!

A moment before, Rafi had asked her again to join the Services Union, and now she was thinking that she had many reasons not to join. The union didn't seem to do very much apart from organising dinners for the few permanent employees, union fees would mean less money, and she was concerned that if the boss found out, she would be given fewer shifts, or worse. Rafi had argued, "Look at how they treat us; if we don't do something, then they'll treat us even worse. It's a step closer to dignity. Think about it, yeah?" Then he changed the topic.

When Mella got home, Ben took her into the kitchen to make coffee and began bragging. There were ants there too. This time their trail went up the space between cupboard doors and onto the counter, passed a 400ml bottle of vanilla, and onto the rim of a tub of margarine. Ben picked up the margarine tub and washed it under the tap, and Mella took advantage of the pause to tell him she was thinking about joining the union.

"They'll never promote you if you do that."

"Well, I don't know if I want to be promoted. Just the other day Valerie—"

"Why wouldn't you want to be promoted? You'd get a higher wage, more flexibility. I mean, do you even know what you're doing with your life? How can your career go anywhere?" He put the margarine tub back in its place and ants with wet legs got up to resume their trail. Others stayed waterglued to the rim.

"I think if I join the union it would be a way of being there for my friends."

"James Bond wasn't in a union, you know."

"No, I can't think of a single TV character that was."

"Exactly!"

The view from the roof

After the police had surprised them, Damjan had been to a nightclub just once. He danced hard but couldn't get into it and went home at eleven thirty. Today he had watched six hours of hospital and crime dramas, then had shaved strips of his arms and legs. He should have been looking for work, but was finding it hard enough to stay excited about living. So he did what was easiest—stayed on the ant trail. He followed the other ants, chose margarine because that's where the scent took him, and when something fell across the path, such as a late night police visit, he did the easiest thing and walked around it. He ignored it.

"Come up to the roof," Paz called to him. It was evening and the tiles were still warm. Damjan left the television reluctantly, and climbed up. Then, as Paz talked to him, he imagined what ads would be playing, recited their catchphrases to himself, and wondered how the hospital show would resolve. Paz wanted to know how he was. Damjan, looking at his limbs and their strips of stubbly hair, his unwashed shirt with one sleeve rolled up and the other just folded over at the corner of a cuff, didn't want to tell Paz that he was concrete. He was heavy bones covered in soggy biscuit dough. Brain of biscuit mush, and a lumpen body that sometimes had to be dragged out of his room. How did he feel? He felt Styrofoam-eyed, white fluffplastic eyed, seeing a world that was a pixelated stage with well-rehearsed dialogue.

But Damjan didn't have to speak out loud for Paz to understand him. "Look out there," Paz said, pointing at the whole town. Tracey had said she liked the beach because there the ocean was so big and she was so small, and that put her problems in perspective. Paz hoped Damjan would feel the same sense of big picture up there on the roof. But he looked where Paz pointed and saw more of the same. Grass grew in stubbly strips; some of it cut months ago, some of it never. Drains were clogged with plastic and Styrofoam rubbish. A bus bench had one plank missing so that the ones on either side had become crooked and met at one end. A hungry discarded cat flopped over a corner shop rain pipe. The sky was mushy, and faded with wear. He saw nothing he cared about.

Things noticeboards say

Mella spat out toothpaste, rinsed her mouth, washed her face, picked up her shoulder bag from the couch and dashed towards the door. At the same time, Ben glossed his hair with gel, double knotted his shoe laces, picked up his briefcase, and headed for the door. He held it open for Mella, gesturing that she should go out first, but she insisted, and he insisted, and they did the dance of accepting at the same time, until Ben pushed in front. They skipped down two stairs at a time, and walked out the main apartment doors together. He headed to his car and she towards the station, then they remembered that they should probably do what couples usually do, according to the television, and they turned back to quickpeck each other goodbye, and then rushed off again.

At work, Ben felt the satisfying sensation of thumbtacks penetrating corkboard. He used a different coloured one on each corner of his notice. Then he walked quickly out of sight, just as the secretaries, cleaners, attendants, door people, and cooks arrived and filed past the noticeboard, each pausing to skim Ben's note, shake his or her head, and hurry off.

"It should be fine," he told the manager in his office. He felt cunning triumph and tried to hold down a smirk. But keeping his mouth flat pushed the smirk upwards, and his eyes and brows lifted at strange, delighted angles. "They'll all work the long weekend without loaded pay, so we can cope with the extra clients. I've put an announcement on the board, rather than taking it through a meeting. That way they won't be able to get all heated up in the same room together."

"You've certainly earned your bonus," the manager said.

When Mella arrived at work there was a small crowd being bees around the noticeboard. They were buzzing, whispering, from the front towards the back, "It says..." and their whispering attracted more people. The notice said that too many people wanted shifts over the long weekend, hence all shifts would be three hours long only, and those over twenty-five wouldn't get double pay. The notice pointed out the generosity of this system, BBB looks after its staff. Rafi stood on his tiptoes and said in a loud voice, "What great news, this calls for a drink at the pub after closing. See you all there." The bees understood.

Ben recited James Bond to himself: "Now he's your enemy and you will kill him. It is that simple?"

"In a word, yes."

Bond killed 006. Quick action, no thought; that's how Bond worked.

Meanwhile, a front desk worker was talking to Ben. She had sinking eyes, and an orange juice that she had quickly put in her desk drawer so that Ben wouldn't see it. She kept looking at the drawer so that she wouldn't bump it with her knee. She spilled out nerovuswords and a clumsy story. "I can't work over the long weekend. You know I'm going to Greece to see my sisters and brothers. The dates on the tickets are unchangeable, and you approved my leave last month," she said.

"If you're having doubts, perhaps you shouldn't be working here."

"I haven't seen my siblings in almost fifteen years."

"Then I suggest you find somewhere else to work," Ben said. It was important to set an example.

Bond straightened his tie as he sped ahead in his gadgetcar. Behind him, a trail of overturned cars and ruined grocery stores, their fruit spilling onto the battered street.

At the back of the pub, they arranged four tables into a bigger square, then put pub stools and chairs around it, bought beers, cups of cask wine, or water, and sat down to start their meeting. The cold glasses left water marks in the shape of three quarter moons on the wooden table surface, and people smeared their elbows in those watermoons.

Rafi was angry. He felt like standing on the table and

waving his arms around. Instead he sat on the edge of his stool, rocking it forward, and talked gently, as though narrating a solemn travel story. People were quiet. All that could be heard from their section of the pub was Rafi speaking deliberately and someone trying her best to do the impossible and open a chip packet silently.

"We're used to making sacrifices; eating less and not going out in order to save for decent shoes, not doing well at school or university because we have to work, then not having time to relax, think, love. We take what jobs we can get, and spend double the time and an hour's wage on the bus because we can't afford a car and the government deprioritises transport in the poorer suburbs," he said.

A night stocker walked in late and pulled a stool up to the tables with apologetic quietness. He hung his head as he did, as though to duck under people's line of vision and therefore disturb them as little as possible. Mella made finger doodles on the misted cold glass, and then changed the watermoons into vines that hung onto her fingertips then rolled away.

"We're the ones that get injured lifting heavy loads, spending eight hours standing at a check out; we're the ones who make the roads, run the schools, save patients in hospitals, collect the garbage, make the clothes, and grow the food, yet they treat us like this."

The night stocker started to smoke. He held the cigarette down at his side, but the smoke still wound round his arm and into the air. Next to Mella, a teenager was busting to go to the toilet, but dared not while Rafi was talking.

"We accept their crappy pay because it's that or nothing, but how bad do things have to get before we stop accepting?"

Mella, fingertips wet, looked around. She saw the film and photo counter guy, and noticed that he became someone else with the brown pub wall and paintings behind him now rather than the posters with the photo printing prices. He was forty, and had once told Mella, "I've reached my peak wage. I'll never earn more than I'm earning now. I won't ever be able to get a house."

Rafi was finishing up: "BBB wants to divide us, pit the older people against the younger ones. Like that, they think they can take away our right to public holiday loading. Then, maybe next they'll take away our fifteen-minute breaks. We already work unpaid overtime when we pack away the store after closing. Some of us may think it's not our problem, like we do with many things in this world, but then the next time it might be. So I'm going to propose that we write a petition and demand that we all get the double pay."

Valerie called out, "Let's vote!" Photo counter guy called out, "All in favour?" and the air filled with hands. The rest of the pub looked over with halfcuriosity to see what was happening then turned quickly back to the soccer on the big television.

They left the multi-table square, and a barperson came over and wiped away the watermoons. Mella lingered behind and asked Rafi where she could get a form to join the union. When she asked, she felt jabs in her lower back as wings grew a little. Her cheeks went warm and her back straightened up. Rafi beamed and his grass hair stood straighter and he shoulder-hugged her because in his world good news was rare. They walked out together.

The night outside was changed because of the meeting. It was deeper, longer, thicker. It wrapped around them, so they folded their arms high on their chests against the chill, and because they felt thoughtful. They walked fast to the train station.

Mella and Ben met at the front door.

"Ha ha, you first."

"No, you."

Straight away, Ben peeled off his clothes and went to

sleep. He snored the sounds of breakfast cereal and heavy trucks. He dreamed about tailored suits and cocktail umbrellas. Mella thought his sleep noises sounded like creeping drums. She sat up in bed, back straight, mind rushing.

Three weddings in Afghanistan

1. Wheat, apple, and grape growers made up the ten families who lived in the housing complex where Inzar, blushing and smiling and whistling, was preparing to get married. The families had had hundreds and hundreds of everyday days, but this one was special, so they celebrated in every way that they could. They wore their best clothes, decorated the complex, and covered tables with special dishes and sweets. They danced and danced, until sometime after midnight the families and their guests— over a hundred people in total—finally slept. At 3:30 am, United States B-52 and B-1B bombers used precision guided bombs to eliminate the complex. An hour later, as a few survivors twitched and twisted among the rubble, a second wave of bombs hit them. Coughing puddle-holes were all that was left of that wedding night. As well as some children's shoes, skirts, flapping school books, the scalp of a woman with braided grey hair, butter toffees in broken red wrappers, and severed paper decorations caught on the wind. —Qalai Niazi, eastern Afghanistan, December 2001.

2. In the house of Mohammed Sherif, women and children sang and danced in the courtyard, and men argued and joked in another compound nearby. A few children dozed on the roof, while others ran around setting off firecrackers. Ahmed Jan Agha played the drum, and lamb stew cooked in large pots. Late that night, US jets and helicopters arrived and made more coughing holes in the houses, in limbs and faces. According to tradition, the groom, Abdul Malk and his bride weren't at the celebration. But twenty-five members of his extended

family, including his father, died. Laik, a thirty-five-year-old farmer, had been drinking with two of his friends. One died; he ran out of the building with the other, who also died. By the end of the attack, his wife and three children were dead too. Fifteen-year-old Naseema told reporters how a piece of iron sliced a woman's neck and her head fell off. —Village of Kakarak, southern Afghanistan, 1 July 2002.

3. This time it was a double wedding, and one of the brides, who was on her way to meet her future husband, was accompanied by a large party of villagers. The children impatiently skipped ahead along the sketchy mountain paths, and the women skipped on the inside. They talked loudly, walked calmly, if a little faster than normal. Then a US jet flew low and dropped a bomb next to the group of children who were sitting and waiting for the women to catch up. Shah Zareen picked up one of the injured children and ran down to the village, calling out to report the attack. As he did, there was a second blast on the group of women. Three escaped, including the bride, but as they ran down the mountain another bomb dropped on them. Three more puddled, coughing holes, ninety less people. —Deh Bala district, eastern Afghanistan, 6 July 2008

On the offensive
The police increased their efforts on the Macquarie Fields side of the railway line. They combed the suburb with their dogs and instigated pest control. They patrolled the poor and the suburb hung its head in shame. Sorry.

Undeclared war 4
A brown jumper over his shoulders, a chicken bone next to him, and his memories left by the river. He sat among the nightlife, among the fights, the flirting, the drunken philosophies spat and sprayed over new shirts, and he sipped from his bottle. Then the police came and told him

he couldn't drink in a public place. He refused to get rid of his drink—what a waste that would be. So the police grabbed his brown jumper and forced him to the ground. They kicked him, punched him, searched his bag, and charged him.

"I just want to get somewhere to live one day so I can stay away from everything, that's all," he told the press. Police do not have the power to arrest someone for drinking in public, nor to search property without a warrant. (20 March 2008, Fortitude Valley, Brisbane, Australia)

He was sixty-five and a little cold, a little dirty, a little without home. He started to get dressed in some public toilets, and a cleaner called the police. Six of them escorted him out of the toilets and pinned him down, pressed his head into the concrete, pulled his legs apart and kneed him. (July 2006, Queen Street Mall, Brisbane)

A child of nine with her singlet slipping off her shoulders, a man who lost his house after caring for his sick father for twelve years, an ex -Ford worker, and a fifty-five-year-old man who went to jail for stealing a guitar (and wrote sixty songs while he was there), were among those living in the little tent city. Then the police came with box cutters and slit their tents at the base in two quick cuts. Like efficiently gutting a fish. They pulled out belongings and threw them into a heap in the gutter. Turned them into rubbish. (June and July 2008, St Petersburg, US, and many other times and places)

It was a campaign to combat visual pollution that consisted of little human beings who accidentally got in the way. The police used helicopters to scour more than one hundred and fifty parks for homeless camps. Two officers also patrolled the parks every day, looking for campers. When they found one, they took the belongings: tarps, clothes, backpacks, and left a note with contact information. (June 2008, Saanich, Canada)

Four hundred and forty private security guards, three hundred and twenty government staff, and three hundred and fifty police officers went to Utsubo Park and Osaka Castle Park to destroy tarpaulin shelters and evict a small group of homeless men in preparation for the World Rose Convention. (January 2006, Osaka, Japan).

When Eddie Felix Franco first became homeless he felt like a lost caged bird. He didn't know where to go for food, showers, or shelter. Night time was scary, so he bought a cheap toy gun. One day he was confronted in the street by seven police officers. He touched the toy gun and they shot him forty-seven times. (August 2008, California, US)

Golf course people fibro house people

Morning rush hour in Macquarie Fields. From the surrounds of the apple green golf course, from the triple story houses, glossed and manicured people flowed like easy rivers towards the station. From the broken windows and echoing fibro walls on the other side, the other people, all covered in clothes and shoes and things with holes and covered-up stains and zipper flies that didn't work, tumbled, plummeted, plunged unstably towards the station with quick regular anxious glances behind them. Both groups ascended the station stairs on their respective sides and arrived at the top then passed through the six buzzing ticket gates as though the gates were combing them, straightening them out into neat little lines that then filed on to the platform. At the top of the stairs, midway between both of them and facing the ticket machines, Ashley, her small backpack on the floor against the back wall, was singing. Her white MacDonald's cup begged for spare change.

The same two police officers that had walked through their backyard were standing at the ticket gates, monitoring those who passed through, and watching her too, openly, obviously. Ashley had bought a ticket; a single to the next station, which meant that she was legally allowed to be in the station and the police couldn't ask her to move on. The golf course people walked straight past her to the ticket gates, their tickets ready and in position in their right hands, while those from fibro walls paused for a few seconds. They saw the police watching her, and they wondered. Ashley closed her eyes so that she could leave the station and the accusing police observation, and she pictured Paz. She sang with gentle breathing. Then she thought about the bills, the food they needed, her growing child, and she became anxious. Her voice became tinged in howlwind.

"That's very good," someone said, and dropped a fiver in her cup. She opened her eyes, but he was already mixed into the combed crowd. The cops walked away.

What is a criminal?
He was responsible for the death of hundreds of thousands of innocent people, and he spent his retirement playing golf and painting dogs. George Bush stole the presidency in 2000 and spent the next eight years lying time and again to the people of the US and the world, and then during his retirement was paid millions to give private cellophane-speeches, with more lies served on long-ribboned phrases at one thousand dollar dinners. As president he pulled out of the Kyoto Protocol, which set requirements for thirty-eight countries to lower greenhouse gas emissions, invaded Afghanistan, and in Iraq his policy led to the torture, abuse, rape, and killing of prisoners in Abu Ghraib prison. He also created the Guantanamo prison, where untried journalists, poets, and cattle farmers were tortured. He ignored basic civil liberties at home, launching a large scale domestic spying program

where citizen's online activity was monitored, as well as slashing the right to overtime pay, and refusing to raise the minimum wage. He opened the US wilderness to logging and mining, and was involved in corporate scandals. Then he entered UN assemblies, parliaments, and palaces and received a standing ovation.

Coordinated

Seventy-two corellas lifted off the trees, and in one morphing shape twisted and glided along the invisible windpaths in the sky. They were one cloud, one scene, one large bird.

People though, walked in a mess, their life links tripping and tangled. Their struggle and sadness were unjoined, their happiness uncoordinated.

Bags in cages

As Mella got ready to go to work, surrounded by a hazy yellow morning and the smell of lentils from the apartment next door, she slipped a paper corella into a small inside pocket in her backpack. Ben walked past her, yawning widely, and her hand jumped a bit too fast. She was glad he didn't see it.

"Looks like the fridge is broken," he yelled from the kitchen. "It keeps freezing things. I'll call the repair guy today; you can chip in half, right?"

Mella said yes, and left the apartment with a new worry. Then she arrived at work and things were different. They had handed in their petition yesterday, and now there was a new security guard and a new giant metal cage in the loading docks, where she and the others were told to put their bags.

After her shift, because many other workers on different levels finished at the same time, there was a queue for the bag cage. The new security guard stood in front of it dressed in a black uniform, a gun in his holster.

The old security guard, George, had worn jeans, and said their names in rhyme over the PA system when they were being moved to a different area. The new guard went through their bags before handing them back, and Mella wondered why, when they had been locked up the entire shift. She saw Valerie's ear tops turn red when the guard pulled a packet of pads out of her bag, and dropped one on the floor. The line shuffled forward and they said little; the only sound that could be heard was the bag cage chain banging about. Mella thought about the fridge, and how she had little savings, and that maybe Ben was right about her needing the promotion, and that that was unlikely now that she had joined the union and signed the petition. She remembered the induction video about security. It had said that searching bags was only legal with a warrant or the person's permission. She knew that they were being punished, and she considered saying she didn't give her permission. But then her turn came and she couldn't say anything at all. The guard took her bag out of the cage, opened the main zipper swiftly, and pulled her notebooks and jumper out in a big handful. He peered into its gutted interior, not noticing the inside pocket with the paper corella. He handed it all to her and she whispered, "Thank you." The line behind her shuffled forward again, and Mella looked behind her, at their feet. She thought she heard chains rattling on their ankles.

The guard searched Rafi's bag and found a left wing newspaper. "I've got my eye on you, young man," he said. Rafi ran after Mella and they walked together. Rafi's jokes went away. A fly bumped into his nose and buzzed around his ear and he swore at it. Mella felt another person who was heavy, bitter, tempered, and she stepped away and watched him, concerned. He looked back at her; his face was dark clouds. Around them, the wind crawled about on the ground and kicked at rubbish. Their conversation and glances were paused as they crossed at the intersection, slipping awkwardly through the crowd then coming together again on the other side. Mella's long look left warmdust on Rafi's shoulders and neck. He brought his tone down a little, softened it, sighed roughly, and then vented to her. He talked about what luck was and about people forced to climb steep mountains. He said that where he came from the battle was raw and messy. "Here it is lined with leather, but it is still a battle." And with that comment, Mella thought that here was a person that knew she was struggling. And one person made her a little less invisible. She touched his dusted shoulder, slung her bag around to her front and opened it, and gave him the paper corella. It fell open; a chain of birds. Then her phone rang: "Hey, Mella, turns out the fridge is completely stuffed; we'll have to get a new one. Might cost as much as nine hundred; you can still chip in, right?"

Bribes in boxes

Hoyan received an unexpected visit. He had been sitting on his unmade bed in his plain rented room after being laid off. The mine where he had worked had been privatised, sold by the Liberal Party, and many had lost their jobs as a result. There was a little table in the corner of his room with a pile of overdue bills and two empty plates. He sat and stared and sat and stared until the knock of the visitor forced him to get up and open the door. It was a man from the Liberal Party. "I have something for you," he said in a big voice, with a big smile, and held out a cologne bottle shaped like a wine bottle, made of pastel white glass. "Normally these cost one hundred and forty dollars, but I'll give it to you for twenty dollars," the big voice, big smile man said. Hoyan didn't need the cologne, but he did need cheering up, so he bought the bottle and placed it on the empty table next to the bills. He thanked the man and promised to vote for the Liberal Party.

Decoy

They gave out peace prizes as the invasions went on.

They sanitised shopping centres with indoor potted plants in token reference to the forests that had once been there.

They put elaborate dresses and rings on the woman being handed over from father to husband

They put sports matches on television when unemployment increased.

They advertised the Australian Army Reserve as an "adventure" with "exciting outdoor activities" and the "chance to meet great friends".

They dressed the torero in a "suit of lights" as he killed and tortured the bull.

And they dressed thugs in uniforms, tuxes and crowns.

They dressed vegetable oil, maltodextrin, whey powder, and flavour enhancers in bold packaging and sold it as food.

They gave trophies to people who won eating competitions as other people counted their food stamps, and others still, starved.

The media and politicians used refugees and immigrants to distract from unemployment, and the unemployed to distract from exploitation.

The business people used charity fundraisers to distract from their robbery and organised corruption.

Dawn talk

Paz was walking home from another one-off 7/11 shift. It was almost dawn, when morning and night overlap and the first few birds sense the proximity of thin orange light skystretching, and call out. The street was empty and Paz chattered to unnamed, genderless people in his head. "It's unreal," he said out loud. He walked fast, then gestured with one hand, chopping the air up and down to emphasise his point. Then two police officers in an unmarked car pulled up alongside him, and the officer in the passenger seat wound down his window and called out, "Hey, what's wrong with you?"

Paz didn't hear him, and kept walking. The officer got out of the car, slammed the door hard, and told Paz to stop. Then he heard, and he turned around and looked at them, surprised, because they weren't part of the conversation he was having.

"Retard! You slow or something?" said the other officer, also now getting out of the car. Paz still didn't reply. There had been few customers during his shift, and he had been talking to genderless people in his head for a while. It was a mode that had to be shut off and left before he could start vocal talking again.

"Over here, down on the car, hands up," the first officer said, pushing Paz onto the car bonnet, and quickly patting him down. Paz's ear tops turned red, and finally he began to speak.

"What'd I do?"

"We'll ask the questions," the second officer said. He pushed the left side of Paz's face into the cold bonnet metal, and then let him go.

Waterbang

And the day before that, when light was instead a solid yellow blanket brushing head tops, Ashley had been busking again at the top of the station stairs. Eva was holding her pointer finger and running in circles, turning her mum into a maypole. Then she played Window and stuck her head between Ashley's knees. She watched the people walk past and saw squiggle aliens, moonbugs, dolphins, knobbly-kneed magicians and gentle geniuses. Ashley looked down at her daughter, smiled, and sang a song for her. She sang up 1350 steps, and then tumbled down again. The station's aliens, moonbugs, dolphins, and geniuses slowed down to listen. The ticket sellers peered around the short queues and watched her. Then a train pulled in around the bend, and as though someone had pressed fast forward on the people-remote, the aliens, moonbugs, dolphins, and geniuses ran down the steps and jumped through carriage doors.

Ashley kept singing. She heard that symphony music that Paz had put on that time and she was in the rivercurtain dress. She was in a stream and her hands played the water like drums and her feet tapped the sand underneath them, shaking it into round puffs of sandcloud. The crunchy tree leaves rattled a rhythm... waterbang, sandsplash and rattle, said her riverworld. At the station though, she was mostly still. There was a three-year-old's head between her knees, and a very small twitch in her feet; dance awakening in her like a baby bird trembling inside its egg before it pecks its way out.

1350 steps

The small old woman walked up 1350 steps to work each day. At the top of the mountain, a giant statue of Jesus opened his arms wide over the drought city of Cochabamba. At the top of the stairs, the woman sold roasted beans and sweets to tourists, then with sunset, she walked all the way back down again.

Dawn talk 2

Paz was walking home from a night shift again. He was unshaved and humming and playing at stepping between footpath cracks. Again, two police officers walked towards him and stopped him. They were taller than him, and he could see that they both had tiny nostrils and that their nostril hairs flapped like flags as they breathed heavily down on him. They told him they were going to pat him down, and this time Paz said no.

"Don't be cheeky."

"You can't search me for no reason; I have rights."

"What rights? You're scum."

Paz could no longer see the four tiny nostrils. His cheek this time was on the footpath square, right on the crack he had been playing at avoiding. With sideways eyes he saw a boot come down and rest on his other cheek. The second cop, who had been quiet so far, twisted his arm behind his back and dislocated his shoulder. The boot of the other came down harder and a sliver of blood trickled out his ear. The police left him like that, on the ground and watching the moon seem to bounce up and down behind the houses and trees.

What is a criminal?
Billionaire Donald Trump once demanded that an elderly widow give up her home so that he could build a limousine parking lot near his Atlantic City hotels. He also set up the Trump University, which wasn't actually a university and which charged for courses which turned out to be publicity for taking more of the 'courses'. He reportedly received US$1.5 million for each one-hour presentation he did for the Learning Annex. He also owned, developed, ran, or put his name to Miss USA, Miss Universe, hotels, golf courses, residential towers, the Trump Taj Mahal Casino Resort and other casinos, mortgage firm Trump Financial, Trump Sales and Leasing, Trump Restaurants, travel website GoTrump, a line of menswear and accessories called Donald J Trump Signature Collection, Donald Trump The Fragrance, Trump Ice bottled water, Trump Magazine, Trump Chocolate, home furnishings, Trump Productions, Trump The Game, Trump Model Management, Trump Shuttle, Trump Vodka, and Trump Steaks. His resource wasting Trump empire was built on, for example, the two hundred immigrants who were paid four dollars an hour to work twelve hour days, seven days a week, unprotected from asbestos dust, to demolish the old Bonwit Teller building in order for the Trump Tower to be built in its place.

The patchwork patterns of places
Pueblo Nuevo in the Venezuelan Andes was a town that appeared on most maps as just a river. They said that's where drugs were bought and sold and where robberies

with broken bottles occurred. Tourists didn't go there, students walked over the bridge to the university to avoid passing through it, taxis went as far as the giant staircase leading into it, but no further. Few wanted to live there, despite the cheap rent. Pueblo Nuevo was where green iron roofs overlapped, roadside soccer games lasted past dark, quick greetings turned into long debates, *quinceañeras* (fifteenth birthdays) were held, and plastic bag kites became stuck among the electricity wires, next to the wasps' nests. It was where there were aloe vera pot plants under dripping washing, body rhythm classes with cups and clapping, teenagers posing on motorbikes, dogs wandering into the school or barking at the cranky hairdresser, people framed by windows and doors as they watched the street, the young man in the wheelchair who would be able to walk if he took his medicine playing chess with whomever, where corner stores were conjured out of the front door entrances of houses where four families lived, where music boomed from the backs of cars and kids robot-danced for passersby, and black plastic bags of rubbish accumulated against the wall, under the hand-painted sign that said it was prohibited to leave rubbish there.

Then there were the northern suburbs of Sydney, where pruned parks had city and harbour views, high salaried workers and business people took coffee under big white umbrellas in the street, shopping centres formed the hub around which residential towers and office buildings loomed over ornate streets with bins that looked like monuments to something. Greyscale spiritless architecture, colour forgotten, birds missing, geometry but no murals rapping along the sidewalls. The trains arrived every three minutes at the stations in the Northern Suburbs. Money went where money was, and services went where taxes were paid.

In Macquarie Fields, the bus that had gone through the suburb to the station once an hour changed its route and skipped the suburb all together. Ashley got up forty-five minutes earlier and walked to the station. Then the trains to the outer suburbs changed from half hourly to every fifty minutes. No tourists went to Macquarie Fields, no restaurant reviewers, no visitors, no shoppers, or people just getting out for a day. The only new people were the police, who seemed to increase their patrol size regularly.

A night the colour of police uniforms

At 7:23 pm, three police officers walked through the unlocked front door of Paz's place and ordered everyone down onto the floor. At first all of them (except Tracey, who was out) just stood there, looking at the figures in the open doorway sceptically. Then one officer put his hand on his gun, and another kicked the door closed and yelled again, "Down, now!"

As they dropped to the floor, Paz looked at Damjan anxiously and tried to read in him some clue as to where his pot stash was kept. Matt eyed the washing machine, a corner of it just visible in the laundry. Damjan didn't look at anyone. He sat down slowly, and then lay on the floor on his back, putting his hands behind his head. He felt comfortable like that, and tempted to sleep. Eva froze, just like she had that time playing soccer, but then she saw that everyone else was lying on the floor, and she sheepishly joined them.

"Something's going on in this house, and we're going to find out what," said the police officer that had kicked the door closed. He pointed his gun at them, while the other two went into the bedrooms. They heard blankets being pulled off beds and thrown into corners, mattresses being lifted, and posters and pictures torn off the walls. Paz imagined the corners of them where the sticky tape was, staying behind on the walls. From where he lay, all he could see were the boots of the officer aiming the gun. They were well polished, laced all the way up, and had grass and gum stuck to the bottom. Behind a chair leg, he saw the pea from ages ago. One police officer came out of Ashley's room and stepped on it. The other came out of Matt and Tracey's room, and the two of them started on the lounge room, taking the throws off the lounges and improvised milk crate furniture, pulling the curtains down, upturning the milk crate table. One sat down and tried to open the DVD player, but he couldn't because it was off, so he broke the casing with the aid of a thump from his nightstick. The other officer went into the laundry, and rubbing his hand over the washing machine as though it were a new car, yelled out, "Get a look at this... Pretty nice."

"Where'd you get it from, eh?" he said to the bodies sprawled on the floor, but didn't wait for an answer. He went to the backyard and threw the barbeque bricks around the yard. Some of them broke against the concrete porch as they landed. Butterflies hid, and Eva, who was lying near the back door, was incredulous. She had assumed bricks were unbreakable.

Matt, meanwhile, lying nearest to the kitchen, watched the front door hoping Tracey would appear. He was used to her being with him now, and it felt wrong to go through this without her. His hand didn't feel empty, because they rarely held hands, rather the space next to him felt vacant. He looked at the space and frowned.

The police made their way to the door, leaving war-rubble and broken air behind them.

"You can't get away with this," Paz said, throwing words at their backs.

One officer looked around. "You think? What will you do? Go to the local reps? They employ us. Go to the media? They wouldn't care, or listen to the likes of you. Complain to the police? Ha ha ha!" He left the door open behind him.

Damjan stayed where he was on the floor, and reached over and took the remote, which had been pushed off the table. He turned on the television. It was the late news. It recapped an acting award ceremony with glitter actors who said vague things to the cameras, then it moved on to the World Economic Forum, where big business owners said a few things to the cameras, then the Pope, visiting Brazil, said things, and the poor did not say things, and then it moved on to sport, weather, and a pregnant dolphin. The butterflies in the backyard stayed in hiding. Underground clocks counted everything without glitter in life. Ashley went to make coffee. She made one cup, and forgot to filter it. So she made another, and forgot to filter that too.

"I can't believe they didn't find your pot, Dammo. Where on earth did you hide it?" Matt asked, as he bent over the DVD, piecing it together with nail scissors for a screwdriver.

"Ha, I've run out."

"Gee. Man, we've got to be careful," Ashley said, her teeth freeing her lip for just that moment.

In twenty minutes Matt had the DVD player working. But, like a folded shirt from a packet that won't go back inside the wrapper, the machine rattled and was a little crooked, with four wide pieces of brown tape holding it together. There was a meteor shower that night, but Matt forgot about it. Eva went around announcing to each house member individually that she would "plant" the broken bricks. She hadn't learnt the word for 'bury' yet, and she thought it was the same thing, and that when the dead were placed under the ground they were being planted, like seeds.

A day the colour of bathwater

"You wrote the petition, didn't you?"

"No..."

"Who did then?"

"I don't know..." Mella hesitated. All of them had. "I just signed it."

The shop manager had brought each of them to his

office, alone. He told them that they didn't appreciate the job they'd been given. He was generous; they were ungrateful. He glared and paused and made them wait. He leaned back in his executive chair. They curled their shoulders and curled their eyes inside. He said they didn't have to have the job if they didn't want it.

And that afternoon butterflies left work alone and parked themselves in separate mailboxes. Mella, in her mailbox, sat on the toilet with the bathroom door locked. She rested her elbows on her knees and her head in her hands and made three patches of red skin. "I just signed it," she remembered herself saying. Distancing herself from responsibility, leaving Rafi vulnerable. Put her job first. Felt her wing stubs recede. The bathroom muffled outside sound. Long stress, that type that clung to clothes and hurt your head in the morning, then followed you into the shower, sunk itself into Mella's nerves and bones. She sat there on the toilet and reached conclusions. The management was countering their intimidation strategy with its own. It was working. It was a plan. She hadn't expected the management to plan.

Party eyes in her mailbox put an MP3 list on loud and got into bed. She had gummy eyes and gluggy skin and a twitching eyebrow. For the next few days at work her eyes avoided people.

Rafi was in his bathroom too. He rested his head against the open window and watched the speechless sky. He had called the union and told them about the public holiday pay issue and the harassment, but the representative had told him he should have gone to her first. She said she could see where the management was coming from, and that the law stipulated that problems had to be discussed with the company first before any actions were taken.

"They never discuss anything with us," he'd responded. His teeth had pins and needles now. Because he was remembering, experiencing, the impotency a friend had felt. He wanted to scratch his teeth, or hit them. He breathed out cubes of air that stuck to the window frame. Who would help them? Should he confess he wrote the petition and take the blame, or try to convince everyone to take things to the next level?

Colours ran away

Paz made a photo. It was black and army green, and grainy. There were guns scrunched up as though they were paper and thrown randomly about their backyard. The guns hummed monotonously. At the back of the yard, someone looked back at him. It was Ashley. No, it was Matt. Paz held the photo in his hands and inspected it. Some of the colour ran down it, collected at the bottom edge, and then dripped off. Colour suicide into his lap. He touched a finger to the drops and tried to spread them back onto the image.

Pillowish

It was just before a 3:00 pm to 11:00 pm shift, and Mella was home alone. She had time to think, and to feel, and her sadness about the state of the world could fill her as though she were sponge. But she took her heavy sponge body and her creeping feet and her face that she wanted to look away from for a ten-minute holiday. She sat cross-legged on the couch and retreated to fantasyland. There, she had her own little place with a big bed and lots of fluffy u-shaped pillows. The walls were blue, green, and purple, and there were bean bags to sit on and seat hammocks too. There was a balcony with vegetables, herbs, and flowers growing out of yoghurt containers and old shoes, and baby lorikeets and sugar gliders would land on her shoulders or sleep in her lap as she read in the seat hammock. There was a big bathtub with a little table next to it, and she had a shelf full of board games.

Your skin remembers your smiles, sulks, and shouts, and marks them with little wrinkles. When you dream at night the image is burnt faintly into your mood the next day, just like the images burnt onto old computer screens. Daydreams, too, leave behind a feeling of softness, of hope, of dark red peaches. Mella picked up her soft sponge body and fetched her bag to go to work.

Dawn talk 3

A young woman with a four-month foetus growing in her womb and a bottle of wine sticking out of her handbag yelled and swayed in the fading night. The police told her to stop being a nuisance, so she turned to them and aimed her swaying words in their direction. "Fffuck youuuu Sunzvvvv...." she said. The police un-delicately put her on the ground so that she rolled onto that four-month foetus. One officer squeezed her breast, but in the commotion, she didn't notice.

"You're under arrest for disturbing the peace," he said.

"You're the ones who disturb the peace," Paz said. He was watching from under a nearby bus shelter. The police arrested him too, and held his head as they pushed him into the paddy van. They said they were arresting him for jumping the turnstiles at Central Station. He didn't insist that he never went near Central Station, and spent the rest of fading night not sleeping in a small cell. They released him the next morning without charge.

How houses die

Cows walked in its doors and out its wall holes and pulled out the grass growing like beard hair from its windows and floor cracks. Slowly, the house fell inside itself. Posters hung by one corner, then fell off the wall. Dust piled up next to chair legs. Walls grew mould, the ceiling flaked, a door rusted off its hinges. Like a camel corpse exposed in a desert, the house rotted, the ceiling fell, wind and rain swept in.

The same thing happened to the neglected people,

those who had to live outside the world of careers and restaurants and central business districts. Slowly, their voices cracked, their nails crumbled, their arguments and memories flaked. Their hearts pumped hard, but cows walked through them.

House cracks and people itches

The raid and the night in prison had left Paz feeling unsettled and upset. He walked around the house, the place that was meant to shelter them, and he saw cracks everywhere, cracks he hadn't seen before. There was a brown-coloured crack that split in two in the glass of their op-shop blender. A cereal bowl had a hairline crack that Eva tried curiously to feel, but couldn't. The front door steps were broken and wobbled like loose teeth, and there was a missing plank in the back fence that hadn't bothered him before, and now did. The DVD growled hoarsely when they put rentals into it. The hole in the roof in Ashley's room seemed to be getting bigger. He peaked outside and imagined that he could see the crack in the sky that was letting all the ozone in. He stepped out onto the teeth-steps and the sun touched his bare toes and lit up a button, half embedded in the garden dirt. Lizards with half and quarter toes, having lost bits of their body in the roughness of tree and ground life, peaked at his toes from the stair cracks. Paz crouched down and dipped his fingers into the rain that slept in the semi-permanent puddles in the uneven concrete at the base of the steps.

His heart was beating too fast. He went back inside to his room, and with Damjan out, gently closed the door—something they rarely did—and then flopped belly first on to his mattress. He felt that he put so much effort into trying to keep his life together that there wasn't time or energy to read, or go places, or take real photos, or paint real pictures. They got knocked down, they got up, then they got knocked down again, they got back up, then again knocked down, and for now he felt like lying there on his stomach and taking a short rest from the constant fight.

On the other side of the wall, Ashley was in her room also remembering the raid. Paz had a tingling itch on his forehead, which he rubbed. Like catching yawns, Ashley, too, was suddenly itchy. Her shirt tag irritated her back, and she hit at it to quieten the sensation.

Tracey had an itch too. It was a fallen out public hair, but she didn't want to scratch it while Matt was next to her. He was very quiet, so just to get him to talk, she said, "We should get out of here soon, get to Bolivia and stay in a tent next to a river. Or do that road trip you guys always talk about, go to Uluru and Darwin and talk to people with real hard Aussie accents, the ones who sound like cockatoos. Camp out with kangaroos peering into our tents."

"Sounds awesome," Matt said, scratching his earlobe and knowing that no one ever leaves Macquarie Fields except to go to prison. Or by stealing a big van and travelling about for a bit then getting caught and going to prison.

Damjan didn't catch the itchiness. He was out buying more scratchies. Since the raid, he'd been sleeping in more, sometimes till as late as 1:00 or 2:00 pm. He'd wake up with a headache, eat crackers for breakfast, and either go back to bed at 9:00 pm, or watch television all night until he fell asleep on the couch, one arm hanging down, the other flopped over his aching head. His legs took him running around the backyard with Eva, overtaking her, and then tagging her from behind to her delight, but not much more. One of his three scratchies won him forty dollars. He put twenty dollars aside for household bills, and then bought two beers and a packet of individually wrapped chocolates. Back at home, with a barely restrained face of mischief, he hid the chocolates all over the house, and said nothing to anyone.

Road cracks

In 2003, US and Polish forces occupied the ruins of the ancient city of Babylon, eighty-five kilometres south of Baghdad, to use it as a military depot. Babylon arose four thousand years ago, and is estimated to have been one of the largest cities in the world from 1770 BC to 1670 BC and from 612 BC to 320 BC. The signs of the zodiac and the sixty second clock originated there. In the blue brick ruins of its gates, the dragon-snake and lion are depicted. The invading forces drove tanks and military vehicles over Babylon's roads, some of the oldest in the world. They damaged the Ishtar Gate dragons, and broken bricks with the name of Nebuchadnezzar carved in them were found lying in the spoils. The invaders covered large archaeological areas with imported gravel, and filled sandbags and mesh crates with thousands of tonnes of archaeological material, including bones. They dug trenches into the Ziggurat, one of the stepped pyramids which probably forms part of the legendary Tower of Babel. The roof of the Ninmakh Temple collapsed, most likely because of the vibrations from the busy helipad the invaders built nearby.

Matt's wings

Matt found a wrapped chocolate in the cracked blender. He raised an eyebrow, opened it and ate it, then scratched the bottom of his foot. That tickled and at the same time made the itch more urgent, so he kicked his thong off and rubbed his foot hard on the corner of a crate in the lounge room. He rubbed so hard that the crate fell off the one below it and manila folders, stapled booklets, and individual papers spilled out. A thick yellow piece of A4 paper caught his attention and made him blush and forget his itchy foot. Eleven years ago he had shown his dad that piece of paper and his dad had slapped him hard on the cheek. Then he'd pulled his belt out of his jeans and chased him around the house, hitting what parts of his fleeing legs and arms that he could. He hadn't shown anyone else that paper, and had forgotten about it.

Matt was three years old when he fixed something for the first time. He folded paper until it was the right thickness, then put it under one of the legs of their dining table; a portable folding table in the corner of the kitchen, to make it stop rocking.

When he was four he made an Ant and All Bugs Wonderland. He stuck thick leaves and husks of tree bark together to make a slide that ran down the dining table, down the back steps, and into the empty flower pot. He put bugs at the top of the slide and carefully poured water behind them. He imagined they were screaming with delight.

When he was five he fixed the television when it wouldn't "talk", and when he was six he imagined how he would make a telescope for looking into things. Instead of the moons or planets, he could point it at the centre of his own planet, and see its core beating, worms moving around, the soil turning.

When Matt was seven though, he started to adjust to the idea that the world wasn't interested in x-ray telescopes, and by the time he was eight, he was easily distracted. His childish grin began to fall away. His eyes alone would light up, as though from a weak current, when he hung out with his mate-from-up-the-road, Paz.

When he was nine, he showed his dad the piece of paper. It turned out that his dad had lost another job that day. Over time Matt felt less like thinking about telescopes. His dad, tired and drunk, fed him oven baked, no-frills fries, instant lasagne, canned pasta, and other convenient and cheap food, and his nutrition levels and thinking suffered. Inventing things wasn't encouraged at school. There, they added and subtracted and wrote lists of spelling words, and beat each other up in rugby. Unlike Paz, he finished year twelve and got into university, though his marks weren't high enough for a science degree. The nearest university was two hours away by public transport, the enrolment fee was unaffordable, and by the age of seventeen he couldn't see the point of studying anyway. Because Matt's heart was connected to his head, he eventually found it hard to think about why paint dried and how plants could eat sun rays. He stopped noticing the cracks in the road which could be fixed with a certain stretchy material, or the noisy machines that would be quieter if they only thought to...

Now, at twenty, Matt was still the first person in the house to fix anything, relishing pulling it apart and putting the pieces back where they so clearly belonged, but he no longer imagined what was possible. Still, he decided he wanted to show Paz the yellow paper. Shoulders hunched, head hanging, he walked into his room, not wondering why, on this day, the door was closed.

"Do you remember when we all did that basic skills test in primary school?" Matt asked Paz. "Well, I did really well in the science section. They said...well, actually, they wrote a letter to mum and said I was...well, I got a really high score, man. They said technically the score meant I was a..." Matt finished there. The word embarrassed him and felt unconnected to the present. He looked at Paz's mattress, pulled a sheet corner back into place. "I used to really like inventing things, you know. I really understood how different materials affected each other, how it all worked. Now the whole bloody world is blurry."

Paz stretched out of his curl and looked directly at Matt. "You fix things like the wind, mate," he said, smiling. Then he began to scheme; Matt's birthday was coming up, and he had a few ideas.

The canvas is a mirror
"Mum, what's Paz doing?" Eva asked, touching window with her finger directly where she saw Paz's head outside. Ashley saw Paz sitting cross-legged on the footpath, bent over, drawing with large pieces of chalk.

"Crikey, he's lost it," she said, grinning, and took Eva by the hand and went outside. Tracey saw Ashley walk outside with a big grin, and curious, she got up to follow her. Matt followed Tracey, and Damjan, peering over the couch, saw that everyone seemed to be going outside, so he got up too. They found Paz drawing giant ants. Brown ones now. No pink ones. Eva inspected the drawings seriously; she considered herself the drawing expert of the house. She looked at the path where they were all standing and sitting and followed its line to the horizon. "Oh, that's a big piece of paper," she said.

"What's this, Eva?" Paz asked, pointing at one of the ants.

"Peas, potatoes, and carrots," she replied confidently.

"Ha! Let's see your ant then!"

Concentrating, Eva drew a round head, a big smile that broke slightly out of the boundaries, and lines from the mouth that looked like teeth, but were in fact grass. Eva thought ants ate grass. Ashley, standing behind her, bent over her. "That's very good."

"Mum, your face is upside-down. Your mouth is at the top of your head."

Across the road and down a few houses, two police officers sat in an unmarked car and watched.

Packaging 1

Ben walked like a car. He drove himself through the city streets and around the corners mechanically, calculating shortest distances, stopping impatiently, merging smoothly, maintaining his perfect speed. At the same time, he glanced in window displays and calculated quickly the value of discounts. Then he paused in front of a jewellery store, eyes jumping from one item to another, five-second calculations. He went inside, and came out forty-three minutes later with a small cube-shaped object in his shirt pocket. He drove on, past an underweight man sitting against a bank wall with his hand held out and his left pant leg pulled up to show a shin half eaten by yellowstuff. Ben made an even square around the obstacle. "Lazy and useless," he thought to himself. "They should all be melted down and used as glue."

Before he entered the BBB loading dock to surprise Mella, he glanced at his reflection in the window, flattened down stray hairs, adjusted his sport jacket, and turned sideways to note the slight shape his bicep made under his sleeves. But Mella had already left work, turned the corner from the loading dock and found him. Rafi overtook them, waving goodbye, and Ben told Mella that Rafi was bad news, that he could always spot the type. Mella should ignore him and work "harder than they ask you to", move up to section supervisor, then floor supervisor, then maybe a manager. He put one hand on her shoulder and steered her across the intersection and towards the Queen Victoria Building. It was mid-afternoon, and there were curly bits of wind, and the Town Hall clock was all tall and strict. Sunlight filtered through the skyscrapers and small squares of it managed to touch the ground. Streets cleaned with precision, plants potted, gutters measured. And a man with a suitcase and blue tie walked past them, an eyelid quivering. A couple sat down on the Town Hall steps and forced laughter the same way people forced smiles for photos. A woman with an orange dress that ballooned around her knees said 'Fuck' to a stranger, leaning her whole body towards him and putting so much air and teeth into the 'F' that Mella thought she was trying to blow out her frustration. And she imagined that everyone who was angry did the same, and the street air filled with clouds of hard-breathed 'F'.

She was steered into a street level hairdresser in the QVB—a place with dark green walls and long mirrors and a woman with a too-tight belt who placed her in a chair. Ben told the woman that Mella's hair was too long and needed more style, and Mella just looked at her reflection and saw uglybits all over the place. But she liked her unruly long hair, which soon became a tamed oval shape with a long fringe. It was gelled and blow-dried, and Mella stood up feeling like her hair was a wig that didn't fit her. She wanted to take it off.

Ben steered her then to a bank and rubbertalked to her about loans and cars and the value of money and safe investing and got her to apply for a credit card. Lastly, he took her to a large department store on Pitt Street. It had four floors, gold escalator railings, slippery marble floors, and products displayed on white columns. He guided her through the shop as if leading the blind, past the fine bone china, past frangipani bath cream and crock print shoulder bags and gold coffee machines. He told her that the things you wore said something about what you were worth, and got her to use her new credit card to buy a lady's watch and a black dinner dress. The watch was heavy, a weight where her wrist hadn't had one, and now she was wearing two things that weren't right.

At home she tried on the black dress and it felt cool and soft. Ben told her to clean the house and use the meat he'd bought to bake a large meat pie. As she worked, she imagined him plotting her life on a graph; promotion, children, house paid off, new car, work, buy, work, buy, less wings more work, buy, die. She was in debt now, for a black dress, and the next two weeks she wouldn't be saving anything. The next two weeks she wouldn't have pillowish fantasies about her own little place with all the plants and flowers that birds liked, about time to read adventure books, about helping to make the skyloads of injustice go away, about being happy and being able to dance like the wind. Not city wind, she clarified. The wind of beaches, the wind above oceans, the wind that was free.

How he held his head

He was a young bull, just four. He had black skin with some brown, big eyes, wet nostrils, and off-white horns. His head and neck were typically big, and his legs short;

standing he was just a metre and a half. He sat now among the dandelions and clover and long grass. Occasionally, he blinked his half-open eyes.

Five days later, at the Sun Festival in Merida, Venezuela, they locked him in a dark concrete cage in the bull fighting stadium. They beat his testicles and kidneys, put grass in his eyes and shaved his horns. He went without light and water for twenty-four hours. And then they made him fight. A trumpet siren. A contingent of fighters entered the arena in silver uniforms. Matador, two horseback picadors, three banderillos. Then the small bull ran into it all, half blind from the surprise of bright left. The matador tested him, the picador stabbed his neck with his lance, weakening his muscles; blood spurted out. And the bull held his head a little lower. Each of the three *banderillos* stuck two razor-barbed sticks into his side. More rolling blood; he was in shock. He gasped for breath, and his head hung further. Then the final stage in the rigged fight, and the matador waved his red cape and

finished it

with a swift sword thrust between the bull's shoulder blades. The bull wobbled around the arena floor and vomited blood in awkward spouts, wobbled more, then fell onto the ground, off-white stomach exposed. He threw up as the fighters took out the stakes and cut off his ear as a trophy for Braveness. The bull's head lay back down on red sand, and spectators stood up and cheered.

How he held his head 2

Paz sat in the backyard, on the sun-warmed lawn, and plaited the grass. Macquarie Fields neighbours were doing their Sunday lawn mowing at snorepace, after 10:00 am Wheetbix breakfasts. Inside Paz's house, the flip-flop sound of thongs could be heard. On each side of the short concrete path in the front yard there were eight ten-centimetre-high conical piles of yellow dandelions and white clover that Eva had made earlier in the morning. She said they were castles for the ants and caterpillars. Damjan stood at the bathroom mirror and pulled his left cheek taught to shave it. Tracey was in her room, trying out meditation. She had one hand on her chest and another on her stomach, and she counted her deep breaths as she fought noisy thought. Matt had all his t-shirts in a bundle in the lounge room, and his t-shirt drawer on the floor. He was enjoying folding each t-shirt in half, rolling it, and then placing it next to the previous one inside the drawer. "Like pieces of gum," he said to Ashley, who walked around looking for something to clean, with Eva, petal-cheeked, following close behind.

Paz made some photos of the backyard, in fragmented sections. One photo half-filled with tree trunk; another caught the edge of the barbeque. He liked photos with slices of things. And he liked Ashley, he thought. She gave him waveworld and longthought, and he liked her smell of raw sky and raw sun and the way her eyes widened when he kissed her nose tip.

Then Damjan yelled, "Oh Fuck!" Tracey opened her eyes and saw two guns pointing at her through the window. More police cars parked outside the house, their sirens turning off abruptly, and seventy police officers in total surrounded the house. All of them were wearing heavy helmets, bullet proof vests and holding riot shields. On call, half separated then entered the house, while those remaining outside kept their guns aimed through the windows. Matt dropped to the floor, in the same position as he had during the last raid, his hands above his head. Tracey ran out and fell down next to him. Ashley, Eva, and Paz also ran to the lounge room and dived on to the floor. Eva, accustomed to talking to people's legs, asked one of the boots its name. The police officer lifted his boot and stomped it down again on a tuft of her hair. Eva struggled, and the tuft ripped out making an audible sound of uprooting. Her displaced hair stayed on the boot, and a one and a half-centimetre bald spot began to bleed tiny red dots. She screamed, but the shrillmetal batons kept the housemates away from her. Police were again going through the crates, the papers, the mattresses. Matt's yellow paper was again tipped on to the floor. He remembered the telescope that looked inside the earth and wanted to point it at all the police to see what was inside them. Then six officers took the housemates' elbows and steered them outside and into the paddy wagon. It seemed darker outside. Eva tripped on her feet as she tried to keep up. Blood dripped from her newly-made bald spot down her arm. The neighbour whose arguments rattled their windows came outside and yelled out, "What the bloody hell is going on?"

"Go back to your housing, you fucking houso," one of the officers shouted back. Paz started to tell him that the man owned his house, and that the government housing was several streets over, but stopped himself.

They were put in a holding cell at the local police station. They squeezed onto the metal bench and through the bars watched the area outside and waited for someone to tell them what was going on and how long they would be there. After three hours, a police officer came and told them to put their fingerprints on the corner of a piece of paper and then to open their mouths to be swabbed. Then he left again. Ashley dabbed at Eva's head with her sleeve, wiping off dried blood.

Back at the house, the police hid RF bugs—little round listening devices—under window sills, above light bulbs, in cupboard corners. The street was closed off all morning and well into the afternoon. People would turn the corner, then stop at the police cordon and look at the cars, the house, with faces that people often have when taking in a change to their unchanging surroundings. Mild surprise. They stood on tiptoes, as though that would help them see, and then turned back.

The housemates were released at five o'clock. Paz walked around the house quietly, socksonfloor, catting around the corners of the house as he had when they'd first moved in. Inside the changed house he was cautious, he poked at things, moved things aside, and looked underneath them. He did broad sweeps of each room, then honed into furniture that had been altered. He found the bug under his bedroom window sill. Damjan went to squash it with the end of a meat knife, but Paz looked at him hard, and silently shook his head. He went to Ashley's room and looked under her window sill and found another bug, and he motioned everyone outside.

Standing around the barbeque, all sombre-faced and hunch-shouldered and head's hanging, with Eva trying to scratch her bald bit and Ashley taking her hand away, they talked.

"Even if we find all the bugs and destroy them, they'll just plant more," Paz said.

"I really think we should do something about all this harassment, though. Seems to me like they were trying to rig a fight," Ashley said.

Paz, stressed, unhappy and prickly, snapped, "It's better we don't, we don't want to make things worse." Justsaynothing.

The vampire houses

Plasmaferesis, owned by the Nicaraguan dictator Somoza in the 1970s, was one of the private centres in third world countries which sold blood to United States companies. The poor, the homeless, the drug addicted, and famished adults and children would line up all day outside the Plasmaferesis building to sell their blood for five dollars a litre. The company then sold it to US pharmaceutical companies for $25 a litre. People said that now and then someone would pass out in the building, and disappear. They called it "the vampire house". It was the place where the rich and the first world literally sucked the blood from the poor.

The temptation of tiredness

Rafi sat on a pub stool, waiting for the rest of the workers to arrive. He felt worn out, and he hung a thumb in each of his pants pockets. His grass hair slumped, his cheeky smile was now just a patient one, and his stories and jokes tasted lately like over processed olives. He who had envied the air because it went where it wanted to go, now just noticed the humidity and fanned his chest with his shirt. He ordered a light beer, and looked again at the door, in case someone was arriving. He knew, though, that he just needed a few days to be tired, to try a little less, to lean on someone else, on Mella, and then he would be his energetic, prankster, driven self again.

Finally, people began to trickle into the pub, and they moved four tables together as usual. Rafi stayed on his stool, a few others used bar stools, while the rest sat on chairs. Mella looked at his pupils and his slanted shoulders and saw his tiredness. She smiled at him, and with that said everything she needed to say. Rafi sat up a little straighter. Party eyes, however, rested her head on one arm on the table and with her other hand massaged her sore neck. A few others also seemed to have sore necks, and they rolled their heads from side to side.

"Guys, I called this meeting today so that we can decide collectively how we want to proceed," Rafi began. "I really don't want anyone to lose their jobs, but as I see it, we only have two choices. I can take full responsibility for the petition, and all your jobs will be safe. Or we can keep things up, perhaps with a picket of all the main shop entrances, or something like that. They'll probably fire some of us, but we'd be standing up for ourselves and future workers."

It was quiet. People looked at each other, and their eyebrows asked, 'What do you think?' A shelf stocker called Andrew stood up and clapped his hands once to kill a mosquito. Everyone looked at his hand now stained with a spot of blood and mosquito legs. Someone passed him a serviette.

"We really should do something," Andrew said, "even if the fight is rigged."

Rafi could have explained more, argued, weighed the issues in more detail. But his tiredness urged him to finish now. "Let's take some time to think about it, and put it to a vote this weekend," he said.

A final stage

Connected words: to ransack, to subdue, to pacify, to control, to intimidate, to criminalise, to mollify, to discipline, to restrain, to tame, to conquer, to overcome, to overpower, to defeat, to destroy...

The police raided the house again the next day, at 5:37 in the morning. The same cars, same sirens, same guns, same boots. This time the police took them outside—dressed in whatever they were wearing—and sat them down on the front fence and told them not to move. A little cold, they crossed their arms, and squinted at the lucid sunrise.

Then there were sounds from inside the house. The sound of tearing at all its different pitches for all the different materials, for the air that tore, for the memories and bits of hesitant hope that were shredded. Mattresses cut open, pillows eviscerated. The sound of posters torn had a slightly higher pitch. And the sound of capsicum spray burning Eva's drawings that were stuck on the kitchen cabinets and of their own throats starting to tighten as the spray drifted outside. Things ripped off hinges, turned over, opened, undone too quickly. The efficient breaking of everything except the little black bugs. They were allowed back in soon, and they found mattresses moved against the wall and big Vs scored into their middlebelly, pillows in a pile in the kitchen, crates turned over, cupboard doors open, the washing machine and fridge open, the taped-up video player undone again, and unravelled toilet paper swelling in the toilet bowl, becoming a paste, cornflakes spilt in the hallway and pieces of boot-crushed flakes trailing into the lounge room and bathroom. The plastic bag they tied to a cupboard handle in the kitchen and used as a rubbish bin was spilled into the kitchen sink. Long knife lines scraping all across the lounge room walls like some sort of giant sharp monster claw, and the curtains also clawed by the giant monster, their corners turned to split-end hair. And the hole in Ashley's room was a little bigger. Ashley stood on her toes on a chair and peered at it. A cockroach came to the hole's edge and looked back at her, and she swatted at it.

"Looks like the cockroaches are back," she said, the first to speak. But they wanted to be away from all the noisy tearing. Damjan put the otto against the house sidewall, heaved himself onto it, then onto the roof, and the others followed, passing Eva up. Looking down, they could see that the two trees in the backyard were broken too. The police seemed to have suspected that drugs, or whatever they were looking for, could be stored absolutely anywhere. One branch of the orange tree, with its oranges that only made it to green tiny oranges then fell off, was cut vertically where it joined the trunk so that it bowed down and seemed to be climbing back into the ground. The green oranges were scattered about so that the air smelt of capsicum spray and immature orange juice. Out front, the ant castles were trampled.

"My neck hurts," Paz said.

"Me too," said the others. And they sat there, on the roof, for hours, with their sore necks, resting their heads on their knees and looking at the houses and yards below. They were quiet, and Ashley squinted and bit the skin around her fingernails.

Finally, "Well, I guess we better go down and get this shit cleaned up and fixed; we don't want the real estate people seeing it," Paz said, standing.

"Nah, man, let's just watch a bunch of movies; we can clean it tomorrow," Damjan replied, not standing. But he'd forgotten that the video player was broken again. When he got down, Matt kicked it, and then had an afternoon sleep on his sliced-open mattress.

Street angst

She tried to overtake him, leaning forward as she pushed the pram. She wanted him to be behind her, out of her sight, but she had to turn around and yell out one last thing. "Yeah, well I don't even fucken know April," she said. He responded, the argument raged on. It didn't matter what they said. They'd been lovers once. But under stress it died quickly, and now, heard in the spaces between their words, seen in the emphatic way she pushed that pram, they blamed each other for the disappointment that something beautiful hadn't lasted and never seemed to last.

Damaged 3

A woman lay on her bed in her shack in Namibia. She felt miserable: her mouth sagged, her arms flopped, her dreams limited to a decent meal, some cigarettes, to tonight, and to tomorrow. In her room that was a house, there were dots of light where the sun poked through holes in the walls. When it rained, the dots leaked. She listened to the sounds outside, a slum movie of a different kind.

Slum movie: Curtain door and sewage path, waterless, doctorless, daily disease, depression, theft, rape, edge of the world rubbish river. Rat bite, cat bite, crooked everything, petrochemicals or agrochemicals seeping with sewage through the floor. Goats, and flirting and fighting, a brothel queue, glue to sniff on better nights, to snuff out hunger. Gangs of street dogs, sheep grazing on garbage, flooded, collapsed sides of buildings for a house and a railway for a backyard. Everything falling apart, crumbling, from shoes to walls to relationships. Then, the tanneries, pottery, drums, guitar, and long nightdance, creative string solutions to the broken bike and lack of shoes, then back in the morning to the uncle with AIDS and the always-coughing neighbour heard clear as day through the holes in the walls. Would have people: would have studied, would have wondered, would have loved more, would have mistaken, would have written, would have met, would have grown old.

So it was, roughly, in the slums of Phnom Pen, Cairo, Colombo, Mumbai, New Delhi, Sadr City, Cape Flats, Kibera, Rio de Janeiro, Jakarta, Johannesburg, Okandundu, Somulu, Lahore, Cite Soleil.

When the chase started

"You could interview every Aboriginal kid from the block, and the majority would tell you that they've been bashed by the police," a Redfern activist said. TJ, a seventeen-year-old Aboriginal boy, had been bashed by the police a few weeks ago. Then, on Valentine's Day 2004, he was cycling from his girlfriend's place through the quiet, tense streets of Redfern, on his way to his mum's house. A police car drew up alongside him and began to follow him. Like anyone chased, he fled. He cycled through the car park, down a road, through a gate, and towards one of the high-rise government housing buildings. He fled fast. His bike caught, and he was flung over the handlebars and impaled on the building's steel picket fence.

The police didn't call an ambulance, but they did call for police backup. Then they removed the dying boy from the fence, against the basic rules of first aid. Then they searched him.

TJ died the next morning in hospital. Or perhaps he died when the chase started. When did the chase start? At the bashing a few weeks ago? The first time the police called him names, or the first time they arrested his mother, or his aunt? What if death isn't just the stopping of a heart or the stopping of a brain, but the exit of curiosity and yearning? If so, then perhaps he died when the long chase started.

The long term impracticality of denial

Mella didn't move for a whole day, and not because she had another decision to make. She was balled up on the end of the lounge room couch near the window, her back to the outside and her head on her knees. Sirens from three police cars rolled over each other like stressed choirs singing in rounds. Mella heard the sound in Doppler Effect as the cars neared Ben's flat, and then passed it. It was early morning and the rising sun sifted through the windows and cast long furniture shadows across the room. Mella's own shadow reached the other end of the couch. Missing Thing, giant hole in the air, was wrapped around her like a snake, holding her down. Thumping headache pounded through her right eye. Last night she had dreamed over and over of blocked toilets, buildings without exits, birds in cages. Her subconscious was screaming at her that she was angry and sad, and she needed to stop putting those feelings into the cardboard packing boxes in the attic of her mind. But she closed herself even more, tightened her bodyball and let herself sulk, "I don't want this, I don't want this".

Then, finally, she started to peer into those packing boxes, and she listed all the things she didn't want. She didn't want Parramatta station and the trains that were always late or cancelled, or its tunnel that took passengers straight to the Westfield's shopping centre, which unlike public transport, was always open and always working. She didn't want Samuel, the work supervisor who made homophobic jokes about some workmates and who stared at her legs that day she didn't wear stockings. Or the mirrors that reminded her that she had a face and a body that she didn't like. Or the maps that scaled North

America and Europe bigger than they in fact were, and Africa smaller than it really was. Maps lied. She didn't want the shrill, trite news with its murder stories and Hollywood gossip, ignoring the poverty pandemic because it wasn't titillating. Didn't want the pollution congesting the earth's system like clogged arteries, or the irreversible global warming, or the strip of harbour leading to the Opera House that had once been grass and public space and was now sold off and turned into luxury apartments and cafes, or the seagulls fighting for food and the people fighting for freebies at Town Hall station. She didn't want refugees locked up in prison for the crime of fleeing for their lives, or Aboriginals in prison for the crime of reminding the rich that someone else was here first. Or the normalised violence and domestic and verbal abuse she heard in the staffroom jokes and gossip. Or nightclub competitions to determine who was prettier, whose clothes were better. Life seemed a choice between hanging by a string, or a contrived theatre. And there she was, doing a bit of both, pretending to enjoy a job she hated. She looked up from her knees, and said it out loud, "I hate my job!" She felt that at work, on the trains, in the streets, in shops, she was being moved through them rather than her moving anything. A helpless dust particle on a reckless wave.

Time passed like smoke. Mella didn't move. She had no urge to eat or wash or stretch and feel her muscles tighten all the way down to her toes. She bodyballed, and the afternoon sun brought blurred shadows and softer light so the room mellowed as the lines of the walls and the edges of the furniture lost the morning sharpness and gained gentle strokes of definition that slightly separated one thing from another. She curled up more, twisted her toes and her fingers. Missing Thing hole pushed her head harder onto her knees. The walls leaned out and shouted at each other, flung the shouts across the room and left hard bruises throughout the lounge room. She pinched herself, and the pain was soothing. She did it up and down the bare underneath of her arm, and it relaxed her somewhat. And she wondered, was her not thinking about the list of things she didn't a kind of denial? Or was it a defence against things too hard to accept? Rafi had once told her that there were three kinds of denial: Simple denial, where an unpleasant thing was denied altogether; minimalisation, where the thing was admitted but its seriousness denied; or projection, where the thing and its seriousness were admitted but responsibility was denied. Mella didn't want to deny, and she didn't want any more packaging boxes to pile up, and she knew she couldn't have too many more days like this, pinching herself on the couch, so she began a train of thought that involved, in the end, a big decision. She could try to like the world, the one Ben pushed on her, to be excited about new clothes and believe that other people's problems weren't her own; she could aim for that house she dreamt about, for some peace. Or she could...and then there was Rafi, effectively offering to sacrifice his own job to save theirs, and how she didn't want to accept that offer.

Fear

An upright silver suitcase in the middle of the square. People hurried past it, leaving invisible intersecting trails. Then a few people stopped and pointed, whispering, "It could be a bomb..."

More people gathered, stopped and stared. They stared sideways, with one foot pointed in the other direction, ready to run. Then a magpie swooped down and landed on the suitcase, making it wobble a little. The crowd wobbled a little too. The bird walked up and down the top part and pecked at the handle with its long beak. Someone got out a phone and fiddled with it. It was on all their minds to call the police, but no one wanted to be foolish; what if it wasn't?

Soon there were almost two hundred people standing in a circle around the silver suitcase as though watching a busker about to perform a final trick. A few people waved their arms, trying to shoo the magpie away, but it kept walking up and down and pecking at the shiny rivets. And then the trick was performed. The magpie must have caught its beak on the lock, for the suitcase swung open. People saw red and began to run. Hundreds of leafwing butterflies flew out, and the magpie bowed on the silver suitcase, but no one saw. The plaza was empty now.

The shapes of flowers

Another day, after they'd cleaned the house up, after coffee was boiled and drunk and the cereal bowls were drying in piles next to the sink, Matt, Damjan, Tracey, and Eva went down to the supermarket car park where they'd heard there'd be clown face painters and checkers competitions. Ashley and Paz were alone in the house. Paz tore a piece of paper off the notepad that was always on the crate-table in the lounge room, the one where they wrote down phone messages, money borrowed or owed, and TV movies not to be missed.

He drew Ashley a bouquet of flowers. She sat next to him on the floor and looked over his shoulder, one hand on his knee. She took the paper from his hand and held the bouquet close to her eyes, and realised that the flowers weren't flowers. They were nipples on stems. Lips, eyes, hands, suns, mini-houses, mini-elephants, umbrellas, parrots, storm clouds, snowy mountains, little vaginas and little penises all on stems. The nipples, of varying shapes, sizes, and ambiguous gender, dotted the bouquet throughout. Ashley smiled, sighed, and leaned against the couch. Paz, laughing, peaked into her underpants. Her vagina was curled up and sleeping and not really ready to be looked at. He touched it though, counted its petals, and it woke up, blinked, and smiled.

"Where's the stem?" she joked.

"Here," he said, drawing a line up her middle, finishing at her head, where he drew lots of lines, for the roots.

Then he took off her clothes, opening her more. He kissed her thighs and massaged them. He kissed the underneath of her feet, her knuckles, her earlobes, and then the space below her belly button. He kissed and tongued her clitoris, then slid one finger inside her, and moaned a little at the feel of her internal heat. Soft fire... He was so close to her. With tongue, fingers, and lips he massaged her inside and outside, gently, then more intensely...and finally, for the first time ever, Ashley stopped thinking. Her body arched, quivered, and warmth quaked from the focal point and flushed her cheeks. She shook some more, then relaxed.

They slept. Her feet spooned his; his hand cupped her stomach, and Ashley drifted, opened her eyes and closed them again. She thought that she had been given happiness that was on loan and that could be taken away at any time.

Packaging 2

Two big boxes, two small boxes, and an envelope. Ben used different coloured paper to wrap each box, and then different coloured raffia ribbon around each small box, and sheer, wide fabric ribbon for the big boxes. He finished them off with speciality bows of "pink and silver fireworks", as they were called on the packet. He hid the four boxes in suitcases underneath his bed.

Threaded drumbeats

A few days later it was just Paz and music in the house. He was lying on his back on the floor, his feet on a crate, looking at the blank wall and ceiling above and around the television. His foot tapped to the music and he sang with it, and then laughed at himself and his out-of-tune voice. He imagined that he was throwing paint onto the wall, because that would be fun. Woosh! He threw orange at the centre and green to the left. And he saw the two colours take on a life of their own and eddy towards each other, dripping long vertical lines as they went.

Paz chuckled. Then he curled up his fist, aimed it at the

middle-right side of the wall, and this time threw a sun tangled in string. Then waterfalls of cotton. Drumbeats threaded on strings and hanging from street lights. Trees which had little fingers that tickled and stroked the air that passed them. Big to small koalas piled up on each other like babushkas. His favourite image of worms whistling as they made the earth go round. People with moons held close to their chest or tucked underneath their arms.

He beamed. He could see it all. But the wall mural was too colourful. He wanted now to add some melancholy, some sensitivity, and some grey complexity. He breathed in and blew charcoal disappointment onto the wall, just below the people with moons. Then, morning horniness— pink and as touchable as cave humidity. Ancient whales mimicking the sound of forests shrivelling and of continental masses creaking against each other. In the corners of the room, he put bird calls drifting down through branches and difficult times to then lie on the floor, as resigned as decaying autumn leaves. He aimed his hands at the air between the wall and ceiling and put the little sounds of pea pods opening in the sun, of rain on empty lakes, of how an ant hears wax drying.

Paz stood back from the canvas that he had made, adjusted it and perfected it. He pointed at the wall to move one image, or make another a bit bigger; he deepened contrast, brought one image forward, and pushed another back. He poured some light in one corner and a bit of darkness in the opposite one. With two hands, he pointed; longer, wider, brighter, stronger. He was conducting colours, memories, smells, and textures.

He felt calm. He stopped thinking for a minute, and simply listened to the imagery, then he went back to his simpler photos. He imagined them, framed them in black serrated cardboard that he took from the shelves of colours and materials in his mind, and stuck them neatly onto the bedroom doors. He made some close-up photos—one of his favourites; the marble patterns on ants' faces with the softness of egg carton cardboard in the background. Paw paw seeds germinating; the seeds covered in transparent film, the sprout squishing out of it, green, new, and happy. It was a photo about a process, about life, about growing, and about change. Finally, various close-ups of animals' eyes; each eye a different mosaic of colours and patterns and bordered by lashes, skin, fins, or fur. Oh, and one special photo; Ashley, dancing and playing the violin.

Packaging 3

"You could call it an investment," Ben said to the "reception ladies", as he called them. They kept typing, looked up at him and raised an eyebrow now and then, or nodded and said, "uh-ha". Ben stood behind one of the women and looked at his reflection in the computer monitor. He tidied his fringe and smiled at himself. "I was thinking about getting her cooking classes—she really can't cook—and I need someone who can. But then I thought, no, better this. She can't refuse this. I can get her the classes later."

Telescoping

Matt found his birthday present in a large cardboard box outside his bedroom door. At first he thought it was a prank; a box of rubbish. But then he rummaged through the contents and discovered four magnifying glasses of different sizes, two unframed mirrors, cardboard tubes and toilet paper roles, a craft knife, a tape measure, some bits of black plastic, wire, a small tube of superglue, polystyrene, and some other odds and ends. He knew straight away that it was a telescope. And now he knew why Paz had lately been looking out the corner of his eye at rubbish bins and the piles of old household stuff awaiting collection.

Matt sat down on the floor with his legs wrapped around the box. He picked up the magnifying glasses, pushed their lenses out of the plastic holders, then, looking at the patterns in the carpet and at dots and stains on the ceiling, he moved each lens away from his eye to gauge its strength. He combined pairs of lenses, understanding that he needed one to magnify, and a second one closer to his eye to correct the blur and focus the image. He moved the lenses apart, and then closer together, until he found just the right distance, which he marked on the cardboard tubing. He cut slots at the marks, then shaped the wire into rings, and with the help of the polystyrene, he secured the lenses into place. He cut the black plastic into a disc to put in front of the lens to reduce image brightness. Then he went outside to try the telescope but noticed that it was hard to keep the image steady. As it was so zoomed-in, the slightest movement of his hands was magnified, so he picked up some broken tree branches and used them, along with some string, to build a tripod to support the telescope.

That night they ate sponge cake, sang songs, and everyone punched the birthday boy twenty-one times. They joked about old age and beer and the eighties, and Eva reminded everyone twenty-one times that her birthday was in just three months. Matt showed them his telescope, and sceptically they fetched a blanket and spread it over the grass. They lay on their backs and passed the telescope between them like a shared cigarette, placing the tripod over their legs. It did indeed work.

Matt pointed north: "See how it looks like a guy with a belt, holding a bow and arrow? That's Orion. That red star in his left shoulder is Betelgeuse. Yeah man, that's a big star. They say if you put it where the sun is, it would be as big as Jupiter's orbit. And it's about to explode, sometime in the next thousand years."

"Orion is shooting a giant ant," Tracey said.

"Yeah, that's Taurus."

Through the telescope, despite some light refraction,

they could see thousands of stars between the stars they normally saw without it. They saw Sirius, and just made out Sirius B, when Matt described it. Stars circled stars, moons circled moons. They pointed the telescope at earth's moon and saw its seas of long dead lava flows, its pockmarked face, scarred permanently by comets, asteroids, and meteorites. Quietly, they passed the telescope, pointed at something, and passed it on again. Eva, now that she knew that the white night dots that seemed tiny but were actually bigger than anything you could imagine, had names, wanted to know all of them. Matt patiently answered her, either remembering or inventing, "Theta, Al Gazeeb, Aldebaran, Pirolus, Oobidae, Bundlebop," he said.

Meanwhile, Tracey asked questions out loud: "If the atmosphere burns meteors, why doesn't it burn planes or birds? Why does the earth have an atmosphere and the moon doesn't?" Matt explained that the moon didn't have enough gravity to hold an atmosphere down. "Does Betelgeuse have a heap of atmosphere then?" She pronounced it Beetle juice. And for a while they lay there, six bodies on a blanket, stuck to the ground by gravity, throwing out questions and not worrying too much about answers.

"The earth is like love," Tracey said suddenly.

Matt glanced at her, "What?"

"You know how when you fall in love and it feels like everything has just worked out and happened so that you could meet that person? Well, the earth has just worked out so that it made life. All the millions of other rocks and planets and things out there haven't managed to make life, but here the earth is the right distance from the sun, the right temperature, the right size to have gravity and create an atmosphere that protects us, the magnetic field protects life from harmful radiation, the tilt of the earth makes seasons and the moon gives us tides, and then evolution, and it all just worked out, to make life, and humans."

"Yeah, it took about a billion years after the earth formed for life to start appearing; that was about 3.5 billion years ago," Matt said.

They looked at the yard, at the lemon tree that "didn't work" and those small common things seemed amazing.

"Boy, I just suddenly got why you hate cars and are always banging on about the ozone layer, Ash," Damjan said.

Crickets, tentacle grass, lemon tree smell, stars with names, a moon with no name, and the silence of the star-gazing kind... the silence of people contemplating how small they are. A silence that can never last too long.

"I don't think animals look up much. They don't look at the stars, and stars can't see, so maybe humans are the only ones in the universe, or at least the solar system, who can see all this," Paz said. "And when life on this planet is gone, there'll be no one in the solar system to know about it."

Tracey wanted to see the earth. A month ago she had bought a big camping backpack. They used it to go to the supermarket and carry groceries home, but she hadn't told anyone that she'd bought it as a commitment to herself that one day she would camp in Australia's forests, see its coastal mangroves and wetlands, its reefs, white beaches and yellow beaches, and the mulga trees of the arid inland. And one day, she wanted to see snow falling and frozen lakes, and finally, the pink dolphins of Bolivia. She was soft Tracey tonight, especially with Matt finally lighting up about something. She pulled his ear towards her and whispered, "There was something big missing from you before, and now I feel like I see the whole you, and I know I love you." It was the first time she'd said it. And the first time in his life that he'd heard it.

Packaging 4
Mella came home from work not expecting anything. She

had foggy eyes and her tired arms hung by her side, so that her bag slipped halfway off her shoulder. She did come home dressed for *him* though. She had his haircut, and that morning she'd put on a work shirt he'd picked out, the heels he'd suggested, and her nails painted as he liked. The bag though, an old faded-pink canvas thing, was hers. It fell all the way down her arm and into the corner when she closed the door. Then she turned towards the lounge room, and saw the four presents in a line on the floor.

He had arranged them with the two biggest presents nearest the door, then one of the smaller ones. He was sitting at the end of the line with the smallest present in his hand.

It was sunset. Light was blurry, and with most of the apartment lights off, the LED light on the microwave that she could see in the kitchen seemed very loud. She looked at it; it was 7:23 pm. Then 7:24. And still 7:24. She looked again, at the boxes, at Ben, at the microwave time, still 7:24. She conjured cheerfulness, forced a smile. Just like those women had forced laughs for a photo.

"Open them..."

The first big box: A dinner plate set with James Bond themed cutlery and crystal glass salt and pepper shakers...from the department store with the gold escalator railings.

The second box: A blue silk scarf, also from the department store. She had stroked the palm of her hand with its tassels.

The third box: Two keys, and underneath them, a carefully folded photo of a house; a house with a porch, a front garden, and a red wooden letterbox.

Mella got flies. Flies rattling and crashing in her throat and inside her organs. It was cold. There was wind outside, but the windows were closed, and inside there was no wind and no sound and no words ready to be spoken in the right way. Just Ben, there, with the last unopened little box, and coloured paper and ribbon scattered about the floor as if a clown had exploded.

"Mella, I want you to live in that house with me. I put down a deposit, and with our combined income, we'll pay off the loan quicker. We'll put a pool out back and a mini gym in the shed. When the loan's paid off, we can have kids; you can stay at home and look after them and take care of the house, and you won't need to work anymore."

Flies buzzed among the exploded clowns. She had to decide now, at 7:25.

"Be my wife, Mella. Together, we'll have safety and security. Our own personal business arrangement, a contract really, which would be of mutual benefit to both parties. It would be like economic insurance. Mella, will you marry me?" He opened the cube-shaped box and held out the ring.

Crossroads

Mella was on one train, and Paz was on another. It was hot, and the air-conditioning fogged up the windows. They both used the side of their hands to wipe away the vapour. The window glass was cold, and their hands dirty now, but outside was rendered in crisp and shifting detail.

Mella sat back and pressed her face against the glass. Her red skirt and orange singlet shouted. Today, she had volcanoes going off inside her.

Paz sat curved, but he too pressed his face against the glass. His blue jeans and somewhat-white t-shirt were soundless. He bit his lip and struggled to keep his eyes open.

Then the two trains entered a tunnel from opposite ends, and passed each other. Their wheels clicked over the joints in the track and made a bumda-bum-bumda-bum sound. Their windows framed portraits of people nodding off to sleep on their chests, staring vacantly, reading the back page of a newspaper, or texting a friend. Mella continued to look out the window. She was unafraid to stare at the people in the other train because they were gone in a second. Others, including Paz, stared back.

Mella saw him and thought that his tiredness looked enduring and raspy, and that his glance at her was gentle. He saw her and he saw her volcanoes.

Her eyes moved to the left to follow him as he passed.

His eyes moved to the left to follow her as she passed.

Rigged

They all wore their favourite clothes. The party was the twenty-first birthday of one of Damjan's ex-girlfriends, in a house on the other side of Macquarie Fields. Ashley stayed at home with Eva, but the others were excited about a night of music, beer, new people, and some craziness. Tracey put on her long red bead earring; Damjan hand-washed his 'Get rid of the British flag' t-shirt; Paz wore a long sleeve black shirt with metal buttons, and Matt, who rarely combed his hair, combed it with water and a bit of gel.

Already at 8:00 pm no buses were running, so they went to the party on foot. Damjan walked ahead, reached a crossing and turned around to implore the others, "Come on!" He maypoled round the traffic light as they caught up. The roads were mostly empty and made no comment. Tracey stopped at the 7/11 and bough a pack of milk biscuits, which they shared as a late dinner.

The party house had its back to the bush and its front to a broad street the colour of mournful rainclouds, as it reflected the overcast sky above. A white Mazda was parked in front of the house. The car was often left outside parties, the mall, or the station late at night, with a door or two unlocked. The entire suburb knew that the car was a police set-up, and that it had a tracker on it, but people used it now and then for transport, leaving it abandoned afterwards near the police station.

Inside the house, music boomed, making the fridge full of beer dance on its broken fridge feet. The party had been going for a while now, and there were wet foot prints going through the dining room, a blocked toilet, and vomit drying along the sides of the laundry sink. Balloons had drifted from different rooms of the house into the dining room, and then had been shoved underneath the dining room table. Two boxes of cask wine had been left on the table outside, and drops of it soaked into the table wood. There were shoutchats inside, and more intimate two or three-person chats outside, where the music wasn't as loud. Damjan, Tracey, Matt and Paz went inside, and came out three hours later smelling of party and palm sweat. They had all drunk as much as they could because the beer was free, except Paz. He didn't like the taste of beer, hadn't found out about the cask wine, and so in order to be sociable had held on to the one beer the entire time. Damjan was jellylegged, and his torso fell to the ground: "Because of the gravity," he said. Matt was so sleepy that he held just one eye open so that he could see where he was going. Paz imagined trying to get them to walk the three kilometres home, and suggested a taxi, but no one had enough money. Damjan tried a door of the Mazda; it opened and he fell inside. Tracey went around to the other side, pushed Damjan upright, and got into the car. Matt got in the front, and Paz shrugged. He would drive them home, bring the car back to the party, and then walk home by himself.

Matt rested his cheek against the window and slept lightly, occasionally opening his eyes a little to enjoy the feeling of being in a car and the strange perspective caused when one cheek is squashed against one eye. His toes curled in and out inside his shoes, and his breathing made fogclouds on the window. Tracey's head bobbed as she too started to fall asleep, then jerked awake, then fell back asleep. Paz imagined kites tied to the ceiling of the car, flying in the wind above them. He saw Tracey's bobbing in the mirror, and smiled. Then he saw the police car chasing them.

"Damn the cops. The car has a tracker and they know

where we live. Why don't they just meet us there?" Paz said under his breath, trying not to wake Matt. He turned a corner without slowing down, and the police car turned it more smoothly and gained on them. Soon it was so close, as though one of Paz's kites had fallen down and was pulling the police car behind them. He accelerated, and the police car accelerated too. At the next intersection, Paz tried to turn at the last minute, but the car didn't turn well, as though the steering was stuck. He then had to accelerate in order to avoid being rammed by the police car. Their house was now four blocks away and he wanted to stop, but couldn't. The police sped up; he sped up more and then the car stopped suddenly, its path blocked by a tree. And the people in the car kept moving sometime after it had stopped. Paz's seatbelt pulled him back into his seat. Damjan and Tracey hit the seats in front of them, distorting their necks and bruising their faces, and Damjan broke his nose. Tracey's mouth closed too quickly, and she bit her tongue and broke two teeth.

Matt was thrown through the windscreen. Matt, who had carefully fixed things, broke easily, and his skull split down the middle. The windscreen fractured in rings around his body, suspending his body halfway through it. Blood trickled from his mouth down his neck and onto the ground, where it was quickly absorbed like the wine on the wooden table. His curled-up toes twitched, and the stars twinkling inside him went out. On the ground near the front of the car, as though they had been vomited out, two half-grown butterfly wings. Shoots of fogbreath on the window faded, and then were gone.

Matt died at 11.52. Or did he? Maybe he died when the chase started, or after the first raid, or the first day of school, the first cigarette, or when he committed the crime of being born into unemployment and poverty in a world where the poor are framed for the crimes of the rich.

MELLA

Impractical

There was an eight-year-old girl who always carried a calculator in her pocket. Her dog had died that morning and she had spent two hours crying in the playground after everyone else had gone back to class.

But after all the tears had come out and her throat was parched and tight, she thought about the children that were stuck in the middle of wars for oil, and how sad they must feel when their friends or family died. She felt the ground and it was scarred and bruised from the messed up mountain ranges of shanty housing, pockmarked from fracking. It was drumming from the feet of refugees running. Trafficked teenagers went thirsty, and the corrugated faces of the overworked climbed onto truckbuses headed home. The hungry waited and the invaded wilted. Her eyes were dry now; she realised she could no longer cry. She calculated that it simply was not practical.

The sound of objection

"I want to protest," Mella told Rafi.

It was a typical Tuesday, a day without the anticipation

of Fridays or the resignation of Mondays or the lightness of Saturdays. The city lived its usual tiled rhythm of still big things and moving little things. The Town Hall, the Queen Victoria Building, BBB were all unmoving giant blocks, while around them people waited, met friends, left, and were replaced by others who sat, waited, met someone, and left. The traffic lights changed, cars stopped, people crossed, traffic lights changed, cars started, people waited. It was a play regulated by traffic lights. The Town Hall clock chimed every fifteen minutes, underground trains pulled in and pulled out, and inside BBB the cash register scanners beeped.

'Job security! Full time jobs not ongoing casual!' read their placards. 'Without the staff, you're fucked,' read Rafi's sign. He was feeling despondent, because in the end most staff hadn't made a decision. No one had wanted Rafi to take the blame, but they hadn't wanted to picket either. So Rafi's job was gone, and he held his placard high above his head.

T-shirts were on special for three dollars each, and chocolate was going at two for five dollars, and the customers chatted and elbowed their way into BBB, barely noticing the five picketers with their placards. Mella felt obliged to constantly step out of the way and to apologise. She held her placard high, like an umbrella, so customers could pass underneath it. She squeezed her free arm close to her side to make herself smaller. When someone trod on her foot and didn't notice, she apologised to them, too. She looked through the crowd at Rafi, and he saw her face. He yelled back at her through the throng of people, "It's just the first step, Mella, so that people know." He stood up straighter.

Then a tall skinny man with long black hair, and a shorter autumn-coloured woman walked up to Mella. "Sorry we're late," the woman said. Mella cocked her head at her, unsure. "I'm Alice," she said, and offered Mella her hand.

"I'm Rain. Well, people call me that," and another hand. "We're just dropping by to give support. We're mates with Rafi. Is he here?"

Rafi was sideways walking through the customers towards them. He gave Alice and Rain a placard, and then they were seven, and that felt a little better. Later, six more of Rafi's mates arrived, and then they were thirteen. People could no longer elbow and chat and peer their way past them. They looked up at the placards and read them, then looked down at the faces that held them, and then looked at the shop where they were about to buy cheap chocolate, and where people were working under unfair conditions. The thirteen picketers chanted, "Dignified wages! No ten-hour shifts! Double pay for overtime!" The group's chanting had a very different rhythm than the city's. It was urgent, angry, and determined.

The chants grew louder, climbed mountains and stood on top of them. The cashiers and stockers inside the shop paused, hands mid-scan and midway to the shelves, and all at once, like meerkats, they looked towards the main door where the picket was. Then heads sensed other heads pointing in a particular direction, and looked there too. For seven seconds the shop paused. Then information was processed, opinions were formed (how nice, how immature, how brave, I wish I had joined them, I'm glad I didn't), and the scanner beeping resumed, queues moved forward, someone asked a shop assistant what aisle the batteries were in, and occasionally people looked back at the doors. But the atmosphere in the shop was now flustered and unsettled; the cashiers scanned a little faster, queuing customers shifted from foot to foot, the manager drank his coffee too fast and burnt his tongue. One layer of pretence, one thin glamour curtain, was removed. Now customers noticed that the floor was a bit dirty, the stock not quite straight, and there were two packets of Tim Tams in the t-shirt bin, and the cashiers were tired and hungshouldered.

Outside, the city rhythm wasn't broken, but it was dented, a little. The people walking fast towards the station couldn't make even squares around the obstacle, the small but loud picket. The picketers handed out leaflets; quarter A4 black and white photocopies promoting a public meeting on Saturday, with 'Defend the rights of workers' in big letters at the top. Mella tapped her placard with her fingernails to the rhythm of the chants as she realised she was discovering something new and important. She asked Rain for some leaflets, leaned her placard against the wall, and went inside the shop to hand them out to the other workers. "There's a public meeting about workers' rights on Saturday in the library," she said. Then the manager told her to leave.

Evening came. A new rhythm; the sun setting peak hour rhythm. Faster faster, everyone home. As Mella handed out leaflets, she felt her throat getting sore, the air cooling and creeping underneath her light t-shirt, and she finally thought of tomorrow. She wouldn't get fired; her name, Rafi's name, and the others, simply wouldn't appear any more on the shift roster. So she was unemployed, again. And of course, after Mella had told him 'no', Ben had told her to leave. He had broken things, and then tried to pick her up and break her on the floor. So she needed a place to live as well. She had packed her things, feeling all the while a strong sense of déjà vu, and gone to Rafi's place and slept on his couch.

They ended the picket just after 7:00 pm; ready to collapse in a heap like dropped puppets. The city-rhythm went on.

Moments

A leader of the Metal Workers Union, a man with a huge build, a thick moustache, and a careful and tender way of talking addressed the gathering. People leaned towards the panel of speakers seated behind the table at the front as though moving their ears that little bit closer might help them hear and understand things better. They sat on blue and green plastic chairs that were arranged in rows which became closer together towards the back wall. It reminded Mella of stories she had written when she was a child where the lines of writing sloped more and more and got closer together as she ran out of page, the last words curling up the right hand edge. Likewise, there were a few people forced to stand squashed in the doorway. Rain, that strange and kind person from the picket, stood at the back of the room, behind a table draped in a red cloth, with leaflets, books and a stack of newspapers spread across it. She wanted to talk to him after the meeting to ask him about his group, and if she might join it. But she worried she would be too shy, and her voice would twitch and tumble and squeak awkwardwords.

One more person spoke, and then there was a round of questions, comments, and a response from each of the panel members. Then everyone got up and stacked the chairs at the side of the room. Mella picked up her bag and hung it over her shoulder, then started to lift piles of chairs, when Rain called out to her.

"Hey, Mella," he said, waving from behind his table. He remembered her name. "Would you like a copy of the latest?" he asked, holding out one of the newspapers. "I know you've just lost your job, so any old donation is fine."

Mella looked at the cover of the newspaper. There was a large skull filled in with the US flag, a dark blue background, and the words, 'How the US armed Saddam Hussein' in bold impact font at the top. In a green strip at the bottom it said, 'Free the refugees'.

"What is it?" she said.

"It's an alternative paper. We put it out to counter the lies and distortions of the mainstream press, and we use it to campaign."

"Okay, I'll get a copy. And I'd like to know more about your group," she said, looking at him then looking at the other people in the room.

"Cool, well, come to the Western Sydney Resist centre tomorrow, if you like. We can keep chatting; I'll tell you about what we do, show you the ropes." He handed her a leaflet for a Stop the War meeting and pointed at the bottom: "There, that's our address." Then he scrawled a phone number in the margin. "And that's my number."

"Okay, I will." Mella put the newspaper in her bag then helped with the last few chairs.

It was a moment that is often easily forgotten, or becomes a few softened frames of memory, ordinary in its emotion. Later though, it is brought out and recalled; not for what it was, but for how it would change what followed.

What is a hero?

Is it the Hollywood stars posing with their jewellery and just-for-one-night gowns on the red carpet, or is it more understated than that, quieter, more modest, and with long term impact? Was Rain a hero?

Rain, who after getting home from the meeting was now lying on his back on a seventh-hand couch with his head on his partner Ramona's lap. Ramona was reading from Open Veins of Latin America and sighing, pausing, commenting, and re-reading some lines. Rain, whose view was filled with the book cover, its spine almost touching his nose, was telling her to "underline that" and "read that again, please", and "show me" so that he could mark a paragraph with a five-pointed star.

Rain believed that books were lyrical guns, that they were dangerously powerful weapons. They had been burnt and banned throughout history, and the best authors, those who upset and questioned the very fabric of society, had often been exiled, imprisoned, or assassinated. He craved their lessons, stories, brave ideas, the borders they crossed, the time they spanned, and the way they made his world and context so big. He was continuously coming across concepts, historical events, economic dynamics, and political situations that he wanted to understand. So he read, alone or with Ramona or other mates, even though he was dyslexic.

He also took life very seriously, more seriously than some take their own professions. "Life is a profession," he would tell people. It needed structure, planning, consideration, and commitment. When he had finally worked out that he was dyslexic, at seventeen after he had barely passed the university entrance exams, he dealt with it methodically. He researched the condition on the Internet and learnt that he needed to read words by their sounds, so he taught himself all the phonics, and re-learned to read. It was still hard for him though, and he read slowly, out loud, and gave himself a break every fifteen minutes. He had lists of books he wanted to read on his computer, with symbols next to each book (fiction, nonfiction, local writer, writer from a colonised country, modern and not modern, and topics), and numbers for their priority. He had a personal preference for the classics, and a schedule to make sure he got through his list by a certain date. He also read the national and international news each morning, and Resist's newspaper each Sunday. As he read, he noted questions and observations in his little black leather bound notebook. Later, he would walk into the Resist centre and ask everyone their opinion about the things he'd learned. Once, when they were making Stop the War t-shirts in the office using spray paint and cardboard stencils, Rafi made him a 'What do you think of...?' t-shirt. "Oh great," Rain had said, putting it on. "Now I can just say words; Inflation? Objective love? The idea that technology causes culture?"

Rain read because he knew that understanding history, economics, and world issues was essential to being able to remedy injustice. But he was also fascinated by absolutely everything, and he thought that each person was a mysterious world full of contradictions and hidden beauty.

When he met Mella, he took her nervousness in his hands and was tender with it. He wanted to understand her too, to read her chapter by chapter.

Worlds inside worlds

The Resist centre was located in Parramatta, in the western suburbs, where the workers, migrants, and middle and lower classes tended to live. The wealthy people lived in the east, by the beaches. Parramatta, the centre of the west, was known as the "second CBD of Sydney". It was one of the first colonial settlements in Australia, and a site of murder and displacement of, and resistance by, the Aboriginal people already living there. Now Parramatta was a transport hub, residential area, and shopping centre, with some of Sydney's lowest income suburbs like Granville, Harris Park and Auburn within walking distance. Parramatta councillors were proud of its "colonial heritage", its old government house, churches, Elizabeth Farm, and Hambledon cottage. They boasted through the press of the ongoing rejuvenation of the area; the flowerbeds in the mall were uprooted and replanted seasonally, the streets were re-paved, the signage re-painted, the lighting adorned, the bus terminal upgraded, the river ferry wharf remodelled. Despite the embellishments, the professionals who walked through the main mall at 5:00 pm to the station had tired and blank faces, and stoned and drunk young homeless people watched them from the benches that lined the mall. At 3:30 pm, groups of high school students ran into Westfield's shopping centre, eager to leave learning. An Iraqi refugee sat alone each morning sipping coffee in DeliFrance.

Mella caught the train from Granville where Rafi lived, to Parramatta station, walked through the ticket gates, past the police with the two sniffer dogs searching every "suspicious" person for drugs. Two of them pressed the face of a teenager against the ticket machine and patted him down. Two others singled out a Muslim Indian man from the crowd and asked him for his ticket and ID.

The Resist centre was near the station, up some stairs in a small arcade, but Mella wanted to walk around before she went there. She headed for the mall and sat on a free bench, and for a while just watched the people walking past. She felt ennui in the air, in the very bricks of the lethargic shops, in the billboards, window displays, and in the buses pulling out from the terminal with a sound of I-guess-I-have-to coming from their engines. It was grey cottonwool, this ennui. A feeling of tiredness and of reluctance to fix broken things, an unhappy relationship or an unfulfilling job because it was easier to stay slumped in them. It was listless legs that needed strings to pick them up and make them walk. It was the ease of buying almost anything, if you could afford it.

In the street outside the Resist centre was an orange A-frame with a black arrow pointing up, and the text, 'Join us in stopping the war'. Mella followed the arrow up the stairs.

"Hey, Mella!" Rafi and Rain greeted her as she walked through the door and into another world.

The centre was the size of a large bedroom. It smelt like the natural smell of humans after sleep, but somewhat rougher. There was a computer in one corner, a long desk near the window that overlooked the station, and some wooden chairs with fake leather upholstery tucked into the desk. The leather was peeling off at the corners, and yellow sponge poked out. More fold-up chairs and card tables were stacked next to the door. On the ambiguously blue or grey or green carpeted floor Mella saw half a red letter 'S' where someone had been painting a banner and had forgotten to put newspaper down first. The walls were covered in flags, posters, and old covers of the alternative newspaper, like a pictorial history of the movements and political issues the centre had seen. There were 'No War' t-shirts in boxes, badges on boards, charts drawn in green marker and a whiteboard with a map of the greater Parramatta region stuck onto it. An open card table was covered in leaflets bunched together with elastic bands, as well as petitions and pamphlets. There was a pair of shoes under the table in the corner with the computer, and Rafi was walking around in his socks, describing how a lizard had looked at him, then jumped off the wall.

"It looked at me, I tell you, then it jumped and its little hands moved in the air," he said, demonstrating the hand movements.

Rain stapled the last corner of a placard and walked over to Mella. He was wearing a white, anti-uranium mining t-shirt, untucked over jeans, and with one sleave folded over a few times and the other not. Behind him, someone sat down at the computer and began entering data into an excel spreadsheet, unbothered by the pink line right down the computer screen. Two other people were making placards as well, and an older man sat talking to them with a book in his hand and a foot on the table. A teenager was sitting on the floor near him listening to the conversation as he cut up raffle tickets. Mella also saw Alice from the picket. She was standing at the whiteboard, her long thick black plait tucked underneath a cotton rainbow scarf. Mella liked her pierced eyebrow. Alice paced up and down, looking at the whiteboard and holding a piece of cheese in her hand. She took a bite, looked up and exclaimed, "Ha!" then, "Oh, nah, that wouldn't work."

"Alice loves cheese," Rafi explained to Mella, and looked at Rain for confirmation.

"She was a cheese eating animal in her past life," Rain said.

"No animal eats...oh, so you're saying I was a mouse? Nice." She smiled at Mella, "How are things? Looking for work too?"

"Yep, and a room."

"Are you? Rafi, how could you not tell me?"

"Now you know," he said, grinning. "Rain, are you

going to give Mella the tour already?" he asked, and then busied himself tidying things, whistling as he did. "My word," he said to himself, looking at the bookshelves. He straightened them, and then asked himself, "What else?" After re-organising the leaflets and putting some of the old ones in the recycling box ("These are expired!" he said), he took the toilet key with the world 'toilet' written on a piece of cardboard and tied to it with a string, off a hook on the side of the bookshelf, and announced, "I'll be back!" He walked down the hallway, humming and spinning the key like some kind of fast boat propeller that pulled him along.

The Resist centre was busy, and Mella watched the activity and the stark lack of ennui, with curiosity. But she was also reminded of the day of the picket when she'd wanted to make herself smaller to get out of everyone's way. Rain gave her the tour. He explained the various clipboards where members wrote down newspaper sales, donations, book sales and other money received. He took her down to the kitchen where the larger banners were stored, and where there was a portable cooker and a big pot for all the soups and pastas that they made for Tuesday dinners. He explained that they charged a small amount for meals ($3.00 for students and unemployed, $4.00 for workers) to raise money to cover the cost of renting the space, the campaign expenses and so on. He showed her the car park out back and where the toilets were, then took her back to the office and explained some of the newspaper covers on the wall, introduced her to the others, and impatiently tapped the excel user on the shoulder, demanding she take a short break so he could show Mella all the things they used the computer for.

"Look at this!" he said, pointing at three different coloured filing trays used as 'in' and 'out' boxes. They were piled on top of each other, but wobbly and crooked. "We need to start buying our trays from just one manufacturer. That's capitalism for you; nothing's made to fit anything from another company!" he said, fumbling with them to try to align them.

As he talked, Mella looked at the things he pointed at; she read the posters and the book titles. She tried to keep her eyes busy because she felt nervous and she wanted to avoid Rain's eyes, bottomless lakes that seemed to contain half the world, compressed. Compressed like stars are compressed, she thought; deep and bright at the same time.

Alice interrupted Rain's tour: "This is the light switch," she said, laughing. "I point it out because people have a rather annoying habit of accidentally leaning on it and turning off the lights during meetings."

Mella smiled. She liked these people, and she wanted to relax her shoulders and her spine and her face and just poke them all playfully. And she had an urge to touch things, to feel the carpet, play with Alice's plait, to run her fingernail along the book spines and make funny noises with it. But she didn't know these people yet.

"Basically," Rain was saying, seriously and gently, "this group is a way for us to change this fucked up world. That's all we are. Of course, there are the details: How do you do that? And what kind of world do we want? Well, we want a world that puts the planet and the people before profits. If you like, you can join. It costs five dollars, and like the dinner money, it goes to pay for all this stuff." He gestured around the room, at books, the table with leaflets, the computer. "And you get this little red card that says you're a member, and this booklet."

"I'd like to join."

Alice turned around from the whiteboard. "Why don't we spray paint the mall with real big letters: "Make Love not War"? That'd get everyone's attention, and then we can leaflet the end of the mall for the 'Stop the War' Parramatta group!"

"Not a bad idea. But let's paint it on a banner and drop it off the bridge instead. It'll last longer, be easier to see, and we won't run the risk of getting fined for vandalism, which we really can't afford."

"So practical, Rain. Good. Let's do it. Mella, we'll have to discuss it of course, but it'd be great if you could help out with the 'Stop the War' Parramatta group. We're really quite short of people and there's a lot to do."

At that moment Rafi walked back in, still whistling and spinning the toilet key.

"Fall in?" Alice asked.

"Once, I fell off a twenty-metre ladder," he announced in response.

"No way! Do you know how far that is? That's like four storeys!" Rain said.

"Off the first step!" Rafi laughed, and went back to tidying up the office.

Mella joined in. She worked slowly, and as she did she watched Rafi, there in that space, in that world, and noticed that when they caught the train back to Granville he brought that world with him. But exactly what it was that went home with him, she couldn't identify yet.

A promise

Two in the morning, and Mella was sitting on Rafi's lime green couch. It was so dark and quiet that if day were to arrive suddenly, she would have covered her ears from all the noise and her eyes from the light. Her brain was recapping the last week or so and not letting her sleep. So she turned on the television with the volume at two notches above mute. It was broadcasting a re-run of the late news; footage of the riots in Macquarie Fields. A few days ago a youth had been killed in a police chase, and that night fifty young, grieving, drunk people, taunted by the police, had rioted. The police had responded violently, arresting many, and the next night there were three hundred people and even more police. Mella watched the footage with heavyhead, and she tucked her knees up and rested the heaviness on them. She remembered an article she had read in the Resist paper about a closely related issue; Aboriginal deaths in custody; Aboriginals killed by police in jails, chases, or during the arrest or transportation to prison. Five hundred Aboriginals had been killed so far, few police tried, and not one found guilty. Hugging her legs, Mella remembered her recent days of hopeless depression.

Now she wasn't so sure that things were that hopeless, and she wondered where her certainty before had come from, given the pile of books Rain had lent her, given how much she had to learn. Rain had made her coffee after they'd finished tidying the office the other day. He'd chatted to her about the organisation, the movement to stop the war on Iraq, and he had shown her the Seeds; little hints of a better world that had been drifting and whispering around her all that time, seeds she had failed to see. He'd unwittingly used Eva's logic; that anything that is planted, if sunned and watered, would grow. In just that conversation he'd given her doubt seeds, knowledge seeds (lots of questions), and one small resilience seed. Based on that conversation and her experiences at the picket and the meeting, she made a few basic, but new conclusions: 1) people could be nice (kindness seeds); 2) there were things that could be done about injustice; 3) people cooperating seemed to have the most impact.

On the television the footage of police shoving barely-adults into police vans continued. There was a photo of the man that had died in the crash, and then a photo of the driver, who was missing and wanted by police. Then there was brief footage of a suburb that was burning and angry. Then the news moved on to the war in Iraq, an entire country that was burning and angry. She turned off the television and decided to make a pledge.

I promise the unjust dead and those who live but suffer, a lifetime of struggle. I promise to be a serious, dedicated fighter for a better world.

PAZ

Waste Mountain

The tallest mountain in the world was a mountain of waste. It was the graveyard of everything, a conical collection of the world's unwanted. Located in the middle of the Pacific Ocean, it stuck out of the earth like a giant tumour and was surrounded by a ring of putrid brown stain with dolphin and parrot fish carcases floating in it. The air above it revolted, causing birds to fall out of the sky and wind to run away and crash into the rain, whipping it into torrential floods.

All the world's broken cars, plastic plates, killed land, discarded televisions, discarded lives, lost potential, wasted time, went to that mountain. Lying right on its peak was the newest addition; the young body of Matt.

Undeclared bomb

Not all bombs are made of metal, not all wars are fought over borders by soldiers with guns and uniforms. The chase that ended in a crash, Matt's butterfly wings flung about on the ground, was a kind of bomb. It hit the Macquarie Fields household with a long metallic piercing sound and spread them far, changing everything. The cracks in the house turned into a giant crater, and they took that crater with them as they ran from it, as they shattered while they ran, as they drank and drank, as they exploded and kept exploding, as they ran into the streets screaming and wanting to destroy something...anything, to take the destruction, the ruin, out of their own bodies and lives and put it outside themselves. All the other people in the area with ruin going on inside them, those that had been walked over and run over by the police and by the world, came out into the streets too, and joined the riot. The metaphorical bomb that hit Macquarie Fields was a manoeuvre in the long, undeclared war.

The role of the mainstream media
Here are some excerpts from the media about what happened in Macquarie Fields after police chased a car, leading to the death of, in this case, two people.

ABC local radio, 8:00 am 28 February, 2005; Riots break out in Macquarie Fields

Eleanor Hall: But first to the rioting on the streets of suburban Sydney overnight.

(Sound of yelling, screaming, swearing and objects)

For the third night in a row, at least one hundred teenagers have clashed with police in Macquarie Fields, in Sydney's southwest. Rioters set a car alight in a public housing area of the suburb, and attacked a squad of fifty police officers with stones and Molotov cocktails, breaking one officer's hand. Four people have been arrested and charged; one was bitten by a police dog in the process...

Claire Mathie: They've told us that it has stemmed from the...or has been triggered by...a car crash at Macquarie Fields on Friday evening of last week. The teenagers were in a stolen car, they were passengers in a stolen car, it was being driven by a third person who hasn't yet come forward to police...

Sydney Morning Herald, 1 March, 2005; **Not disadvantaged, just bad, says Carr**

As riots erupted for a fourth night at Macquarie Fields last night, [NSW state premier], Bob Carr laid the blame solely on the individuals who ran amok, and denied it was the fault of governments which had thrown poor jobless people together in a run-down housing estate.

"Listen, reality check," the Premier said yesterday. "There are no excuses for this behaviour, and I am not going to have it said that this behaviour is caused by social disadvantage.

"A lot of people grew up in circumstances of social disadvantage and they did not go out and attack police with bricks and light fires in the streets... There is one blame [sic] here, and that is the people who went out and threw bricks and caused riots. There's only one thing to say to them: the police will get them, because they are engaged in illegal behaviour."

Daily Telegraph, 1 March, 2005; **Scenes that bring shame to our city**

These are the rioters who must be stopped... Faces twisted in hate, they have set Macquarie Fields ablaze... They are trouble-makers who have travelled into the area and should hang their heads in shame. The violent group has incited public unrest, injured members of the police force, and brought disgrace on the suburb... They should be named and shamed.

Criminalised

At midday, the day after the crash, Ashley, Eva, Tracey, Damjan and others went to the crash tree and tied flowers to it. Someone nailed together a cross out of white painted fence wood and leaned it against the tree. Some relatives stuck photos of Matt among the flowers. Then they all took turns emptying beer cans around the base of the tree. "Sorry, mate," they said.

They sat around the tree and had a barbeque, and they drank more beer because the heavy sky was falling down on top of them and pushing them into the ground. They drank beer because their mate was dead. They drank beer because they knew that this was just another hard thing they had to swallow and accept.

Then the media arrived. Vans, suits, microphones with chunky mic flags, cameras and long chords, unnaturally paced voices. They walked around the people at the tree and put the microphones into their faces and asked, "How do you feel about your friend being dead?"

The next day, after the riots became headlines, they found Paz's aunt and offered to bake dinner for her if she could help get Paz on Ray Martin. When she herself finally went on the show a few days later, they brought her a big tray of muffins and grapes. False rumours then spread that she'd received twenty-eight thousand dollars for the story.

The journalists never asked them though, how they'd like things to be. Perhaps it was better, because most of the people by the tree were long past imagining. The idea of a better future was for other people.

It was around 1:00 pm when the police came. They could see the crowd was drunk. There were empty beer cans spread about the tree like erupted tears and sad tantrums.

"What are yous all upset about?" one police officer said to them as he approached, hands on hips.

"That's one less crim on the street," another officer said.

"You got no right being here, time to go home," said another.

Then, as it got darker, the police started to chase them away from the tree with dogs and batons. They pushed the growing crowd towards the end of the road. And that's when the riot started.

Ashley wondered where Paz had gone; he seemed to have completely disappeared.

Battles 1

On the first day of the riots the police brought ten horses and a water cannon, and they used the pressurised water to flick the rioters off the road and off the pavement, and eventually out of the media spotlight. After the first day they also brought buses, vans, four-wheel drives, and electronic surveillance. They filled the shopping centre car park that was next to the police station with their police vans, and they manned the roads, not letting anyone in or out of the suburb without ID.

During the day and into the evenings they would kick down house doors and use four-year-old infringement notices and unpaid petty fines to arrest people. Fifty police raided Paz's previous next door neighbour and her five children. They burst in and knocked her over as she opened the door. Dazed, she got up and pushed one of the police officers. So they beat her with their batons in front of her children, then hit her twelve-year-old, and pointed their guns at the others. They shackled her by her hands and feet and dragged her to the police van.

At night people would gather on the road near the tree, while others watched from their yards. It started with booing. The police shouted back, "Youse all gunna end up like your mate." and, "He's dead. What are you going to do about it?" And people threw things back at them; empty beer bottles and beer cans filled with dirt or water. They burnt dumped mattresses and abandoned cars and rubbish, and threw bricks and stones.

On the second day, Damjan watched the smoke curl around the air and spiral towards the sky, and he imitated its movement with his middle finger, then pointed it at the police. Someone near him coughed and wheezed and took out a Ventolin puffer. A kid with blue glasses took to pulling the planks off an abandoned house's fence and making a pile of them where others gathered and picked up the planks and threw them like javelins towards the armed and shielded police. The kid with glasses sneezed three times, sniffed, and the phlegm slid down his throat. He wrinkled his face, then kept pulling planks. Someone else, a middle-aged woman, tried to fart silently, but then thinking that all the noise would cover it up, let it rip, enjoyed it, and then noticed that everyone had heard it after all. She shrugged, nodded at them, and didn't see that the line of police had moved much closer. Others ran; she was grabbed from behind and led away.

For four nights the sound of glass smashing, horse hooves, booing, car breaks, screaming and shouting and projectiles crashing perforated the fabric of the suburb's nightspace. By the last night though, the rioters had thrown out their salty rage, their sour pain. It was 4:00 am and they dared not simply walk home, but they needed sleep.

When it was all over, seventy young, or poor, or tired people were in jail, and one man, the driver, still hadn't been found. The police won that small part of the ongoing undeclared war, and people sat down on the jail floor or went back home or back to work and back to television and back to their personal battles with spouses or children or neighbours.

Battles 2
In Redfern, Sydney, a year before the Macquarie Field riots, there was another riot. It came after the police chase that caused young TJ to die impaled on the steel picket fence. His girlfriend, a fourteen-year-old with no permanent home or family, declared the day after he died, "I don't dream any more..."

The day of the Redfern riots, people were also grieving by a tree when the police came and taunted them and called them names. Later, the police sealed off the street with cars and gathered in large numbers at both ends of it, visors shielding their faces. Then they waited for a riot. Staged it, rigged it. They watched, doing nothing, as kids loaded wheelbarrows with bricks for a few hours and set fire to the Redfern station entrance. They claimed they were waiting for back-up, yet it hadn't taken that long for back-up to arrive when TJ was impaled. Then the riot, or the protest, began. Kids as young as eleven wore t-shirts over their heads and charged at the police. The line moved back and forth for hours, until two hundred and fifty police in riot gear dispersed the crowds with a fire hose.

The fact was, Redfern was right near the city and they would have liked to have just flicked the Aboriginals there away and built hotels and shopping centres and high-rise apartments and made a lot of money. Indeed, after the riot, the Liberal Party called for the area to be bulldozed. Bulldoze Palestine, bulldoze the slums of India, bulldoze all the poverty and protest out of sight, out of the way, stick all the homeless people and the things gone wrong into the intolerable desert and leave the harbours and beaches and trains and restaurants for the well-off, to the people who never complain and never riot and who plan their next trip to India to photograph the palaces and dodge the poverty as though it were inconvenient roadkill.

After the riot in Redfern, some media wrote and talked about the "brave police". The policeman driving the car that had chased TJ was promoted.

Undeclared war on the land
In the middle of a barren red-yellow desert, under a white sky, there was a living fan. With broad and long ribbons flying from her many arms, she spun them eternally, creating a wind that lifted the sand so that it danced in circles around her head and fell in ever-changing hills around her feet.

Then a heavy, tall black cloud appeared on the horizon. Perhaps it came from Waste Mountain, or perhaps from the war on the land, where mining, forestry, and industry tore up layers of the land as though it were sponge cake, picked up green hills and snow-capped mountains and smashed them into the ground, painted rivers new, dull colours, stripped the coral reefs, ripped waterfalls to pieces.

As the cloud came closer, she saw that it was made of old cars, plastic bags, sauce bottles, chip packets, agrochemicals, tree bodies, plane exhaust, rotten food, landcrust and asphalt and concrete. The cloud blocked the sky and rained its juices on her. Desperately, she tried to keep spinning her arms, but they were heavy and slowed, then finally stopped. Her mouth filled with slime, her hair became knotted, and the thick ribbons tore. Her wind hills fell flat, and all about her, dotted around the desert landscape, were bird skeletons. Their ribcages were full of plastic toys and coke lids. They had died because the rubbish they ate where food and trees used to be had weighed them down and stopped them flying.

The price of being remembered
Restless one morning, with an urge to walk wherever her legs would take her, the elderly woman set out, and found herself in the local cemetery. It was quiet there, and the white of the statues of posing angels erected over some of the headstones stood out from the flat blue sky. Little yellow birds flitted about among the rows of headstones, as though they were giant, hard flowers, and as the woman walked towards the birds, they would lift up and fly a little further off. She walked slowly, looking at each grave, and she noticed that some were marble blocks with elaborate statues and gold-plated inscriptions, while others had wooden headstones or crosses, with roughly painted names and dates. The latter ones decomposed quickly; the names became hard to read within a few years, and the headstones broke or fell off within ten years. If the idea of graves was to make the memory of the dead last longer, it

seemed to her that even in death there were those who were apparently more worth remembering.

Burying

At the crematorium just outside Macquarie Fields, the sky was flat blue and the grass was so evenly cut and such a consistent apple-green that it seemed unnatural. The crematorium itself sat still and clean and perfect like an unused but preserved colonial house. And in front of it, to the left, a garden of trimmed hedges, bordered with a fence of long flat pebbles. Mourners were uncomfortable in ironed shirts and with empty hands. Damjan, Tracey, Ashley and Eva stood in a group somewhat apart from the rest, and the journalists waited with their telescopic lens cameras poised.

Paz was there too. Because he didn't care anymore if the police caught him, and because hiding was not living, and because he missed Matt and he wanted to say something to him. He sat in the back seat of his grandmother's car and watched people walk into the crematorium through tinted windows. He saw a black and white film funeral. Black and white perfect grass, silent, deadpan people with their hair combed and gelled and decorated. Black and white flowers that would be placed on the box that held Matt's body. As though it were all designed to turn death into sleep, to package the sadness and make it pretty. Paz watched them walk inside the doll house crematorium. Ashley held Eva's hand and chewed on her bottom lip, drawing a small part of the bottom of her face into her mouth. Damjan, behind her, looked at the walls and at everything except the box. He put his hands deep inside his pockets and decided to go to the pub that night.

Paz watched them walk out again. He saw the human-sized, Matt-shaped empty space next to Tracey, which made her right arm feel cold. That space had been there since the crash, and it would follow her around for a long time.

Bits

Strands of cloth dangled over the bridge handrail, spaced apart like uneven teeth. The woman walked along the bridge collecting the strands, which were almost dry. Left and right she turned her body, taking first a strand, then watching the traffic, and then taking another. She talked to herself. "Quite. Quite right. Quite might sight." The words were spoken in time with her turning, her plucking, her piling. "About tout, about doubt lout, About smout pout," she said.

Rag collector woman, her own memory dangling and scattered; every morning she spread the multi-coloured bits of cloth across the bridge. Cars passed. Some people wondered about the cloth; most didn't. In the evening she collected the rags again, plaited them, and made her night's bed, parked between the base of the bridge tower and a brick wall. She slept, dreaming scattered dreams. Then morning came yet again, bringing the police who would not let her stay there, and because she didn't want to carry her bed and her dreams around over her shoulder during the day, she scattered them over the bridge's handrails.

Paz in a box

Paz was in hiding, but with Matt gone and the household inevitably splitting up, he had nowhere to go. The loss of his closest friend meant that walking felt slow for him. His air was gone, and he couldn't read signs. His internal butterfly was still. So eventually, after two weeks of hiding and going nowhere, he met the police in a paddock. He heard the approaching sirens, then the brakes of the three police vehicles, doors opening, and he stayed there, lying on his back on the grass, for just one more moment. He felt the hot grass itching him and the solid ground and the life throbbing modestly within it; the ants and crickets, the energetic dirt. He remembered Sunday mornings when he had wondered about everything, and the way his heart had drummed with each new touch on Ashley's soft body. He remembered how he'd planned Matt's present.

Then it was over, and he stood up, brushed the bits of foliage off his back, and with his hands in the air, walked towards the police van.

They cuffed Paz's hands behind him, put a gloved hand on his head, and pushed him into the back of the van.

At the processing wing of Parklea Prison they took his keys, wallet, a handmade plaited friendship band, his belt, and his cap. They told him to wait but didn't say for how long. He sat still, thought little and looked at his knees. Because it was that kind of waiting; rather than waiting with expectation, or waiting in a queue and gradually getting to the front, or where the free time is enjoyed and the mind wanders, he waited in absentia. He didn't realise it, but he waited for nearly four hours. Then they told him they were going to search him, and to take off his clothing. They told him to wiggle his fingers and open his mouth and pull his ears down so they could see behind them, then to squat and cough three times, and to comb his fingers through his hair. They sent him to take a shower, put his civilian clothes in a plastic bag and gave him his prison greens. As they watched, he put on his new uniform. Then he waited again. Eventually, they photographed him, and he waited some more. Then they took his fingerprints and did some medical tests. He waited one more time, until they called him and issued his prison number, which they told him to memorise. They didn't tell him he had been arrested for aggravated dangerous driving occasioning death, nor when his trial would be or how long he would be in prison.

Parklea was a male maximum security prison with a capacity of eight hundred and twenty-three inmates. In October 2009, the government would sell it to a private company, the GEO group. But for now, it was government-employed guards who led Paz through three metal hallways and up the stairs in the common area, then slid open the barred door of his cell and left him there. And he sat on the thin mattress, in a 4 x 3 metre box with cream painted walls and sallow green tiles around the bottom half. Two broad planks attached to the wall at different heights and distances formed a desk and chair, and a stainless steel toilet-sink, with the tap running straight into the cistern, let off a smell that clung with sharp nails to his skin. Paz wasn't allowed to stick posters, photos, or notes onto the walls, and he felt that the cell had a blankness to it, like a person with no face. Security cameras hanging from the ceiling in the corridor pointed at him and other inmates through the barred cell doors.

Putting people in boxes was like tying their arms and legs and covering their eyes; because what people do, how and what they see, hear, think and decide, was the essence of who they were. Now Paz's being was limited. He took the pale blue sheet, the itchy grey woollen blanket, and the thin pillow that had been placed at the end of the bed, and lay down, curling his body around them. Then he looked at the blank walls and tried to project the people with moons tucked close to their chest onto them. He tried to print out the photos in his mind and stick them onto the cream paint. But the walls rejected them, the images curled into themselves and rolled down the walls onto the floor. He coiled his body tighter; clenched his toes, packed away his spine, rested his head inside the grey blanket. Then he talked himself into acceptance; this was no different than hiding in his grandma's car or in the bushes, or crouching on the ground during the police raids, or working alone in that big office block, hoping that he'd finally get paid. Not a new world, this box. A very heavy hole lay on top of his bodyball and made his head ache. It was the Missing Thing.

What is a criminal?

Silvio Berlusconi, prime minister of Italy for nine years and also controlling shareholder of Mediaset, the largest media company in the country, had been convicted by the final appeal in just one out of thirty-two court cases. Over his career he was accused of defamation, extortion, child sexual abuse, perjury, mafia collusion, embezzlement, money laundering, drug trafficking, false accounting, corruption, and bribery; some of those on multiple occasions. He used his parliamentary majority to shorten the time limit for prosecuting many of his crimes, he paid for the top lawyers and publicists, and some of his lawyers were also members of parliament. He was eventually convicted of tax fraud, with a one year jail sentence to be served doing unpaid community service, and he remained one of the richest people in the country. Perhaps a criminal is someone who can't afford a lawyer.

Criminalised 2

In 2008 Berlusconi referred to non European migrants who were unemployed or homeless as an "army of evil". He passed laws where undocumented migrants (described by politicians and the media as "illegal") could be fined $14,000 and jailed for up to six months. Those who offered them lodging could be sent to jail for three years. So thousands of people lived in an underworld; they arrived in broken boats, lived in dark park shadows, abandoned buildings, and in the sewers under Rome station, just near the Colosseum. Above them, tourists who bought plastic Colosseum key rings from people dressed as centurions, were oblivious. Yet the Italian authorities knew, and they permitted it, because "illegal" workers were much cheaper. They performed a large proportion of the country's agriculture work.

MELLA

It was a poem with three legs

It was a poem with three legs and two languages, that was written like life was written. It was struggled for and the verses came and went and changed. It was dreamt about before it was written, and it was written by him and her and them and while kissing and between heartbeats. It didn't follow straight lines; instead it imagined its many authors singing in choirs and finishing the poem on a bare city wall.

Mella snug in a notbox

Mella used the pair of copied keys that Alice had given her to enter her new home. When she walked in, she saw Lives. Everywhere she saw evidence of people living in the five bedrooms and among the house's odd accumulation of furniture left by people as they moved in, moved out, and were replaced by others. It was a crooked, uneven house, with sloping floors, steam stains above the stove, and faded wine stains that blended into the lounge room's carpet pattern. Located near Granville station, it was rumoured that the rent was low because the previous occupants had been caught using the place to grow pot.

But for years now it had been an activist share house, with people moving in and out as their studies, relationships and jobs demanded.

Mella explored. Green and purple cotton sheets being used as curtains in the lounge room blew about, covered the television, and knocked an old puppet off it. Sometimes they got caught in each other, like seahorse lovers. There were more wraps and shawls draped across the couches and the coffee table, and black and white photos, old calendars, and political posters were stuck to the walls in the hallway and on bedroom doors. There was a laminated photo of a sugar glider on the inside of the bathroom door, which fell down and got re-taped there about once a week. The rental bond long gone, someone had painted in pastel purple, yellow, green, and blue, lines from Benedetti's poem along the tops of the walls, "... my love, my accomplice, my everything, in the street elbow to elbow, we are more than two people".

There were deflated balloons in the hallway and dining room. That was from when someone had stayed over one night, tired and tipsy after a party, and slept in the hallway covered in the balloons. There was a bathroom door that locked from the outside but not the inside. Housemates had gotten used to looking at the line of light below the closed door to determine if it was occupied. Once though, Sussie was in there and Alice had pattered down the hallway in a towel and white socks and called out, "Are you having a shower? Can I pop in and use the toilet before you do?" Sussie hadn't responded, and Alice had repeated, "Hello? Are you showering?"

Sussie had whispered, "Hello?" There was a pause, a flush, and she popped her head around the door. "Oh! I thought I was hearing voices."

Sussie loved small children and being an auntie. She had organised a strike of contract call centre workers, cried easily, fell in love easily, and had just moved to Perth to get involved in student activism there. It was her room that

Mella would move into. Sussie's name was still on the house cleaning roster, and she had left a note on her door for Mella that said, 'Welcome!'

Mella saw life in the fliers for rallies that were taped underneath the roster, in the couches where people often draped about like flung washing; reading and chatting, in the gaps under the bedroom doors where the muffled sounds of private lives sometimes trickled out. She saw that two of the housemates had got dressed up once and danced with their umbrellas in the dining room, and she heard the gentle clocksound of the Sunday morning house meetings. There was the wallmemory of someone getting locked out and climbing back in through a window, and the sound of someone arriving late and the couch-draped housemates taking turns to guess who it was by the sound of the keys. There was a computer in the dining room, and Mella imagined she would get into the habit of reading it while perched on a chair, weaving a scrap piece of soft material in and out of her bare toes.

The door to Alice's room was wide open, and Mella peaked inside, knowing she would see the story of a person there. There was a queen-size mattress in the middle of the room, sheets in knots and pillows at both ends. Around the mattress there were piles of books, scrap books, comics, and newspapers. Alice drew her own zines, and her latest one was spread about on the pillows. It was full of unconventional characters that looked like real people; she gave them sag, stretchmarks, hips, hair, baldness, bad posture, and wiry fingers. When she needed to relax, she folded origami, and she had hung folded frogs, turtles, flowers, fish, and koalas, as well as some other ink drawings with string from a thin rope that went from a nail in one wall over to the window. Origami waterfall. There was also an old record player, a cardboard box of records, a red and purple violin, and behind the door, a badge board from the Resist centre. Mella looked forward to getting to know Alice.

In her room there was a similar mattress, also in the middle of the floor, and Sussie had left a few magazines and books behind. Mella sat on the bed and smiled. She felt better in this house; she felt the fear of not doing things right slipping away. She would do this room her way; for now making some shelves out of planks and bricks, and tying a bamboo stick to the ceiling for something to hang clothes and her towel on. She would go to the two-dollar shop and buy some long coloured candles and arrange them around the room. Over time the rest would take shape. She browsed through Sussie's magazines and found some pictures of flying lorikeets and crimson rosellas. She cut them out and stuck them on the middle of her door. Then, although it was midday, she lay down on the mattress, arms and legs starspread, and relaxed. She had no headache, and the heavy missing thing hole had gone away for a little while. She felt that if she didn't cover herself in a blanket, she might float away from lightness. She pulled it over her and she was snug. Inside her, cells grew, rearranged, changed, and her wings kicked with an urge to collect colour and grow. Finally, she had a very deep sleep.

Chairs and custard

Alice sat on a spinning chair at the computer in the Resist office and made some last minute notes before the fortnightly meeting started. The chair was very old, and had five legs that spiked out from the centre pole, but just four wheels. Umpteen times Alice had taken it out into the street for it to be collected, and umpteen times Lar (who always drew made-up maps during meetings) or Hassan (who was always in a hurry, talked very fast and walked very fast) would enthusiastically bring the chair back to the office, proud of finding some new furniture.

Alice leaned forward to turn the computer screen off, and as she did the chair moved backwards and she almost fell onto Rain's feet. "That's enough!" Mella laughed, and with Rafi following her, she took the chair out to the stairs that led down to the car park. She tried to throw it down the stairs, but it got caught on a railing. Rafi peered below the staircase, checking for people.

"Okay, all clear, try again."

The chair landed at the bottom of the stairs with a metallic clang. Rafi and Mella ran down after it and examined it. It was still in one piece, but the wheels had broken off.

"Wow, we could probably use it now," Mella said.

Chairs, in many regions of the world such as Egypt, Rome, and Greece, started out as thrones; they were large, ornate, made of marble, bronze, or wood, with tall straight backs and legs carved in the shapes of animal feet. They were used by the most privileged people to show their status. Later, the wealthy would use them, while most people used backless stools or long benches, or they sat on the floor on mats. These days, in Sydney, there were large stores dedicated just to chairs; chairs for one person, for two, for eating, studying, consulting, for a front porch, for sitting on the beach.

In the Resist office, the chairs were for working, and for organising people into rows to facilitate group decision making. There were three ergonomic chairs that someone had found or donated, and the rest were stackable plastic ones. Now, as it struck 7:00 pm, people began unstacking the chairs and placing them in tight rows with a narrow aisle in the middle. They were meticulous, as though laying a table for an important meal.

Mella sat near the back, and Alice asked an older woman, Marg, to chair the meeting, and a teenage boy to take minutes. Marg proposed that to the meeting, all raised their hands in favour, and then she proposed an agenda and time limits for each item. There was some discussion about which item should go first, then it was decided, voted on, and the meeting began.

"The first agenda item is building the Stop the War collective in the west," Marg said. Alice stood at the front of the room and gave a short report, with general perspectives and some concrete proposals, then Marg opened the meeting for discussion, and people raised their hands to go on the call list. Each time someone got up to speak, in order to let them pass, everyone in their row would tuck their feet under the chairs, though it made little difference.

"We aren't against the troops..."

"But the slogan, 'Bring the troops home'... it's like we care more about the Australians than the Iraqis..."

"It's a useful rallying point because it's a concrete way we can oppose the war..."

Someone dropped their pen, and it rolled across the aisle towards another row. A sort of soccer game of passes followed, where one person used their foot to manoeuvre the pen backwards, another person leaned around and, monkey-like, scooped up the pen, then passed it to their neighbour, who passed it across the aisle to the owner.

"Here in Western Sydney, we need to involve more people in the committee, so that the movement can go beyond the inner city... Mella, the new resistance member, has agreed to help out with the committee, and that's an important boost there. We also need to make sure other groups, no matter their positions on other things, if they are against the war, they should send at least one rep to the committee," Alice argued.

Mella tried to swallow smiles. She would be useful, and they were talking about and organising important things.

At nine o'clock the meeting was still going. It had started to drizzle a while ago, but suddenly the rain turned loud and heavy, pounding onto car tops, the roof, and against the glass of the office windows. Marg turned around and looked outside with a disgusted expression, as though the rain was intentionally disrupting the meeting.

"One minute left," she said.

"Time to wrap up now," she said.

Rafi listened to everything, but was also fond of moving around. He would get up now and then and take the toilet key off its hook and go to the toilet. Then he would stand in the open doorway, then sit, concentrate, stand up again, straighten some books, raise his hand to go on the call list, run to the front when it was his turn, talk on his toes and slice the air with his left hand for every important point, and would be surprised every single time he was told his time was up. However, he always stopped talking as soon as he was told, even refusing to finish his sentence. He usually voted against the time extensions, arguing that it was fair that everyone have the same amount. Alice, on the other hand, almost always voted for them, and would turn her head a little to point her right ear at the speaker after each granted extension, sure that something important would be said.

"Three more people on the list and we've run out of time for this agenda item. I'm going to propose we close the call list," said Marg. "All in favour?"

The rain weakened and the meeting drew to a close. The chairs were collected and stacked again at the back of the room.

Rafi stayed back in the office to finish an article, and Alice asked Mella to do a paste-up to promote the 'Stop the War' committee.

"Why don't we just put an ad in the paper?" Mella asked.

"It's not a bad idea; the thing is we don't have much money, Mella. We barely manage to pay the office rent with the money we raise. 'Free speech' is a funny term, because the fact is that speech is very expensive. Only the rich, the big businesses can afford to advertise, have billboards, and all that."

They mixed flour and hot water in a bucket with a branch, and Alice carried it downstairs, trying not to let it slosh back and forth. Mella carried the posters in a roll, and they crossed the road to the bus terminal. Using a large brush, Alice painted a square of glue on the first bus stop window, and each time the brush reached a corner, drops of glue would spray onto the ground, their shoes, and drip down her fingers. Mella pulled out a poster and pressed it down on the square, and then Alice painted more glue over the top, while Mella looked up and down the road, watching for police.

"Have you heard the Tim story?" Alice asked. "He was doing a paste-up one day when he walked straight into some cops. The cops acted all macho, and asked, 'What do you think you're doing? What's in that bucket?' 'Custard,' says Tim, with this very straight face. And the cops think he's being a smart ass. 'It's true, have a taste!' Tim insists. One of the cops smells the bucket and is like, 'Omigod, it IS custard.'"

Alice picked up her own bucket, indicated a closed down shop where there was space for many posters, and they walked over to it.

"That day the branch had run out of corn flour, so they used custard instead," Alice said, laughing as she dipped the brush into the glue again.

"Does custard even stick?" Mella asked.

"It sticks to the stovetop, that's for sure!"

What is a hero?

Was it Marg, who got angry with the rain for interrupting their meeting? Marg, who despite suffering midnight beatings and morning bruises, worried about the Palestinians, and about improving Sydney's public transport. She took Mella, Alice, and Rain to a campaign stall in her car, and on the way she told them about her violent ex-husband. He had kicked down doors and told her it was her fault when he got into one of his war-tempers, or when he cheated on her, or when their twenty-three-year-old daughter hit her. The daughter, enraged once, had stabbed and almost killed someone. That was after her boyfriend had shot himself in her room a few years ago. His body was taken away under a white sheet. A neighbour later said to Marg, "I thought it was you under there".

Eventually, Marg left her husband. Now, when she wasn't working as a high school teacher or looking after her kids, she was an activist. She screamed at the traitor politicians who crossed the picket lines, soggy in corruption, taking back promises, voting for war when they'd said they wouldn't. She screamed back at the racists who jeered at her on the street while she was campaigning.

"My daughter came home one day and told me she was dating a woman. She thought I would be shocked, but I just said, 'Oh, when can I meet her?'" Marg said, then screamed at a car which cut her off.

What is a hero?

Colin Fox told this story: It was 2003 in Scotland, and he was a tall confident man with mop hair and a pierced ear. He was a leading campaigner against the poll tax which taxed the rich the same as the poor, a member of the Scottish Socialist Party, and was elected to the Scottish Parliament.

In order to take their seats in parliament, Scottish MPs had to swear an oath to the Queen. Colin's fellow party member, Rosie Kane, who had also been elected, held up her hand with "My oath is to the people" written on it. Colin sang a Robert Burns song instead of the oath, and was promptly kicked out.

"I got a letter from the Queen inviting me to a reception, and it was addressed to Mr and Mrs Fox. I don't have a wife, so my mum thought it must be addressed to her. She asked me what I'd wear. 'I'm not going mum,' I said. Everyone went though, including the Scottish republicans. Only the SSP and one other person didn't go," Colin said.

"We're not prepared to live by their rules... Parliamentary democracy is a means to an end, it's cheaper than a military dictatorship, and that's why they use it."

"In Edinburgh we have a castle, and at one o'clock a cannon goes off, boom. And we decided to mark the war in Iraq by dying in Princes Street at the one o'clock gun. And we organised it, and there was probably about two hundred people there, and we marched. But unbeknownst to me, we were joined by four thousand five hundred school kids who had gone on strike that day. Here we are, trying to stop the traffic with two hundred people. The school kids came down, and they were looking for something to do. And I said, 'Hey come along, there's plenty of room' and we sat down, four thousand five hundred of us. Blocking traffic all day. The chief constable of Edinburgh would come up to me and say, 'Oh, Colin, yes, how long will you be staying here?' I'm used to the chief constable saying, 'Move the fuck off or I'll arrest you'. Not good PR for the chief constable to be moving fifteen and sixteen-year-old kids around with horses and police batons. So for that week the constable would ring me up and ask, 'Colin, where will you be protesting today?'"

No chairs and a disappearing suit
Was Bomba a hero? In 2003, in Harare, Zimbabwe, he and thirty other activists met in the corner of a yard surrounded by a brick and barbed wire fence. They had travelled to the capital from around the country, spending up to eight hours squeezed into the back of an old combi van. Now, ten people crammed onto a bench as though huddling against the cold, even though it was extremely hot. The others sat on the rough gravel floor, or on newspapers.

(The butterflies of Zimbabwe were trying to fly, beating the ground over and over until there was a few seconds of lift-off. Their wings filled with dry dirt and tore.)

Bomba brought the meeting together, and they all listened to his analysis of the economic situation; inflation rising, the MDC, Mugabe's repressive tactics. People raised their hands to agree and disagree. Tfadzwa, the only woman there, used a mixture of Shona and English to argue that the MDC would eventually capitulate to Mugabe, therefore Gwisai should run in the elections independently. "But without using our name. For our safety."

Bomba nodded agreement. He remembered the last national elections when students were detained after leading a class boycott in solidarity with the stay-away called by the Zimbabwe Congress of Trade Unions. The police reaction unit raided the students' offices, pulled down their posters, and rounded him and other students into police trucks. At the central police station, the police beat and harassed them for hours, and by the time they were thrown into cells they could hardly sit. There was no food or toilets, but they refused to sign the prepared statements. It was only because of a huge crowd at their hearing that they were released three days later.

"Can I borrow a pen comrade?" Biko whispered to him. "One day I'll get one of my own."

(In central Harare there was a large sign, 'Sunshine city—Harare, help keep our city clean'. It was adorned with a large Coca-Cola logo, as was the standard for most street and police signs. In Highfield, outside the centre, there was a sign that said, 'Welcome to Paradise, the promised land - Nyika ye Chipikirwa, llizwe Lesi te Mbiso'. There, the green maize grew higher than the houses and some of the balancing rocks. On the main road a woman and her two babies sat under a table, their stall with one onion on it, placed perfectly in the centre. Back in the city, two four-year-old children cupped their hands and asked for food. An older boy sold hand-painted cards. A man with many things on his mind apologised, "No thanks," and the boy smiled, laughed, and waved goodbye. People ate Tsadza fast in a humid room in Mbare. They ate fast because it had been a while since their last meal, but they didn't talk about the hunger.)

Bomba tapped on the wall to tell Tfadzwa she should wrap up. "Comrade, please finish now," he said softly. "Ok," Tfadzwa replied, and leaned back against the wall.

Biko's turn; he pointed and gestured: "If we get a small vote, people will be disappointed."

"Sharp!"

"But Gwisai was elected before, and he could be elected again. Is that useful coms?"

"Yes, it is a big opportunity to get our messages in the papers."

The meeting lasted four hours. Because of the heat, those sitting on the ground steadily shuffled sideways as the fence's shadow shifted.

(Another funeral...in a field of newly dug graves. After the ceremony, people chatted and hid their eyes from the sun, then piled into the waiting vans. Their mood was like the end of a long day at work.)

It was late, and Bomba gently shut the door to the small room he rented, and hundreds of cockroaches scuttled down the walls and under his bed. His room was almost empty, with a small electric cooker in one corner, the narrow bed, a cupboard with three shirts, and about twenty books; the ISO's library.

"Com, how is it?" It was his unhappy neighbour, come to talk. Bomba was tired, but he invited the neighbour to come inside and sit on the bed.

"How long do you think it will last?" the neighbour asked, referring to the hunger and lack of jobs. Almost every night he visited Bomba with a new solution. Sometimes he felt the only way it could be made better was to bomb them, to "give them back what they deserve". Often it was suicide, or immigration to Australia. And he hoped Mugabe would die of old age, he hoped it was that simple. But that night he was quiet, as though exhausted of all possibilities. Then he asked, "Where is Briggs?"

"Ah, comrade Briggs, he was given money; he bought a suit and disappeared. It's a shame."

(The Highfield combi stopped at the flea market. The fare collector yelled out, "Three! Highfield!" and three people squeezed into a seat for two. The others who were waiting waited a little longer, and then hitched a ride on the back of a truck.)

Bomba and Hopewell wrote up a poster for a campus meeting that afternoon, and stuck it up around the university. At 2:00 pm the lecture room was full. Bomba stood on the stage, and read the words of "Imagine", then talked about why there were wars and what that had to do with the money shortage in Zimbabwe. He encouraged discussion, but the room was silent. Everyone knew there were at least a few plain clothes police in the audience, as it was common practice, and a police car was parked outside the hall.

Hopewell, sitting at the very back of the lecture theatre, decided to try to spark discussion about the US's justification for invading Iraq. "Yes I think Saddam is a dictator and should be removed, but does it take massive missiles from across the globe?" he asked.

Everyone laughed. A few people put their hands up.

"I say to all the police here, this was an academic submission, not an attempt to mobilise people," Hopewell said, as he sat back down.

"We can't afford to eat lunch; these days the tsadza is too expensive. So our lunch are made more interesting by having meetings like this," Bomba explained.

(In Harare, like an over-rehearsed play, the police waited outside the union office on their horses, batons ready. The union leaders arrived for a meeting and were arrested straight away. People hovered nearby, watching with one foot pointed in the other direction, ready to run. Because in the play that was real, that was put on over and over again, there was usually tear gas and bashing by now. Then the people were Shut Down.)

What is dance?

Venezuela. The day Florcita understood what dance was, she was waiting for a Communist Party meeting to start. Two comrades arrived in their car. They were in their eighties, and had been active for decades, including when the party was underground and repressed. The woman had had a stroke a year ago, and with help from Cuban doctors, was gradually walking again. To cross the six metres from their car to the office, she faced her partner and placed one hand on his shoulder, and one on his waist. He did the same to her, and walking backwards, slowly and patiently, they made their way. She lifted one foot carefully, dragged it, put it down, and then the other. He supported her, moved with her. In the office he arranged a pillow behind her back, and the meeting began.

Mella's battles

(The tender Venezuelan Andes and their wise peaks and silent patience roused an urge to stroke them and fall asleep on their downy green slopes. And the soon to be firefighters, who were hiking up the slopes for two days as part of their training, were even more tempted, as they felt their sore legs, the mud worming in through the holes in their shoes, their coin-size heel blisters, their asthmatic wheezing and their sunburnt noses. They wanted food, hot showers, blankets, and movies. They couldn't perceive their lungs, heart, and leg muscles becoming stronger, nor the build-up of physical and emotional endurance. What if they walked on flat streets, or took taxis instead? What if they looked at the mountains, their battles, and decided to watch television instead?)

In a Western Sydney backyard, rain sprinkled down, cleaning the streets and the air, then gliding off to other suburbs. Two activists parked out the front, then carried bags of long rolls and sausages into the house. Alice came out, greeted them, and ran over to the car to bring in the boxes of soft drinks and beer. Rafi arrived on foot and took the cask wine he'd bought into the kitchen. Marg parked behind the first car, and brought in onions, tomatoes, sauces, and an old red sheet to cover the serving table. The kitchen became chatterhub as they cut up onions and one of the teenagers got a barbeque going. Lar, the made-up map drawer, in order to be useful, took to sweeping up the dirt people walked in and the sesame seeds that bounded off the bread and onto the floor. As soon as he had swept, the floor was covered in more shoe dirt and more sesame seeds, and map drawer was so keen that he broom stalked Alice's feet as she brought more things inside. The chatter was like a pinball machine, spreading bright laughter and big eyes as it bounced and rebounded. Outside, bees imitated them, moving busily from one yellow dandelion to another, helping the weeds to invade the front yard footpath and gradually break it apart.

Mella got to the fundraiser later, when people were already eating. Everything needing to be done had already been done, and Mella fidgeted with her empty hands. She didn't know what to do, didn't know how to start talking to people. Her tongue felt like a piece of salted fish. She watched Marg sell drinks, then leave the table; then she saw people pay for their drinks on their own, dropping coins into the washed-out mayonnaise jar. She saw Rain and Ramona holding each other, passing earthsecrets and soulstroke back and forth with their eyes. Like someone tongue-tied in the middle of a public speech, she was party-tied to the ground, stuck in watching mode, until Rafi came up to her.

"Hey, you look lost," he said, holding her shoulder. "Come, we need someone to wash the plates so we can use them again; we don't have enough," He lead her into the kitchen.

She was wiping the bench down when night began to arrive. Casting a softspell, it covered day with a cloak of purple, and a yellow moon, and said to the activists, 'Now you can relax. Day is over, work is over; it's time to dance'.

Music was turned up. Moths hit themselves against the outdoor lights then settled on the windows and walls the same way people had settled onto chairs at the meeting. The sky drizzled rain again. Rafi said, "Even when the rain is being affectionate, it moves too fast to poke", as he poked two fingers at the cooling air. Rags and soap sprays were put away, conversations about 80s music, heatwaves, and theories of inclusive participation were wrapped up and stored away, and everyone went to the centre of the yard to dance.

And Mella watched again. She saw Rafi dancing in the middle of the crowd. He was still poking the too-fast rain, and he stomped the ground and punched the night cover, his rhythm his own invention, completely unrelated to the music. But he was happy. And he laughed and jumped and hip-knocked and high-fived the people around him.

Mella couldn't do that. She stood on the edge of the dancing area, and on the edge of the world, and watched. Because she still had feet of socksonfloor, and still needed to hide what wasn't worth showing. If she danced, it would magnify her insecurity. If she talked, her lack of things to say would be deafening. Her little wings craved colour now, but she was still in the never ending queue of colourless people, the faceless ones.

Rafi came up to her and asked her to dance with him. She shook her head. "No worries, compa, maybe later, eh?" he said. Then, even though he didn't seem bothered, Mella felt guilty. There were a few people who weren't dancing, but she didn't know how to start talking to them. It was too hard.

She socksonfloor snuck down the hallway, through the small front yard with the dandelion weeds defeating the footpath, and out into the street. Two houses down she came across a vacant house with a lot of long grass, and she sat on it, trying not to cry.

An ambulance went past. Then two police officers on bikes. Rain dripping inside her shirt and down her back. The sound of the party behind her. Then the sound of the front door opening and closing.

"Mella? Hey, possum, come sit here," Alice said, indicating a large tree root on the other side of the footpath.

Mella wiped away the tearbits that had congregated in the corners of her eyes and sat by Alice on the root. She was quiet for a while, and then said, "I don't know if I can do this. I don't know if I'm the right person to be fighting for another world."

"Growing up, we aren't taught how to organise. We're taught to be passive, to consume products and television, rather than to be active and express our opinions. We're also treated like we're not worth much, as humans. That money is more important. So that means it's a hard fight, Mella. For all of us."

Mella listened with little face furrows. Alice hugged her, and then let her be alone for a while. She transported herself back to Rafi's lime green couch and to her midnight oath—her oath to try. Now, a battle to be a person who could dance...

She walked, shoesonfloor, back to the house, down the hallway and into the yard of dancers. She saw someone standing alone, introduced herself, and started to talk to him. In a few hours the night would wind down, close up, and when all was quiet, the street sweeper truck would move slowly down the road, gather the rubbish and wrap up the streets, putting them away for a few hours until dawn.

Invisible battles

The undeclared war and its forty million fronts; its mudslides, landmines, racism, blockages and borders; so many insecurities, so many insults hurled like grenades. Just as children played at guns during times of war, and the veins of a leaf imitated the branches of a tree, people carried a small version of the world inside themselves; their own personal battles a mirror of the bigger ones happening in the world.

John's battle

"I need a favour," said John. There was panic and perspiration in his voice.

In life, John had done some of the hardest things. Since the 70s in the US, he had organised solidarity with Latin America, fought union battles, campaigned for gay rights, and marched against wars, always going against the tide.

Then in 2009, he went somewhere else for a while. He used cocaine for instant euphoria, instant escape. He tied himself in knots, became bitter, sagged. He complained more and did less. He and his partner broke up and got back together about once a week. His partner, two teeth missing and his fist in a bandage, beat him, threatened him, and then pleaded with him. Then they broke up for good, and his ex walked the streets unbathed, hungry, with new bandages over two gunshot wounds, telling strangers their fortune for food.

Fortune for food.

John tripped, crawled, and finally crumbled. Then one day he called. He was in a psychiatric hospital that was actually a pale prison cell with four beds to a room. It was time to stay down or to get up, and he started to get up.

(A big global scam: A broken society, inaccessible mental health care, and drugs.)

Elena's battle
Elena was a serious, sharp-minded young woman who worked for a government institution in Venezuela and who liked to invite friends over on Friday nights for beer, bread, and long conversations around the kitchen table. In the days leading up to the local beauty competition, she and five friends got on motorbikes and went around the city spray-painting blank walls, clothing shop windows, and billboards with 'A woman's place is in the struggle' and 'My body is not for advertising'.

She had a five-year-old girl, Ana, whose laughter rolled in dizzy circles and who played loudly, chattered loudly, and pulled her adult friends along behind her as she ran to the park. Her godparents gave her light-skinned Barbies to play with, in a country where most people were shades of brown. At pre-school she played kitchen, dress-up, and watched television, believing it was something to aspire to.

One of Elena's battles was to let her child be free, let her make mistakes and grow in her own way, but to also to protect her from society's negative messages.

One Saturday, Ana came to breakfast with her eyelids painted blue. She looked up at her mum, and asked, "Am I pretty?"

(A war front where small girls aspired to be dolls instead of humans.)

Leonardo's battle
The room that Leonardo rented was his entire home. He slept on a thin mattress that sagged in the middle. He had a camping cooker on a plastic red table in one corner, and

pans and implements hanging off nails on the wall. His paintings on squares of cardboard covered stains on the walls, rags stuck in the holes in the green tin roof only half stopped water leaking in, and his clothes hung from a pipe that crossed diagonally from the small window to the wall. He stacked all his books in piles against the wall. He could only see the bottoms of the books, but he knew them all by the colour of their paper and their size. He washed his dishes under the pipe outside, and used the same pipe to fill the ice cream container to flush the toilet.

Leonardo was a teacher, a volunteer forest fire fighter, and a brilliant guitar player. He spoke Spanish, English, and read French, and would read the news in each language in the mornings. He liked black and white movies, and he missed his nephew, who had moved to Colombia. He said that when he was five he had stood on the couch and looked out the window at a TV antenna, sucking on toothpaste.

The children at the school where he taught told him their stories; abuse, confusion, parents who sold drugs, a father in prison, bad food, boredom. Maria, fourteen, told him about her three brothers who had been killed. He said that death was different for her, not part of a natural life cycle, rather it was violent, common, expected, and it happened when you were young. His own father had kept a gun, had cheated repeatedly on his mother, and now retired, spent all day watching Mexican comedy. Leonardo said it hurt him when he thought about how much his father had worked, and that "society gave nothing back". His uncle died on the streets, and another had diabetes, then gangrene, and ended life in a mental institution.

Leo had no dreams. His battle was with sadness, and with sleep. He became depressed because he felt that he couldn't do much about the problems he saw everywhere. He walked out of school meetings to smoke, and then he came back inside and sat down, his back rounded, his eyes falling to the floor. He massaged his aching head, started to speak, and then changed his mind.

And he was exhausted. He would have liked a holiday. "But," he said, "I'll never be able to travel. For one night in a hostel, I'd have to go hungry for a week. To travel to the coast, another week of hunger, then another week for the trip back. One day at the beach, three weeks of hunger; it's impossible."

He could never sleep. While the whole town slept and dreamed, he lay awake. "Beast of the night," he said.

Maria saw death differently, and he saw daytime differently.

One August afternoon, he played Silvio on the guitar, under the sound of the rain on the green tin roof. The fingers of the beast danced. Come lunchtime, he made too much lentils on purpose, so he could give some to his neighbour who was out of work. That week he painted and painted. He cut up boxes into A5 pieces, and studying the colours of trees, he painted hills, houses, trees and leaves. The next week he played more with the colours, and his mountains were purple, his trees full of yellow and red. At night he looked at the landscapes and imagined he could go there, and it helped him to finally sleep. He felt a little better for a while. Then one of the children's uncles was shot dead under the barrio bridge. And three days later he walked past a stranger, shot at the top of the barrio stairs. He described how the blood soaked into the concrete. And then he disappeared for four weeks.

(And another front: Billions forced to work long shifts with few or no holidays, especially the casuals, informals, and rural workers. Mentally and physically burnt out, stressed for years, struggling to stay awake then struggling to sleep, full of bodyhurt and unfocused eyes and clockwatch, missing out on life, rest, time to recharge, reflect, read, enjoy the world. No time to organise).

Mella's ten questions

Mella had been accumulating doubts. Doubts that were questions, braintickles that beseeched her. So one Saturday morning, on the back of a supermarket receipt, she wrote down the most urgent ones. Then she knocked on Alice's bedroom door and said, "Alice, I have ten questions."

Alice glanced at the receipt. "Questions are one of the loveliest gifts one can give. Ask me your first one now, and I'll make you breakfast. Then let's see if tomorrow we can look at the second."

Alice made rice pudding and Mella asked her, "Why are some people so greedy?"

The next morning Alice made a banana smoothie and Mella asked her, "What is freedom?"

Then on Monday Alice cut up two large slices of watermelon, and Mella asked her, "Isn't it logistically impossible to include everyone's opinions and needs and be totally democratic?"

On Tuesday, Alice made toasted Lebanese bread with fried tomato and onion for breakfast, and Mella asked her, "Where does apathy come from?"

On Wednesday, Alice made them mint milk tea and crumpets and Mella asked her, "Why are politicians so dull; is it strategic?"

On Thursday, Alice served Wheatbix with sultanas, and Mella asked her, "What types of power are there, and do they all corrupt?"

And so it went, until Mella had asked all ten questions. Each time, Alice wouldn't answer directly. Instead she suggested that Mella read a certain article or a certain chapter of a book, and she countered with more questions that would help Mella think through the issue. On the tenth day, though, Alice didn't make breakfast. She asked Mella to cook, and said that she had a story that might help her with some of her questions. Mella made thin pancakes and cooked some aging strawberries into a thick sweet sauce. Alice quietly watched Mella cook and played with her rainbow cotton scarf, eventually wrapping it around her forehead, then plaiting it into her long hair. When Mella brought the pancakes, Alice rested her forearms on the table, and never taking her eyes of Mella, she began.

"This is the story of a few weeks when Sydney woke up. On 15 February 2003, half a million people marched in Sydney as part of a global protest against starting a war in Iraq. They believed they could stop the war. I remember it clearly. The trains to the city were full, everyone had homemade placards, and everyone was excited, strangers talking to each other. And the tourists, Mella, who come here for koalas and the beach and food and fashion and seafood restaurants, walked around completely surprised, because they didn't know about this aspect of Sydney. The few workers and shoppers that hadn't come to the city to march were surprised too. Their eyes were like plates. There were just so many people.

"Then, a few weeks later, the US bombed Iraq. The 'Stop the War' collectives had said that if bombing began, we would march at 5:00 pm that day. I was at uni, and we handed out leaflets and the NTEU called a stop work. Random students took our leaflets and photocopied them and handed them out too. People wrote on the walls with chalk. The cleaner who normally removed our posters left them there that day, and crowds gathered around them. I remember how sad people felt, how concerned they were, asking us for more information about the bombing. We only had three hours to organise that protest, but twenty thousand people turned up. I stood on a fence and got the people around me chanting, 'One, two, three, four, we don't want your racist war!' and 'George Bush go to hell, we won't fight a war for Shell!' A tiny old woman blew hard into a whistle, over and over. The chants took on their own energy, moved from where we were to another area, grew bigger, then smaller, then a different one from somewhere else was taken up. On the other side of the road was a bus stuck in traffic, and the driver honked his horn, and the passengers waved at us. We chanted even louder, and I swear, Mella, that it echoed off the glass fronts of the buildings. And those few weeks, the city changed. It became about marching and protesting, chalk-writing, graffiti, posters, instead of shops. People weren't packed away in their houses, and politics wasn't up to Someone Else. Everyone tried to do something to stop the war; artists made t-shirts, singers stood on crates in the park, writers wrote articles and blogs, people organised meetings, and donated money. The idea that 'it will always be like this' was abandoned. People were hopeful, and things became clearer. Unjust death stopped being peaceful sleep, it became death again, Mella. The statue of liberty in New York cried black oil, and people noticed.

"After the war started though, some people felt defeated and the protests became gradually smaller. Also, the government didn't want the movement to get any stronger, and MPs and the media started to criminalise the protestors. We organised a student strike, and it was big, but by the time we got to John Howard's office, there were only about five hundred people left. They were the energetic ones, and we all jumped and chanted and danced. Then ten or so cops on horses blocked off the road, and hundreds of riot police formed lines around us so we couldn't go anywhere. A few people tried to get past, and the police tackled them and arrested them. We were detained there for two hours. The police pushed us around, trying to get us angry so that they could arrest us and make us look bad. Eventually they let us go, five at a time. They'd let us through one line, then they'd search us. A friend of mine who is a law student told one of the cops that they couldn't legally search us without reasonable suspicion, and the cop said, 'Yeah, well, one of our radios has gone missing, I suspect you stole it'. Channel 7 News announced that night that 'young protestors caused massive disruptions' and Current Affair on Channel 9 said, 'Up next, thugs and mugs...a disgrace, they don't give a damn'. Premier Bob Car called us 'violent extremists'. They showed footage of a cop holding a knife that they supposedly found on a protestor.

"So, on 2 April, we organised a rally in defence of our right to protest. Lots of parents came, older people, lawyers. But two hours before the rally was due to start, the police formed a double line barricade around the Town Hall square. It was a bit surreal, Mella. The head cop marched up and down the line, talking importantly on his phone, acting like some kind of army general about to go to war. And there we were, blowing bubbles, chatting, and painting peace signs. Then there was a group of teenage boys who looked a bit Middle Eastern and were hanging around a tree, talking. A line of police walked over and got into position behind them, I guess wanting to provoke them, but the teenagers just walked away. Then the police brought in a large cage for arresting people and announced over a PA every five minutes, "Attention, this protest is illegal, should you proceed to march you will be arrested." They really went to a lot of effort to stop us marching, and only a trickle of people could squeeze out through their lines anyway. So we stayed there and chanted and sang for three hours, and then a plain clothes cop sprayed capsicum spray into the air. It was mostly high school students that were closest to him, and they panicked and ran around in circles trying to open their eyes. And that's how it is; the more we resist, the more they do too."

Lists that don't exist
In June 2004, Durban, South Africa, nineteen-year-old Marcel King was defending his mother, who was trying to stop ANC council security guards from disconnecting their electricity. A guard shot him at point blank range, in his mouth.

And in August that year, in Harrismith, a town on the N3 highway from Durban, four thousand five hundred kids marched to protest the state of housing and public services, and an entire people's slow suffocation. Police shot at them with plastic bullets, pellet guns, and stun grenades. A stun grenade is a 'flash and bang'; a blinding, deafening explosion, and the Military Police Corps of the US Army used it as a way of neutralising and disorientating what they called "enemy personal, kidnappers, and terrorists". The enemy kids panicked and ran back into town, and a few threw stones back at the police. The police arrested thirty-eight of them, and charged them with public violence. They also shot seventeen-year-old Teboho Mkhonza, and while he was wounded from birdshot, they kicked him in the ribs and put him in a police van. He died from internal bleeding the next morning.

"There was no other way of controlling them," Policeman Kubheka said.

"That's all that's left of him," said Teboho's mother, throwing his bloodstained clothing on the floor.

Marcel and Teboho: just two more on the list that doesn't exist of those killed by the police with impunity.

Genoa

When a G8 Summit was held in July 2001, in Genoa, Italy, in a castle surrounded by a walled and fortified "red zone" which no one could enter, people came from around Europe to protest. They held a massive social forum, organised camping venues and accommodation, set up an eating area for a thousand people, information points, a three-storey stage and a media centre in a primary school. Before the summit, sixty thousand of them marched for migrant and refugee rights, and they held other protests for women's and worker rights. Peace protestors tried to enter the red zone with balloons. Two thousand nuns held a hunger strike demanding the cancelation of third world debt. There was a medical team, a team to provide water, and a team of fifty to pick up the tear gas canisters that they knew the police would use, and throw them away from the protestors. A team of seven was elected to make tactical decisions. Protestors sang and chanted in different languages. The police threw the gas canisters, which caused bodycrush as people found it hard to flee. They also raided the media centre and the social forum, leaving sixty injured and bloodstains on the walls and floors of the primary school. They drove their dark blue vans into the marchers, and shot twenty-three-year-old Carlo Giuliani at close range in the forehead and the cheek. Then they ran over him twice. Another person was added to the list that didn't exist.

Mella's one hundred questions

The more questions Mella asked, the more questions she had. They multiplied like dandelions...became fields of flowers expanding in yellow waves, curiosity unclenching, unravelling. Some of the questions were whole and ready to come out, others were vague trails of words that she shifted around inside her until they became clearer, more focused. She was realising she needed to know the world better. Know it in the way one knows a close friend, oneself, or a community. She felt she owed the world that, but also that not knowing the world now was like not knowing the streets of your own suburb, your local transport system, your local language. It made her feel vulnerable. She could be told that crime was high or floods were coming and to be afraid and she, in her present state, had to believe it. She had to go where she was told.

Then there was that thing Rafi had said to her recently: "I can't imagine how many people die with their eyes still closed."

eyes closed
ears closed
mouth closed...

She imagined people drowning in mud. And living then dying without ever wondering where they fitted into the global economy and power structures, or perhaps without imagining unobligated love, or knowing where their food came from. She wanted to take the world in her arms, open it up and look inside. Just like one might look inside a car. To find out how it worked, why things were happening. So she decided to study for two hours every night, on top of her classes with Rafi, and the books that Rain and Alice had suggested to her. Sometimes she went to the library to study, always sitting at the table in the furthest corner where the skinks hung out, watching her and dodging the air conditioning. A few times she went to the Botanical Gardens with Rafi. They sat on moist grass under hundreds of sleeping bats that dangled from the trees like ripe fruit, and they talked about Neruda's poems, the life of Sor Juana, the Egyptian rebellions, the development of capitalism, political earthquakes, evolution, icecaps, farming methods, and rap music.

"It's about which forces are doing things, and why, and in what context," Rafi said. Mella nodded and watched the bats sleep. It must be nice to wrap yourself in your own wings. Or in the soft wings of another. She was quiet for a while and hardly moved. But inside she had found fireworks. Her mind was sun. Her body tingled, blushed, ran, explored. And started to love, perhaps...

PAZ

Watching

The GEO Group, previously known as Wackenhut Corrections Corporation, would eventually take over Parklea Prison, where Paz was. It was a company that courts had found responsible for the death of inmates on a number of occasions. In Raymondville prison in 2001, Wackenhut was negligent in the death of Gregorio De la Rosa Jr. As he died, his body seizing and rattling as two inmates beat him, the guards had just watched. They had smirked and their laughter threw rifle shot up and down the walls, breaking flesh in its own way because their doing nothing meant everything.

Gregorio was thirty-three and had just four days left to serve on a six month sentence for possession of less than a quarter gram of cocaine. When a young person dies before their body and cells have decided to succumb, the universe makes a sound much like ripe fruit being run over by a train.

The game

Prison: where fairies, goblins, and curious critters suffocate slowly.

Dependence: A subtle, cunning, and invisible abuse, where the powerless depend on the powerful. A taught helplessness, reliance, and lack of self-sustainability. When, for example, rich governments provide conditional "aid" to poor countries, subordinating them in the process.

Paz was passed, drive-through style, through the first hearing. A judge who did not talk to him, a lawyer who did not ask or explain. He was refused bail. Now, Ward 24, a new home without a housewarming. They wouldn't move him again, which was uncommon. There was a formal policy, written down on papers: Move the prisoners around the prison circuit to different cells. Make them feel unstable, at the will of others. Also, a policy of divide to conquer—they put certain prisoners with certain skin colours in certain cells in order to set up gangs, so that they would fight amongst themselves, and not fight the guards. Paz, though, would never move from Ward 24.

He sat outside. Outside being outside his cell, not what it used to mean. Not trees and traffic lights and streets that carry people up hills and down them again. Paz sat in the common area looking at his reduced world and tried to work out how to make a phone call. He needed to talk to Ashley.

Who to ask, how to ask... He surveyed three floors of cells and focused on the observation pod above the hall with the guard moving in circles just like a goldfish, but with a gun. Tables, and their steel tube legs and the stools around them, four stools to a table, nailed to the floor. Another day, one with less copper anxiety to make one phone call, he would see the nooks and crannies, he'd see the odd bits of this militarised filing cabinet of a home. He would memorise the mattress stains and find rhythm in the sounds of the kitchen. He'd notice the irregularities in the bricks—chipped teeth. And he'd see the scraps of grass that had managed to squeeze through the concrete ground, bragging with wagging tongues of nature's resistance, or was it persistence? But no, not now. Now this place was a two-dimensional computer game. A beep-beep-music platform game from the 90s, without any magic diamonds.

Two character units in this game. One was the prisoners ghosting about in their three sizes of ill-fitting uniforms: asparagus green track pants (one), asparagus green t-shirts (two), asparagus green shorts (one), and their own strictly plain underwear. Also, closed black Velcro volleyball shoes. Velcro was safe. Can't hang yourself or choke someone with that. The prisoners were the edible dots of the computer game, moving, but without any function. Just there; hovered lives. Then a whistle would blow and they lined up at 6:00 am for the morning count, then again at 11:00 am for the second count. They worked in the laundry, in the kitchen and they cleaned the toilets and showers. They queued for their meals. They played cards every night during wing time. Finally, a last count, and into the cells for lockdown. Good sheep. Good computer game dots.

The other unit was the guards. Multi-coloured monsters, they'd eat you if you bumped into them. Computer game would make a deep wao-wao-wao sound, and then you died. The guards here, though, were not multi-coloured. They wore dark blue-grey uniforms, just like those of the police. But more grey, and 'GUARD' was written in bold yellow at the top of the backs of their shirts. And they had powers. They had watches (information), walkie-talkies in their holsters with a small speaker stuck just underneath their collars (quick coordination), whistles (control), pepper spray and batons (control level 2), a like for random room searches where they opened up beds, took off pillow cases, scattered personal effects over the floor, and accidently trod on sentimental photos (intimidation), and they had the keys (power).

First step of game, find the phone. Find the guard with the keys to the phone.

One guard unlocked the roller shutter to the prison shop, the hour-a-day canteen. As he lifted the bulky cluster of keys from his belt and inserted one, the smooth sound sequence of slide-in-turn-CLICK travelled around the hall, jabbing prisoners in the ribcage, and causing them to pause. Pause, just for a half-second, then resume (resume game, resume hoverlife). Because that sound, just like the shrill whistle that called them to count time, meant something. It was guard entering your cell, door being opened to visitors' room, door being shut on soft cell or solitary. It was morning wake-up and night lockdown. It was permission, or it was intrusion. It was locked inside and locked outside. Their ears were tuned to it; they heard it even above the unremitting prison shouting and the rhythmic screech of kitchen metal.

This guard, as guard of the shop, would know something about a phone call. Paz had few powers, just a range of greetings. He picked one, he talked to the guard.

"How can I make a phone call?"

"You need phone credit."

"How do I get that?"

"Work pay or from allowances transferred by your family."

And the game's beep-beep tripped. It threatened danger, but Paz asked anyway. "How can I ask someone to transfer me money if I just got here and I can't make a phone call?"

Then a prisoner with mop posture sitting at a table nearby said to Paz with a chin nod, "Come here..." Paz sat, then waited some, as the prisoner bent over scrap paper and coloured his boredom in with a graphite pencil.

The prisoner had three minutes left on his phone card and told Paz that he could pay him back later. An awkward thanks, but nothing else. No introduction; no name. Paz though, stayed a little too long, and observed the man's eyes. So many types of eyes he'd noticed in his life—eyes of the about-to-die, eyes of the young and unjaded, eyes of the 'been through love too many times', eyes of the settled into how it is. But eyes here were all very similar, injected with opaque glass. Paz said he would ask to borrow the card once he had permission, and then added another awkward thanks.

Paz tried another way. He walked over to the barred steel door leading to the guards' quarters, where the phone was located. He tried to get a guard's attention. A security camera pointed straight at his head. The security camera saw him, but the guard at the end of the hallway pretended he didn't. Paz leaned against the wall. He waited. The security camera rotated, refocused. And the guard finally walked over to the barred door.

"Yes?"

"I need to make a phone call. Another prisoner said he would lend me a phone card." Paz tugged on his earlobe, tried to hide a bit of nervousness behind his ear. The guard glanced at the phone on the wall. No one else was in the hallway.

"Okay. You can use it when it's free."

And Paz walked back to the hall, and waited again (waiting was his thing now, it was what prisoners did). He tried not to walk around in circles, or to look too closely at anything. After an hour, he returned to the barred hallway door. The same guard was there. "Yeah, the phone's not working," he said. As Paz turned around, he saw another guard come out of one of the offices and use the phone. A decision then: to try again after the guard shift changed.

One final time today, just before lockdown. Paz returned again to the hallway door, this time with his bar of expectation running low. Almost out of hope, almost out of fuel. He told the new guard he needed to make a phone call.

"Only with your own phone card," he replied.

For a few minutes the prison was quiet. Prisoners lined up outside their cells performing well-rehearsed, chemical conversions. Yellow frustration expressed as hostile negativity, or a fight in three days' time. Paz in his cell, appeared calm. An unaffected type, this one: the no-phone-call didn't bother him. But actually he was silently shouting all the things he wanted to say to Ashley down the blue mountains of his imagination. He looked at the small barred window, a tiny tunnel to the World, where she lived, where Matt did not. He and Ashley had sewn each other together one stitch per day, one stitch per late night conversation over cereal with banana. Now broken stitches waved around like sea anemone along the side of his body, and it was raw, red, and untouched.

Who holds the keys
In Haiti, after the earthquake, a retired bus driver pressed his face against the chain link fence of the airport to see what was happening on the other side. His sunburnt fingers held onto the gauge wire and budgiewhispered questions to the people on the other side.

"Which people hold the keys to the world? Who holds the keys to communication, to our resources, to health, to technological development?"

"If those people aren't elected, then why don't we call them dictators?"

On the other side of the fence, the U.S soldiers who had taken control of Haiti's Port-au-Prince airport were preventing aid planes from landing and were guarding the water, food, and medicine that had arrived days ago. The retired bus driver pressed his dry lips together. The soldiers didn't answer his questions.

Markers, chess sets, and chewing gum
"Three permanent markers for ten pesos! Three permanent markers for ten pesos!" he yelled out all day,

every day, standing in the middle of the busy stairs to Mexico City's Zocolo metro station.

His throat, legs, and feet hurt. And he was duplicated millions of times over; as the teenagers selling pirated music, chocolates, and gum on the trains below, as the middle-aged man who sold wooden chess sets in the tourist section of New Delhi, as other informal sellers of all sorts of mostly useless, plastic things: tea towels, plastic jewellery, phone covers, hair ties, badly translated children's books, light sticks. They lost their voice on the buses of Bolivia, on the median strips of Argentina, outside the universities of South Africa, and anywhere they could in Thailand. They were the world's unorganised army of the unemployed and uncounted.

Soldiering alone

"Got a dollar, luv?" the woman called out to each person that passed. She was sitting on a street bench, with her plump legs dangling, her white hair worn haphazardly, her clothes discordant. She coughed out her chant like a tennis ball machine, firing the balls at each person. She had to do it like that, because otherwise she would have felt as if she were talking to each person and being rejected over and over again.

Her bench was opposite a Vietnamese take-away shop with roasted ducks hung by their necks in the window. The owner stood in the shop doorway and contemplated the woman.

"Can't you go somewhere else?"

"No, luv. Got a dollar?"

"You're driving away my customers."

"Not me, luv. Those headless ducks are."

The owner tightened his face. "Go on, get out of here!"

"There's a bench here, so I can sit on it. Got a..." Her eyes chased a person who'd managed to sneak past.

"Got a dollar, luv, got a dollar, luv?" Two people walked past her together.

The owner shook his head, shrugged, and went back inside.

For sale

Three small children were selling pirated pornography in Tepito, one of the oldest barrios of Mexico City. Dressed in white and blue school uniforms, aged six to nine, they were climbing up and down the wire grid display, adding a few new DVDs to the stall. On one DVD cover was a woman sucking a penis. Another had a woman with her legs wide apart, her feet touching the bottom corners of the cover, a penis inside her. The youngest sister carefully arranged the DVDS, and reprimanded her brother for stopping to play. Their stall was located at the start of the maze of stalls of cheap, pirated, and stolen goods; of phones, imitation brand clothing, and mp3 compilations on USB sticks.

"These days the youth don't produce anything when they work; they don't make anything, they just unload stuff off trucks and sell it," Juancho from the local cultural collective said. His group organised craft workshops and played music in a small plaza near the station as part of what he called the war of culture against consumerism. A few old couples danced, the loud speaker squealed with feedback, and Juancho seemed tired.

Psychological weapon

Fear: the calloused accomplice of dependence, the psychological gun to people's heads making them act in discordance with their desires.

There was an unusual quietness in the prison, even lightweight optimism. It had just stopped raining, the concrete was wet and exciting, and most prisoners were in the wing area playing cards. Ashley had called and was coming to visit on Saturday. Paz, in his cell, thinking he was alone, tried to tap dance. Buppity-buppity-bup, boom. He wasn't good. He couldn't move fast like the pros, he couldn't vary the rhythm. He tried just stamping his feet up and down as fast as he could.

A head popped out from under a sheet: "Dude, you cold or something?"

His cellmate, glasses, hair to his chin and tucked behind his ears, and coat hanger shoulders, had been on and occasionally off drugs and alcohol for most of his life. He had also been in jail on and off for a decade, mostly for trumped-up charges. This time the police had arrested him for wielding a knife in public after searching his car and finding a camping pocket knife. He was now mildly brain damaged, and thought slowly. This afternoon his younger sister was coming to visit; just six and a half hours to go.

"So, can't believe you've never been on a motorbike," he said. He talked a lot about motorbikes. Paz knew a long spiel was coming so he sat down on his bed to listen.

"Scooters are all the rage now, but they're for novices. Motorbikes are the real deal, with bigger engines, mate. No scooters on the freeways! My mate used to buy old motorbikes and fix them up. He'd give them all the features: Mp3 player and radio, liquid cooling, CVT transmission, the rear top box..."

"A motorbike would be great for travelling around Australia," Paz said.

"Well, mate, when we get out of here, we'll each get us one and off we go!" He described which features would be the best for long distance travel. As his cellmate chatted, paused for minutes at a time, and resumed, Paz listed things in his head that he missed. Cottage cheese, documentaries about camels, waves, news of floods, sunburnt legs and the delight of peeling off the skin, fried mushrooms, barbeque smoke, Ashley's stomach.

Then, suddenly, a long whistle sounded. Paz sat up quickly; his cellmate stood up quickly. Cards were put down on tables. 'Random cell search' screamed the metal wind. And no one moved, because moving could be misinterpreted.

"Everyone into prisoner count positions!"

And everyone moved.

Guards stood at points along the count line with their guns aimed at the prisoners, while other guards with blue rubber gloves patted them down then entered the cells. The prisoners had their backs to their cells, but they could hear the guards picking things up and throwing them down, knifing mattresses and pillows open, and going through notebooks and magazines. Then the guards came out, all at once, and spat bruises and blankets onto the corridor floor.

"Prisoner 2909, step forward!" It was Paz's cellmate.

"Personal photos are not allowed, prisoner 2909!" said a guard, waving a photo of the cellmate's younger sister.

"That photo has been approved..."

"Are you speaking back to me?"

The guard pulled the cellmate's arm behind his back, and grabbing him by the hair, marched him down to the wing area. He twisted him down onto the floor and four more guards surrounded him so that all that could be seen were five dark, blue-grey uniforms moving their arms and elbows in rapid jabbing and stabbing towards softthing in the middle of their circle.

(Briefly back to convict Australia, when the British poor who had stolen bread or cloth or sold their bodies, were punished with transportation to Australia, and their labour was used to build the invasion, the colony, and dig its roads. If the convicts pretended to be sick in order to get out of work, or if they ran away or got drunk, they were punished. That is, the once-punished were punished again by being strapped to wooden beams and lashed with a whip or cat-o-nine-tails fifty or a hundred times until their flesh was mincemeat.)

One guard got up and said to a bit of the cellmate's shoe that was sticking out of the guard-huddle, "Stand up!"

The shoe twitched, but it didn't seem able to stand up. For his lack of obedience, a guard sprayed tear gas into his eyes.

(Watching from the count line, Paz imagined that he was Ned Kelly, and it was 1880, and he was walking towards the guards in the 44-kilogram metal suit, and they were shooting at him and the bullets bounced off and they were running away screaming, "It's a bullet proof bunyip!," just as they did with the real Ned Kelly. Then, like Ned Kelly, Paz locked up the police in their own cells.)

With his cellmate on the floor, and a guard making declarations over him, "For violating rule number...I sentence you to seven days segregation and loss of visiting privileges..." Prisoners picked up the blankets and bruises and put them back in their places. They swept up the bits of broken butterfly parts scattered like glass where the guard huddle had been. They straightened their crooked shirts and their crooked cells and went back to the previous quietness.

No high rise twin towers fell that day. No media went crazy, jumping over each other for the best shot of the pain. It was a short earthquake that came, and passed, and all the prisoners thought it didn't matter and they didn't care because you can't care about a violence that is daily.

With visiting privileges revoked, his cell mate, at that moment picking dried blood from his nose and flicking it around the segregation cell, didn't get to see his sister. Paz thought about Ashley's visit in a few days. And he was thinking that Punishment is not something inflicted by the good upon the bad, but rather by the powerful upon the powerless.

War front: fear battled rationality

Fear took its fight to a new level when the people of the US watched the twin towers fall forty thousand times on the television, and they still couldn't believe it, because war was something their government did to everyone else.

They were in shock, and the US government and CNN and Fox television took that shock and puttied it into fear. Bush declared a War on Terrorism and the media chorused hysterically, hypnotically: Terrorists! Al Qaeda! Bin Ladin! Terror threat! Enemy! Muslims! And there was anthrax and poisoned pens, and a terror thermometer set to red, and sometimes lowed to orange. Colour-coded simplicity for the people turned children by shock. A world turned red and orange. Dangerworld! And seven hundred and sixty-two mostly Muslim so-called suspects were detained, but never charged, and thousands more foreigners were detained and held incommunicado. Rationality stood on a street corner and called for analysis, reflection, logic, history, and more information, and was arrested, locked up, and covered by a large white sheet like an unwanted memory.

Many red and orange people tolerated the increased airport security, bought, if they could afford it, solid steel safe-rooms, hesitated to open mail, ran away when someone left a backpack in a shop, tried not to go outside, and stopped criticising their government. Some verbally abused Muslims, attacked mosques, and even a Hindu temple, and murdered Balbir Singh Sodhi, a gas station attendant and a Sikh, not a Muslim, but with a turban and a beard it was enough to shoot him five times. The same day they killed an Egyptian born man and a Pakistani man, the next day a twenty-year-old Saudi Arabian student. They had chanted anti-Arab abuse as he left a night club, and so it went on.

Rationality cried.

Fear celebrated in the empty streets and empty airports.

Bush told people he would put them in a cage, and they said okay, because they thought they'd be safer there. He passed the USA PATRIOT Act seven weeks after the towers fell, when his support was at ninety percent. Red and orange support. The act allowed the government to deport foreigners for association with any group the attorney general didn't like. The government could freeze the assets of any entity without having to prove anything. Civil liberties remanded, various Muslim charities shut down. People put pillows and televisions in their cages and got comfortable.

Pillows in cages

Fourteen hours until Ashley's visit. Paz was counting, playing with maths, lying on his back on his cell bunk bed, pointing at the rungs of the bed above as he counted. Two more hours of wing time, an hour in the cell before lights out, seven hours of sleep, morning count and breakfast, three hours of laundry work.

Then he went over his list. His hungerlist of insidequestions about how she was right now, how Eva was, and the others... Touching the rungs he imagined he was taking them out and moving them around; revising his list, re-prioritising. He wanted a detailed answer for this question, so maybe last was best. But he wanted time for her to respond, so perhaps second.

Then there was a noise outside, and he held the question in the air as he looked towards his cell door and the wing area. A guard had stopped outside the cell to the left.

"Ya lazy Abo scum... I know your type, you like it up the ass... Your little mate...hanged himself...one less Abo for us to worry about," he was saying.

The guard was bored. It sounded like he would keep going until he got an explosive reaction. Paz dropped his question onto the floor and sat up. He shuffled backwards on his bed away from the cell door. He should say something, something that would make the guard stop the abuse. But there was his list of questions. She was coming tomorrow. And he wanted to get out of prison as soon as he could; he didn't want any parole strikes.

In that moment he made a decision that every prisoner, and most human beings, make once, or over and over again. The decision between doing what you believe is right and what is expedient, between speaking out or being subordinate.

Paz folded his thin pillow in two and put his head on it, facing the wall. He put his free arm over his one exposed ear, and closed his eyes.

Another little piece of him died.

And when he tried to dream, to imagine something far away and amazing; orange-yellow dragons with kind eyes and flute tails, they fell to the floor, deflated. Try something else. Try the past. The past couldn't deflate, could it? He tried to remember the time that they'd all danced in the living room, all of them except Ashley. The memory did not deflate, but it was cardboard shaped and cardboard flavoured.

Thirteen hours to go.

Waste Mountain

Waste Mountain grumbled with greed. The sound that emanated from its entrails of exhaust pipes, its inner knots and tunnels of the unused, the rejected, was a deep haunting sound, rather like the word 'more'. More more more, it said. And people obliged. Time split and splintered as it landed on top of the mountain. Dignity fell and flopped and rolled down the mountainside. Possibilities were scattered upon it, and independence, smelling of burnt skin, fell, together with rationality, poetry and platonic love, around its base. Play and sensitivity sank right into its centre.

Waste Mountain grew and grew, and the little earth sneezed. It had fever.

MELLA

What is beauty? Mella's fish in tanks

Time passed and it seemed to be a race, with the days flip-flopping over each other and even the months spooning the next with rushed affection. Six months, then seven, each day gone, leaving just a few skid marks and trails of silver dust in its path. Mella wanted to hold time by its waist and stop it running so fast, but it would have been useless; she would have dangled behind it like an origami bird tied to a bullet train.

And as the salty night angled over the city's profile, this day was almost over too. The Rock for Refugees was wrapping up and the ones-who-always-stay-till-the-very-end had moved outside the dancehall where the lack of walls and the sweetair allowed them to dance as they wanted. Mella watched from the doorway as huge and hairy Vladimir bounced around like an electric bowling ball. A woman did the steam engine dance, and her child copied her. Rafi, in his tigerdance traintoot chimneypuff world at one point slowed down a little and pointed at her and winked. She forced a wink back, a wink without chimneypuff. A little while later he came back, and glittering sweat, said, "Let's help pack up, then we can go to the train together."

It was a long walk to Town Hall station, so when they reached the George Street cinema entrance to the network of underground pedestrian shopping tunnels, they decided to take a short cut. Past midnight, all the shops were closed, their lights and signage dark and the window displays and doors covered with metal shutters. In the tunnel, Rafi and Mella felt like they should talk quietly. About important things. If it had been day, and the tunnel had been filled with its usual clamour of thousands of high-heels and office shoes rushing to work, they wouldn't have been able to talk at all. But now, in the quiet and after the night of energetic dancing, things needed to be said.

"Rafi, I often feel ugly, pathetic, shy, and incapable of talking to anyone."

Rafi smiled. When Mella did talk, she said things straight, and he liked that. He pointed down a tunnel at a seat where the Town Hall Square fountain splashed after hours, starting at ground level and falling down a large square opening into the tunnel. "Let's sit for a bit," he said.

She sat close to him, it was cold. A pigeon flew down the opening and into the tunnel and proceeded to walk around in curlypaths as though exploring. It had an apple sticker on its head. Mella followed it with her eyes, welcoming an excuse to not look at Rafi, because she felt ashamed. "These feelings make it hard to function. How can I do contact work if I can't even talk to people?"

Rafi knew what he needed her to understand, but he didn't know how to explain it. He looked around, stalling. There was a greeting card shop opposite them. Slightly slanted shelves displayed $4.95 and $6.95 cards in a range of categories. Mass produced messages of blueprint love. The shop to the left had its shutter down, but they both knew it was the pendant and bracelet shop, where identity came with its own assembly kit. Rafi was thinking about these things and he wanted to tell Mella that she was raw, gentle, and selfless. But he searched for better arguments.

A music store. Pop music, made to a commercially-defined pattern with lyrics snapped apart and stuck back together again in slightly different combinations. Fast food music.

"This is how it is, Mella," Rafi finally said. "They put fish in tiny tanks and sell them, while at the same time contaminating and poisoning the ocean. They reduce wellbeing and happiness to advertising concepts. They would pluck the stars out of the sky and put them in packages and onto shelves if they could, and if eventually the sky had almost no stars, it wouldn't stop them. They do the same to human beings, especially women. They try to package you. But, if you think of yourself in those terms, if you commercialise your own incredible beauty, you will probably feel a bit unattractive. Most of us will. But we're more interesting and more meaningful than their packaged love, their factory lyrics. Mella, hunt for what is truly interesting."

The pigeon with the apple sticker circled around and walked right under their legs. Mella watched it as it walked towards the card shop, then back towards them. Then in a corner of the fountain it fluffed its feathers to ready itself for sleep. Rafi talked. He mentioned some strange phone calls about his residency visa. But Mella was cold and curled up, as if imitating the pigeon. Rafi touched her shoulder, and they both got up to go. The pigeon slept.

The global indignity

People uncomfortable because the bed is broken and sewage surges outside and the buses are overcrowded, and they are living between corrugated walls—card houses about to fall. They are living in slums, or in the slums of their minds, the slums of work cubicles or assembly lines. People in second hand clothes compelled to be quiet. People ashamed and hiding themselves beneath their roofs made of tin or asbestos or one old sheet. The rain is louder on some roofs, and leaks down the walls onto a thin mattress. People having secret abortions, missing out on dental care, missing teeth, tired faces, bent backs.

A global low self esteem. Global anxiety. Global insomnia. Disposable people. Disposable in war, disposable in work, like plastic cups and plates. People exposed, naked, unprotected, without privacy, shamed, powerless. Shades of indignity from overcrowded housing to those wearing ties and suits and carrying smartphones; but they all live in one box in the end, the one outside the boardrooms where the decisions are made. A global feeling of ugliness, and a global urge to give up. Globalised apathy sometimes broken by a scream, broken by a poem, broken by a guitar, by a song, broken by a united protest, broken by a strike, broken by an insurrection. Broken by an 'ugly' person refusing to be ugly. Standing up and saying, "You can't fucking treat us like that."

Stealing

There were rich people with neckties instead of crowns who went around at night and used straws to steal. In mosquito-like ways, they sucked out the essence of things and left the husks behind. They stole the world's flowers and replaced them with plastic ones. They stole real food and replaced it with GMOs and junk food (plastic food). They stole art and replaced it with pomposity. They stole free speech and replaced it with advertising. They stole the mountains and replaced them with mines. They stole talent and replaced it with human resources. They stole delight and replaced it with canned laughter.

They stole beauty.

The many moons in Rafi's fingers

Rain strolled, long steps, into the Resist office and dropped four newspapers onto the table. Rafi was giving Mella a class on the relationship between education and economic systems, and they both looked up at the source of the softbang and horizontal gust of air made as the newspapers landed in front of them.

"Hi!" Rain said, grinning proudly at what he had brought.

"Anything interesting? Anything for the kids?" Rafi asked, picking up the top one.

"Comics? No, that's Sundays, ya doof."

Rain went over to the computer to design a leaflet, and Rafi sprung up to scan the bookshelf, and brought back three books. Studying, Mella was becoming more aware of things around her. She was catching trains and wondering how long the drivers' shifts were. She was buying cereal and wondering where it was produced, if any trade agreements were involved, and if the corn farmers received subsidies. But her senses were also opening up, and now she heard the sincerity in Rafi's eyes, saw the small cracks and fissures in the words he tried to hold together, and felt the coldness of her exercise book paper as she wrote. She felt a warmth stretch up her back, because though she was worried about the cracks in Rafi's words, she was also enjoying their class together.

Rafi had been arguing that there were two kinds of education; one that encouraged conformity and acceptance through a focus on fact memorising, and another that encouraged participation in society through a focus on critical thinking and active, community based, learning. Mella had two columns on her page and was writing words in each, and now she noted the names of the three books on the next page.

"Freire called it the banking concept of education, where the student is basically an empty vessel that the teacher tries to pack full of information," Rafi said, tapping the column in her book. He spoke softly, and when she said something he listened intensely. The warmth in her back spread up her shoulders and down her arms. Rain typed away on the very old, yellowing keyboard, and she heard the distinctive click-thud sound each letter made as he pressed them. She liked the sound of heavy typing, it had determination. Rafi and Mella talked about what they'd been taught and not taught at school, "how to be good workers but not how to be good humans," Mella said. Rafi pointed out that only certain types or classes of people were studied in history. "They even teach economics as though a few incredible individuals are the only actors and no one else does anything," he said. "They make out history and economics to be abstract incidents that have nothing to do with our current lives, and we're not made aware of how they influence us or how we influence them," he added. Mella watched how Rafi's slight sadness and some 3:00 pm drowsiness shaded his eyelids. She noticed the faint discolorations where sticky-tape had been, in contorted patterns around the office walls, echoed in character by a few coffee rings on the table where they worked. A haunted little moth swung from a spider web between two bookshelves. Wet parrot feather smell came out of the carpet. And she saw Rafi's hands, pen marks on his left fingers, recently cut nails with pale sleeping moons at their bases. No freckles, few hairs, no watch.

"It seems that awareness gives our life context and connects us to the world and its peoples, and that as we learn, we remake ourselves over and over again. That puts a lot of responsibility on teachers," Mella said, and paused. She looked at Rafi's finger moons and at his loudeyes. A medium-size red balloon, like a ghost passing through walls, entered her chest and lodged itself there. Her crush whispered 'hello' to her, and settled in.

"Are you alright?" Rafi asked, touching her hand.

"Yeah, I... really enjoy these classes with you, and I've been thinking lately that I'd like to be a teacher. It wouldn't be easy though; I really need work now, and I'd have to do a TAFE bridging course on top of that, and then apply for university."

"You should do that," he beamed. She beamed back, maybe for a bit too long, and her glance became a gaze.

She heard that Rain's keyboard sounds were different now. They were slower and broken by mouse clicks. He had finished typing the leaflet and was going through a contact list. It had over three hundred names on it, and one by one he was clicking a name and assigning it an A, B, or C, according to priority. Though Rain sometimes became grumpy in long bank queues or when trains were delayed, he was patient with social change. Some people said too much so, that he fell into the trap of routines. Yet everyone also knew that he wouldn't become tired and frustrated after a few years of activism, and give up.

Mella decided she wanted to invite Rafi over for a movie and a couscous dinner. Just because it would be nice. But the red balloon was poking out goosebumps and forcing swallows, and telling her that it was actually something more than that. She started to ask, but hesitated. She would ask him later.

"Have you noticed how simplistic advertising is?" she asked. "It talks to us like children. Maybe because they don't have profound arguments as to why we should buy their stuff, so they appeal to our emotions instead. And because of the way our education system works, and the slogan-based advertising we consume every day, we become simple thinkers, and lazy, and we want things quick and easy. We shy away from complexity."

Rafi agreed, and talked about the importance of debate, doubt, and analysis. "When fear controls us, things become cloudy. Which brings me to the practical part of today's lesson," he said, laughing excitedly. "I'd like you to take another small step in confronting your fear of talking to people. You're going to go downstairs and ask the first stranger you see if they think education here is getting worse. But first, analyse the situation." Then, without meaning to, he gazed instead of glanced. And made Mella's warm back quite hot. She tried to focus on the present and reasoned that the worst that could go wrong was that the person wouldn't want to talk to her. Perhaps they'd had a bad day, and it wasn't personal. There was also a good possibility that it would be fine and that she'd have an interesting conversation. Rain and Rafi were already standing at the window, waiting for her to go downstairs.

"Good thinking, Mella. Now go!" Rafi said.

The first person Mella saw was a man in a long beige coat, walking very fast. She decided he was busy, and waited for the next. The next was a man with three small children, and she passed on him, too. He seemed agitated. He was pulling the kids along, jerking at their arms. She would talk to the next person, no matter what. He turned out to be a policeman. Mella approached him, and he seemed confused, but answered her. She got high-fives when she went back to the office. She laughed, hiding her face, but she didn't ask Rafi over for couscous that day.

Underneath the concrete footpath

And underneath the concrete city, lay the bones of man-made deaths and the rubble and remains and last dusty evidence of so much organised injustice. And organised resistance. All of it was covered up, silenced, invisible under concrete, quicklime lies and seven o'clock sitcoms. Real history buried under skyscrapers that would never scrape the sky. Giant obelisks, trophies to the egos of a few. A mathematical equation; the taller the tower, the more was forgotten.

Ways of educating

In the barrios of Merida, that mountain city of no wind and purple night clouds, there was an alternative school. The people of the barrios had spent years held hostage to the slavery and abuse they inherited down the generations. They'd become accustomed to the violence and they beat their children, who passed on the beatings.

At the alternative school, tiny little Isa, seven years old, always sticking her tongue out and pulling the most outrageous faces, was asking the doctor there to pick her up and spin her around. Isa, who was afraid of no one, who talked to anyone, and who would stand up in class and scream for as long as she could, grinning...always grinning.

Then the school meeting began, and the teachers and the doctor talked about the history of the barrio, about how it had started off as a temporary place for rural workers to camp before they sold in the market, then it had become a more permanent settlement. Later, drugs had arrived, brought by the students at the university nearby, and by people wanting to wipe out political movements.

Isa sat in on the meeting. Like the others, she raised her hand to go on the call list. When it was her turn, she became shy. She ummed and ahhed and looked at the table.

A teacher helped her: "Where are we?"

"In Merida."

"Where in Merida?"

"At the bottom."

"What's our barrio like?"

"I like the teachers."

She went on the call list several more times, more confident each time. "My contribution is going to be short!" she said, with her usual big grin.

She sat through the whole six-hour meeting, quietly listening, sometimes pulling faces, and sometimes winking, in turn, at each teacher. She didn't know it, but she was learning how to organise. A few years later she and other youth of the barrio organised their own cultural group, supported by their own fundraising. The older ones in the group quickly became community leaders.

Ways of seeing

1. When a couple broke up, the woman's friend told her to look at life from very far away. He said, "Go to Pluto and

look at yourself, at the earth, at history". She did, and she calmed down, a little.

2. The couple had loved each other deeply because they had looked at each other very closely. They learnt details, like his red and blue nightmares, her sensitivity, his appreciation of religious art, her strange sleeping habits, his back moles, her problems with her father. By looking at things close-up they came to understand that normality did not exist. That human beings were much more interesting than that.

3. Then there was looking at something as though it wasn't there at all. Imagine life without water, without the sun, a friend, television, salt and vinegar chips, and you become aware of how important or unimportant that thing is. She tried to imagine a world without words. She realised that with words, we made love, got angry, showed empathy, remembered our history and made our future. Words were magical.

Love without salt or cinnamon

Cold days of dry tongues
    Computer anger, faceless people
    at factory funerals
    Crying, passion, burning jealousy
    Rotting under our fingernails
    Drying up between our teeth
    Falling from the sky as unvented acid rain
    Unused kisses wandering the streets
    Missing their mark
    In a world without poetry

Where planes go

Hundreds of pink and purple planes with down feathers on their plane underarms flew overhead, making holes in clouds. Rafi had brought her books, and she talked with him in the streets as the holes from the clouds fell out of the sky and landed in piles nearby. She had hot toes and he gave her chest stars. She gave him kiss smoke. Rafi waved and backed away.

Mella twisted awake out of afternoon couch siesta, put on her sandals and got ready to go to the Resist office for another class with Rafi, stuffing her little dream out of sight in a small pocket in her jeans.

The office door was unlocked when she got there, but the light was off and no one was inside. She walked around in the barely-lit, dyingsun office and thought how strange it was that Rafi wasn't there yet. Something was wrong, like it wasn't just the lights that were off but the books, the chairs, the tables, the walls, and even the posters were off.

The phone rang and Mella answered.

"Who's this?" said the voice.

"It's Mella. Alice? Are you at work?"

"Ah, Mella... Rafi's been deported."

Ice filled her chest. For a minute she was justbones.

"What? But... I thought he had a permanent visa. I don't understand, and he..."

"I know, not much warning. Spent last night in the detention centre. He told them he wouldn't go back to Iran voluntarily, so they issued a deportation order. They took him to the airport this morning. He suspected that it was because of his political organising; the main way of cancelling a permanent visa is for failing a character test."

Rafi's fingers, with their white sleeping moons, in handcuffs. Planes not purple flying off to a far-away place...

Loud

Mella was back in the Town Hall square, this time without Rafi. She stood by the top of the fountain that fell into the tunnel shops and looked down at the spot where they had sat. The shadow of a metal chair, part of café furniture brought out during the day, cut across the spot.

Around her, the square was filling with people for a

rally for refugee rights. The weather had been hot and humid all day and even the trees had seemed to sweat, and now grey sky and strong wind arrived. Soon, in an hour or so, the storm would wash the city. Cars would pull away, leaving dry rectangles of road behind them that were quickly obliterated by the road rivers. Now though, the crowd, with hair lashing their faces, was holding down hats and skirts and slitting its eyes against dust and grit. Wind currents of rubbish; cigarette butts, torn corners of chip packets, straws and napkins, darted around legs.

Mella had been asked to speak at the rally, and she looked up from the fountain to the crowd that was growing bigger and bigger. Near her stood a middle-aged woman with dyed red hair, a man tying a brown scarf into knots because it kept flapping off and flying onto the tree, and a young man with a handful of fliers. He had been handing them out and now half the crowd was holding the A5 black and white piece of paper in their hands, reading it, or folding it up for later. Someone sipped coffee, someone held their child's hand, someone smoked, someone texted, and a kid on a bike paused on the edge of the sea of people to see what was happening. And there were placards being buffeted by the wind, big word signs displaying quick summaries of their Objections. Today: border and immigration policy, and the policy (and acceptability) of treating people, due to the location of their birth, like shit.

Mella became a body of out-of-time drums. All hammer-heart, pressure cooker breath, sweat streamlets. She was a list of 'what ifs'. What if I get up there and my voice is squeaky; what if they laugh; what if I can't remember what I was going to say? It's too hard, I can't. She counted the reasons, hoping to find a good one to withdraw. Her hammer-heart counted with her. She wasn't good enough; someone else should do it.

"Someone else always means nobody. It's shedding one's responsibility," Rafi argued back from inside her head. And he told her to analyse the fear away, and she did. And she remembered her decision to struggle and to not be subordinate.

Alice came over and squeezed her hand. "Ready?" she asked. Clouds crossed the sun and the wind relaxed. The darting rubbish dropped to the ground. Hats, hair, skirts, banners and placards settled.

Mella walked up the steps on the side of the Town Hall building to the place they used as a stage. One of the co-chairs of the rally handed her the microphone. Mella began, "The Australian government deports refugees back to the countries from which they have fled in terror. Some are sent forcibly, others are offered money to return to countries like Afghanistan and Iran, and if they refuse the offer, they will be forcibly deported anyway. We're here today to make a strong and clear statement. Refugees are welcome here."

And then a plane flew overhead. It had just taken off and the sound cut her off for a few seconds. She thought about where planes went, and how crossing borders was easier for some, impossible for others, and forced for others. And so she shouted for the first time in her life, "Refugees are welcome here!"

Wind again flapped hair, gently now, and man with scarf, woman with red hair, person holding coffee, even boy on bike, cheered to say, Yes! Yes they are welcome here.

That night in bed, Mella piled up pillows and looked at the ceiling and imagined a world without borders. The poor majority pulling down its leaking roofs, taking over five-star hotels, taking over factories. Erasing the numbers etched upon their foreheads that declared them just another death, just another worker, just another disease. She imagined flower petals tumbling from their lips, colours exploding in the air around them. Red, blue, pink; sun yellow, sun orange. Eyes, previously blank, turned off, hypnotised, painted on... now trembling, crying viscous flames. Eight billion daytime stars leaping, skipping, meeting, arguing. She imagined what unafraid looked like. She imagined an enormous sense of *Finally*.

The number of colours

The known story of the world was a monotone cartoon. Western television and media ignored most of the world, and simplified and stereotyped the rest of it. Tunisia, Egypt, Ecuador and Zimbabwe didn't exist, and people in Iraq were irrationally angry, bearded people, and everyone talked funny except themselves. It was a ridiculous narrative, yet accepted by too many.

In Tunisia on 17 December 2010, Mohamed Bouazizi, 26 years old, no beard, and the sole income earner in his family of eight, set himself on fire. That day he had been working, selling vegetables from a cart, and a policewoman confiscated the cart. When he tried to pay the fine— equivalent to a day's earnings—the police slapped him and spat in his face. When he tried to complain, he was refused an audience. So he doused himself in petrol and he burnt himself in public because it wasn't just about the policewoman, it was about unemployment, poverty, corruption, invisibility, and monotone cartoons.

Bouazizi died in hospital on 4 January, but his immolation sparked daily nationwide protests. Lawyers rallied, were beaten, and went on strike, and then the teachers joined them. Police repressed the protests and killed hundreds, but on 14 January, Tunisian President Zine El Abidine Ben Ali fled to Saudi Arabia after twenty-three years in power.

The protests spread to nearby Egypt. Hundreds of thousands, and later millions, demonstrated around the country. In Cairo's huge Tahrir Square, people formed a pulsating sea of accumulated grievances. A small teenage woman chanted and the nearby crowd repeated. A father with a son on his shoulders handed out water. We won't go until the dictator goes, they all insisted, and set up tents. The government imposed a curfew that the protestors defied, and the sea in Tahrir Square grew each day.

On 28 January 2011, "The day Egyptians lost their fear" Al Jazeera called it, after hours of marching forward and tolerating water cannon, protestors retook the two-kilometre-long Kasr al Nile Bridge from the police.

In all, eight hundred and forty-six protestors were killed and finally, on 11 February 2011, President Hosni Mubarak resigned, ending his thirty-year rule. The Egyptians managed to topple a dictator that many had known since they were born, a dictator that they had assumed was Part of Life. There was an after party, and it was televised. From a balcony an elderly woman looked out at the crowd. Then she ran downstairs and danced. The world watched multi-coloured faces shout and cry.

Merida, Venezuela, 2010
They met on Wednesday nights at the local school. Tropical rain blew cold air in and forced them to raise their voices. Sometimes, there were blackouts. Those days, while seated in an awkward circle of chairs that accommodated the strange shape of the small school dining room, they talked by the light of the moon, or the dim fairy lights of mobile phones.

The slogan of their communal council was 'the community working for the community'. Their council was one of thirty thousand such councils in Venezuela, created so communities could solve their own problems. In the little school dining room, they made new kinds of decisions. Not what to buy, what to wear, or what to eat decisions, but how to live decisions. For the first time, neighbours got to know each other.

Saramago, in his novel about everyone going blind and the resulting chaos, wrote, "And how can a society of blind people organise itself in order to survive? By organising itself, to organise oneself is, in a way, to begin to have eyes."

Kinds of decisions

"George Bush will be visiting Australia for bilateral talks at the end of October," said the radio, the television, the internet news alerts, said Mella to Alice, turning up the dining room radio.

By the next night, eighty people, including Alice and Mella, had formed a protest coordinating group. Meeting in a dimly-lit function room above a city pub, they debated whether the protest should be the day that Bush visited, or the day before, at what time, and where. Then a vote; hands in the air, two people standing at the front counting, decisions made. An initial division of labour on the whiteboard; media (press releases, press contact lists, media stunts), publicity (design, printing, handing out the leaflets and sticking up the posters, stalls), logistics (sound equipment, legal team, donations and fundraising to pay for the equipment, rally speakers), networking, the next meeting. That night Mella went to bed at 12:30 am. That night no one coloured boredom in with graphite pencils.

That night drywhitebread politicians made the old kind of decisions. Security, numbers of police, budget. A quick drywhitebread statement to the press. Hard to imagine them painting murals at night, singing trova, whispering long poetry, getting angry at injustice. Not them. Democracy was a parliament play, and not one character in it had a beard or was a young woman or an Iraqi refugee or travelled by public transport.

Apathy bombs

They cast a spell of ash. It was a bomb of apathy that they dropped onto Sydney, dimming people's senses and sprinkling 'whatevers' into ashen lungs. Ashwords and subtle messages clouded the media, television, classrooms, and workplaces. People shrugged.

Mella tried to do a campaign spot at the entrance to a Sunday farmers' market. Set-up in a school parking lot, stalls sold organic fruits and vegetables, homemade cheeses and yoghurts, jams, chocolates, sourdough bread, coffee, flavoured olive oils, Thai chilli plants, handicrafts, and more. Mella held out her leaflets for the 'Stop Bush' protest. In four hours, a few people looked interested and stopped to talk; many took the leaflet and put it in their bag or pocket without reading it, and quite a few threw it in the bin on the other side of the fence where Mella stood. Many people refused to take it, saying "no thanks" or "not interested" or "why would I do that?" Others ignored her. Mella saw ash in their hair and under their eyes as they walked past her to taste or touch the products, to pull out their wallets and buy another thing. She felt like she was begging, "Would you like to stop a war, please? Or protest a murderer touring the world in style?" She watched ashen fingers draw blinds across the world, search for the strawberry panadol to ease a worldmigraine, buy things and bathe in that easy anaesthetic for the saddened soul. Elsewhere, people had apathy in their throat. Ashvoices. Mella thought of the way apathy fogged the streets near where she lived, where the long term unemployed and the usurped kept their eyes to the ground. Pissed off and uninterested, their voices croaking out quick streams of swear words, their fingers searching for a cigarette instead of Panadol.

Mella finished handing out the rest of the leaflets. It was just the beginning of building the protest, and she knew that. Still, for just a few minutes she let herself sit in the spotty shade of a eucalyptus tree and imagine that she had the magic to break the spell.

Birth of a placard
They would need placards for the protest, but they were all out of materials. While one team walked the streets

looking for discarded cardboard boxes to use, four others got into Vladamir's car and drove around until they found a street full of 'For Sale' signs. Alice got right into it, taking down one sign quicker than the other three working on another sign. Then she charged down the street to the next sign, ripping it off its wooden stakes without even using a pocket knife. Mella imagined someone walking down the street the next day wondering where all the signs had gone.

Weighing rocks

Mella sat on a bench next to a bin. Someone had said: "Have a good day" at the end of another job interview, and she had said nothing. Her mouth hadn't even wanted to give a smile. Still Unemployed. Like breathing in and out, life seemed to need its ups and downs to keep it moving forward. Today was down, and Mella felt her head throb and her face flop. Toothache too, but no money to see the dentist. Barely enough for the train to the city for the job interview. She wanted to marvel at today's cloudshapes. She wanted to sleepndream and nightskip and lovealot, but today, all she got when she tried to daydream were monotone cartoons, squeaky mockeries.

Alice said, "You poor thing." Hugwords for her; soothing tea.

"Okay, let's go for a walk then. Lend me one of your rainbow scarves," Mella said, and Alice was delighted.

"Of course!"

Down the street at 4:00 pm, the otto bins out for Tuesday otto day, cars parked perfectly, lawns trimmed, trees trimmed, passion trimmed. Mella and Alice chatted like gentle leaf rustle. Two budgerigars; one blue, one green. Their sandals pattered. Mella's long hair fluttered. She would never cut it, never.

"Not even when you're old?" Alice asked.

"Not even then."

Mella talked about her rocks. Her little loads of worries tied from her arms and legs, from everywhere, pulling her earlobes down, her eyelids down, pulling at her teeth. Alice held the rocks and examined them, played with them, joked, and Mella felt better. Ready for an up-day. Ready to go home and make a plan. As it seemed she wouldn't be able to study teaching, she'd make a list of other jobs. And an hour each morning of job searching, calling, and cover letter writing. But no more than that, because she couldn't let Unemployed become her life. There was so much more to do.

The many worlds we live in
The untouched world of the unloved

The semi-silent world of the ignored

The uncounted world of those without bank accounts

The always raining world for those who live outside what is considered society, who live in informal housing on muddy river banks, mountainsides and under bridges

The shaky world of the always drunk

The overcrowded world of people who think they are ugly

The little-less-sun world of people hiding something

The life lived one or two days a week world of workers

The endless ladder to the sky world of those who think they have Careers

The fun park world of polished cars, high wine, fashionable food and new outfits for every occasion of the rich

The planet is my theatre world of the powerful

They try to tell us that the worlds we live in are contained within dotted borders on maps, and that you can travel between worlds with a passport and a bus or plane ticket. It's true that the walls between some of the unacknowledged worlds are crossable, with the right decision, an action, and raw courage. But the barricade between the small world of the rich and the giant world of the poor reaches up to the sky. It's made of cement, money, and power, topped with barbed wire and equipped with screaming alarms.

One night, for just an hour, she dared to enter the world of the borderline rich. She went to an expensive restaurant in downtown Bucaramanga in Colombia. The lights were dimmed and all the tables had fresh flowers and candles. Diners ordered main meals and wine, paying twenty times the minimum hourly wage, each. A waiter in a suit ghosted around them, carefully pouring iced water into long glasses and arranging their plates, the red silk napkins, and the cutlery. The diners ignored him.

Another waiter brought her fried yucca with guacamole, then ravioli in mushroom sauce with parmesan, and complementary garlic bread. She asked for water and he asked her if she preferred fragrant water. She didn't know what he meant, but she thanked him for the food and that seemed to surprise him.

It was clear that she was in a world that was not hers because of her lack of a watch or expensive jewellery, her unironed plain white t-shirt, tights, un-styled hair, her dog-eared notebook on the table, and her excitement. She ate hurriedly and cut the ravioli awkwardly. The complimentary entree surprised her.

She was aware that this world had never been hers, because you learn worlds, and she hadn't learnt this one. She didn't know how to dress up or how to use a knife and fork together. Nor did the rich know how to play the guitar on a plaza bench, sell in the street, use public transport, or live in just one room.

Campaign on

This time Mella was at a campaign stall outside Merrylands shopping centre. She and Ramona had set up two card tables and covered them in a red cloth, alternative newspapers, leaflets, 'Stop the War' badges and stickers, and stuck 'Stop Bush' posters to the sides of the tables. A well-dressed woman and her kid, carrying a large black toy gun, approached the stall. The woman told Mella her husband was in Afghanistan. "We're really not getting the whole story here," she said. She bought her son a badge, which he pinned onto his jacket. They walked into the shopping centre, and the son accidently left his gun at the stall. When they came out again, Mella would give them the toy back, but for now she looked at it on the table with alarm. Passers-by also eyed the 'Stop the War' posters and stickers then the large gun with confusion.

A woman had a different story to the papers.

There was a little less apathy-ash in the air.

Banner paint in the wind

Alice and Mella had spread the white fabric, one and a half metres by four metres, across their front porch over a layer of old, yellow newspapers, in order to paint a banner for the upcoming protest. A mobile of coloured metal tubes hanging by the door chimed in the wind. The banner fluttered a little too, despite the water bottles and books they'd put around its edges to keep it down. Seven of them kneeled or squatted around it, painting in the outlined letters, sometimes inadvertently adding small bumps to the lettering as their brushes tripped on the creases in the material.

Every now and then someone would take a break. Rachel and Bec, both small with short hair and a little plump, one light-skinned and one dark, rolled around on the lawn. Rachel grabbed Bec's nose between her fingers and pulled at it. Baby pandas, Mella thought, and she picked up the pink ukulele with an urge to play around as well. She tap-touch stroked the strings, then experimented with a rhythm that combined string strumming and tapping the wooden body. Sayuri painted carefully, slow enough to watch the black paint sink into the fabric, to watch it touch the yellow and the red and change them slightly at the line where the colours came together. Sayuri was just out of a mental hospital, after two months there, and there was an unspoken awareness there on the veranda that Sayuri was still sad. Bec put blue dots on top of yellow. Too much for a banner. So she put yellow on the blue and the yellow disappeared. "Blue's a greedy colour," she said.

The chimes, the wind, the slow paint... Mella relaxed and saw life in slowmotion, saw Bec and Rachel back at the banner, their arms dodging and twisting about each other to reach the letters, saw knuckles clenching paint brushes: knucklehills, explorefingers. Alice there too, her paint strokes sharp, giving the letters clean edges, making them bold, making them shout. But Alice was thinking about something far away. Someone going to the bathroom. Barefeet, coldfeet tapping chipped tiles. Puncholand colours and a banner almost complete.

Alice, shaken out of far-away world, stood up and stretched, then said, "Mella, let me play with your hair?" Alice, quick fingers, quick with paint, with origami, with phone, typing at a computer, drawing, and now making many tiny plaits with Mella's long hair. Feathermassage. Touch of twenty tiny flowers. Mella's eyes closed and Alice saying gently, "You have nice hair. Soft..."

Alice finished, and Mella went back to work. But with questions: "Why don't we get goose bumps on our hands, feet, or face?" she asked. Hands paused and heads popped up with suggestions. Someone speculated that it had to do with where hair grew. But Mella wanted to check - part of her urge lately to look things up, decode complex mysteries.

Bec needed more paint. Mella passed her the pot. Bec said thanks, and Mella gave a small smile and looked down at the banner shyly.

Little big things

As the sea and sky bumped together and made the

horizon, they giggled and shivered. Orange sand or yellow sand or white or grey, chipped spiral shells, clouds chasing tails, wind song, grapefruit blossoms, undersea volcanos, midnight snowfall, sugarcane, salt deserts, ancient cactus, finger monkeys, hot garlic, a continent of ice and penguins, coral wonderlands. Someone as big as a city sat cross-legged on the land, and with playful curiosity, stroked the hills, traced the rivers, and tasted the ocean.

Campaign on 2

This time Mella and Alice were in Auburn, a suburb two stations away from their own, where a large number of Middle Eastern migrants lived.

"George Bush is coming to Australia! Join the protest!" Alice called out. A young woman grinned and took the leaflet, almost bumping into another person as she read it. "I hate that man," she said.

Ten minutes into the campaign and two police officers approached the stall. "I'm going to have to ask you to move on," said one.

"You're not allowed to be here; you need council permission," said the other. "We'll need some ID and your address, then I'll have to ask you to pack up and go away, otherwise we'll arrest you."

Passers-by stopped to watch, and a small crowd formed. A large man came up to the police and said, "Ay, you leave them alone! They're doing good stuff!" He waved around his leaflet with George Bush's face on it. "This man is up to no good!"

"I dunno about that," muttered the first policewoman, and she wrote down Alice's address. Mella took a few steps backwards to take a photo with the Resist centre's pocket digital camera.

Then a council ranger approached the police and talked quietly with them. "It's okay; they're allowed to be here. As long as they don't make any money, there are no more than three people, and they move back against that wall there, its fine."

Alice grinned at the ranger, and said, "Thanks for that; what's your name?" and the officer walked over to Mella. "Oi, what were you taking photos for?"

"Umm, general interest, I guess."

"Well, don't do it. You think people around here want their photo taken? People around here are sensitive to that kind of thing." Sure, Mella thought, you mean *you* are. You mean you're annoyed because you didn't get to shut down our stall.

"So don't let me catch you doing that again," said the first officer.

"It's my political right, actually. Read the constitution."

"Don't get cheeky; if I catch you clicking your camera again, the lot of you will be arrested."

With just a few days to go until the protest, and press releases to write, posters to stick up, and buses to organise, that day was a long one. Mella, her body leadbones, lay down in the lounge room to read a little before bed, but quickly fell asleep. A slight awareness of the sound of footsteps, of someone arranging her legs and covering her with a sheet. She murmured something, but not words. Then there might have been a kiss, on a cheek. Or maybe she dreamt it. The next morning she wouldn't remember.

Four things police did

1. In Circular Quay at around 10:30 am, police arrested a homeless man for being homeless. And that day there happened to be a small rally at the Quay against the war in Iraq. So around two hundred protestors, together with some people passing by, crowded around the police car and tried to block it. "Shame police, shame!" they yelled, and the police got out their batons and broke up the crowd.

2. Prime Minister John Howard spoke in Parramatta Town Hall. The police road around the building on bikes

and horses to keep the protestors out. To stop them from listening to, or speaking to their prime minister.

3. Rain and Ramona were sitting outside on the curb one night, kissing. Police road up to them and asked them what they were doing, then told them to move on.

4. A postie wrote PEACE with chalk on the pavement near Parramatta station and police threatened to fine her.

The quality of anger

On 23 October, the day of the protest, Mella, Alice, Rain, Ramona, Sayuri, Marg and the others got up at 4:30 am when morning was raw and night diminishing, the first news coming on the radio, and the CBD office cleaners were finally going home. Because George Bush's visit had been moved to Canberra, at 5:10 am eight buses full of protestors pulled away from Sydney Central Station.

The protestors had been chanting anti-war slogans for forty minutes when the cavalcade of black limousines with US flags on the hoods pulled up in front of Parliament House. The protestors, behind blockades and several lines of police set up one hundred and fifty metres away, craned and pointed and speculated on which car Bush was in. Later, the mainstream media reported that Australian security had even planted flowers at the entrance to parliament so that no one would be able to see Bush when he got out of his car and entered the building. Nevertheless, Mella and the others knew that he was there somewhere, and that he could hear them, but anger took hold and all they could chant was "Shame!" and boo until their voices were sore.

Once Bush was inside, the protestors gathered around the stage to listen to speakers, comedians, and singers. Then, knowing that he would soon be going to the Lodge—to the prime minister's house, they packed their campaign stalls, the stage, brushed grass off their legs and bums, and marched the short route there. Clapping, playing tambourines, they held up their hand-painted banners and waved their placards that said, 'Occupation isn't liberation', 'He lied, they died', 'Stop Bush, dump Howard', 'Bush is a murderer', 'He thinks he's in Austria'. Mella chanted hard, her body straight, sweating, and her wind-combed hair flagging behind her. It was hot and she undid an extra button on her shirt and rolled her jeans up below her knees.

The march route took them through a road tunnel which amplified their voices, so that thousands of them sat down there for a while and chanted. Then they continued until they reached a large white building that looked like a mansion and had three tiers of orange plastic security fencing erected around it, with police posted at intervals along the first fence. The plastic fencing was held into the ground with metal stakes, recently purchased with their barcode stickers still on. Douglas, a lover of meat and of theory, later said, "We all thought it had to be the Lodge!" Actually, it was the US embassy. The marchers walked up to the first line of fencing and pulled it out. At the third line of fencing though, where the police were, they paused. The police, having been informed that the march would go to the Lodge, were few, and they looked at the crowd facing them with confusion and fright. One officer grabbed a person from the crowd and told him to go back, but the person looked at him with surprise and followed the others who were walking through and over the third fence. Eventually, the protestors worked out that the building was not the Lodge, and marched off again. One person rolled up some of the orange fencing and took it away. Mella said to the people near her that perhaps he wanted it for his garden at home. Marg guessed that he was concerned about the mess and was cleaning things up.

Outside the Lodge the protestors sat down and chanted and sang, "He's got the whole world in his hands, we want the whole world in our hands, we want democracy in our hands." The singing crowd felt unstoppable. The bar of expectation was high. Fuel tank full. Mella noticed that anger became something dignified when it was collective and planned. It had a different quality to the anger of ashen apathy, of desperate plate throwing and door slamming.

A jogging couple turned the corner and approached the protest, unaware of what was going on. They tried to pass the police line, but the police wouldn't let them. So the protestors chanted, "Let them through, let them through!" and the joggers laughed, embarrassed, and jogged back the other way.

Bush, meanwhile, had entered the Lodge via the back, through the servants' entrance. Various people on megaphones proposed to the crowd that they march back to parliament where the buses were waiting. It was then that the police attacked. They formed a line to push the protestors, already turning around and walking away, back towards the Lodge. They battened those in reach, grabbed and pushed, and kneed one man onto the ground, rubbed his face on the concrete, and arrested him. The mainstream media journalists got up from where they had been sitting and rushed over, the cameras hanging from their shoulders clattering in the tight huddle they formed around the arrested man. The headlines the next day read, "Protestors Turn Violent".

As Mella rested her head on the seat in front of her on the bus, intermittently sleeping, back in Canberra, placards left leaning against the fence erected around parliament formed a kind of ad hock gallery of desires.

Types of sleep

Warm, relaxed, wrapped-up sleep. Constant rain rhythm tickling the roof and its pattershadow stroking the top of her bodyball. All night blanket hugs, pillow-dreams, and waking up smiling and stretching.

Then there was another kind of sleep. Awake, but eyes shut, working without softness, making the world without thought, creating without creativity. Like a person eating something delicious, but forgetting to taste it. Autopilot life, ashen, someone else pressing the buttons.

Mella, in her bodyball, dreamt of a world waking up from that second kind of sleep. She imagined a blackout, that televisions stopped working, and a sudden mass exit, into the street. Storytelling and street football matches by moonlight. Learning, finally, the names of neighbours. Walking about in darkening streets, millions of new suns, more subtle their goodnight, their smile without fanfare. They tickled the world, gently.

Mella's list of things she had discovered
The lines her fingernails made on flower petals, and the mellowbitter taste of roses

The joy of listening to music alone, pretending she was the one who was singing.

The placid hairsmell of birds

The barely-noticed death of some words

The moon's freckles

That backs weren't flat. That hers had undersholder shadows, and lower back dimples

The pinched dashes behind her knees, and the old faint stretch marks weaving sand patterns around her hips. Her body a beach, its form slowly changing with the passing of time

A strong sense of being a woman now

That impotency was one of the hardest things. She couldn't find anything out about Rafi, and she missed her first friend

That people who did the most useful work tended to be the most humble

The satisfaction of drawing small pictures to illustrate how she was feeling. The day at the farmers' market she drew a very little thing

The places where you can write poems: gum wrappers, toilet paper rolls (the sentences wound around and met their start and so could be never ending), in the margins of second hand books, public toilet doors—one of the best places. And one day, on someone's stomach...

What it takes

On 17 January 2006, French Prime Minister Villepin announced the creation of a new employment law that allowed companies to fire people under twenty-six years of age during their first two years on the job without explanation. The parliament approved the law on 8 February.

On 7 February to 4 April 2006, millions participated in hundreds of strikes, university occupations, and marches. As they filled the streets, they changed the aerial view of the towns and cities. The buses and trains stayed sleeping in their depots and the planes parked at airports, the newsstands were empty, as were the universities, and the radio stations put music on repeat. Some marchers dressed up in rubbish bags. They were saying, "If you treat us like rubbish, as disposable, this country won't go on." In Paris, one march was led by a saxophonist playing jazz music from a truck. Rain arrived suddenly, and the entire march cheered. The police ended the protests with water cannon and tear gas. In the two months of protesting, they arrested four thousand five hundred people.

10 April 2006: President Chirac scrapped the employment law.

Responsibility

He was eighty-seven when he realised it for the first time. He'd been smoking in the hospital car park, leaning against a lamp post, breathing in deeply, puffing out, and staring at the tidy sky. First he heard the chants, and then he looked over, through his smoke rings, at the scene of nurses, whistles, and placards. With the nurses outside, the hospital was all slowed down and in a state of confusion. They were striking because they were overworked. And it was then that he understood that we decide if we do something about injustice or if we don't. We're responsible for this world. For its midnight migraines, its thrashing fevers, its fallen trees and fallen masses of third world, their voices stolen and put in a box somewhere. The box vibrating, trembling, shaking because the voices inside were locked down and silenced. And one day, it would explode, that trembling box, and confetti-ed sounds would burst forth and paint the planet a different colour, a colour we don't yet know or can't yet see.

Eighty-seven years and now he was clear. It's we who are responsible for whether a war starts or stops, for if our history is remembered lies and forgotten struggles, forgotten songs and forgotten peoples. We're responsible for each other, who else is there?

At eighty-seven, lung cancer and resigned to it, he joined his first protest. He marched with the nurses.

The woman in the flying red dress

Standing with her feet submerged in the mud
    Of humanity
    In the sludge of sick slavery, of sleeping with rain
poverty
    In the waste dump of all the disgusting things
    Among the mud, people bent over
    Half dead, crying something or other
    And the sky was brown-green-urgh-sick-fucking hell
colour
    All fogged up with car breath and coal spew and
    Beneath it nuclear botox plastic bag soil
    And there was that woman in her
    Flying red dress
    Standing
    Her fist up high
    Her eyes wide open
    Pointed towards the future
    *Her flying red dress

*Malalai Joya (Afghanistan): dismissed from the Afghan parliament after she publically denounced warlords and war criminals within it.

*Nanny of the Maroons (Jamaica): founded communities of escaped and ex-slaves then led raids against plantations in order to liberate more. The British attacked her community on a number of occasions over many years. Nanny and her people faced constant attack and hunger, but in 1739—1740, the British were forced to sign a peace treaty with her, giving the Maroons five hundred acres of land.

*Angela Davis (US): opposed the Vietnam War, fought for gay rights, women's rights and against racism. Was a teacher who believed that learning was about being able to think. Campaigned to abolish the prison-industrial complex after her experiences in prison.

*Inessa Armand (France, Russia): wrote and edited against the First World War and domestic slavery, organised national and international women's conferences, was arrested and went into exile, then arrested and imprisoned.

*Ayat Al-Qarmezi (Bahrain): sentenced to one year in prison for reading a poem at a protest against the monarchy of her country.

*Sor Juana Ines de la Cruz (Mexico): wrote at a time when women couldn't, in the seventeenth century.

*Gladys Baez (Nicaragua): guerrilla before and during the Nicaraguan revolution, helped organise women and peasants, sometimes walking for days to talk to them. Tortured in jail, the doctors said she wouldn't survive, but she spent two years recovering, and then fought on.

*Eva Haule (Germany): after twenty-one years in prison for fighting imperialism, the first thing she did when she was released was travel to Venezuela. In jail, then in Venezuela, she took photos of people, capturing their battles and the complexity in their faces. She kept living after her imprisonment, showing that it was possible to make it through the Long Struggle.

*And millions more...

When battles change from I to we

Mella took a migraine to her Job Seeker training session. She had been searching for work for so long now that she was used to her morning ritual. But the daily fight to not take the rejections personally affected her sometimes, and the migraines came, rampaging on the right side of her head, once a week or so. Today, one had attacked her after breakfast and she'd gone back to bed, the sheets storming around her writhing snake body. The urge to vomit had hung out in a vague place near her stomach and throat, never quite finalising itself. But an hour later she got up again because missing her Centrelink sessions meant temporarily losing her unemployment payments. She'd walked to the Centrelink office with her hands squeezing her head and breathing deeply to repress the urge to throw up.

When she arrived she was told to wait in one of the workshop rooms, a glass panelled square area with green carpet and pinging air-conditioning. Chairs lined three of the walls and were nailed to the ground and upholstered in the same green carpet material as the floor. Twelve people were positioned unevenly on the chairs, like abandoned marionettes. *If only I could get a job* was written in the furrowed foreheads of each, their life's music turned into a single repeated note: *If only...* The marionettes avoided eye contact while the Centrelink woman who was to run the workshop stood outside the room chatting to a colleague, flashing stiff smiles, and in no rush to start. Mella, massaging her head with her thumbs, wanted to ask them all who they were, and what their story was. And a few times she started to talk, but then stopped. She felt awkward. But the woman with the stiff smile kept chatting, so Mella finally asked.

The marionettes moved then, looked around, gave names, talked, and in doing so, stopped being marionettes. A few had accents, a few talked softly, others in a tumble with their words sticky-taped together, one talked in two-word sentences, and another like an injured race car.

"I was fired after thirteen years on the job, not even allowed to say goodbye to my workmates, had to mortgage the house."

"My boss thought kissing him was one of my duties. I left, and Centrelink wouldn't give me payments because I'd left voluntarily, they said."

"I'm way behind in my rent. I'm so desperate for work that I've started responding to those business from home ads, but they're all scams."

"I've worked two jobs—a night job and a day one—most of my life, but people really look down on you when you're unemployed; they call me lazy, and I'm starting to hate myself."

"I get temp work now and again. I'm registered with three different contract agencies, but it barely keeps me going and I never stay at any job long enough to get to know anyone."

"I've been living in my car for a while now, sometimes I think about closing the windows and leaving the engine on."

Mella's migraine softened, but she felt nailbite instead. Because there was a never ending list of damaged, hurt and hidden people, statistics of injustices normalised and printed on pretty paper, tent cities of unemployed, shanty towns of informal workers, the nowhere to go of slavewives, the night meat packers, the MacDonald's workers uniformed into Happymeals, factories of robot workers, all the lives that didn't count, all the 8:00 am to 7:00 pm exhaustion. It was the longest list.

In came the stiffsmile woman. She said 'good morning' like an electric doorbell, then turned on the overhead projector and pointed at different parts of a flow chart. It was her rehearsed play, put on a stage once a week for years. She talked about how to behave at job interviews, and the importance of "clean and hygienic presentation", and Mella got the message. We're dysfunctional and disgusting, and it's our fault that we can't get jobs.

She raised her hand. "I read last night in an article that there are currently eight times more jobseekers than jobs. That is, for every eighty job seekers, there are ten jobs." Non-marionettes tilted their heads, nodded together.

"Why are we here?" Mella asked, stressing the 'we'. "Shouldn't it be the companies receiving workshops on how not to downsize, on how not to put insane amounts of profits before people's jobs, on how to treat workers with respect?"

Battles

In the house where Mella and Alice lived there were all kinds of conversations. There were the morning coffee conversations in the dining room, the occasional shared cask wine and salted peanuts conversations in the lounge room, intimate conversations sitting on the floor in someone's bedroom, the intervallic half-conversations while watching the news, the random ones where someone would lie on the couch and someone else would come home or come out of their room and they would just start, the conversations around the oven, stirring different pans, arms everywhere like pick-up sticks, and the more solemn veranda conversations. Mella and Alice were having one of those, sitting on second-hand couch pillows on the tiled veranda floor, looking out at the dark, quiet street. Alice was holding her pink ukulele on her lap, like it was her cat, stroking it gently in slowstrum. Mella wiggled her toes in a pair of rainbow socks. Rain had knitted them for her after a conversation where she'd said she would love it if her body had the colours of a rainbow lorikeet. They were a heartgift and Mella felt warm, despite the day she'd had at Centrelink. Quiet minutes passed where all that could be heard was the air, the strumming, and that sound of faraway cars. But Mella was thinking many things quickly; her thousands of thoughts sounded like a city under construction.

Then she said, "Alice, today after Centrelink, I had an idea."

Alice rested her hands on the strings of the ukulele and tilted her head towards Mella, "Oh yeah?"

"I thought, the rich wage this war against us, but we're all tied up fighting our tiny personal battles. And there's just so many of us, Alice; so many, everywhere. We're like lost soldiers who've forgotten what they were doing. So I thought, we need one army, a global one, to unite all our battles, defend ourselves in an organised way, and eventually build a new sort of world that isn't run by the rich," she said. *The used n abused, the mess lickers, the ripped up, the fingertrodden, the toleratingalltoomuch, the livinginthedark, the avoided, the peoplethings, the cannonfodder united to become something else.*

"An army of the poor." *Organisation of the invisible and the ignored. Army of poets, graffiti artists, farmers, construction workers, nurses, checkout workers.*

Alice smiled and pulled on her chin.

"It wouldn't be a typical army, though." *Sweet tasting. Millions of pawns fighting a few kings.* "I'm not talking about uniforms, chains of command, orders obeyed without a second thought, none of that. But seriousness, plans and strategies, yes."

"Yes, an army without borders rather than one that guards those imaginary lines with guns, telling people where they can and can't walk," Alice said.

"One that sets up its own radio stations and schools, visits its neighbours and makes sure everyone is okay," Mella said. They added more and more things to the list.

"That fosters critical thinking." *Arguments in oilpaint. Discussions by coffee and candlelight. An electricity grid of new warm ideas.*

"That votes on all positions of responsibility." *Stadium decisions.*

"It's not a completely new idea, I know," Mella said. "Forms of it already exist. We have Resist, we have 'Stop the War' groups and unions—the non-corrupt ones, and women's organisations."

Alice played a few chords.

"It's just an idea," Mella said again.

Opening
A flower in rocks, its seedroots tarred over with Road Cities. But it pushed itself up through a small crack, and the little plant tasted saltystorm. The stem sprouted new leaves and grew taller, firmer, while its roots grew deeper, thickened, and multiplied. Root straws sucked up soil vitamins and soil-filtered rain. Leaves licked light.

Budpoint snuggled out through the wet leaves and in quickspin the emerging flower racqueted its wingpetals. Colour unrolled.

And the flower's stamens stretched out their naked bodies, half draped in pollen blankets. This was the flower opening. Breezeheart, sky-scratcher flower. And some crumpled tar.

PAZ

Drugs and music as weapons of war

US soldiers blasted rock music at deafening levels at the Vatican diplomatic mission in Panama City for ten days. It was December 1989, and they were trying to get General Manuel Noriega, Panamanian dictator, to come out and surrender. Called Operation Nifty Package, they used other psychological torture techniques, such as gunning the engines of armoured vehicles against the mission fence, and they set fire to a neighbouring field in order to create a helicopter landing zone.

Noriega had taken refuge in the mission after the US government tried to capture him when he became a public relations liability. He had been giving military assistance to the contras to wage war against the Nicaraguan revolution, at the request of the US. In exchange, the US allowed him to continue his drug trafficking activities. When a CIA pilot was shot down over Nicaragua, documents on the plane revealed many of the CIA's activities in Latin America, and the US's connection with Noriega became embarrassing.

Especially because the US was pretending to wage a War on Drugs. Richard Nixon declared it in 1971, and it went on for decades in the US, Mexico, and Colombia. Yet in the end, wars can't be waged on inanimate objects such as pills, powders, and leaves. They can only be waged on people, and it was the poor, migrants, Latinos, and indigenous people who were sent to prison, while the big drug traffickers remained free and even grew richer as illegality increased sale price. The war on drugs was just another war by the greedy against the poor. And like the other US wars, its pretext bore no fruit. In over forty years, the war still hadn't managed to decrease drug use.

Damjan's legs

Drugs were an excuse for war, but they were also a tool; their abuse was encouraged by an absence of alternatives, of help, and their good use discouraged by misinformation and illegality.

After Matt's death, Damjan began to turn off feeling in order to keep functioning. Around him, police patrolled...in reality, occupied, Macquarie Fields. There were twenty around the supermarket, twenty with dogs at the station, five patrol cars constantly going up and down the streets, and more scattered about the streets on foot. Damjan felt that he was marked. Marked for being poor and angry—the biggest crime. The supermarket wouldn't hire him, real estate agents wouldn't consider him and the groups of friends he got together, and the government, despite the media attention on the area, still wouldn't provide it with a decent bus service.

Damjan moved back in with his parents. He stopped jogging, and instead walked the short way to some of the local pubs and sat on their sides, in the shadowbits, and watched the footie on the plasma screens. Plasma bright-sharp images, high-definition, amazing resolution. And his eyes glazed over in lazy low resolution. Now and then some lonely pub dweller would start to chat to him, and he would keep glazing his eyes and not respond because he'd figured out that friends in this world were just too hard.

The world was built and rigged for money and dazzle and millions of people climbing endless ladders, trying to push the others off, not for friends. It sent friends to jail. Or to the grave.

When the pubs closed and his parents' constant arguing got to be too much, at first he'd spend a night or two at Melissa's place. But her current boyfriend didn't like that, so he bought a second hand TV, set it up in his room and would put it on loud at all hours to drown out the chalk and metal sound of arguing, or of silence, or of memories. So went his desensitisation. The ashen process by which he blocked it all out, convinced himself not to care, became numb. It helped him feel free from anxiety, sadness, and indignity. Yet he didn't realise that that wasn't the same as freedom. That in fact, his denial of reality would ultimately have the opposite effect, and he would end up inhabiting a space, a world, smaller than that of Paz.

At first it was just the television, light drugs, and beer. Pubs filling up with exhausted seven-day-a-week construction workers, train drivers, and teachers who let toomuchbeer take the edge off a rusty world. Another kind of pharmacy altogether, the pub. And the drugs were similar. They put Damjan in a sailing boat, took the storm out from under him. Things were cool breeze, blue breeze and gentle swaywater. Bleak world coloured in mandarin orange and smelling of banana. So pretty. He sniffed, or he smoked, and his head candled out. Awake-dreaming, with nothing in focus. But the high always wore off, and the storm came back and capsized his boat and tipped him into...drowning. So then he'd watch TV, which was certainly cheaper and at least kept out the horrid glare of life. Once he was surprised to see trampoline dancing on Channel 10: synchronised twists and leaps of beautiful bodies; some kind of competition. I'll be darned, he'd thought, and switched the channel. Ah, a Bond movie. Halfway through it he fell asleep, a young potbelly poking out from underneath his t-shirt.

About six months after the riots, he took up serious gambling. Though he constantly had to borrow his parents' or friends' toothpaste, or spare change for the bus, or pasta or coffee, he always found something for gambling. It was quick horse coloured adrenalin, it was excitement, and it was the impossible possibility of easyrich. Now and then, he won something: $50, $250, $15. Then he could buy Stuff. And when he didn't win, he dreamed of buying Stuff. Damjan, with his trolley zooming around town putting all the hundreds of things he wanted into it. Mine! Mine! Mine! Mine! He would have things, he would bath in all his things, count them, display them.

And he'd be happy...

But still bored, with a stomach full of all the TV you could watch in one day, full of all the things one could own. He picked away at the ingrown hairs on his knees. Flew away without the flying. And the hair goose bumps on his unused legs, the hairs that buried themselves, multiplied.

His invisible leg, the extra magic one that made him a super soccer player, shrivelled up, became a dried up carrot left in the fridge for months. It twisted, shrank, became limp, and was gone. Left rubbishjuice drip stains over the lounge room floor. The springs in his real legs rusted and clanked. Until one day when he rolled out of bed and stepped on a beer can pull tab on the floor. He pulled it straight out again, and bandaged his foot, but it became infected. Reluctantly, and limping, using only the toes of his injured foot, he made his way to the local medical centre where a doctor applied an antibiotic cream and rewrapped the wound. Damjan limped back to his parents' place, and though the wound healed in two weeks, he had no desire to walk again.

He changed. He went from an all-out effort to making the world tolerable and pretty to simply ignoring it. He hardly left his room. The TV became the window he looked out of, and it in turn reduced the outside world to the few rooms of Two and a Half Men or the dolphins, sport, and entertainment of "news" programs, and the ads arguing buy stuff buy stuff buy stuff in a complicated hypnosis to persuade its chicken audience everything is good everything is good everything is good... Keep watching; find out what happens next. So he did. And day changed into night, then back again. And who was Damjan? The television series he liked most. TV was his emotions, his small manageable world.

And one night, a little tipsy and a lot whatevered, he fell asleep murmuring "money, money, money" with a faux gold chain dangling from his neck, a cigarette burning out in his fingers and empty beer cans, chocolate wrappers, and a cereal box, strewn around him. No longer quite human, the few times he did leave the house to buy something for himself or for his parents he felt like a stray dog. In people's way. He'd grown a full beard, because it covered him up; the skin around his eyes was puckering, his bottom lip fell forward and his feet shuffled. His heart shuffled too.

Finally, about nine months after the riots, while lying on his bed he rolled onto his back, and like a flipped-over dung beetle, could no longer move. A voice somewhere called him a slob and a loser.

Why they moved
In the Zocolo, the giant plaza in Mexico City, two girls dressed as fairies placed a basket between them on the ground, and stood still. A crowd gathered around them. A boy dropped a coin into the basket and one fairy did a little dance, took off her hat, and let him choose a small piece of coloured paper from it. Then she went back to her position and stood still. She fixed her face into a smile and held it there. A man dropped a coin into the basket and the other fairy came to life, spun on her toe, then handed

him a lollypop. And it went on. Two girls dressed as fairies. Money made them move.

Petrol air
Not just pollution, not just car-identity.

Also a ten-year-old boy in Central Australia with a plastic bottle swathed in his sleeves and held up to his nose. Breathing in forget.

The sex holiday industry
In Thailand, Philippines, Costa Rica. A binge on women, a shopping spree on people who have been bought, sold, imported, trafficked, and resold for a discount. Price tags and expiration dates stamped into their lowered eyes.

Why he smiled
There was a clown waiting for a train at Bellas Artes station in Mexico City. He carried a backpack, an expression of slight impatience, and a sniffle. Like others, he was catching a peak hour train home from work. It was no longer necessary to joke and smile.

Not so bad
The rotation of shadows outside and the repetition of wake-eat-work-sleep were the surest indicators that time was actually passing, and that Paz's sentence was passing. It had been over six months in prisonstorage. Six months since Ashley should have come to visit him, but never did.

Every day he wondered where she was, what she was doing, thinking, and feeling, and why she hadn't come, and he recited his list of things to talk to her about in the mornings, almost like prayer, hoping that she would surprise him that day with a visit.

Today he was extra hopeful, because it was his birthday. He had drawn another bouquet for her, and this time the flowers were flowers, not lips or clouds. But they were unusual flowers that curled around each other like spiral staircases, that stretched their necks up and breathed out blue dot clouds, that winked, shivered, and whistled. One flower grew up the side of the piece of paper in a grapevine of petals which at the top corner drooped down a bit, and then shed its petals onto the rest of the bouquet. Another flower was shaped like a toucan beak, another like a parasol, and another like an upside down jellyfish. One final one, small, at the side of the bunch, was a home; two of its petals pointed together to form a roof, another opened horizontally as a door.

Paz put the drawing in his shirt pocket and went downstairs for breakfast. It was one slice of almost stale bread and half a cold hardboiled egg. The same every morning. Likewise, lunch was always a cold meat pie. Twenty-five percent animal fat, a bit of muscle, snout, ear, tongue roots, tendons, blood vessels and muscle of various farm animals (as the industry standard prescribed) and the rest was gravy (cooked meat liquid with a bit of corn starch), inside a soggy pastry crust. Dinner, too, was a meat pie, but with coleslaw.

Paz ate hungrily. From the start he'd convinced himself it wasn't so bad. Not so bad. He missed cooking, being able to play with flavours and colours, combine sweet and spicy, watch cakes rise. But here he enjoyed sitting down with the other prisoners and joining in with the chatter, a chatter which went well with the cling-clang of the metal food trays and chairs. Still, the food that the prison provided was never enough, and prisoners always had to spend some of their small wages on canteen snacks. Paz tried to buy less food so that he had money for phone calls, and for pen and paper, or even the newspaper. He was impressed with what was available at the canteen; there was even a choice of pens: red, blue, or black ink, and felt-tip.

After breakfast he went straight to work in the laundry, and it was for that that he was paid twenty-eight dollars a week. He worked in the sorting stage of the process, opening the bags of prisoners' clothes and linens as well as the large bundles they received from the hospital (the prison had paid contracts with three nearby hospitals to do their laundry), and removing any objects such as coins, cards, or paper that had been left in pockets, or needles, bandaids and other things left in the hospital linens. After that he sorted it all into piles according to type of wash; the most soiled articles—those soiled in blood, vomit, faeces, urine, puss, or food—went into one pile. Whites and underwear into another, and so on... He did this daily, until dinner. Because of the various machines involved—steam presses, dryers and washing machines—the laundry room was hot, humid, and very noisy. The lack of windows made it worse and kept in the chemical smells, occasionally giving the workers nausea. The work was repetitive and tedious, and Paz stood up all day, which caused him mild back and foot pain. He often felt like a marionette on an assembly line, his arms moving about in puppet fashion, opening bags and sorting, while his body stood inert. Still, it wasn't so bad, he told himself. It was better than doing nothing, than lying around all day. He felt useful, and though there was too much noise to talk, and the supervisor was constantly on his back to work faster, he felt like part of a team. But because the prison itself was also very noisy with its constant clatter of metal doors, the whistling and shouting (most conversations were shouted), he sometimes craved large outside spaces and simple quietness. Still, he told himself that working in the laundry was exciting, the noise was lively, and if he was exhausted afterwards, it was okay because the exhaustion helped him to sleep.

A guard blew the whistle to mark the end of work, and the afternoon count. Paz stood in his place in the count line and took advantage of the brief window of quietude to try to make a photo. It was something he remembered seeing once, but he wanted to frame it and get the contrast and colouring just right. It was on a train. A little girl, light skinned, really skinny, perhaps six years old, with a serious sulky face and blond wavy hair was holding a pair of large adult sunglasses. She was sitting on the lap of a dark skinned Aboriginal teenager in a singlet and a black bra that lifted her small breasts horizontal. She had her arm around the child, who looked up at her and pulled at her singlet to cover her bra. Paz had seen tenderness, had seen maturity in an unexpected place; he had seen longstories. He tried to take the photo but his camera lens seemed stuck. It clicked and jerked as he tried to adjust the focus. It was his heart shuffling, like Damjan's. The aperture too was sleepy, wouldn't open all the way, and his photo came out too dark, with diluted colours. Six months in prison and he was finding it hard to remember those burning reds, drenched greens, edible yellows and sleepy blues that had filled the world he experienced. That world had been a canvas, its energy felt in the paint colours and vivid strokes that covered it. Now...he sighed and followed the others downstairs to dinner.

After dinner it was wing time. Paz moved to his regular table where he almost always sat alone, although sometimes someone would come over with a pack of cards in hand and start talking to him. This ritual was established as Paz became the prison listener. It was never acknowledged, no nickname was given to him, but everyone knew that if they needed to vent, they could talk to Paz during wing time. The prisoner would always pick up the cards, deal them, but they'd never get around to playing. Today, it was a nineteen-year-old with a mullet and a gentle face. He'd been sentenced to two years for stealing credit cards, but while in prison he'd seen another inmate raped, and now he constantly had nightmares with that "crazy scream". Paz listened by nodding, showing his concern, occasionally asking questions, now and then mentioning something similar that had happened to him, but rarely giving advice. They didn't want advice, and usually there wasn't much they could do. But by listening he could share their sadness and make it a little more bearable because it wasn't theirs alone anymore. Before entering prison Paz was already skilled in the forgotten art of listening, but in prison he had become a master. And over time, he was able to put together a kind of social map of NSW, based on where all the prisoners came from, what they told him about their lives and towns or suburbs, what kind of drugs they used, where the police were worse, where they were more corrupt, and where some of the different gangs were located. After the prisoner left, Paz put his head down on his arms, because all the bits of sadness he was sharing were heavy when added together.

Then, he insisted. No, it wasn't so bad. There were nice things. There were the holes in the prison ceiling where the clouds burst through. Hushed clouds, swimming silently. And there was a butterfly. It was a blue that glowed.

"Paz, you're talking out loud," someone said to him as they walked past.

"Ha?"

"Those aren't clouds; they're ceiling stains. And those aren't butterflies; they're the blue security camera lights, mate."

Never mind. Soon he would be released on parole, if he was good. He had just pleaded guilty to aggravated dangerous driving occasioning death, on the recommendation of the public defender assigned to him, but because he hadn't done it at the "earliest opportunity", the Crown submitted that a fifteen percent discount on his sentence was "generous", but then gave it to him. Seven years, six and a half to go. It was a fraction of his life. And when he got out (he replayed his favourite dream) he'd finally drive around Australia. Ashley and Eva would come too. They'd busk, and meet people, and learn the names of the plants and animals.

His birthday was over and Ashley hadn't come. But she would soon. He stored the drawing of the bouquet under his mattress. He'd be out soon. It wasn't so bad.

What is robbery?

In 2013, Warren Buffet had an income of US$12.7 billion dollars. In 2012, Haiti, population 10.4 million people, had an income (GDP) of US$7.2 billion dollars. Burkino Faso, population 17 million, had an income of US$10.7 billion dollars. Rwanda, population 10.5 million, had an income of US$7.1 billion dollars, and Madagascar, population of 21 million, had an income of US$10 billion dollars.

Tracey's doors

When Tracey was a toddler she had loved doors. She opened and entered every one she came across; the washing machine door, the fridge door, drain gates, the doors of houses and shops she passed. She wanted to be the one to open car doors, or to be the first to pass through the door onto the train. When visiting, she ran to the kitchen and opened all the cupboard doors, peering behind each one, delighted.

She wanted to touch things, to roll up the beach and look under it, to pick the ocean apart, to play with the shape of everything. It was a feeling of internal skipping and wildface, of loving caves, corners, and complexity, of playing in life. It was a state that was essential to freedom, and to growth, because it implied trying things, making mistakes, discovery, and activity.

After Matt's funeral, Tracey went back to their house and packed his belongings into a cardboard box with Queensland Bananas printed in yellow on the side. She packed up his t-shirts, his homemade telescope, his affection, stars, and the lounge room moments. After that, what was left was a hard Tracey with that human-sized empty space always at her side.

She took over Paz's job at the 7/11, and she got stuck there. Working ten-hour shifts, she found comfort in being told what to do, in not having to think, in always being tired. Her plan to see the world became a silly dream, a childish notion. In her armourskin, she never gazesmiled. She looked fixedly at each customer and told them, "That's ten dollars fifty. Plastic bag? Here's your receipt. Next."

One night, Tracey logged out of the register at the end of her shift. "You can all go fuck yourselves," she said to no one, or to everyone. She slammed the door on the way out.

Doors were for slamming now. And a backpack and a cardboard Queensland Banana box collected dust underneath her bed.

Things missing

Paz tried to make portrait photos of the other prisoners. Each photo depicted, with sharp contrast, their varied wrinkles, eyelashes, moles, teeth, and earlobes. But each one had a bit of his face missing; a nose, the top of the skull, a bit of ear ridge, the iris of an eye. It usually had something to do with the story they'd just told him. Later, he made portraits of some of his friends and the people from his town, and put the photos into the series. They too had things missing.

The worst thing of all

"I think it must be when you lie on your death bed, and you realise you wasted your entire life," said the first man.

"I think it's when you're young and poor and you know already that the rest of your life will be a waste," replied the second.

Lissa

Her name was Lissa. She had feet freckles. Damjan had enjoyed watching her, but she had wanted to leave the quicksand suburb. A year or so later, in the middle of an even-colder-than-last-year winter, she was found glassy-eyed and stiff in Parramatta Park. They had made her do things from porno magazines, because they thought that that was how women really were. She'd run away and slept on flattened-out cardboard boxes. She had talked only of practicalities.

Ashley

"You have a visitor."

Paz looked up, and she was standing in his cell doorway. "Ashley!"

She was wearing a yellow cotton dress. Around her eyes there was hardwork, but they were still a little cheeky, angry, yet kind. Her hair was shorter and she had a fringe now. It made her softer.

She told him that she was sorry that it had been so long, and rubbed her eye to stop it twitching. He bit his lip for the same reason.

No, Ashley, no words. The list of questions...erase that. Just come closer.

She stepped towards him. And Paz thought of when he would touch dew hanging from a leaf and it would drop and break on his finger tip. They held hands and pulled each other into a hug.

Then their hug swayed a little, did small little sideways rocking. He asked her with his eyes, again, and this time she seemed to say yes.

His hand on her shoulder and hers on his, they seahorsed—small grazes, slide, hip click. Both of them smiled for the first time in too long. They were salt-skinned and dancing to no song and no rhythm, only heartbeat. They moved as a storm. Then calm. They stepped seaweedslowly into a silent liquorice night.

"You're dancing, Ashley! You dance beautifully," he said. Then there was a banging on the cell door. A guard yelled out to him, "Hey, who you talking to, crazy man?"

Paz's ears cleared, then refilled with the ongoing clatterscream of the prison. The yellow dress turned back into an orange prison towel, and he noticed his sweat smelt not of salt but of enzyme laundry detergent. He kicked at the toilet basin sink and its constant drip, and disappointment pulled him like a heavy rope, slam, onto his bed.

Ashley 2

After Paz went to prison, Ashley put up fences around the past. Brick fences with broken glass bottles at the top. She returned to not trusting, to not allowing herself to let go, to expecting disappointment, like expecting rain during a monsoon. As well as biting her lip, she started to grate her teeth day and night, and to bite the insides of her cheeks. Sometimes her cheeks bled, she often had tooth pain, and eventually many of her teeth became worn down, chipped and cracked. She continued busking on the trains, changing train lines constantly so no one would remember her, her Macdonald's cup in one hand and the other hand held to her jaw to press away the pain. She sang without singing now, she sang in straight lines.

Dental bills became her prison, keeping her in debt and on the trains at all hours. When she was at home, wherever that home was, like Tracey she slammed doors, and sometimes she slammed Eva too.

Eva started smoking at thirteen to relieve her anxiety, and as a way of being nonchalantly pissed off. She grew up, worked as a private cleaner, then in call centres, then in banks, back to private cleaning when she lost a job, then back to banks, moving every three to nine months because the rent was raised, or the landlord kicked her out in order to raise the rent, or housemates wanted her room for a friend, or because she was late on the rent. She left most of her stuff in boxes, to save all the packing, and with each move or job loss her anxiety grew worse. She became paranoid and depressed but couldn't afford mental healthcare, a luxury in a world of sick and sad people.

What is robbery?

Monarchs with business suits instead of crowns spent four thousand American dollars per day on accommodation at the APEC summit in Busan, South Korea, in November 2005. US President George Bush occupied the entire Westin Chosun Hotel, at a price of ten thousand dollars per night. The luxury banquet for summit participants cost 1.5 million dollars. It surely must have been Rollsroycefood, swan toilet paper, musical champagne.

Meanwhile, the city government closed the street stalls near the venue and walled off the poor quarters, saying, according to press reports, "these things shouldn't be shown to world leaders". Thirty-five thousand police kept protestors away. If they could, the government would have gathered up the sun too and put it inside a crystal cage in the centre of the summit, leaving just the crumbs of yellow light scattered about for the rest.

Where wealth comes from

For almost two weeks the cities of Bagh and Muzaffarabad in Pakistan-administered Kashmir were in darkness. After the October 2005 earthquake, when buildings and bridges roared then fell into shards and scraps, when five hundred villages disappeared and sixty thousand people died instantly, businessman-dictator Pervez Musharraf's government spent more time talking toywords to the press than they spent financiallyon relief. Despite thirty percent of its budget allocated to the military, Pakistan failed to use military equipment and resources to rescue the thousands of injured and trapped people, repair services, or to bring food, medicine, or shelter to the needy.

Natural disasters and wars were good news for business people. The more that was destroyed, the higher the demand and desperation. The owner of an Islamabad tent company, a man with gel hair and lots of pen pockets in his ironed shirts, sent teams to Muzaffarabad to sell his merchandise. He charged the wandering, dazed, newly homeless people double the normal price, but said it was "very cheap, considering..." Two weeks later he bought four new business suits and a fifteen thousand-dollar watch.

And in rubbish dumps too
In those graveyards of things
    The ghosts of poverty
    Were seen
    Only by the vultures.

Where stolen beauty went
For weeks leading up to Christmas, the wealthier neighbourhoods of Sydney draped thousands of tiny coloured lights on their rooftops and around the trees in their front yards. One night, after seeing the houses from the train, little Eva asked her mother why the lights were there.

"They're fairy lights."

Eva frowned. "Who put the fairies in there?"

Ashley had been thinking about Lissa, and about the up to four million people trafficked for labour, prostitution, and organs each year.

"People who buy them," she replied.

Unlimited
The monarchs in business suits wanted to make money out of the water, so in Bolivia they put padlocks on community water wells and made it illegal to collect rain water from roofs. They wanted the streets, so the streets around private shops were made private too. They wanted the parks and plazas so they contemplated high security fences. They wanted the beaches, and considered charging entrance fees. They wanted the air, and proposed a breathing tax. They wanted the mountains and lakes, so they designed corporate flags to plant. They wanted the rights to all information, ideas, and dreams, so they broadened copyright law. They wanted to own the wind, so they set up toll gates for it to pass through.

So bad

The night after Ashley didn't dance, Paz brushed his teeth and washed the drawing of the bouquet down the sink with the spat out toothpaste. Then he got into bed, pulled the thin prison sheet over him, and curled up into winter sleep position, chin touching knees, hands sandwiched between the soft warm flesh of calf and thigh, shoulders hunched. In a few minutes he changed to the foetal position, but with one arm under his pillow. Then he changed again, onto his back, his hands by his sides like a soldier, staring, eyes wide open, at the rungs of the bunk above.

In washing the drawing down the sink he had turned off the TV version of life that had been running through his head, and he had admitted that it was so bad. He admitted that he hated working in the laundry, and that the prison food was giving him constipation and stomach aches. He admitted that he missed affection and the sound of trains and being able to draw cows with brown chalk. He was in prison. He was walled off, out of sight, out of the way, abandoned. His cell was a damning all day all night criticism of who he was, and he was reduced to the result of a decision between buying a red pen or blue pen, between responding to the guard's taunts, or not.

He kicked his feet a little, bringing air under the sheet. Too much grey heat inside the cell. He closed his eyes again and tried too hard to sleep. His hair twisted, his knuckles cracked on their own, his sweat fought with him, made him itch, the creaking bed called out road screeches. He changed his position again, onto his stomach with one arm flopped off the bed, his fingertips grazing the floor.

Even that didn't work, so he tried to make a photo. Something simple, calming, a flower. Orange petals with a red furry middle. But the flower wouldn't stand up. It kept falling over then trying to bury its head in the ground, ingrown, then it was gone. I can do this, he thought. A flower. Orange petals. He tried, but he felt sick, and there was a flashing red low-battery symbol. His lens whined and frothed. Again. A flower, orange petals. Hold it there, the image, simple but wonderful, strong even. He tried to let the photo breath, vibrate, but it choked like a fish in a dried-up lake. He admitted that his photos were lifeless lately. More often he was brainstuck, and during laundry work he was brainoff. His photos were without wings. The flower was cold and dry. Flat flower desperate to go underground.

Paz buried his head in his pillow. He swept his arms and legs around until he was tangled up in sheetknot. The future now was laundryhours and prisoners, colourless mock-ups of human beings walking in straight lines, heads bowed, wings folded as so ordered. And the future for many was learning how to work, then working and making fifteen fucking phones per hour for fucking ever, then retiring and being ignored; and his future was asking permission to use the phone, to breathe, to walk outside certain doors. The future for many was asking permission to walk outside borders. You can walk here but not there. Why? Because someone said so. A future of buy a tent, or health, or a university degree at double the price. A future of without; eyes without movement, waking up without yearning, conversations without discovery, reading without amazement, talking without tumbling, shitting without meditation, orchids without stalks or red guitars without strings: skeletons of what they were meant to be. He, too, was a skeleton of what it meant to be human.

Future of littlelight; and with littlelight his photos wouldn't develop. They would come out underexposed on an all-black background.

More sleep positions without sleep. The pillow between his knees and arms as though it were his prey. Straight limbs then bent limbs. Back, side, front; nothing worked.

Prison morning; a dark and soundless sunrise, without birds. And because of the direction the cell faced; even without shadows. Day's arrival was marked only by the prison bustle and the yelling and whistles of the guards.

Morning count was at 6:00 am, but Paz was still in bed. His cellmate was brushing his teeth. He always did it three times; brush hard, fill mouth with white froth, spit, rinse, then brush again. Paz watched him, and his cellmate said, "Get up then, mate; it's almost six. You know what could happen if you miss the count."

The cellmate splashed water on his face, rubbed his eyes, picked the sleepgoo out of the corners. Paz turned and faced the wall. He stared at it and finally fell asleep.

What is torture?

He was two years old, a very small person, when thirty armed men under the command of Alvaro Corbalan burst into his house and arrested his father. They also detained his mother, his sister and himself in the house, interrogated them and physically abused them, because his father had resisted the Pinochet dictatorship. Decades later, people talked about the disappearances, executions and torture of that period, but the children who had had to watch it, or who had been smalltortured—put on hot grills or beaten—felt that their torture was minor, and therefore irrelevant. Because others had been through much more. But he was still hurt, and he realised that torture wasn't understandable in grades of physical suffering, but rather, he said, in its aim to eradicate the victim as a person, to remove respect.

All the quiet pain. All the pain that was felt to be Not So Bad because it was common, because it was less extreme. Was racism, sexism, deprivation of education, lack of access to healthcare, torture?

Dull mind

When the morning call was over and a prisoner had failed to turn up, four guards stormed into Paz's cell where they found him on his bed, facing the wall, sleeping. His skin was slightly sunken and he had beads of sweat across his forehead, shoulders, around his neck, down his legs, and on his palms. He was hotter than a human should be; his mouth was ajar and each hot breath dried it more.

The guards tore the sheet off him and told him to stand up. Paz responded with flakes of moans; he was sorry, he was sick. They then pulled him out of bed and held his floppy body up and noted that he was vertical, he was standing up, he was fine and could have come to morning call; such a violation of prison procedure, and furthermore, subordination to guards wouldn't be tolerated. And they put his hands behind him and cuffed him and lead him out of the cell.

The solitary confinement cell was two metres by three metres. With off-white ceiling, walls, and floor, it had a thin concrete bed against the wall, a stainless steel sink-toilet in the corner, a portal at the bottom of its metal door for the twice daily plastic food trays, and a four centimetre by sixteen centimetre stained glass window at the top of the back wall. Paz would stay in this cell for twenty-two and a half hours a day, spending one and a half hours alone in the exercise yard; a cell about double the size of his own. Sixteen hours a day his cell was filled with sort-of light: a blend of artificial lighting and what scant bits of the sun managed to squeeze through the tiny sortofwindow, or snake their way in from the outside, through the corridor, and in through the tray flap.

Straight away Paz fell onto the bed, and in some kind of coincidental solidarity with his pathetic window, he sortofslept for the next three days, sweating unsymmetrical stains onto the concrete of the bed, which then slowly dried.

His three-day sleep ended when he vomited on the floor. His fever subsided, then his headache dulled, and he opened his eyes, craving water. He splashed his face then cupped his hands to drink from the sink. Then he surveyed his new place. He yelled, to see if any other prisoners could hear him and talk with him: no response. He looked at the stained glass window, but couldn't see through it. He got down on his stomach and tried to look out through the food tray portal, but whatever he could see, it wasn't enough to know if it were a door edge or a brick in a wall. He wasn't even sure what part of the prison he was in, and when his lunch arrived through the portal, the guard delivering it didn't speak, and Paz had no idea who made the food, where it came from, or who washed the tray afterwards.

Returning his food tray to no sound and to no person was when Paz started to realise just how disconnected from everything he was now, even more so than back in regular prison. Even if they had allowed him television or books, it would only have slightly relieved his inability to interact, affect, cause, create, and react to his surroundings. He was cut off from the worldly processes of production, decision making, climate, and relationships. Perhaps he always had been, but now it was clearest.

So it was in solitary confinement that Paz began to understand that who he was had nothing to do with his hair, or body, and everything to do with his world, his surroundings. In solitary, without any surroundings at all, he was reduced to just a few thoughts about not much of anything, to wondering, for the umpteenth time, how much longer it would last.

With life censored, his first illness was replaced by something much worse: a bored mind. He spent the next days, weeks, then months pacing, sortofsleeping, eating without tasting, and flopped on his back on the bed, his arm hanging off the side of it and his head hanging off the end. He could have invented games, played with the sounds of the flushing toilet, created fantasies so that he could travel into forests or into romances or into happier times. He could have reflected and analysed the past, but he didn't, because boredmind made it difficult. After three months in solitary, he also found it hard to do basic subtractions, or name three words starting with 'p', to remember things clearly or to form cohesive thoughts and sentences. He found it even harder to wonder, or criticise. He suffered from eye atrophy, lost too much weight, and developed a regular tic on the left side of his mouth.

His boredmind became dullmind, helpless, bland, and clumsy. It got used to the rectangles and off-white colour of the cell, and it started to think in off-white rectangles. Then, when he got out, he would speak rectangle. A language of damaged sentences.

After one hundred and twelve days in solitary, the same four guards opened the cell door, handcuffed him, and walked Paz back to ward 24. Paz dragged his feet and rolled his atrophied eyes.

"Four months is nothing; most get five years," the guards told him.

"What are you sulking about?" the prisoners said to him.

He saw no point in telling them that he couldn't make photos anymore.

Waste Mountain

Imagination and colour lay spread eagled across the slopes of Waste Mountain, their bruises dissolving into yellow rubbish as they became part of the unwanted and abandoned. Analysis was scattered about on the side of the mountain too, as well as unread and unwritten books, bound into tight cubic bundles. Nearby, amazement, connection, and compassion slumped and wilted. Hope, sold at the price of war on the poor, was stacked on top of those.

Waste Mountain was growing so big, and so fast that the little earth wretched and shuddered and swaggered with the burden.

MELLA

Excited mind
The meeting. That most basic means of human connection. In some Australian Aboriginal paintings - aerial map views of dreamtime stories, the meeting place was represented as concentric circles. Perhaps because that was how they would sit around the campfire, everyone facing everyone.

A few of Mella's years passed. Her years, world years; it was the same thing, though many people still perceived their own ageing as something separate. And time, which was also inseparable from change, saw the new replace the old in a never ending process essential to regeneration. During those years Mella had come to understand that social change, therefore, was also a long term, never ending process, and so she had learnt to balance mountain patience with a concern that it was already too late and that there was too much to do. That dynamic of patience and urgency was similar to the relationship between sadness and happiness, with the opposites cohabiting inside her, acting as her own internal land and sea buffeting and touching each other. Happy and sad, patient and urgent chattered, and that sea's rhythm, its warm ripples breathing inout, inout, inout, inout was what told her she was alive. Nightday, nightday. Time. Change.

Each day Mella either went to a job assigned to her by one of the temp agencies she was registered with, or to work with the Army of the Poor. She did whatever was necessary; contacting, handing out leaflets, writing an article now and then, banner paintings, sticking up posters, and travelling to the more remote towns with leaflets and the alternative newspaper. At night she consumed books, pausing to note something down or to patter into the lounge room to ask someone about what she had just read. Sometimes, when she needed to, she wake-dreamt, and then she had wings, and someone was kissing them, or she was kissing someone else's wings, and there were multi-coloured feathers everywhere. She also sketched sometimes, or she would just lie on the couch with her feet falling over the end and think about the people she had met.

The periods of work and no work were another kind of chattering fluctuation in her life. The temping—mostly secretarial work and filing, was meaningless to her and sent her home struggling to be optimistic. Then when she had less work, and therefore less money for food but more time, she would fight the stomach aches, enjoy more optimism, and improvise with the pasta, flour, two-minute noodles, and cans of Homebrand corn to make up new dishes.

Her other internal fluctuation was the daily arguments with herself over if she could continue, or not, and over her nagging belief that she was ugly. When she was given a list of groups to contact, she thought surely it would be better if someone else did it—she was hopeless at explaining issues over the phone. But she knew that she had to try, so she would do it, and add each tiny victory to her others. The more little victories that she accumulated, the weaker the contrary argument seemed to be. The belief that she was ugly surfaced now and then when she passed a mirror or someone took a photo. It hurt; it ripped up little pieces of her, but she argued then too, "Shush, you know ugly is not that simple."

Besides, according to Rain, the Mella that she had become was now smiling all the time. He said it was a small and tender smile, and coupled with a look of intense concentration in her eyes, it seemed to soften others, making them want to talk to her.

This morning Mella was listening to her housemates as she cooked oats with sultanas for them all. They ate quickly, standing up in the kitchen, holding the bowls of hot oats with the tips of their fingers, then they all got ready to go to one of the largest meetings any of them had ever attended.

Alice dressed quickly and left before the rest so she could walk the eight kilometres to the meeting and think as she went. She sped along the smog streets, her head titled forward, her hands gesticulating and her mouth sketching words. The movement of her legs untangled the clogs in her brain, and she worked out the proposal she would put forward.

Many others were also getting ready. The man with the brightly-coloured suit and flapping hair who had appeared at the Opera house with a megaphone and just one milk crate and a ferry driver who had been teased because he was awkward and tactlessly truthful were helping to fill boxes with cheese and vegemite sandwiches to make sure that no one at the meeting was hungry. The woman who had spray painted "I feel so sad" on a brick wall in Newtown was packing stackable plastic chairs into the back of an old van. A huge man who worked in the changing room section of Kmart, liked animals so much that he refused to have pets, and was in love with someone who lived too far away, together with a slime line worker whose hands were marked with the smell of fish, and a skinny rapper with long grey hair and multiple open relationships, were doing a last minute hand-out of leaflets promoting the meeting at different exits of Parramatta station. A doctor who had just finished a year working in Darwin, was in a last minute meeting with the Medical Workers' Front discussing the larger meeting's agenda and their proposals. A diabetic telemarketer who had recently started studying Chinese so that she could talk to her grandparents, had called in sick to be able to attend the meeting. A man of seventy who was still unable to retire, a relentless swearer, was folding a giant banner up into a manageable square. An immigrant who worked below minimum wage and made up for it by doing strip teasing at night, and who enjoyed making tiny, detailed plasticine animals, drove around in a specially hired van to pick up some of the most elderly people who were eager to attend the meeting.

When Mella got there, the open air mall was already packed. People were backed up into the town hall on one side and into the church gardens on the other, and the small circular fountain with its sculptured dramatic bodies and spare change and lolly wrappers floating in the water, barely dimpled the crowd. A twelve-year-old with a book in one hand chatted to a woman in a wheel chair who had panda-like eyes and a loud voice. A hunched poet helped the telemarketer set up the stage of many milk crates. Other people chatted in their groups; a researchers' front, the refugee rights coalition, High School Students for a Better World, housewives united, and many more, including, Mella was excited to discover, a recently formed Temp Workers' Organisation. Each group held its handmade banner or flag high, creating a garden of flapping colours. This was the Army of the Poor.

Sunlight filtered through the trees, casting an irregular lattice shadow of small triangles across the banners and over the heads of the crowd. A dog with one ear turned inside out wove in between all the legs, receiving attention and pats wherever he went. There was hot cheek anticipation which made laughing easy and eyes eager. It made the giant Westfields nearby seem to sulk in its plainness. It made the breeze felt and the shopkeepers stand in their doorways because *something* was about to happen.

Mella remembered that when she was younger, if she had thought about meetings at all, she had pictured businessmen sitting around boardroom tables in upholstered and swivelling office chairs, and she had assumed that meetings were dull. But walking through the crowd in the fluorescent orange vest assigned to the logistics crew, explaining the call list system and noting down names, Mella felt alert and excited. She had brainskip and wide-eye. She looked at people and saw poems; she asked some of them how they had learned about the meeting or become involved, and she was really interested in their answers. She saw one woman with alopecia areata—bald patches, and admired how the woman owned it, dying what was left of her hair a melange of colours. Like Frida Kahlo painting her casts, she thought. She chatted briefly to someone fixing a broken badge board, and then watched a group of people playing drums. They would invite people nearby to enter their circle and move to the drum beat, which became faster and faster. That sort of thing still intimidated Mella and she scratched her head awkwardly and walked towards a different section of the crowd. There, her excited mind saw two people locked in lipkiss, comastopped in stormtouch. She saw the filtered sun touch bare shoulders gently with its yellow strips. There was a man with a voice like carpetfoam, and so many pigeons taking over the church garden. A baby's rawmind. A hurricane smile. Soft strangers, not hard ones: the unknown kind of stranger rather than hostile kind. Strangers with cinnamon expressions, long songs, lunglaughter. And tender stories told too quickly because the meeting would start very soon.

Hard police (hostile strangers) lined up around the edges of the crowd. Someone tapped the microphone to check if it was working. A homeless man sleeping on his stomach on a green metal bench opened one eye and watched what was going on around him.

"Let's get started," said a person standing on the stage. A silence settled over the crowd, radiating outward from the stage until eventually just a few of the small groups furthest away continued to chat. Inside-out-ear dog sat down as though to listen too, with his new family of thousands. Some people took out notepads or voice recorders. Minute takers volunteered. Mella, in the speakers' queue, talked quietly with one man who was sure there was a mistake and that he should be first to speak. Someone proposed that the Army of the Poor elect a spokesperson so that the mainstream media would have someone to quote. Someone else spoke against the proposal, arguing that it was more participatory to create their own media, and boycott the mainstream, until one day it was just talking to itself. Another agreed that there was no need to see the private media as legitimate. More proposals: someone kept saying that they would "finish on this point", then kept talking and started new points, while another person talked in sign language, with a translator for those who couldn't understand. Another person began her contribution with chants, and jumped up and down as she spoke, while the person that followed found it hard to explain just what it was he wanted to propose.

Proposals were voted on, with six people in fluorescent vests counting the raised hands that were for and against. It started to get dark—they had been meeting for seven hours—and a time limit was set. With the street lights turned on, and thousands of shadows growing longer in the twilight, it was now Alice's turn to take the stage. She made the proposal she had been thinking about: a global blockade of all stock exchanges. "And banks!" someone called out. "And the real estate agents!" yelled someone else. "Shut down the system!"

The thirty-eight hard police officers who until then had stood around the perimeter of the meeting were now reinforced by thirty-eight more. With plaster of Paris expressions, they slow-ghosted among the planning groups, all the while taking notes on pocket-size notepads or on iPhones, assuming the same posture that they would to note down a traffic infringement. They paid special attention to those whom they had identified as "leaders", taking photos of their faces or recording them on video cameras. Mella understood that many battles lay ahead.

The dog with the inside-out ear put his head down on the cool grass of the church garden and fell asleep. Darkness covered the shadows and brought out the crickets.

Missing
That night Mella went to the biggest, emptiest space she could find, because she wanted to see if she could feel the Missing Thing. She went up to the roof, her favourite thinking place, with the big night above it. At the meeting she had looked for that familiar hole that engulfed her head, but she couldn't find it. Yet sometimes it was still there, a little. It was like a memory clinging onto the heels of her shoes by its nails. Still bringing her migraines. She wanted to name that gap, define it, so that it would finally become clear to her. All she knew then was that the air was never soundless now. It was always buzzing.

Notes
And she went about taking mental notes of the things she saw
As if life, as if living, were a new
Language for her

Value
In a world ruled by buying and selling, for those with

power, people were worth what they had. Similarly, the private international media covered a country in proportion to the size of its economy.

What is a criminal?

The giant media conglomerate News Corp owned one hundred and forty-six newspapers in Australia (including the *Australian* and the *Daily Telegraph*), as well as newspapers in Fiji, Papua New Guinea, UK, Ireland, the US (including the *Wall Street Journal*), magazines, radio stations, various film and television production companies, including 20th Century Fox, TV stations including Fox News, satellite and cable companies and channels including Foxtel, Fox Sports and National Geographic, and Internet news sites, among others.

Rupert Murdoch, often referred to as "the man who owns the news" was the chairman, founder, and CEO of News Corp. Another monarch in a business suit, his Media Empire was much bigger than the Roman Empire ever was. Responsible for turning life into uncontextualised fairytales and horror stories read in one minute by an always blond newsreader, one thing Murdoch's media outlets would never report is that dictators weren't limited to countries, but ruled over whole industries, too.

Worth remembering

The morning after the giant meeting was a Saturday. Exhausted, everyone in Mella's household slept in, then at around nine, barefooted their way quietly into the lounge room. One housemate proceeded to panda about in a giant white shirt and black socks on a pillow on the floor, playing with his toes, sticking his face into another pillow that he grabbed off the nearby couch. The others cat-ed the morning, curling up into four balls of pyjamas and oversized t-shirts on the two couches.

Alice turned on the television, and the five different coloured blob people—panda colour, sky blue Mella, patterns of orange and yellow Alice, and two housemates in purple and pink—lifted their heads out of their curled colours and watched as Alice flicked through the channels. She paused at the Ten Network News. A blond newsreader with a plaster of Paris expression and a suit equally as stiff was talking about their meeting: "Hooligan minority groups gathered in Parramatta yesterday... Analysts say this movement, which has captured the imagination of a few radical youth, will burn out quickly."

Alice changed the channel. A replay from Fox News, another newsreader: "... the Army of the Poor, which is said to have links to terrorist organisations, met yesterday. The anti-Australian group disrupted the mall, with this man complaining that it was 'chaos'..."

Switch to Channel Seven, the end of the ten o'clock news: "Police had to control rabble rousers from violently..." then a cut to a bank CEO who hadn't been there, commenting on the meeting, then a quick vox-pop from a Liberal politician, who also hadn't been there, then the news moved on to a celebrity break-up and a new diet, and a sale at Grace Brothers.

The coloured cat-blobs became pointed ones, the pyjamas and legs and feet and faces all rearranging themselves to sit up straighter, to think more clearly. There were frowns, a cramp, swallowed-down swear words, and ink clouds above their heads expressing their anger for them, because they were still half asleep, and because it was an expected anger—they had known the media would cover their meeting like that, but it still hurt to have their efforts lied about. Words that were selected for their connotations in a sweet journalist recipe designed to make them look small, insignificant, rabid.

Mella's black cloud shattered, reformed, and shattered again. Alice's entered her eyes and slid down her throat. Panda housemate's cloud wrapped itself around his neck, and he breathed deeply, calming himself, repeating to himself that of course the media would show it like this, of course it would, that's what the media did during war, and the war on the poor was centuries old, they all knew that.

So they picked up pillows and held them, crossed their legs and straightened their pyjama blob backs, and they talked. They had ideas.

"In the Philippines, people have already proposed a team of translators to achieve more coordination between the alternative media; and Johannesburg has suggested setting up a central Internet site that everyone can contribute to. They've even got a slogan: 'The news about us, by us, for us".

"Us being the poor," Mella said.

"And we should get rid of that," said Alice, pointing at the television with her chin. Yes, they nodded, and they all stood up and placed one hand on the power cord, then together they pulled it out. Panda housemate found several screwdrivers, and they turned the television over, took off the back cover, and began television surgery. Alice discharged the CRT and cut the wires connected to it, and then they took out the circuit board, the copper coil, more wires, plastic and cardboard. TV guts were spread out across the lounge room.

Alice and another housemate took the two halves of the television casing to the side of the house and painted them white, then painted little blue skinks with red eyes and big red lizards with yellow feet and pink tongues on it. They would use the cases as giant planters. The other two housemates sorted through the television guts, putting the screws and wire to one side because they could be used, and looking in the phone book to see where they could take the CRT to be properly recycled.

Mella wake-dreamed of a night of people throwing their televisions off a cliff - a night of raining televisions, a mass unplugging from the fake version of the world with its digitally edited people and lives, the injustice edited out altogether. Then she put on a pair of worn jeans and sat on the front porch with her diary. She had started it a few months ago. In it, she noted the things she thought were worth remembering. Most recently she had made entries about:

-Water springs, *nacientes de agua* in Spanish, the places where water is born. Where it rises to the earth's surface. She noted how springs work and ways to protect them.

-a person she had seen at the train station who was barely adult and barely happy

-the people's history of Western Sydney: the history of the area from the point of view of the women, the indigenous peoples, the prisoners, the workers rather than just the "explorers" and the governors.

-various poems by Neruda, Marti, Dalton

-how six-year-olds jump in and out of their imaginary worlds

-the way Eduardo Galeano had described the IMF and the UN: "The five countries which make decisions regarding *the* world's security—the five countries with veto on the UN security council—are the five principal sellers and produces of weapons in the world...they are the ones in charge of our peace."

-the number of nuclear weapons in each country

-the chords and strum pattern for *Techos de Carton*

-the importance of crisis, according to Einstein

-whalewords

-jokes Rafi had told

-a nightmare she'd had where a stomach eater had entered her room and she had hidden, begging it to not to eat her stomach because she needed it.

Today, she wrote about consciousness. "Consciousness is necessary in order to feel history beating," said Hugo Chavez. "And to know your place and role in history, the economy, the environment," she added. "Without that, you can't know who you really are. And you can't feel close to a stranger."

History beating

At a mass placard painting event in Redfern, a mother and her two and half-year-old child sat facing each other with their placard on the ground between them.

"What's dat?" asked the child.

"Well, it's meant to be the Aboriginal who was killed by the police."

"Is dat Mulruuuunji?"

"Yep, well, I don't know if it really looks like him. Now I'm going to write some words about him."

"Umm... Police! And, Mulrunji, please! And draw police here!"

The mother started to draw a man.

"Are you drawing daddy?"

"Not this time."

"I'm going to draw Maizee!"

Someone nearby asked, "Oh, who's that?"

"She's got a tail!"

"Oh. Is she a dog?"

"No!"

"Is she a cat?"

"Mouse!"

Their placard showed one man killed by police, the police who were still uncharged, and a mouse.

History lessons

2000: In the second row, Henry spread his legs out and looked around the school hall with a huge self-satisfied grin on his face. Conny, short and plump, walked on stage to accept her graduation certificate. She was sweating and stumbling and she lowered her eyes. Henry leaned forward and yelled, "Fuckin' hell, will you look at that ugly tart!"

2003: Henry was marching for free university education. A look on his face then of profound and permanent surprise.

Economy of music

Lucio was a fire twirler from Lima. He wore his only clothes (an off- white t-shirt, rainbow beanie with a long point that flopped down and tapped his shoulder, and pants that hung off his hips in a fashionable rejection of fashion) and carried an old woollen jumper and his fire twirlers in his bag. Like that, he travelled around South America.

He made complicated fire patterns in front of cars stopped at lights, or in plazas full of people waiting for something or someone, then he caught a bus to another city. To avoid paying, he would sleep on the floor in the aisle, then walk quickly through the door when the bus stopped, avoiding the questions of the ticket collector. On his journeys he would chat to strangers and tell them how too much music listened to in Peru came from the United States, and about what indigenous peoples of the world had in common, and then he would follow them to a café and ask them to shout him some food.

Taking back beauty

Days later, Mella wrote in her diary of things worth remembering: "Culture and creativity are tools to understand, question, and explain the world. They also help us imagine another way of doing things. We can't fight for something that we can't imagine."

"Culture bombing" they called it. One Saturday morning, when the sky was full of spiky cirrus clouds gliding about like slow stingrays, they put on costumes and took a train to Merrylands shopping mall. One woman was dressed as The Arts. She had streamers flying from her hair, big blue circles painted around her eyes, her hands and fingers painted cool pastel colours, and her billowing dress was covered in the glittering outlines of shapes and thoughts. She danced around, touching things curiously, approaching strangers and looking at them with sympathy, stroking their hair. She wrote and whistled, and mimed. Then nine people with wire wrapped around their heads and money taped to the end of it so that it dangled in front of their eyes, zombied around in circles, noticing nothing, ignoring the people they bumped into. The Arts watched, started to choke, fell onto the floor, and the zombies walked right over her, pieces of her streamer hair sticking to their shoes.

They went to the coldest areas of the Blue Mountains and debated using night puppets. They painted footpath murals that told stories and history and asked questions all across the city, and the people walked slower over those paths, reading the paintings and pointing out different bits. There were mass screen print workshops in the malls and parks, poetry on stickers stuck on train windows and public toilet doors, spoken word at the pubs, cooperative games, the tour of the retired comedians, outdoor movies projected onto walls and followed by discussion, surprising sculptures made of recycled things dangling from a train carriage ceiling, wrapped around traffic lights, climbing out of drains. A march of many drums organised by the elderly who refused to stay at home all day and out of the way woke up the sleepy inner suburbs at 5:30 am one morning. They pasted philosophy comics over the ads in the bus shelters. Guitar songs and spoken songs at stations where tired trains waited for electronic people. Hip-hop stories on campus before class started, framing the day in a poetic way. Speakouts: quick denunciations, eight-minute announcements of injustices agitated in old towns, on beaches, in video arcades, in crowded fast food restaurants. All the city cleaners put on rainbow uniforms and badges that said 'not invisible anymore', and after that they never went back to the dull grey-brown uniforms that had camouflaged them amidst the dirt that they cleaned up. Call chains to radio stations. Leaflet runs to grinding factories and green carpeted offices. Reams of paper formed into towers where the forests used to be, photographed in black and white and passed around the Internet. Wall animations. And the setting sun disappeared into a volcano mouth then erupted hot red-yellow liquid. Soft clowns, puffs of play, melting beads of autumn, blankets of pineapples, trees imitating the curves of clouds, clouds imitating the urgency of peak hour. Peak hour clouds that were angry, and tired, like many of them were. Anger imitating the inside of shells. Their city anger running like tap water. Dreams running down walls in wet paint drips of the latest imagined future.

Many of the people who watched or participated in the culture bombing got excited mind. Internal wings unravelled. But some didn't. Mella saw the man who muttered under his breath and walked away, she saw the teenager who barely looked up from his phone, she saw the older man who watched it all then walked down the road into a shoe shop and walked out with three pairs of shoes in two bags. She saw the middle-aged woman walk her Pomeranian dog right through the middle of the street performance, and wait there as it squatted down to shit.

Mella felt doubt again that it was possible to win this war, and with doubt came a resurgence of impatience. It came on one of those days when it was harder to be optimistic and a little easier to feel ugly and stupid. She growled her hands into tight fists, then found a friend's arm and wrapped herself around it.

Our butterfly wings

When the butterfly emerged from its pupa, its delicate wings were crinkled, wet, and deflated. They were covered in tiny scales made of chitlin, and each scale was a single colour, or transparent and reflected colour. The butterfly hung upside-down and pumped blood into its wings to inflate them, then waited for them to dry before flying off.

Paused on a sky blue wall, the orange butterfly's thin wings left no shadows. Close-up though, they were rainbow artworks of subtle orange tones on four very fragile canvases.

Each person also had such wings—a life that was a canvas to become an artwork. The artwork evolved as people learnt and grew and shaped their lives, complicated brushstrokes of who they were and what they had done— green ideas, earth-brown kisses, blue hopes. Some people did their art, their life, rigidly but carefully, with great attention to detail. Others painted their lives with more spontaneous strokes of harsh contrasting colours. Leonardo's wings were murky greens and shades of yellow. He painted life roughly, with a loaded brush, drops of paint escaping and trickling down. He painted sharp red and blue and purple lines exploding out of his murky yellow background.

Everyone's wings were different, yet the tragedy—the biggest crime, was that most people in the world didn't get a chance to live an artful life, to fly. Wings stayed closed, wings fell off, wings bled and disintegrated, wings remained as blank canvases.

Maths wings

His mathematics was beautiful. He started a sum within himself, and experimented, adding numbers and other equations so that the lines of maths became further and further indented and ran down his arm, over his hand, and up the other side of his arm. It was raining and he was running, and the numbers at his shoulder smudged and the ink ran down in stripes. There is something in this, he thought. He wrote quicker and ran harder and the rain got heavier and battered him. He swerved, almost falling. Hours passed. The sun dropped closer and closer to the bottom.

Then he fell.

The numbers on the back of his arm slid into the running water at the side of the curve. The sun arrived at the bottom, disappeared. Light changed exactly.

What is a hero?

He was on a sixteen-hour bus trip to the capital for a concert. He had a tattoo on his chest that said "never stop", and he made whispered promises to do anything it would take to make a difference, as the punk rock band earthquaked the crowd, their spines, their minds. He never did stop. Even on the bus back, exhausted, he turned around to the boy behind him and asked about his community problems. He never interrupted, but listened with his head resting on the seat and his heart taking notes. The bus ate road, ate wind.

Mella the teacher

Mella had found it hard to find the time and money to do a bridging course and try to get into university, and had largely given up on the idea of being a teacher. Then, a few weeks after the mass meeting in Parramatta, she volunteered to facilitate army training and study workshops, and was surprised to find herself teaching after all. She had taught four classes so far, and as she taught, she learnt to teach, and she remembered what she had liked about Rafi's classes.

She was a different kind of teacher. She listened much more than she talked. She asked questions that she really wanted to hear the answer to; why somebody thought something, and where their opinions came from. She encouraged them to make suggestions at the end of class, and was delighted when they offered criticisms, because it meant that both she, and the classes, could improve. Likewise, at the start of the class she carefully explained what they would learn, how they would go about learning it, and why. Her classes finished when they felt they had reached their goals, rather than at a specific time.

She used a lot of cooperative games and other dynamic activities that promoted working together and participation. She and the other group members sat in circles and read, or looked at photos, or brainstormed, or took turns writing on the whiteboard; and one member took notes of the conclusions they reached. They had fun, and the class always energised Mella rather than tired her. Unlike many teachers that tried to get their students to admire them, Mella admired her students. She found them fascinating, and told them so. She shared her doubts, mistakes, and weaknesses with them, and let them support her, as well as each other.

Most importantly, she taught them what they most wanted to learn, so they were always keen and motivated. She got them to analyse other ways of being and of thinking, and to question old values and create new ones, and she taught them the many ways of reading: "You don't just read books," she said, "you can read the land and people too". They looked at footprints, erosion, dead fish, breeding mosquitoes, temperatures, wind patterns, and at wrinkles, posture, accents, the sounds of the spaces between words, the rationale of possessiveness, the need to be nice, power, marriage, the history of gods, and they gradually integrated people with land, with economics, and learnt to read them together, dialectically.

Today's class was in a restaurant near Parramatta. It was Sunday morning and the restaurant was closed, and many of the group's members, cooks, dishwashers, and waiters worked there or nearby, so the location was a logical choice. When Mella arrived, she was in a funny mood, and she stood on one foot like a flamingo, watched one of the cooks who was helping arrange chairs in a circle, lost her balance, laughed at herself, then helped to move a large table to one side to create more space. While they waited for everyone to arrive, she chatted to someone who worked in a nearby ice-cream shop, asking her about the hours, the pay, and conditions.

Mella began the class with a brainstorming discussion about the effects a blockade could have. One of the cooks wrote on a small whiteboard with a blue marker the phrases they came up with, such as 'take away an institution's public legitimacy', 'rejection and criticism', 'strengthen the movement', 'communication', 'kick start larger/longer actions'. Then Mella divided the class into three groups and gave each a different hypothetical question to discuss: If there was police violence, what should they do? How could they ensure that everyone had a role to play? In a difficult situation, such as confrontation or mass arrests, how could the blockade best make democratic decisions? One person from each group shared his or her ideas with the rest, then they had an all in question session about the practicalities of a blockade: the legal aspects, first aid, the properties of tear gas, what to wear and not to wear, chants and songs to keep the morale of the blockade high over many hours, and communication and coordination. Finally, they practised blockading techniques, with half the group forming a line in front of the kitchen door, and the other half portraying police and breaking the line.

As they experimented with different formations, Alice walked in. She was visiting all the different classes to deliver handbooks put together by the lawyers' collective. She put a bundle down on one of the chairs, and then watched the class for a minute. Mella was portraying a police officer but wasn't managing to maintain a serious police face, and she started to laugh uncontrollably. The others caught it, but as the law of contagious laughter requires people to have been together for a while, Alice couldn't catch it. But she smiled at the laughtertears smudged around Mella's eyes. How she's changed, Alice thought. She's filled with generosity, sincerity and warmth now. Alice left quietly, blowing travelkisses to police-Mella and the others.

Futureseeds
Breezeheart flower nestled its hundreds of seeds, its new things waiting, then launched them into the air. They

drifted towards abandoned ground. Seed beads cuddled into the soil, sponged up water, and split their coats. Hungry, they stretched out leg roots, shoots, and leaves. Touched sunfood. The flower multiplied, and eventually a carpet of flowers would paint the old abandonment into a colourfeast.

Photo thoughts

How do you take photos of fog? You photograph silhouette people and the soft glow of street lights; you photograph the street under the fog.

How do you take photos of sunlight? You photograph the leaves up close and the dance of colour on their surface.

How do you take photos of bubbling hope? You photograph the old and the new touching as they pass.

How do you photograph injustice? It is the easiest to photograph, for it is as common as the number of people on the earth; each person staggers under its weight.

Kite love

Dozens of kites soared on windroads in the sky, while clouds with an urge to storm loitered above them. There were parrotfish kites with long fins and tails, a centipede with its many coloured feet flailing in different directions, bugs with intricately patterned backs, sailing boats frolicking on windwaves, giant rainbow rings, a kite of scattered blossoms, a multi-coloured shark whose giant mouth swallowed all the air in its path, five giant feathers, and a kite of huge water drops—blue and translucent—which caught the sun's light, played with it, then threw it off again.

Mella and Alice walked away from the others, up over the beach's sand dunes and into the bush behind them, where they followed a thin dirt path for a while, then strayed off it to sit under the shade of a small eucalyptus tree. They felt like some barefoot chatter with basil warmth. But today, their conversation was of a different kind. Instead of talking they looked, and then they touched. Mella wore a large button-down shirt that fit loosely; she could have been anything underneath it. Her breasts were free and outgoing, and Alice was curious. She wore an old, frayed singlet top, and when one strap fell off her shoulder, revealing a small bit of areola colour, she let it stay there. They lay down on the grass and dirt and twigs and decomposing bugs, and Alice slid her hand underneath Mella's shirt and left it resting on her stomach. Mella put her hand over Alice's. The kites dived, ducked, and played above them. And they too played, discovered, tasted different parts of skin, mixed mutual massages with the remembering of their favourite stories, rocked to the lavender rhythm of the music floating up from the beach, and let it tell them when to move faster, or when to slow down. They asked what the other wanted, where, and how, and enjoyed the gentle intimate descriptions they heard. They found new clefts and dips of sensitivity and noted that one could read with fingertips too. They explored the hundreds of ways of touching, rubbing, stroking, kneading, fairy pinching, and hand resting. Why not play with dirt, why not kiss a flower. A sleeping petunia's tip licked and kissed. It opened slowly. Tasted like treacle and salty rain.

And as the storm gathered, the kites moved faster and more abruptly. Blue raindrop kite and pink scattered blossom kite made concentric circles around each other, dived through the loops made by the others' tail, then headed towards each other face-on, sliding over each other at the last minute, getting caught and entangled so that they became a new kite altogether, made of a new colour, moving in new ways.

The ground was warm from spent energy. Alice swore that she would sleep "just for a minute". Mella sat up and felt her heart beating calmly, and she heard everything: the bustling in the grass of the army ants and beetles, and the far off galahs, wrens, and sparrows. She felt well: no headache, no itches or anxiety, and she had an urge to paint or draw.

The storm finally started, and they ran back to the beach, laughing at how heavy their legs were as they tried to stride the sand. The kites dived out of the sky and belly landed around them. Mella caught the bus back with the others, while Alice dashed off to a meeting. As she went she talked out loud to herself, one idea landing on top of another, and her excited body extended itself into excited mind.

Love systems

One night the next week, Mella was at home with the others, when for a moment she remembered Ben. After a long day of meetings, teaching, and contacting, they were sitting down for a 10:00 pm dinner of tomato soup. Rain and Ramona were visiting, and Ramona asked Mella what she was thinking about. Mella looked down at her lap, then said, "Well, I was just remembering my ex, and how he would count the number of times we slept together each week and note it in his planner. Sometimes he even timed himself, and another time he measured me and compared me to supermodels, or he would watch porn and tell me to fix myself up like the women in the movies. For him it was so important to be 'normal', and that meant there was only one way to do things". Her remark started a long conversation about how power and economic and social systems affect human relationships. Rain argued that personal relationships reflected human economic relationships, so under a market economy, people "shopped" for their partners and even their friends, and women were objects to be acquired. Ramona agreed, and said that sex should be about working together, and connecting, and that if society were more about cooperating, relationships would be too. From there, the conversation steered in another direction. Alice and a guy left the group to go for a walk. They held hands. Mella watched them leave and smiled to herself. She suggested a late night game of dominoes to the others.

Taking back dignity

They insisted they couldn't do it. Weren't good enough, didn't know how. We're homeless, where would we organise, and who would listen to us? One in two hundred people in Australia living in one set of stale clothing, each with overgrown salty toenails, worried eyes that rattled silver, ashamed bent backs, sun-spotted, dried-up bruises over older bruises, a beard to hide behind, exhausted spirits, familiar with the coldness of floors, lack of privacy the worst nakedness, sleep disturbed by the rain knocking on the body barely protected by pieces of cardboard, watching the silent movie of the world from a knee-level viewpoint, and dreaming of suicide.

Maybe they felt like a stains on the street. Every Olympics, every World Cup, governments packed them away like the Plague and threw them somewhere out of sight. So the world was pock-marked with the black holes of people who were there but didn't exist.

But Mella thought that they could do it. One of her students designed an invitation to the first meeting to form a homeless people's rights organisation. They printed off hundreds, and she and her class went around to all the parking lots, abandoned cars, station toilets, church doorways, arcade back steps, behind the library, the Parramatta River bridges, the soup queues, the women's refuges, abandoned houses, an old and vacated hair salon, and talked to the homeless people there. Mella noted their names in her diary of things worth remembering. And most of them stored the invitation in a pocket or a sock or in a swag of all things, sure that it was another silly gimmick by another charity or church trying to get cred, scared and intimidated by the idea of walking through the front door of the town hall to talk about things like Organisation and Rights.

Except for Jon, a nineteen-year-old dressed in black jeans and a black t-shirt with the sleaves ripped off, a head of long bleached dreadlocks tied back with a stiff woven headband, and a dry voice. He whispered when he said, "Why the fuck not? Got nothing better to do tomorrow."

And also Samuel, eighty-four years old, seventy-one years homeless, a storyteller of the history of their world—he knew all the burnings, beatings, and good luck stories of the homeless of Sydney, and he was a mapper of their places, with a partner by his side who sang sadly and strongly her own songs in a mixture of English and Ngarrindjeri. They lived in Central, Redfern, and Town Hall stations, and on the trains. He said, "Whaddawe got to lose eh? Give me more of those leaflets and we'll round up our mates."

Fifteen people came to the first meeting. They sat in the furthest corners of the large hall until Samuel barked at them to help Mella arrange the chairs in a circle. They talked, and tumbling over each other in interruptions and lost trains of thought, they insisted, again, "It's pointless; people like us can't do anything." Mella insisted that they could. She talked about when women had first won the vote, or when workers had won the minimum wage, about the long list of struggles that people insisted couldn't be won, and then had been won. Samuel asked each person how many other homeless people they knew. He made a list and put it on the floor in the middle of the circle. Then he asked them to name all the spots Mella and her students hadn't been to, and he made an even longer list. "We'll call another meeting," he said, knowing that when they saw how many they were, all in one place, and that it was they who had brought the others there, they would feel more optimistic.

Around three hundred and thirty people came to the second meeting. They sat on the orange plastic seats, looking up and down the rows, falling silent when Mella turned on the microphone at the front. They slumped in their chairs, preparing themselves for a long speech, as many were accustomed to the obligatory sermons given by religious charities. But Jon proposed an agenda with just two items: What are the problems? And, what do we want to do about them? Everyone voted in favour, but when he invited people to speak, no one did. They were unsure of themselves and kept looking up and down the rows of orange plastic seats. They kept finding the floor fascinating. Then one young woman with short hair got up and said her homelessness was like a punishment for having been abused, and then the people in the street with their non-looks punished her for being homeless. After her, everyone had something to say, and half the hall was in the line for the microphone. Then, when it came to the second agenda item, they resumed their glances at the rows of chairs. Mella had foreseen this, and she invited some members of the Cleaners' Collective, the Bus Drivers' Union, and the High School Organisation to quickly recount some of the things they had done. After that, the short haired woman proposed a "Homeless People's Front", and following her lead, eleven more people queued up for the microphone to make proposals. Someone "proposed" that unity was important, someone else "proposed" that society treat them with more respect, while Samuel proposed that they build a contingent for the global blockade, and have a banner and placard painting working bee. Others proposed some concrete demands, including more public housing and getting rid of police power to make them "move on". They proposed their hearts out, then shuffled out of the halls, leaving the rows of orange chairs uneven, thinking that it had felt good to speak out but had probably been a waste of time, too.

They held the working bee in the Town Hall square, where many of them had spent nights and days trying to blend into the benches, the trees, the carpet of autumn leaves. Everyone did what they could; some nailed together placards, some measured banner material, others mixed paint colours, others drew designs, composed placard wording, or painted. A group of around sixty people divided up the posters among themselves for their blockade contingent, then in pairs, scattered themselves around the city. The hall felt busy: one of the secret seeds of dignity.

A journalist from the new Army of the Poor media arrived, and sitting on the ground next to the banner, asked Samuel if she could interview him. Then she showed him how to clip the small microphone onto the inside of his shirt collar.

"Can you tell me about what you're fighting for?" she asked, angling the camera tripod so that she got his three quarter profile as well as some of the activity in the background.

"Well, now, it's like this. People assume we're lazy, can't be bothered working, but that's never the case. Some of us have been to prison for something trivial, and then we got out but had nowhere to go; others were kicked out of their families for being HIV positive, others for being gay, others flee abuse, others lost their job, many have physical or mental illnesses that make it hard to hang on to a job, or to cope; some have severe stress, and they are sad and started to gamble, drink, or do drugs. But those are fewer than you might think. Usually, people take up drugs afterwards, because it's not easy being totally abandoned by the world. And then, well, housing is expensive, isn't it? Something so basic...shelter. It seems like it should be one of the most basic of human rights, but it costs an arm and a leg."

Samuel paused, but the journalist just smiled a little, and waved her hand in a gesture that suggested he should just keep talking. He talked a little more then paused again, each time expecting to be told to wrap up. But the journalist hardly talked, and only occasionally did she ask for more detail.

"Well so then, once you're homeless, it's even harder to study, get health care, get a job, or recover from addictions. And the saddest thing for me is that we can't participate in anything. We get kicked out of libraries, cultural events, and things like that. We're shut out; some people are even scared of us. I'm done."

"Thank you; that was really useful," the journalist said.

Samuel frowned. "You'll cut it up, of course."

"No."

He frowned more, and pretended to be occupied with taking off the microphone.

When sixteen hundred homeless people turned up at Belmore Park for their contingent's march to the global blockade, they realised that maybe they could do it. They marched up George Street with surprise in their eyes. Little wings sprouted from their backs and their vibrant banners undulated in the wind. They held their placards above their heads, they jumped and ran instead of walking, they blew whistles and beat improvised drums made from empty paint cans, biscuit tins, and red, yellow, and light green buckets. Jon walked long steps, looking every which way, feeling a little awkward because he was stopping himself from skipping. They made up for too many years of no noise. No more street stain, instead they filled the road with their excited chanting and singing. And for once, the other people in the street, those waiting at intersections, those in shop doorways and looking down from fourth floor windows, waved back. Samuel laughed, throwing his head back and punching the air. Because his stories had new endings now. And because new stories were being born. For the first time, they felt pride. Lonely lifelong battles joined together to scream out as they marched, "We exist, and we demand our rights!"

More contingents behind them and in front of them, heading to the blockade. A contingent of people with mental and physical difficulties—thousands upon thousands of people with autism, Down Syndrome, chronic anxiety, insomnia, post-traumatic stress, eyes that didn't work well, marching with arms linked, and distributing leaflets that explained their demands. A contingent of graffiti artists, another of refugees, and one made up of three thousand woman who had been sexually abused.

And on the other side of the city centre, in the echoing spaces of the Sydney Opera House car park, eighteen thousand police checked their rifles and shotguns, put on helmets and bullet proof vests, and grouped into tactical response units.

La lucha

Her name was Lucha and she lived in Cochabamba, Bolivia. She wore a purple polera down to her knees and carried her shop wares in the rainbow coloured aguayo on her back. Her husband had died two years ago, and at twenty-four, she cared for her three children alone. All the Luchas of Cochabamba left home at 4:00 am, and walked to the city centre to quilt its paths with their stalls. Breastfeeding, working, husbands demanding, children on their shoulders, Bolivia's long history of being invaded, and the legalised abuse of its peoples...all those weights linked as chains. Chains they carried quietly, with much strength.

In 2007, they wore their best clothes to march past Evo—the first indigenous president, the first coca farmer president—someone like them. Thousands upon thousands of Luchas had huge smiles on their faces, easily outshining in that moment the boring bright blue sky.

History from far away

Mella had a telescope, but it was different to Matt's. It was an inverse telescope for looking at history from far away;

for zooming out from the chairs, tables, and coffee cups of history to see its patterns. The night before the global blockade Mella sat on her mattress with piles of documents, statements, books, Internet print-outs and photos, and she used her telescope to reach a few conclusions. She read about different times and places:

Ludlow, Colorado, United States, 1913 to 1914: Rockefeller's Fuel and Iron company ran a feudal kingdom of shops, laws, land, doctors, schools, churches, bars, and housing. Thousands of miners went on strike over the domination, the low pay and the dangerous conditions. They were kicked out of the housing and moved into tents set up by the union. Rockefeller hired gunmen to puncture and lacerate the tents and the miners with bullets, yet they still resisted. So he set fire to the tents with the miners' families hiding inside.

Egypt, 1977: Where bread was life and the government ended basic food subsidies as an offering to the IMF and US business monarchs. People responded with strikes, meetings, occupations, marches. Egypt was raging and its police stations, hotels, casinos and government headquarters were burning, and the government quickly caved in and restored the subsidies. But first it deployed the army on the rage and killed around eight hundred people.

Tlatelolco, Mexico City, 1968, ten days before the Olympics: Thousands marched then concentrated in the Plaza de las Tres Culturas, and as dusk dropped, five thousand soldiers, and two hundred tankettes and trucks surrounded the plaza. They fired into the crowd and turned the plaza into moonsurface; pockmarked with the craters of hundreds of students' bodies, and the empty spaces left by the one thousand, three hundred and forty-five that were arrested.

Haiti, 1791 to 1804: Plantation owners squeezed slaves into husks of humans and sent coffee and sugar to France. A hundred thousand slaves rebelled and the plantation monarchs aimed their guns and tried to shoot birds back into cages.

Nicaragua, 1970s and 1980s: It might have started when a poet killed the first Somoza dictator. Then the dictator's son took over and consumed the country; acquired forty percent of the economy and thirty percent of arable land. The revolution—millions of poets this time—toppled him and brought on agrarian reform, healthcare, childcare, books everywhere. New laughter, sunheads, debate; all night long. Then came the US sponsored contras; an army of organised abuse, kidnapping, torture, mutilation, murder, bombing and burning of health care centres, schools, farms, cooperatives, houses, and towns; they amputated the new urge to write.

Guatemala, 1954 to 1990s: When the CIA and Colonel Castillo took power in a coup and reversed years of economic reform, the country atrophied. They painted the country with MacDonald's colours and branded it all over with the flag of US-owned United Fruit Company. US backed death squads and the army killed an estimated two hundred thousand people who had criticised the regime, made the words in newspapers disappear, gathered up the sun, the moon, the colour green, and hid them away where nobody could find them.

Indonesia, 1965 to 1966: Indonesia too lost the sun. PKI members were beheaded, arrested, five hundred thousand to a million killed, with US help. Towns, buildings and houses were burnt; days greyed, trees looked away. "With five hundred thousand to a million communist sympathisers knocked off...I think it's safe to assume a reorientation has taken place," said Australian prime minister Harold Holt while visiting the US.

Vietnam, 1955 to 1976: Again the US stuck its bombsmissilesrocketspoison into other people's weddings, work days, romances, livelihoods. Land, forests, farms: erased by chemical peel. Twenty million bomb craters filled with breeding mosquitoes.

Through her inverse telescope Mella saw the pattern. Every single time the poor demanded dignity, they were attacked, the war on the poor taken up a notch. And every single time, the violence was blamed on the people it was committed against.

Battles

Amidst the overcast light that cities always seemed to have, among the buildings and skyscrapers stubbornly stuck to the ground, harsh in their snobbish silence and their stiff expressionless shades of grey, the homeless people's contingent ended their march. They had arrived at one of the many blockade points around the city; the eight-story head office of the Commonwealth Bank. There, they joined the three thousand who were already standing in six lines of blockade all around the building, including Mella and her students and the casual workers' organisation, and the refugee contingent. Logistical groups were also standing apart from the blockade on the corners of the block: legal observers, Army of the Poor media, people assigned to communicate with other blockades, some food and transport workers, and some roving back-up people. The homeless marchers propped their placards on the ledges of the dark brown tiled and arched windows of the bank building on Elizabeth Street and tied some of their banners to lamps on either side of the main door.

Ten minutes after the homeless contingent arrived, the police followed; led by mounted police, because the riot vans that they would usually have used hadn't been able to get past other blockades that they'd confronted along the way. They, too, numbered just over three thousand. Dressed in full riot gear with helmets with transparent plastic visors and various canisters, batons, and guns hanging from their belts, they set up metal riot fencing, connecting it together like k'nex toys all the way around the blockade, just ten metres away from the blockaders.

Then they stood in formation, staring straight ahead, the mounted police in a line behind them.

Mella walked around to the front of the blockade, answering questions about their various contingency plans and checking everyone's grip to make sure they were linking arms and holding their own wrists, rather than just joining hands, which was less secure. She tried to ignore the hot police glare she felt on her back. She was worried, and excited: the opposites cohabiting that day inside her. The combination worked well: excitement stopped the worry from becoming panic, instead maintaining it at a useful level of alertness; and worry calmed her excitement, helping her to focus, and keeping her sense of proportion; the blockade viewed through an inverse telescope was just one day of many decades, was just one small step.

Chants and songs started in sections of the blockade and wove their way around the bank and back again, growing and shrinking as people tired and reenergised. Above them, above the towers, a flock of starlings turned and dived and glided in unison—in entrainment, to also save energy.

"Bail out hunger, not the banks!" people chanted. "They've got the whole world in their hands!" they sang, pointing at the bank behind them. "But not for long!" they yelled. Mella joined the blockade, standing in the front row between Jon and Samuel. Jon was jumping up and down as he chanted, and he greeted Mella with an elbow poke to her waist.

And the police picked up their riot fence and moved it one metre closer, tightening the perimeter around the blockaders.

And Mella noticed that she was chanting out of time and felt a little pathetic, then forced herself to remember things that mattered, and chanted on but still out of time.

And the police picked up their riot fence and moved it another metre closer.

And the sun rose above the building opposite the bank

and threw its yellow light in the blockaders' eyes. Hundreds of hands moved up simultaneously to shade faces. As if they were suddenly saluting the police.

And the police, still staring straight ahead, moved their fence another metre closer. Samuel said to Mella, "All they're doing is actually helping us keep the bank shut down. Or trying to make it easy to attack us and arrest us."

And the front row of police took out their guns and aimed them at the blockade. Then they were still again.

The blockaders went silent. They looked back at the guns as though it were a staring contest. Then their eyes were distracted by the one thing that was moving, a rotating advertising billboard on the opposite building: a woman made happy by shampoo. Ten seconds and the ad scrolled down. Gold necklace on a black background. Ten seconds and back to happy shampoo. Then a horse sniff. Then a blockader sniff. Eyes back to the guns aimed at their faces. Chanting again, their voices tripping and trembling a little, first shrill, then angry.

Line of guns.

Overcast light again.

And a blue and yellow butterfly, clearly lost.

It fluttered from one gun to the next as though expecting to find pollen inside the barrels.

And Mella realised that the police, the bankers, the big business owners, the government which represented them, were more scared than they were. They had privilege to lose. She started a new chant, "We're not afraid, we're not going anywhere!"

Horse twitch; gun twitch.

With guns lowered, the police in front stepped aside so that the police on horseback, batons in their right hands, could move to the front. Gun police disconnected the riot fence for a moment to allow the horses to pass. The mounted police gave their horses a knee nudge to make them move forward, then a leg squeeze to make them go faster. "Wait!" Mella shouted into the megaphone. "Wait!

Wait! Sit!" she said. The entire blockade sat down, their arms still linked, just as the horses reached them. The horses, disorientated by the sudden obstacle in front of them, raised their front legs, neighed loudly, and snorted, until their riders, struggling to regain control, nudged them to turn around. They straightened their horses, straightened their helmets and clutched their batons. And amidst the upset horses, Mella sensed something else fleeing. She could no longer feel Missing Thing. But she didn't have time to think about that now. The blockaders were high-fiving and fist-knocking everyone around them, and holding up victory fingers at the police. But the police were reforming their lines and moving their fence closer once again. From the fifth floor windows of the bank building, bank managers in blue shirts, ties, and no crowns, watched.

What is a hero?

Are heroes allowed to fail sometimes, or be discouraged? Miguelito loved books; he covered all of his in plastic contact and wrote his name neatly on the inside front cover. He would dance around his girlfriend's room to ska while taking books off her shelf and glancing at their content pages: books about history, philosophy, socialism. He tried to organise a community reading group and walked down the jagged street of his barrio, greeting a man who was almost blind with an "Epa!" and giving him a leaflet. He gave another one to the woman in the small shop on the corner, and another to the kid with the faux silver necklace, and another to the tired man smoking at his window.

He went to the pub that night and argued with his girlfriend about Cuba. Then he went home and she went home and they continued the argument over the Internet. At 11:30, they went to bed, but couldn't help sending just a few more text messages, arguing... The next night they met and sat together in the plaza during a blackout, and they realised that neither of them were completely right. It all depends, they agreed.

Miguelito felt despondent sometimes. After days of organising meetings that people didn't turn up to, he would put his head in his hands and briefly renounce struggle altogether. "I want to go walking in the mountains," he said.

His girlfriend showed him a photo of a line of soldiers in riot gear, holding shields and batons. They were coming to take a woman's land, and she was trying to hold them back, on her own, with a baby under each arm. She physically pushed at them, as one might try to move a huge train.

One photo, but they saw different things: she saw a strong woman in a simple skirt, resisting something big and powerful with determination; he glanced at the photo and asked, "Doesn't that depress you?" He saw her pointless struggle, her defeat.

The importance of failure

They called it a failed coup, when, on 4 February 1992, Hugo Chavez and other military leaders and soldiers rebelled and tried to overthrow the president. After decades of corruption and kleptocracy, then more recently the enforcing of an IMF package, increasing poverty, and the Caracazo of 1989 when the police and army went around killing people in the streets, it was felt by the rebelling soldiers that a coup was the only way. But on that day, someone from within their group alerted the military high command and their communication was cut off. President Carlos Andres Perez, whom they had planned to intercept on his way to the presidential palace, made it there, then went to the Venevision television station and made a speech, effectively defeating the coup attempt. Chavez also addressed the nation, telling his people to cease hostilities and saying that they had only failed "for now". He was sent to Yare prison, but in 1998, he was elected president.

"The coup attempt broke decades of silence," a Venezuelan remembered. "People stopped being scared then to criticise the regime. Finally there was a bit of hope, and Chavez was seen as the leader of that."

The hardest thing

Despite the hot cracked sun scalding and big doubts hurting like gaping holes in the footpath; fall down, graze self-esteem, get back up again. Despite the lies and being called a terrorist and a bludger over and over again, despite being misunderstood, mis-portrayed, despite the heavy exhaustion and the fucking pepper spray at protests, not to mention the arrests, the occasional shooting and a bit of fear about what could happen (you could lose your job; you could get beaten by a cop today or raided tonight). Despite the loneliness of doing things that take a long time, despite the apathy, despite it being unfashionable, despite illness, confusion, headaches, and a bit of helpless hunger...

Despite feeling unworthy of taking on the whole world and its mess...

And despite the lack of recognition. No degree to recognise all that reflection and study. No ceremony, no rewards, no fame or spotlight, no big audience clapping... Despite no retirement age for this sort thing, despite little bits of sadness gnawing away at arms and legs...

Despite no guarantee that the years and decades of commitment would be worth the effort; no contract ensuring that this would turn out okay in the end...

Despite the incessant rain,

They marched.

They went on strike, they boycotted, organised self defence units, they studied, they recruited, they rallied and blockaded more, they took over media outlets, and they took over work places and ran them themselves; then they started new things, and built up their own health systems, new food distribution systems...

The battle lasted many decades. The Army of the Poor fought on, discovering that you can't cut off the wings of time, and some of its members got old and passed away before they could witness major changes.

PAZ

What is freedom?

There's a thing that makes you wake up when something is wrong, and it woke Paz before everyone else. Before the rackety chaos of sounds, feet, drowsy shouts, and running in different directions woke up those who had slept on. It meant that Paz was one of the first, one of the few who got out, before the guards managed to reactivate the security system, put out the fire, re-lock the cell doors, and do a 2:30 am emergency roll call.

Maybe it was the laundry cleaning agents and solvents that caused the fire, or maybe a kitchen boiler, an electrical fault, or a stove left on. Paz would never find out. He would barely remember the non-sound of fire and its aggressive smell and its smoke airbrushing the night. A high pitched ringing in his ears—the sound of screaming closed windows or a police siren—followed him out the prison doors and out the main gate as the guards opened it for the fire trucks.

The screaming sirenwindow followed him as he ran on, not noticing the incense taste of outer-city air, or the slap from sudden cold. Noticing, but not caring, that the air moved—he'd forgotten that air moved. Not noticing that he was only wearing his night-time boxers and that the gravel he ran over was gradually wearing down his bare soles, preparing the way for cuts and blisters and two medium sized infected wounds. When he couldn't walk anymore, he slept. In soldier position, right in the middle of a suburban footpath, his arms at his sides despite the cold slapping.

Four hours later, he woke up stiff and saw the blue sky and felt the warm sun lying gently on his stomach. For a few minutes he remembered happiness. A flicker of a photo—the first in too long—a sun with hands, touching people, patting them on the head. Then he got up. He noticed that he was almost naked, and that the skin on his feet was tattered, and that he not only didn't know where he was but that there was nowhere he wanted to go.

With sirenwindow still wailing in his ears, he set to walking again, taking some sports pants and a singlet off a backyard washing line before he reached the unknown suburb's centre. Asphalt roadlines, broad concrete footpath lines, power lines, lampposts, and shops were all he saw. He looked left and right, at this main road, and saw shops. Shop shop shop like cell cell cell. A few blocks away, a giant windowless shopping centre, another windowless prison. Security guards at its main doors; guards, prison guards. Paz would go there. He dodged the sun now, as if it were shooting its rays at him. And people looked at him. He knew he had crazy eyes and crazy dodgewalk and droopymouth and no shoes, and he felt ashamed. So he dodged people's glances as well. He was out of prison but his mind was wonderclosed. Slugsteps to the shopping centre. Vaguely aware of something very big, missing. His thoughts and sentences a train riding off the rails and diving off a cliff. Another attempt at a thought, but his sentences were trainwrecked, wartorn. They couldn't get back up again. They stayed down, shattered.

He walked through the shopping centre's sliding doors, half expecting to go on with laundry work. But this place had fruitloop music and smelt like blue jelly. And there were more people staring at him, talking about him without moving their mouths. Walking past him and eying him and tossing their comments across the huge jelly floor. "Put your eyes away!" he said suddenly, his voice a quiet sirenwindow, though he had tried to shout.

Back outside now, where the street smelt of salt. He could smell his own hair too. He pulled it out in clumps, blood on the tips like bundles of fibre optic lights. He needed food. He sat down where he was, on the main street but still near the shopping centre, and cupped his hands to beg. His arms tired quickly, so he held out just one hand, resting it on the pavement. A man in a business suit with a designer watch and a five-fold power tie heading towards the shopping centre trod on his hand, looked at his shoe as though to check it for dirt, and hurried on. Two women with fringes combed over one eye, false eyelashes, injected lips, and handbags too small to carry anything, stood right in front of him and chatted to each other about the clothes on display in the window behind him. They laughed in measures. They talked for a long time about prices, and would they wear it? But Paz needed to eat, he needed money, and they were in his way. So he bit one of the legs blocking his view. Bit it hard and got stocking taste in his teeth and a tiny handbag hitting him repeatedly around the ears until he unlocked his jaw. The two women fast-walked away.

Then there were lots of people fast walking. A man with so much steroid muscle he couldn't close his arms in a hug, a woman in heels so high her knees cracked and her legs bent inwards, others with multiple smartphones, using them all at once to say nothing at all. All those people parading, life one long fashion show with each of them competing to be number one. They walked faster and faster, elbowing each other, sticking out a leg to trip a rival, pulling at a wig, cutting off a nose—anything to win the Race.

Behind them in the parade, muttering, with flies undone, and saliva stripes running down chins to necks, tripping on the birds, throwing violent anger into the air and catching it again: the shambolic march of the alwaysdrunk. Then the hunters, shooting pigeon flocks in trees, small grey bodies contorting in the air and crashing onto the hats and heads of the fashion parade. Raining pigeons, and a few dogs, and a couple of kids... Then the multi-national restaurant slaveworkers, uniforms, microphones in their ears, someone in a control room off in paradise giving them orders: sit down, stand up, spin around, smile, smile, smile, repeat have a nice day, sit down. Their parade dance so well coordinated.

Paz looked up at the awful-lot-of-blue sky and saw the businessmen monarchs, dictators without crowns flying about on little dragonplanes, pointing down at the world and deciding without consulting, agreeing to not do anything about global contamination, writing little pieces of manipulation on blue poisoned paper and throwing it at the hoards of rich-hungry followers who imitated them with glee, aspiring to have a dress, or a mansion or a car just like those of their favourite economic dictator.

Sirenwindow growing louder. Inhabiting his nerves. He realised that in a place like this no one would notice his hand held out, one finger already swollen, bruised and flopping down at an unnatural angle.

Beggars not butterflies
In Buenos Aires, children juggled all day on wide roads of traffic and wide clouds of black exhaust hoping for people's leftover money. A boy with the shoes of a doomed old man walked up to tourists in the middle of the dark night, played his accordion for a minute, then cupped one small hand, and with the other, pointed to his mouth.

In Bangalore, people in the beggar colonies died five or six at a time under "mysterious circumstances".

In Bogota, a woman with her disabled child in a

wheelbarrow rattled her tin can by the church door.

In Kenya, the widows begged by day and slept in the park. Occasionally, they talked together about the only thing in their lives; how much money they got that day.

In New Delhi, thousands of beggars blended into the metal beams and the makeshift shanty shops of the main station and the main streets. Many of them were self-mutilated: burns, amputations, untreated and festering wounds, all in order to better compete with the others.

In New York, a woman wore a large straw hat and a scarf to hide her face. Sitting on the ground, her head bowed, her arms flat on the gravel, her hands holding her plastic cup, she didn't move for days.

Other beggars were unaware that they too lived on their knees. They sold their souls to businesses that they didn't care about in order to be able to pay off debts, rent, or to eat. They sold things door to door or bus to bus or over the phone, trading dignity for food. They crawled about on the floor, getting orange dust knees and leaving two knee-wide paths behind them. They formed the slowest parade of drained, burned out people.

They all could have been cello players, passionate orchestra conductors, skateboarders, rappers, muralists, chefs, agro-ecologists, teachers of imagination, water drummers, avid morning readers and nighttime lovers, Trova singers, slow salsa dancers, tree house builders, short documentary makers, animal doctors, night nurses, idea dreamers, melancholy comic drawers... But instead their poemseeds, songseeds, colourseeds rotted in the darkness. They became sellers of ugliness, and beggars of pity. Butterfly wings stolen. What they might have been had died in the dust of degradation, and fell, like abandoned angels, onto waste mountain.

Paz-seed

Paz, don't you remember when you were little and you

asked the homeless man how he was, and asked to touch his nose?

That was a long time ago.

Don't you remember hanging out with the bus drivers at the train station as they rested before starting their next journey? You would sit there, on the metal bus stop bench, listening, fascinated by their bus driving stories. Eventually, they invited you to try the steering wheel, and to share their lunch. You found a magnifying glass buried in grass by the footpath, and after looking at everything close up—at dirt, bugs, bricks, electric plugs, bread, and the bus tires' tread—you took to putting the magnifying glass on people's faces and over hearts, hoping to see those close up too. The bus drivers laughed uncomfortably, self-consciously, as you chirped, "I want to see what you're made of" and held the glass to their ears.

Like I said, that was a long, long time ago.

Not long after that you got into bug caring. You gathered up skinks, caterpillars, garden roaches, slugs, garden snails and tiny snails, and ants, and you put them all together in a glass jar with some leaves, thinking you were giving them a bug party. On Sunday afternoons, when your mother took the washing off the line and dumped it onto the couch, you would climb on top of the clothes, warm from the sun, and fall asleep.

What's the point of this?

To make you remember Paz, who you used to be, and therefore who you could have been. Do you remember why Eva started planting things? Because you showed her how. You planted a pen lid and told her to wait years, and perhaps a pen would grow. When you were her age you had planted a feather, hoping for a bird. You planted a toenail clipping, hoping, for some reason, for a roaring transparent dragon. You planted an oil bolt, hoping to grow a train, and once you planted a match, believing that the next morning a second sun would be growing alongside the first, giving it company. It was around that age, five or six, that you first started to take photos. And you decided to make the whole world colourful, starting with cows on the footpath. Remember, the police called it vandalism, and your first little dream deflated, and the first piece of you died.

Barbarism

Paz, with his swollen blue dangly finger hanging beside him, and both his arms swaying at his sides, wondered-drifted and stumbled about in the shopping centre parking lot, looking for somewhere to pass time away from eyes. The only place that seemed safe enough was between two dumpsters in a far corner, where there were fewer cars parked. He sat there with legs straight out for lack of room, barely glancing at the sides of the bins on either side of him, their lids not quite closed as rubbish filled them to the brim, some of it tumbling out where he sat. Both bins had half-ripped 'caution' stickers, and a large one with a green border read: 'Waste Management Sydney'. Idly, he picked through the rubbish around him. There was a blue sports team cap, some plastic plates, broken bricks, vegetable pastries in wrappers just one day past their expiration date, a mobile phone, some small marigolds in pots, batteries, old fruit, and a bag of coloured mount board scraps and a mount cutter.

The ease with which people threw things away, he thought. The global acceptance of discarding stuff as though the planet had a vacuum somewhere and the things that weren't wanted just disappeared into it.

The three o'clock sun left shade from the bins blanketing his legs, but lit up his face—to no one. Because people near rubbish become invisible, probably also falling into that non-existent vacuum along with all the other unwanted stuff.

(Somewhere else: Soldiers trained to be unthinking and aggressive. In the US it was called brutalisation. Long periods of treading freezing water, special exercises to break down resistance to authority. Break down independent minds. A lot of resources went into creating robotkillers wrapped in patriotic packages. The soldiers marched in lines but their blood and their victims' blood preferred chaos. Some of them committed suicide in undignified splotches around the walls, scattering their letters that had been written with the falseness of a résumé, because there was always just a bit of human left that needed to be hidden.

And the other robot things. From the drugs injected and swallowed as psychological care because the world wasn't helping them and they were drained out and they prowled the streets robbing her, and when they did she saw in their eyes that Life had left. The real inspiration for the movie zombies. They put their hand over her mouth and they yelled at her to hand over her wallet, and another time they put glass to her neck, another time three guns to her head, each time the same non-expression as the soldiers who had kill, kill, kill pounding inside their heads. Soldier robots and street zombies turned off music, undid poetry, packed away dances, locked up hope.)

Paz didn't feel like sleep and he didn't feel like tomorrow. And when he picked up the mount cutter and ran it across his eyebrows, he didn't feel that either. Like that, he cut off amazement, turned off his own expression, put an end to concern, sympathy, surprise.

He cut a straight line across his thigh. Out floated a ghost, a red one that quickly split into smaller versions of itself. Puddle of redghost fit nicely into the pockmarks of the asphalt. With his leg went journeys, and the feel of the ground.

What was he doing? Confirming numbness. All the people shrugging to the sound of ongoing and unnecessary starvation.

Confirming absence. The world of missing things, gaps

left by invisible bombs dropped by robotsoldiers and monarchs without crowns.

Confirming that it was time to turn off the lights. One more cut, deep and jagged, to his waist. To turn off curling up with someone, someday, under a sweet afternoon sun.

(Somewhere else: The private healthcare industry and its bloody art of cutting corners to make money from people's suffering. Patents to make urgent medicine unaffordable. People sick on waiting room floors because they didn't have health insurance.

And diarrhoea: Easy to prevent and to cure, but without access to safe drinking water or basic medicine, so many people got it, went to the toilet every hour, became dehydrated, and in a few days sunken eyes, hollow cheeks, dry mouth, swollen and cracked tongue. After a few more days, the inability to make tears. Decreased skin turgor turning bodies into a desertlands of wrinkles. Seeing white dots, seizures, falling in and out of consciousness, and a face turned into a vacant mask. The body devoured itself desperately, drying out its brain cells, consuming its respiratory tract and stomach lining. Slow motion roadkill; and the flies, fitter than ever, parked on their dried out eyes. Two million people allowed to die like that each year so that money could be spent on cosmetics or wars or bailing out banks. Pharmaceutical and health corporations playing active roles in the Destruction.)

Paz cut a deep gash into his arm, looking for numb inside his flesh, turning off forever hugs and caring for others. He noted ironically how soft things made no sound when they broke, how souls made no sound when they crumbled. His skin parted so smoothly and so easily; he could have been slicing custard. Another cut for his stomach and for his belly button to end all energy and to complete the disconnection from origin, and from history.

(Somewhere else: Monsanto patented what came out of the soil. And it patented pig breeding techniques, owned them, made sharing information illegal. It would have arrested the birds and bees for pollination if it could. It made designer plants so farmers depended on its seeds and on its cancer causing, anxiety causing, contaminating herbicides and pesticides. GMO profit crops and pesticides causing lizard heart attacks, excess slime on fish, birds with hooked beaks, gastrointestinal problems, premature births, impaired liver function. And in India, hundreds of thousands of farmers drinking pesticide to commit suicide. An industry of fake food, instant notmeat and powdered vegetables and junk, with the real food thrown into the sea so people would pay more for what lookslikefood, turning into whatlookslikepeople.)

Paz's thin skin, this package that held him in, contained his organs and his memories. It was so delicate that he could cut line after line into his back, and turn off dignity, just like that. More blood leaking out, just like the thrown-out marigolds. Their colours dripping out, seeping out, gold yellow orange stripes in the rubbish pile. Next, Paz turned off drawings, stroking, photo taking and all creation, once and for all. He cut across his fingers on his already damaged hand, then swapped the mount cutter over and cut the fingers of his other hand. Almost done, almost all turned off.

(Somewhere else: "Turn the dole bludgers into glue," he said. Joking and serious... Yet there were governments already turning the poor, turning people from certain countries, into something more burnt than glue. Bombs, nuclear bombs, guns, grenades, poverty. Four thousand four hundred active nuclear warheads, and twenty-eight thousand in total, waiting, just waiting...their destructive force at least one hundred thousand times that of Hiroshima, or capable of killing seven billion people. The

US had around half of them.

One sad person ripping up paper and throwing it off a balcony so that it flutterdanced on the wind. Many others' lives so easily torn up in the same way and scattered in the street. The list of peoples and countries was long: Iraq, Afghanistan, Libya, Hiroshima, Nagasaki, blown apart. Others fell apart slowly; India, Somalia, Haiti. Shanty cities of cardboard houses and mud cakes for meals. We were breaking

Of a slow death
Or fast destruction
Moon planet and the real ugliness.)

And the fire had gone out
Just one thing left to turn off
Before the all lasting sedative
Paz made a deep cut into his throat and ended opinion, ended being heard though it never had actually started.

All the untaken photos flicked out.

And a pair of butterfly wings fell from his throat the short distance to the ground where he already lay.

El capitalismo mata, continuamente, la Paz

Damaged
When Paz was added to Waste Mountain, along with all the other things that had been turned off and ended, Waste Mountain reached that point of too much, and it exploded. It was the sound of a single earth-humanity scream. And from then on, the earth became one giant graveyard-desert; the grey garden of bombs.

MELLA

Eclosure

Morning emerged from its cacoon. It broke out of the hills with a silent hurrah and sent puffy clouds skipping across the sky. Sweetlight painted yellow tinges along the edges of all things. Mella, already sitting in the community garden that they'd created over the site of a large waste dump, looked up as a cheeky five-minute drizzle sent watersnakes down, head first, towards the seedlings. They wrapped around the little leaves then wandered down the seedling bodies towards the soft and fertile soil.

This morning was Mella's last, and she knew it. She was very old now, though by then the world was calling such age 'advanced' instead. She had clayfeet, tea-eyes, driftwood bones, and complex skin. Her body hurt a little, and she could hear and feel its systems wearing out and grinding towards off.

Other people from the community arrived and sat near her to weed. Mella told them stories as they worked. Her stories were actionmemories that went up hills then tobogganed down them. After, they would reflect, ask questions, and debate, while still gently pulling at the weeds. Their work rhythm and the morning relaxed them.

Mella said that she thought that life was like reading a book. You dived into a book, relishing it, but when the end came, it was okay, because you knew it was there all along. Each chapter of the book built upon the last, and then the end completed the book, made it whole. Yet books were written in constant dialogue with each other, and with the world, in the same way that people built their own uniqueness in dialogue with friends and their relationship to the world. Life, books, friends, at first didn't seem to last, but through their interactions and participation they did last, after all.

Life, as temporary as a kiss on a cheek: already gone, but a little tingle that lingered behind. Mella thought of the things that people of her generation had grown up to believe would last forever: countries, poverty, and capitalism. Yet all those things were gone now. Nothing lasted forever, nothing was so powerful, except for change.

Home of the butterflies

He was seven, and his eyes and cheek bones looked just like Mella's—a great grandson, perhaps. He ran most places rather than walked, and he jumped up stairs rather than stepped. This morning, as usual, he had also tied a very long and colourful kite tail to his back, so that it would flap and fly behind him as he ran. For this, he was called Kite, and today he was in an extra rush to get to the community garden early, as he had something special to do. He had been to all the photography classes on light, focus, balance, proportion, composition, shutter speed, and exposure, and he had borrowed all the cameras, lenses, and flashes available at the technology library, and when he wasn't running and jumping, he was standing very still, taking unique, child's-eye-view photos of expressions and feelings. So, some artists who were planning to paint the back wall of the garden with giant insects in Mexican alebrije style, had asked him to take some macro photos of the garden bugs for them.

Kite ran down the main road, his trailing tail making a kiteline through the city's walls, which had come alive since the poor had won the war, had become people's biggest canvas. There were murals of all sizes and colouring-in walls for kids or people of any age to paint, poem walls, message and information boards, whiteboard walls for more temporary drawings and writings, and street exhibitions of art and photography. All the old billboards and advertising had long since been taken down and used for other things, or had been painted over and incorporated into the city's never ending art-story. The footpaths were part of it too, and people of all ages jumped their way through the giant hopscotch that someone had painted leading into the entrance of Parramatta station. There, next to the stairs going down to the platforms, a slippery slide. Such slides going into the stations were common now, as were slides next to the library stairs, next to the giant staircase that took people up to the cliff parks, next to the stairs of the steep suburban hills, and there were even curly slides in many apartment buildings and towers. A lot of people preferred them as they made their way to wherever they were going, adding a regular 'weeee' followed by a soft bump at the bottom to the gentle and cheerful city rhythm.

The trains transported people between suburbs and cities, and from the stations, trams and solar powered buses took people down a main road into the depths of those suburbs. People could also pick up a bike from most corners and ride it where they liked, leaving it there for someone else to then pick up and ride somewhere. The unused roads had long since been closed to traffic and their asphalt had been ripped up and replaced with grass, trees, flower gardens, benches, and sheltered spaces with pointed roofs and hammocks tied to the beams. People loved the hammock areas, settling down there for a siesta, a read, or a cuddle; the squeaking swing of the hammock ropes not quite birdwhistle, but relaxing nevertheless.

Other people gathered in groups along the green roads, streets, intersections, and the many shops that had been renovated for community use, and practiced circus tricks, debated different issues, played ball games or birribirri, or hidefind, did poetry and rap jamming, storytelling, dance popping, puppetry, mime, liquid dancing, capoeira, slow and sensual paper mache, and impromptu didgeridoo and guitar classes. Now, their homespace was a place to be alone if they wished, or with a few close friends, but mostly it was a place to sleep, because night and day the streets were where life was breathed a never ending adventure.

Unable to resist, Kite took a small detour past the rappers and the dance poppers to the giant instruments. Hanging from rope tied across the street were pipes of various lengths and thicknesses, and glass bottles filled with different amounts of water. Kite picked up one of the sticks in a clay pot, and played the pipes. Nearby, other children and one adult were hitting at the giant drum kit of recycled things that formed a thirty-metre curved line down the road. When it rained and people ran off into shelters, rainsounds would chill the streets after a hot day and the rain drops played the drums—rain patter, and the invisible windslivers, played scales on the pipes.

With the re-building and re-ordering of the world, music had changed too. It was now something to learn and share, for expression or communication, rather than focused on a few commercialised "stars". People experimented with it, some people studied it closely and practiced it, and new music was found and created, while at the same time the forgotten and erased music of invaded peoples was also recovered. Some groups made new songlines, rescuing that wonderful Aboriginal practice of navigating the folds and curls of the land with the melodic contours of a song. In that way they got to know music and land more intimately than ever before, as though stroking their landplaces with their sound.

Kite continued his run. As he did, he let out a stream of little farts, and delighted, made bus noises to go with them. Bus with a kite tail. Amidst early morning bustle; the best kind. The bus in the bustle.

A group of very advanced people skated past him and his little noises, two of them holding hands, laughing, teasing each other with pokes to the belly. Other advanced people swung as high as they could on the tire swings near the hammock shelter. Many other old people were already on their way to teach; no longer kept at home for shame or lack of access to decent health care and physical therapy, they had become one of the most well rounded sectors of society. With all their experience and maturity, they had a particular dignity and an intricate expression in the contours of their face.

Mella was one of these teachers, in fact she was a teacher of teachers—a critical pedagogue, a scientist of education, of that art of the constant process of creating complete human beings. She taught her students to play with new ways of thinking and being; integral thought, critical complex thought, the many, many different ways of seeing things.

New ideas and new words bloomed and breathed. Skipwords, image-thoughts, wovenpoems, excited mind a fever state, a consciously chosen intoxication. Classes for everything; massage, exercise, sport, art, soil reading and biology, travel, argument...an endless list of things to learn. With compulsory work—that work that society really needed to be done—shared among people at fifteen to twenty hours a week, there was plenty of time for such classes—teaching them and attending them—and for other types of recreation and community service.

Kite had almost arrived at the community garden, but he urgently needed to go to the toilet, so he ran into a meeting hall where the city's builders and architects were gathered with some community representatives to discuss slight adjustments to their working hours. As Kite ran through them, his tail snagged on their pants and skirts, then half of it caught on the toilet door as he closed it. Someone in the hall had proposed that the workers increase their weekly work load from eighteen hours to twenty, given the needs of the city right now. One hand held up high among the brisk head nods. The nods looked toward the hand's owner, who argued for a one-year limit on the increase. Some community representatives offered to find more help for the builders. Amidst the chatter, Kite ran out, receiving multiple head pats and handshakes as he went.

His last stop was the community kitchen. A buzzing place, it was one part of what was once a prison. They had knocked holes and bigger windows into it, painted it over, opened it up, and converted it into a community module where there were also nutrition workshops, a health centre, psychological care, and another space which was often used for classes or meetings. As all these things were integrated and related, it was felt to be important that they were located in the same area. During the War of the Poor they had also taken banks and turned them into learning spaces, turned police stations into community run radio stations, casinos into theatres, and hotels into housing for the homeless. In England, even the Queen's palaces had been turned into housing space for those in need, with entire wings or halls being used as libraries, museums and classrooms, and the gardens were used for yoga and dance-exercise therapy. This morning the kitchen smelt of roasting capsicums stuffed with nuts, herbs, beans, rice, and organic vegetables. Kite ran up to the oven, bent down in front of it with his hands on his knees and caught his breath for a few seconds, then picked up twelve capsicums that were ready, cooling on the stovetop on a tray, and ran out again.

Running, skipping, paintdreaming. New laws were written in people's work groups. Meetings determined production, distribution, and the best use of resources and the least amount of damage... This new world without poverty felt less stressful.

There had not been much urge to sleep when the fireworks of a war came and awakened their desire to be alive and to
start to understand what that actually meant
Little wings on their fingertips, aurora borealis flying about inside them, its sky painting a tumbling
out of new humanity of long eyes wide open
It started as a massive outrage
And then it never stopped. Because a revolution doesn't end; it's a better world under constant construction. And so they never retired
from life.

Fortresses, also called borders,
a forced
separation
of sisters
Those lies of lines
that broke the globe up into cracked glass fragments of colour coded places
were destroyed, crashed, brought down
And people walked across them, towards each other like
Old friends
Their legs and their journeys finally free
The fragments, the people sown back together.

And the old coal, nuclear, and thermoelectric generators were gone. Now, expansive lakes of solar panels were built in the deserts, their little solar heads turning to find the sun and eat it like hungry birds. Then, on the edges of the world's desert, they filled old car bodies with good dirt and planted trees. Made an oldcar forest on the desert's edge, and the roots of trees broke out the door windows and clawed into the ground, their natural muscles a resilience that slowly defeated the old way.

Until it was broken apart and buried.

And just before Kite reached the garden, just before it struck seven and pure daylight hit, he bumped smack into the local soilcarer. He was a man with a medium beard with two patches of grey in it on either side of his chin. He was a quiet person, with a resilience inspired by the plants and trees he looked after. Apart from working with the gardeners, teaching them to compost and sheet mulch and other things, he also helped out with recycling, forest replenishing and river clean-ups. He was like an earth doctor, and his art was something that was well respected. He picked Kite up from the ground where he'd fallen from the bump, and tickled him with his kite tail. Kite laughed and jumped and tickled back, then picked up the tray of capsicums—all intact—and entered the garden, shouting out a hellohug to Mella first, then to the others.

New people

On your last day you're aware of everything. The rhythm of the wind, the four thousand smells around you, the slippery mordant taste of the roasted capsicum touching the tip of your tongue... Mella was aware of her weight on the ground, and of the ground itself; so firm, serious, full of conviction. She felt her legs, her hands, and Kite off in the background with the camera and his tail constantly catching on the giant yellow zucchini flowers.

She wanted to write. Because memories and reflections were starting to come at her like shooting stars—comets diving down her throat, one after another. Even on this last day there were things worth remembering that she hadn't noted yet. She took her two hundred and forty-second exercise book out of her knapsack. She spun a sharpened pencil around her fingers. Black and red dirt in her fingernails. A worm half out of the ground wiggling by her toes. She touched it. Soft and cold.

Things worth remembering, she wrote:

—How things used to be, so we can understand how we've changed. The Mella she used to be: the times she had worry doing laps in her head, making it hard to sleep, because she couldn't get a job. At first, she hadn't worried that others couldn't get work either.

—Then later, new Mella. Working with the homeless crew to convert the QVB mall into a living space: meetings, repainting, installing extra showers, toilets, and kitchens, drilling and bashing down walls at 11:00 pm at night, then sitting down on the floor among the paintdust, and sharing coffee from a glass jar they passed around. Mella had brought three long loaves of bread filled with cheese and vegemite, which they also passed around. It was at the time when they hadn't won the war yet, and things were hard. She was hungry, but it hadn't occurred to her to keep some bread at home for herself. A radio sitting on the floor near the power point, singing to itself budgie style. A caterpillar moving in slow moon circles around the light bulb on the ceiling, and their bread and coffee moving around their own circle below it.

—How her day dreams had changed as she did. She dreamt more of being able to help people. Of giving good advice to Saba for his relationship, or being able to massage Carlos' back until his daily pain was cured.

—How the body often knew how you felt before you did. She had eventually learnt to body read too, to see and feel where the pain and tiredness was, to know how to massage it away or to talk to the person. Learnt physical empathy, hand speech.

—The close relationship between perseverance, inner strength, and depth of character. Six years old, sitting with her mum on that brown couch with the buttons. Pulling at the buttons to make them twang as mum read the story of the little blue engine that could. The smallest engine of them all that made it to the top of the hill, chanting, I know I can, I know I can...

—Her mother fluttering about the house, pecking at the furniture, cleaning and cleaning and fluffing and fussing, polishing, mopping, dusting, rearranging, re-waxing the things that sat in their house, their mini-museum of stuff collected from shops. Her mum a slave to the house museum of common and useless objects. In this world, her mother might instead have learnt to sing and play the keyboard. She would have laughed with all the free time she had, a special sort of wealth.

—Complexity. In a pub that time with a young Colombian geologist. He drank three beers. She drank water, and played with some cordate leaves she'd found. She'd pretended to put them in his beer, and he put them for real in her water. She asked him if he'd seen the movie *Vendadora de Rosas*, and he asked why he would watch such a sad movie about his country. He told her about where he'd grown up, how he'd watched bodies floating down the river, how there was no water or electricity, about a neighbour—the government had killed his wife and when he went to complain they killed him too, with his child sitting on his knee. The house his father had just bought fell down in an earthquake. His sad eyes and his face down a little towards the table. She had always wanted to convince people to join the Army of the Poor, but this time she could understand why he preferred not to. He poured some of his beer into her water, they laughed, trying not to let the world get to them.

—Old Mella in high school writing in tiny whispered text on the corner of a thirty-year-old maths book without a spine or back cover, 'We need new maths books'.

—New Mella not whispering anymore.

— What visibility was like: being taken into account, going into an office or the local parliament or a community meeting and being listened to. Being visible was believing that you had the right to say what you thought, and that what you thought was useful. It was sunny, big eyes and big smiles and pride. It was being understood. It was really existing.

Versions of the world

Somewhere else, three people were playing a board game. It had lots of coloured squares, tickling, music, and challenges. Grele landed on a blue square, a story one.

She laughed, "Oh, I've got a great story! Before, people played board games too!"

"Oh really?" said Kez. "I wondered about that! What were they like?"

"They were always competitive. Two of the most popular games were chess and monopoly. Chess was two monarchies fighting each other. The people were represented by pawns, and these were usually sacrificed early in the game. When you lost your king, you lost the game. Monopoly was a simulation of capitalism. Players were given money and bought houses randomly and then got money for it without doing any work. And you could go to jail for no reason."

"Gosh, how horrid! People had fun playing these games?"

Seeds

Tiny seed (embryo, food, a coat and a code) gathered food from the dirt and turned itself, slowly, into a giant tree. Simple thing became complex and strong. But for the embryo to eat and grow, it needed water to activate enzymes to break down storage compounds. Soil poverty also affected plant growth: the seed needed loose soil rich in organic matter, a good soil temperature, oxygen in the soil, and light to germinate. People were like seeds.

What is beauty

And then something that was very much worth remembering; that moment when she had finally worked out what missing thing was.

Mella smiled to herself, and looked around her. With such urge and desire this garden had blossomed and expanded since she and a few others had started it decades ago. After sorting the dump's rubbish for recycling, they had planted sunflowers to clean out elevated levels of heavy metal. Now they had herb spirals near the kitchen, forested fruit and vegetables, a bio pool with ducks and frogs, chickens and goats walking about, bird baths, a worm farm, and dense mounds of flowers around the edge of the garden. Vanilla flowers, cup plants (with their leaves forming cups that collected water for insects and small birds), anise hyssop, daises, roses, blue columbine, fennel and others sugared the air and attracted insects to counter pests, and butterflies to pollinate. Banksias attracted native birds and provided a wind belt.

The garden was busy now, people as busy as their fellow insects in it; some just sitting and chatting, one person sitting among the corn and playing the violin, four-year-olds sifting dirt, half of it falling outside the pots, but no one minded. A group of slightly older children picked mulberries for juice for lunch, their fingers already purple as they noshed on half of what they picked. In one section of the vegetable forest people were mulching for water retention, and Carlitos was massaging the soil; kneading it and turning it slowly, enjoying its rich, wet, soft texture. When the soil was ready they would sprinkle the seeds—a serious ceremony, the seeds passed from the palm of one community member to another with respect and delicacy. Likewise, last week they had transplanted some of the baby lettuces from the nursery over to a vegetable bed—three huge men with deep voices and pony tails cradling the little lettuces in their hands and gently placing them in their new holes. Now, the lettuce leaves were yellow at the corners and floppy, as though expressing soreness from the uprooting. They would recover quickly, as the older ones had. A portion of them wouldn't be harvested, so that the single flower that sprouted from their middle could be used for more seeds. A baby crawled among the lettuce, falling into it a few times, until someone picked him up and put him back on the path. He wandered back in. A young woman whistled. She had a small love, a wee fetish, for the musical note D; it tickled her, so she whistled it again and again. The birds joined in. And somewhere amongst it all it, there were little fairies. No longer stuck in the glamourlights, they were right there, digging out the weeds. The ground breathed, tree leaves shivered.

Mella wrote in her notebook: I realised what that painful hole in the air was when it was completely gone, when life was full and we were starting to win the war. I climbed on top of a bus stop roof in the middle of the day and wrote on the wall in red spray paint: "They stole our humanity, and now we're taking it back."

The super-rich, the owners of all things, of workers, land, information, and production—the monarchs without crowns—had stolen time and stolen dreams. They'd stolen beauty by convincing the world that it was something measurable and buyable. "Step by step we need to reclaim beauty for what it really is, remember our real history, our story," Mella wrote.

(And maybe it was a dream she had, or maybe it happened, metaphorically, during the trembling of revolution; all those millions of people wandered around naked and raw and saw things as they were for the first time, noticing that no one was the same, and that normality and one kind of physical beauty were televised, hypnotised, lies. Like that they saw the butterflies growing inside, cheeks flaming red from conversations, green fingers from touching the land, the magic in their diversity and they understood beauty, finally, as a feeling. As something that makes you want to play and touch and explore, as something relaxing and stimulating, as anything that is amazing).

Some things that are beautiful, Mella wrote.

—the music of the way things change.

—him dreaming up poems in the shower, then leaving wet footprints in the hall as he ran to write them down

—that sadness that hurts in your chest, that's caused purely by knowing someone else is hurting

—Rafi's mind

—the soldiers when they took off their helmets and put down their guns and joined the protesters in Egypt

—the sensual windcrying stormy songs of Chavela Vargas, a person who refused to stop being a woman because she was very old and who always refused to wear high heels, and who made love to other women, who sang in the streets

—babywonder, sleepwarmth, lorikeets

—mindforeplay conversations late at night, going hard places with another person, exploring their past with affection and intimacy.

The soilcarer had gathered some of the newer gardeners around him, at the edge of the fruit and vegetable forest.

"Life flourishes better with diversity. That's why the monoculture farms in the old world would turn rich soil into desert. In order to mass produce food and make large profits, business farmers would plant hectares and hectares of just one crop, and these crops weren't adaptable to changing environmental and weather conditions, they exposed the soil, pests and weeds thrived there, and the farmers used pesticides, herbicides, and fertilisers. These chemicals contaminated the soil and rivers, and were often carcinogenic and therefore made the actual food poisonous too. The monocultures took nutrients from the soil without replacing them, whereas a diversity of plants cycles the nutrients, and the different plants defend each other," he said, as he picked up handfuls of soil.

"And the same goes for humans," said Mella, walking over slowly, and visibly in pain, her notebook and pen in her right hand. "We need the right kind of world, the most just economy and social relations, and a rich diversity of human character in order to flourish".

As the young ones poked and felt the soil, she sat on the ground and wrote some more. 'Things that are beautiful...' Kite read over her shoulder and climbed into her lap. "You are," he said. He saw her age and her accumulation of loves, battles, play, the shed confusion, the inner strength. Kite touched her back and saw her art wings full, enormous, and resting.

She kissed him on top of his head and indicated that she was going to stand up. He scrambled away, and watched as she surveyed the garden, smiling and firm. Blending in with the tall trees off behind her. Kite took a photo. Of the kind that Paz would have loved to have taken but that he'd never even imagined.

The many kinds of love, now

Love of doing: People had time now to dedicate to the things they most enjoyed and appreciated. Ry loved architecture, and would enter old churches and gaze at their ceilings, windows, and the gargoyles outside, while his partner waited in the doorway, impatient to leave. He also loved travelling, and he visited the buildings of the world, noticed all their shapes and colours and character, until his one pair of socks became hard from wear and sweat. It was a love that was accompanied by serious happiness, persistence, and an urge to live.

Intimate love: Love whispered to her, 'Go to him'. It whispered; 'Visit him for five minutes, kiss him in the plaza, in the rain, on the bus, in the doorway.' She tried to pick up the whispering thing and throw it out the window, and get back to work. But it bounced back up and hovered happily behind the glass for a minute, then flew in and sat on her shoulder. It watched her read for a while, then pulled down nighttime like a blind and took her to see him once more.

This love kind involved mental, emotional, and physical intimacy, and seeing one's partner as a maze, each day a journey to know them better. Break-ups were almost as hard in the new world as the old, except they were made a little easier for the lack of judgment, the lack of economic pressures, and an acceptance that change was natural. For that, there was also less or no violence. Each day and each night in the new world, all the millions of orgasms; there but hidden like stars on cloudy nights, the warm cheeks and gasps of joy and much restful sleep.

Brotherfriend or sisterfriend love: Very common now, these mates who let you vent, who worked through your problems with you, swapped philosophies and jokes, compared childhoods, supported you.

Intergenerational love: Now, most people had lots of friends who were much older than them to look up to. The older ones shared their experience, and the younger ones, having grown up in a different way, asked questions that made the older ones stop and think about their lives from a new angle. These relationships were healthy for society, added energy, meaning, and perspective, helped people understand the usefulness of aging and growing, and made history something living, personal, and passed down.

Kite had many people of whom he could ask questions, and who would hug him and rock him when he was upset. He felt safe and unafraid to try new things, and his older friends watched him grow with fondness. He tied his tail around their ears and asked them to tell him again why clouds were round and not triangle. Do horses only greet horses when they are walking around, or do they greet donkeys too? Should he greet the horses? Some years later, he'd ask about the best ways to tell someone that he was in love with them, and then he'd work it out himself, but it helped to have lots of older people to talk to about it.

Community love: It was homestreets, uncles and aunts everywhere, painting a flyingmural on the school fence together, street soccer, each face well known, each person a character in their community with a role to play in it. And when someone travelled for a bit they were missed by the others, and when they came back they had a lot to catch up on—people to visit, and to ask how their homeplace was going, because each community had its own personality and its own history, its own face, and the people within it noticed its little changes, worked together to fix its problems.

Love of the land: When it rained *palos de agua*—sticks of water—people turned eights in bed over and over, not worried about their washing drying or things like that, but about the garlic drowning, or the hillsides collapsing, the riverbanks flooding...and when there were dry spells, they worried about the lettuce browning, the rivers shrinking and their fish flopping about on dry land, and it hurt them, because they were part of all of that, and that sort of connection was just another way of saying love. As you walk along it, the land and your steps kiss quickly (to paraphrase Silvio Rodriguez).

Love for humanity: Caring about the fate of strangers. This last one was a very warm, omnipresent love.

For all the different shades of love, which often overlapped each other, there were no rules, no normal, no hierarchies, no better or worse, no contracts, no expiration dates, no numbers of how many or how long or which gender. There was just respect, and an understanding that love was a kind of art too; it was an action that was practised, developed, and given freely.

Dance

Everyone had gone and it was night now. Deep, soft night, a pastel black because the half moon was making its moonshadows crawl across the ground.

And Mella was in pain; her bones hurt, her mouth was

dry, and she was breathing loudly. Not long now, she thought, as she walked towards a small clearing in the garden. The clearing was surrounded by white roses, which, catching the light of the halfmoon, seemed to glow in the dark like fallen stars. And there was the melody of night—sugar gliders rustling lightly in the trees, tawny frogmouths calling, crickets chirruping, frogs and their monotonous rhythms as they yelled out for mates, and the breeze squeezing its way gently through the plants. Others were silent; the butterflies hanging from the undersides of leaves with their wings closed, chickens sleeping with their heads upon their chests, the goats resting their head on the ground or curled into circles with their heads resting upon a hind leg. One slept with his head in the middle of a lettuce. The daises had closed their petals and hung their heads too, as though they were heavy and exhausted.

And Mella danced...

To the music in her head, and to the sounds and the silence of the garden. She danced to the rhythm of her memories, and to all that was worth remembering. She danced the feeling of freedom. She twirled her arms in front of her and behind her, above her. She skipped in circles, tilting her head towards the sky, relishing the cool breeze underneath her arms. She drummed her bare feet against the soil and damp grass.

And then her breathing clutched, as though her lungs had become two broken zippers. She sank her toes and heels into the soil, and as she danced harder, her feet sank further, and her toes were covered, and her ankles too. Her knees wobbled, yet she danced more.

Sometimes old trees crash and fall in the forest. It means their spot in the sun can be taken by the new, smaller trees, and those new ones can then grow tall. An ongoing process which is good for the health of the forest.